IMMIGRANT VOICES

VOLUME II

IMMIGRANT VOICES

VOLUME II

Edited by Gordon Hutner

 NEW AMERICAN LIBRARY

New American Library
Published by the Penguin Group
Penguin Group (USA) LLC, 375 Hudson Street,
New York, New York 10014

USA | Canada | UK | Ireland | Australia | New Zealand | India | South Africa | China
penguin.com
A Penguin Random House Company

First published by New American Library,
a division of Penguin Group (USA) LLC

First Printing, June 2015

Copyright © Gordon Hutner, 2015
Authors' copyrights and permissions can be found on pages 423–25.

REGISTERED TRADEMARK—MARCA REGISTRADA

NEW AMERICAN LIBRARY TRADE PAPERBACK ISBN: 978-0-451-47281-6

Printed in the United States of America
10 9 8 7 6 5 4 3 2 1

Set in Bembo STD
Designed by Cassandra Garuzzo

PUBLISHER'S NOTE
Penguin is committed to publishing works of quality and integrity. In that spirit, we
are proud to offer this book to our readers; however, the stories, the experiences and
the words are the authors' alone.

To Dale Bauer, as always

CONTENTS

INTRODUCTION

As a kind of birthright, Americans grow up with the idea that theirs is a "nation of immigrants," and of course it has been and continues to be. But does this phrase have the same resonance in every generation or even every century? Questions about what kind of and how many immigrants we should have are now as controversial a subject as they have ever been in our past. For at every stage of the history of American immigration, our vigorous welcome of so many of the world's tired and huddled masses was not something about which everyone agreed. Despite our cherished ideal that this country should be understood as a grand melting pot, there have typically been great detractors throughout our history who have challenged this faith in the vitality of an ever-diverse nation. Yet for all the resentment sometimes greeting newcomers, we should also discern the nation's abiding passion for the potential growth that immigrants carry with them, whether they arrive here to meet a labor shortage or to escape persecution in their homelands or merely to join in the American pursuit of happiness.

A century ago and longer, immigrants from Ireland, Italy, Russia, Eastern Europe, and China were especially viewed as objects of suspicion. Immigration from Asia, the Middle East, as well as Central and South America, was, for many years, discouraged, even denied; the Chinese Exclusion Act of 1882 banned Chinese laborers for ten years, a law renewed in 1892, made permanent in 1902, and not repealed until 1943. A similar statute, the Asian Exclusion Act (1924), forbade immigration from India, Korea, and Japan as well as from the Middle East. And immigration from Africa was nearly as difficult.

What was behind this atmosphere of mistrust? It was less the case, as it is now sometimes expressed, that immigrants would create an undue demand on U.S. social services, largely because social services were not yet federalized in the early years of the twentieth century. Instead, nativist anxieties hinged on two kinds of fears: economic and social. The first focused on the conjecture that immigrants would eventually develop and control wealth and that it would be disposed according to their loyalty to their church, if they were Catholic, or to their homelands, especially if they were non-Europeans. Immigration was also imagined to threaten social stability, especially through racial and ethnic mixing, which would contaminate the American gene pool. This fear of diluting the nation's northern and western European "stock" is a biological and sociological fallacy that has long been discredited, though one can hear it articulated even now. Compounding such concerns was the worry that immigrants would also import dangerous political ideas from abroad, such as views opposing capitalism and the presiding understanding of the nation's democratic ideals. That so many of these despised immigrants were Catholics, Jews, and Asians further contributed to this America-for-Americans prejudice, an anxiety that politicians readily exploited.

Despite these worries, the story of the successful assimilation of a multicultural immigrant population is among the most brilliant chapters in modern U.S. social history. And these immigrants' rise from generally low origins—during the rise of industrialism, they were much more often peasants than people with trades or professions—into the middle class is an epic tale that gives the phrase "a nation of immigrants" its meaning, perhaps even its glory. This tale is recounted time and again in the novels and tales that immigrants wrote about the challenges of achieving cultural citizenship. Perhaps even more popular were the first-person chronicles of coming to America and of becoming Americans. For one crucial way of conducting the argument over who can and ought to be citizens—and who should not—is found in the rich literary record that immigrants have left behind.

Such autobiographies are often written partly as accounts of how to flourish in one's adopted country. So it is unsurprising that they often include practical lessons: say this; don't do that; dress *this* way. But their more enduring value lies in how they also address the mainstream populace, readers who took up these memoirs both for the vitality of the stories they told and for keeping up with changes in the culture. Written as they are in English, these accounts specifically appeal to the host culture's interests, while also advertising an author's mastery of the language as a sign of successful assimilation. Explicitly and implicitly, these books present their authors' case for belonging, as if to demonstrate for the audience of the native-born that immigrants have a great deal to offer and that they in their own way have a vast potential to make the U.S. an even better place. In this sense, such autobiographies are both personal documents—the story of my exemplary past—and public ones—an understanding of our nation's shared future. If so much immigrant writing was spurred by the need to model how success in the U.S. might be achieved, they were also written to inform the native-born how to value the ordeals that immigrants endured, how to appreciate the achievements that they might tally, and how fully the belief in the virtue of the nation's diversity will be rewarded.

Autobiographers probably don't begin with this larger purpose in mind. They begin instead with the hope that their stories might be illuminating and entertaining. And they are. Their narrative form is often drawn from the bildungsroman, a tale of a protagonist's growth and education. Such memoirs start with a figure who must navigate between the crippling marginality of present circumstances and the promise of the future. Typically, these narratives begin with the struggle to leave native lands, where the autobiographer faces more or less intolerable social, economic, or political conditions or their combination. Often, there are hurdles that must be overcome. Sometimes, family is the only source of encouragement; other times, family discord worsens these circumstances.

Next, the writer is likely to describe the bewilderment and bedazzlement greeting the newly arrived immigrant in the U.S., first impressions that turn out to be illusions needing to be modulated or overturned. Writers are likely to record several of their most vivid scenes of instruction, tests that they go through with varying degrees of success, often related with a humorous eye at some bumbling misadventure. Frequently, newly arrived immigrants are aided by a guide of sorts—a kind stranger, a predecessor, a teacher, a benefactor, an investor—who appreciates their talent and helps them to find the opportunity they need to make the next step of their journey. Ultimately, these autobiographers manage to make the most of their chances and define themselves within a new cultural identity, although passing that threshold often comes at a price, like an adjustment in their family relations, and entails a diminishing of their previous sense of identity. By the close, they have come to know more about what America will make of them and what they will make of America.

This is the vision of immigration that has proven such an unshakable force in U.S. culture. In these pages, readers will find examples of many individuals whose stories more or less follow this basic scenario from the nineteenth century and that recount privations borne and persecutions withstood. But in ways both superficial and profound, immigration stories at the end of the twentieth century and the beginning of the twenty-first differ from their predecessors.

A previous volume, *Immigrant Voices*, assembled some of those nineteenth- and early-twentieth-century stories of success and their animating trust in hard work and initiative that Americans believe in with all the force of a national creed. Those narratives of becoming Americans remind us that tales of personal striving are often punctuated with a lucky break, an unpredictable circumstance, even a coincidence, or the intervention of an informal support network, like a benevolent aid society such as immigrants from one country might set up for those who follow. Even so, the overwhelming feeling that such narratives convey is the solitude—the often profound loneliness—of the immigrant. And the first difference between contemporary immigrants and their predecessors may be this crucial one. Today's stories more frequently begin as family tales: families uprooted by war and politics, families denied economic security or legal rights, families needing new opportunities so that they might stay together. Perhaps one family member, the author, has needed to split off and has come as a student or is sent as a sort of emissary to the future. An author's connections to family and homeland may be troubled, but they remain sustaining, much more so than in earlier generations. Family ties and community connections assert themselves more forcefully now than they were generally represented to do in the past. Immigrant stories, at least in this crucial respect, are evolving.

This book assembles, with just one exception, narratives of immigrants entering the U.S. under the Nationality and Immigration Act of 1965. This was the most important piece of immigrant legislation in the second half of the twentieth century, and it was cosponsored by Emanuel Celler, a long-standing congressman from New York City, himself the grandson of immigrants. Celler's tenure in the House was so enduring that he actually began his career, forty years earlier, by opposing the notorious Immigration Act of 1924. Stirred by traditional nativist protest, along with the recent surge in distrust that World War I excited, this reactionary law curtailed immigration from eastern and southern Europe by establishing limits based on the 1890 census. The desired result was achieved by creating geographical quotas: the origins of 70 percent of all future immigrants would be limited to three countries—the United Kingdom, Germany, and Ireland. The Johnson-Reed Act, as it was called, continued to exert control throughout the middle decades of the twentieth century and was invoked to deny refuge to Jews fleeing Nazi-occupied countries. Hart-Celler repealed the McCarran-Walter Act of 1952, which had essentially sustained Johnson-Reed and which had passed despite President Truman's veto—he called it "un-American." The 1965 law struck down these obsolete discriminatory prohibitions, even as it gave new preference to immigrants with special skills. Perhaps even more significantly, it allowed immigration among those who had preexisting family relationships with U.S. citizens and permanent residents. Plus, the 1965 law set aside some 170,000 visas for immigrants from Asia, Africa, the Caribbean, and South and Central America, effectively reversing the percentages from the early part of the twentieth century. It was eventually supplemented by the Refugee Act of 1980, which significantly enhanced immigration for asylum seekers.

So many immigrants since 1965 have turned to the U.S. as a place to practice their talents; so many have come to reunite with their families or to avoid political suppression; and so many have come for their education or to escape poverty. Although many immigrants came from terrible poverty, readers may be surprised by how many enjoyed comfortable, sometimes affluent economic backgrounds. What doesn't change is the exhilaration of freedom that these immigrants find in their new lives, nor does their pleasure in the expansive power of the American promise. We follow them wherever their careers—in business, in various professions, in service to others—may take them. They generally find some help along the way, but they often have to battle prejudice. Immigrant memoirs tend not to see the resistance these newcomers face as being systemic or debilitating, but rather as challenges to surpass. None of these authors cares to be seen as a victim. Especially is this so for women whose multiple sources of vulnerability—being female, being immigrants, being poor, being people of color—compound the obstructions they must surmount.

The stories that immigrants tell are always negotiating between the world they leave behind and the new life upon which they have embarked. "Life on the hyphen," as one autobiographer has termed it, describes how hard it is for immigrants to feel wholly a part of either world. This split can be experienced in a person's heart. Nowhere is that story more vitally encountered than in the tales of generational divide. An older, less malleable generation of immigrants—parents—finds adjusting to contemporary American life too demanding, whereas the children have an easier time making America their own. Often that assimilation is achieved through the grasping of popular culture, like music or slang, even though the child may be torn between full immersion in a new culture and loyalty to parents whose ways represent the values left behind. It's the classic immigration plot. *The Jazz Singer* (1927), the very first "talkie," is about a young Jewish singer who departs from the old-world religious tradition of his father, a cantor. Some of the narratives collected here tell similar stories of what it is like to come as children to the U.S., where they are socialized in school and grow apart from their families, while others record what it is like to start new in a new country without the double bind of opposing allegiances.

That new life is also a story of immigrants finding their niche, their new way of being. Whether they are coming into their own as writers or businesspeople or athletes, these figures make their presence in America felt in various ways. They may do so by cultivating an aptitude they already had or by gaining a skill or expertise they could only attain when given the chance to create themselves anew. Sometimes, the impact that these autobiographers make on the U.S. is modest, their success merely average. Still, the success of immigrants is not merely measured by fortunes or illustrious careers. Rather, we see how indispensable they are to American well-being as people who by reaching their best thus contribute to the sum of the nation's happiness.

Perhaps the interest of these immigrant lives is merely to suggest that the U.S. is still the place where the everyday level of dreams achieved remains possible for newcomers. When this country first understood itself as a nation of immigrants, it was probably true that there really weren't too many other places where immigrants were welcomed, where their lives might be improved and where they, in their turn, might benefit those countries. But now, more than two centuries later, more nations see themselves as heterogeneous and make room for immigrants suffering from upheavals and economic distress around the globe. Yet even as these nations are becoming more diverse, America remains the refuge so many millions continue to seek, certainly in its own hemisphere. The burden this creates can sometimes seem unsustainable. Perhaps, in the near future, another new law will enable the country to strengthen its capacity to bolster itself by absorbing new immigrants. If so, as these autobiographies demonstrate again and again, such a law will help to renew the nation's faith in itself and in its most treasured resource. Once it does, new immigration narratives will then be written, new memoirs recording the rewards and consolations of becoming Americans.

The memoirs selected for this volume are stories we need to know, not just because they help us understand the new challenges facing immigrants, which they do, and not just because they familiarize us with an array of new countries and the reasons immigrants come to the U.S., which they also do. We read these new immigrant autobiographies because the more familiar we are with them, the more we understand this new America, an America made different—better and more fulfilled—as a result of immigration. We read these stories to appreciate the United States we are always in the midst of becoming.

—Gordon Hutner

IMMIGRANT VOICES

VOLUME II

ANDRÉ ACIMAN

Egypt

André Aciman (1951–) was born in Alexandria, Egypt, to a wealthy Jewish family of Turkish and Italian descent. His father's successful textile business supported a luxurious lifestyle of tennis lessons, private tutors, and splendid vacations. As Aciman matured, he became aware of the family's growing concern about the Egyptian government's anti-Semitism, which had intensified with the creation of Israel in 1948 and the subsequent border tensions. Even before Israel's victory in the Six Day War in 1967, Jewish Egyptians faced increasing persecution and expulsion, and the Aciman family moved first to Italy in 1965 and then immigrated to New York in 1968.

Aciman soon enrolled at Lehman College of the City University of New York, where he earned a BA in English and Comparative Literature, followed by an AM and a PhD from Harvard. He has published two sets of essays, False Papers: Essays in Exile and Memory *(2001) and* Alibis: Essays on Elsewhere *(2011), and two novels,* Call Me by Your Name *(2007) and* Eight White Nights *(2010). Aciman is currently the Distinguished Professor of Comparative Literature at the Graduate Center of the City University of New York.*

Published in 1994 to wide acclaim, Out of Egypt *won the Whiting Award for emerging writers. Similar to many of the autobiographies in this anthology, Aciman focuses on his extended family and chronicles his own coming of age. The following passage comes from "The Last Seder," the memoir's final chapter. Before the nationalizing of their textile factory, Aciman's father identified fleeing Jewish Egyptians by the smell of their luggage, linking the scent of leather with stigma and shame. Abattoir—*

slaughterhouse—becomes the word he uses to signal to his son that their own family will soon be leaving Egypt. When his father learns that he's about to be arrested, fifteen-year-old André is thrust into adulthood and must learn to navigate the necessary web of bribes and encoded messages. Aciman's father, however, was not the only family member preparing for their escape; unbeknownst to the author, what appeared to be an afternoon of running errands with his grandmother turns out to disguise her routine for smuggling money out of the country, an activity she had been perform-ing for years. The Acimans thus found themselves financially, though perhaps not emotionally, well prepared for leaving their native country.

Excerpt from

Out of Egypt

— **1994** —

"I want you to sit down and be a big boy now," said my father that night after reading the warrant. "Listen carefully." I wanted to cry. He noticed, stared at me awhile, and then, holding my hand, said, "Cry." I felt a tremor race through my lower lip, down my chin. I struggled with it, bit my tongue, then shook my head to signal that I wasn't going to cry. "It's not easy, I know. But this is what I want you to do. Since it's clear they'll arrest me tomorrow," he said, "the most important thing is to help your mother sell everything, have everyone pack as much as they can, and purchase tickets for all of us. It's easier than you think. But in case I am detained, I want you to leave anyway. I'll follow later. You must pass one message to Uncle Vili and another to Uncle Isaac in Europe." I said I would remember them. "Yes, but I also want each message encoded, in case you forget. It will take an hour, no more." He asked me to bring him a book I would want to take to Europe and might read on the ship. There were two: *The Idiot* and Kitto's *The Greeks*. "Bring Kitto," he said, "and we'll pretend to underline all the difficult words, so that if customs officials decide to inspect the book, they will think you've underlined them for vocabulary reasons." He pored over the first page of the book and underlined *Thracian, luxurious, barbaroi, Scythians, Ecclesiastes*. "But I already know what they all mean." "Doesn't matter what *you* know. What's important is what *they* think. *Ecclesiastes* is a good word. Always use the fifth letter of the fifth word you've underlined—in this case, *e*, and discard the rest. It's a code in the Lydian mode, do you see?" That evening he also taught me to forge his signature. Then, as they did in the movies, we burned the page on which I had practiced it.

By two o'clock in the morning, we had written five sentences. Everybody had gone to bed already. Someone had dimmed the lamp in the hallway and turned off all the lights in the house. Father offered me a cigarette. He drew the curtains that had been shut so that no one outside might see what we were doing and flung open the window. Then, after letting a spring breeze heave through the dining room, he stood by the window, facing the night, his chin propped on the palms of his hands, with his elbows resting on the window ledge. "It's a small city, but I hate to lose her," he finally said. "Where else can you see the stars like this?" Then, after a few seconds of silence, "Are you ready for tomorrow?" I nodded. I looked at his face and thought to myself: They might torture him, and I may never see him again. I forced myself to believe it—maybe that would bring him good luck.

"Good night, then." "Good night," I said. I asked him if

he was going to go to bed as well. "No, not yet. You go. I'll sit here and think awhile." He had said the same thing years before, when we visited his father's tomb and, silently, he had propped his chin on one hand, his elbow resting on the large marble slab. I had been asking him questions about the cemetery, about death, about what the dead did when we were not thinking of them. Patiently, he had answered each one, saying death was like a quiet sleep, but very long, with long, peaceful dreams. When I began to feel restless and asked whether we could go, he answered, "No, not yet. I'll stand here and think awhile." Before leaving, we both leaned down and kissed the slab.

The next morning, I awoke at six. My list of errands was long. First the travel agency, then the consulate, then the telegrams to everyone around the world, then the agent in charge of bribing all the customs people, then a few words with Signor Rosenthal, the jeweler whose brother-in-law lived in Geneva. "Don't worry if he pretends not to understand you," my father had said. After that, I was to see our lawyer and await further instructions.

My father had left the house at dawn, I was told. Mother had been put in charge of buying suitcases. My grandmother took a look at me and grumbled something about my clothes, especially those "long blue trousers with copper snaps all over them." "What snaps?" I asked. "These," she said, pointing to my blue jeans. I barely had time to gulp down her orange juice before rushing out of the house and hopping on the tram, headed downtown—something I had never done before, as the American School was in the opposite direction. Suddenly, I was a grown-up going to work, and the novelty thrilled me.

Alexandria on that spring weekday morning had its customary dappled sky. Brisk and brackish scents blew in from the coast, and the tumult of trade on the main thoroughfares spilled over into narrow side-lanes where throngs and stands and jostling trinket men cluttered the bazaars under awnings striped yellow and green. Then, as always at a certain moment, just before the sunlight began to pound the flagstones, things quieted down for a while, a cool breeze swept through the streets, and something like a distilled, airy light spread over the city, bright but without glare, light you could stare into.

The wait to renew the passports at the consulate was brief: the man at the counter knew my mother. As for the travel agent, he already seemed apprised of our plans. His question was: "Do you want to go to Naples or to Bari? From Bari you can go to Greece; from Naples to Marseilles." The image of an abandoned Greek temple overlooking the Aegean popped into my head. "Naples," I said, "but do not put the date yet." "I understand," he said discreetly. I told him that if he called a certain number, funds would be made available to him. In fact, I had the money in my pocket but had been instructed not to use it unless absolutely necessary.

The telegrams took forever. The telegraph building was old, dark, and dirty, a remnant of colonial grandeur fading into a wizened piece of masonry. The clerk at the booth complained that there were too many telegrams going to too many countries on too many continents. He eyed me suspiciously and told me to go away. I insisted. He threatened to hit me. I mustered the courage and told the clerk we were friends of So-and-so, whose name was in the news. Immediately he extended that inimitably unctuous grace that passes for deference in the Middle East.

By half past ten I was indeed proud of myself. One more errand was left, and then Signor Rosenthal. Franco Molkho, the agent in charge of bribing customs officials, was himself a notorious crook who took advantage of everyone precisely by protesting that he was not cunning enough to do so. "I'm always up front about what I do, madame." He was rude and gruff, and if he saw something in your home that struck his fancy, he would grab and pocket it in front of you. If you took it away from him and placed it back where it belonged—which is what my mother

did—then he would steal it later at the customs shed, again before your very eyes. Franco Molkho lived in a kind of disemboweled garage, with a makeshift cot, a tattered sink, and a litter
of grimy gear boxes strewn about the floor. He wanted to negotiate. I did not know how to negotiate. I told him my father's
instructions. "You Jews," he snickered, "it's impossible to beat
you at this game." I blushed. Once outside, I wanted to spit out
the tea he had offered me.

Still, I thought of myself as the rescuer of my entire family.
Intricate scenarios raced through my mind, scenarios in which I
pounded the desk of the chief of police and threatened all sorts
of abominable reprisals unless my father was released instantly.
"Instantly! Now! Immediately!" I yelled, slapping my palm on
the inspector's desk. According to Aunt Elsa, the more you
treated such people like your servants, the more they behaved
accordingly. "And bring me a glass of water, I'm hot." I was busily scheming all sorts of arcane missions when I heard someone
call my name. It was my father.

He was returning from the barber and was ambling at a
leisurely pace, headed for his favorite café near the stock exchange building. "Why aren't you in jail?" I asked, scarcely con-
cealing my disappointment. "Jail!" he exclaimed, as if to say,
"Whoever gave you such a silly notion?" "All they wanted was
to ask me a few questions. Denunciations, always these false
denunciations. Did you do everything I told you?" "All except
Signor Rosenthal." "Very good. Leave the rest to me. By the
way, did Molkho agree?" I told him he did. "Wonderful." Then
he remembered. "Do you have the money?" "Yes." "Come,
then. I'll buy you coffee. You do drink coffee, don't you? Remember to give it to me under the table." A young woman
passed in front of us and father turned. "See? Those are what I
call perfect ankles."

At the café, my father introduced me to everyone. They
were all businessmen, bankers, and industrialists who would

meet at around eleven in the morning. All of them had either lost everything they owned or were about to. "He's even read all of *Plutarch's Lives*," boasted my father. "Wonderful," said one of them, who, by his accent, was Greek. "Then surely you remember Themistocles." "Of course he does," said my father, seeing I was blushing. "Let me explain to you, then, how Themistocles won the battle at Salamis, because that, my dear, they won't teach you in school." Monsieur Panos took out a Parker pen and proceeded to draw naval formations on the corner of his newspaper. "And do you know who taught me all this?" he asked, with a self-satisfied glint flickering in his glazed eyes, his hand pawing my hair all the while. "Do you know who? Me," he said, "I did, all by myself. Because I wanted to be an admiral in the Greek navy. Then I discovered there was no Greek navy, so I joined the Red Cross at Alamein."

Everyone burst out laughing, and Monsieur Panos, who probably did not understand why, joined them. "I still have the Luger a dying German soldier gave me. It had three bullets left, and now I know who they're for: one for President Nasser. One for my wife, because, God knows, she deserves it. And one for me. *Jamais deux sans trois*." Again a burst of laughter. "Not so loud," the Greek interrupted. But I continued to laugh heartily. While I was wiping my eyes, I caught one of the men nudging my father's arm. I was not supposed to see the gesture, but I watched as my father turned and looked uneasily at a table behind him. It was the woman with the beautiful ankles. "Weren't you going to tell me something?" asked my father, tapping me on the knee under the table. "Only about going to the swimming pool this morning." "By all means," he said, taking the money I was secretly passing to him. "Why don't you go now?"

Two days later the third blow fell.

My father telephoned in the morning. "They don't want us anymore," he said in English. I didn't understand him. "They don't want us in Egypt." But we had always known that, I thought. Then he blurted it out: we had been officially expelled and had a week to get our things together. "Abattoir?" I asked. "Abattoir," he replied.

The first thing one did when *abattoir* came was to get vaccinated. No country would allow us across its border without papers certifying we had been properly immunized against a slew of Third World diseases.

My father had asked me to take my grandmother to the government vaccine office. The office was near the harbor. She hated the thought of being vaccinated by an Egyptian orderly— "Not even a doctor," she said. I told her we would stop and have tea and pastries afterward at Athinéos. "Don't hurt me," she told the balding woman who held her arm. "But I'm not hurting you," protested the woman in Arabic. "You're not hurting me? You *are* hurting me!" The woman ordered her to keep still. Then came my turn. She reminded me of Miss Badawi when she scraped my scalp with her fingernails looking for lice. Would they really ask us to undress at the customs desk when the time came and search us to our shame?

After the ordeal, my grandmother was still grumbling as we came down the stairs of the government building, her voice echoing loudly as I tried to hush her. She said she wanted to buy me ties.

Outside the building, I immediately hailed a hansom, helped my grandmother up, and then heard her give an obscure address on Place Mohammed Ali. As soon as we were seated, she removed a small vial of alcohol and, like her Marrano ancestors who wiped off all traces of baptismal water as soon as they had left the church, she sprinkled the alcohol on the site of the injection—to *kill* the vaccine, she said, and all the germs that came with it!

It was a glorious day, and as we rode along my grandmother suddenly tapped me on the leg as she had done years earlier on our way to Rouchdy and said, "Definitely a beach day." I took off my sweater and began to feel that uncomfortable, palling touch of wool flannel against my thighs. Time for shorts. The mere thought of light cotton made the wool unbearable. We cut through a dark street, then a square, got on the Corniche, and, in less than ten minutes, came face-to-face with the statue of Mohammed Ali, the Albanian founder of Egypt's last ruling dynasty.

We proceeded past a series of old, decrepit stores that looked like improvised warehouses and workshops until we reached one tiny, extremely cluttered shop. "Sidi Daoud," shouted my grandmother. No answer. She took out a coin and used it to knock on the glass door several times. "Sidi Daoud is here," a tired figure finally uttered, emerging from the dark. He recognized her immediately, calling her his "favorite *mazmazelle*."

Sidi Daoud was a one-eyed, portly Egyptian who dressed in traditional garb—a white *galabiya* and on top of it a grossly oversized, gray, double-breasted jacket. My grandmother, speaking to him in Arabic, said she wanted to buy me some good ties. "Ties? I have ties," he said, pointing to a huge old closet whose doors had been completely removed; it was stuffed with paper bags and dirty cardboard boxes. "What sort of ties?" "Show me," she said. "Show me, she says," he muttered as he paced about, "so I'll show her."

He brought a stool, climbed up with a series of groans and cringes, reached up to the top of the closet, and brought down a cardboard box whose corners were reinforced with rusted metal. "These are the best," he said as he took out tie after tie. "You'll never find these for sale anywhere in the city, or in Cairo, or anywhere else in Egypt." He removed a tie from a long sheath. It was dark blue with intricate light-blue and pale-orange patterns. He took it in his hands and brought it close to the entrance of the store that I might see it better in the sunlight, hold-

ing it out to me with both hands the way a cook might display
a poached fish on a salver before serving it. "Let me see," said
my grandmother as though she were about to lift and examine
its gills. I recognized the tie immediately: it had the sheen of
Signor Ugo's ties.

This was a stupendous piece of work. My grandmother
looked at the loop and the brand name on the rear apron and
remarked that it was not a bad make. "I'll show you another,"
he said, not even waiting for me to pass judgment on the first.
The second was a light burgundy, bearing an identical pattern
to the first. "Take it to the door," he told me, "I'm too old to
come and go all day." This one was lovelier than the first, I
thought, as I studied both together. A moment later, my grandmother joined me at the door and held the burgundy one in her
hands and examined it, tilting her head left and right, as though
looking for concealed blemishes which she was almost sure to
catch if she looked hard enough. Then, placing the fabric between thumb and forefinger, she rubbed them together to test
the quality of the silk, peeving the salesman. "Show me better."
"Better than this?" he replied. "*Mafish*, there isn't!" He showed
us other ties, but none compared to the first. I said I was happy
with the dark-blue one; it would go with my new blazer. "Don't
match your clothes like a pauper," said my grandmother. The
Egyptian unsheathed two more ties from a different box.
One with a green background, the other light blue. "Do you
like them?" she asked. I liked them all, I said. "He likes them
all," she repeated with indulgent irony in her voice.

"This is the black market," she said to me as soon as we left
the store, the precious package clutched in my hand, as I squinted
in the sunlight, scanning the crowded Place Mohammed Ali for
another horse-drawn carriage. We had spent half an hour in Sidi
Daoud's store and had probably looked at a hundred ties before
choosing these four. No shop I ever saw, before or since—not
even the shop in the Faubourg Saint Honoré where my grand-

mother took me years later—had as many ties as Sidi Daoud's little hovel. I spotted an empty hansom and shouted to the driver from across the square. The *arbaghi*, who heard me and immediately stood up in the driver's box, signaled he would have to turn around the square, motioning us to wait for him.

Fifteen minutes later, we arrived at Athinéos. The old Spaniard was gone. Instead, a surly Greek doing a weak impersonation of a well-mannered waiter took our order. We were seated in a very quiet corner, next to a window with thick white linen drapes, and spoke about the French plays due to open in a few days. "Such a pity," she said. "Things are beginning to improve just when we are leaving." The Comédie Française had finally returned to Egypt after an absence of at least ten years. La Scala was also due to come again and open in Cairo's old opera house with a production of *Otello*. Madame Darwish, our seamstress, had told my grandmother of a young actor from the Comédie who had knocked at her door saying this was where he had lived as a boy; she let him in, offered him coffee, and the young man burst out crying, then said goodbye. "Could all this talk of expulsion be mere bluffing?" my grandmother mused aloud, only to respond, "I don't think so."

After a second round of mango ice cream, she said, "And now we'll buy you a good book and then we might stop a while at the museum." By "good book" she meant either difficult to come by or one she approved of. It was to be my fourteenth-birthday present. We left the restaurant and were about to hail another carriage when my grandmother told me to make a quick left turn. "We'll pretend we're going to eat a pastry at Flückiger's." I didn't realize why we were *pretending* until much later in the day when I heard my father yell at my grandmother. "We could all go to jail for what you did, thinking you're so clever!" Indeed, she had succeeded in losing the man who had been tailing us after—and probably before—we entered Athinéos. I knew nothing about it when we were inside the secondhand bookstore. On one of the stacks I had found exactly what I wanted. "Are you sure you're going to read all this?" she asked.

She paid for the books absentmindedly and did not return the salesman's greeting. She had suddenly realized that a second agent might have been following us all along. "Let's leave now," she said, trying to be polite. "Why?" "Because." We hopped in a taxi and told the driver to take us to Ramleh station. On our way we passed a series of familiar shops and restaurants, a stretch of saplings leaning against a sunny wall, and, beyond the buildings, an angular view of the afternoon sea.

As soon as we arrived at Sporting, I told my grandmother I was going straight to the Corniche. "No, you're coming home with me." I was about to argue. "Do as I tell you, please. There could be trouble." Standing on the platform was our familiar tail. As soon as I heard the word *trouble*, I must have frozen on the spot, because she immediately added, "Now don't go about looking so frightened!"

My grandmother, it turned out, had been smuggling money out of the country for years and had done so on that very day. I will never know whether her contact was Sidi Daoud, or the owner of the secondhand bookstore, or maybe one of the many coachmen we hired that day. When I asked her in Paris many years later, all she volunteered was, "One needed nerves of steel."

Despite the frantic packing and last-minute sale of all the furniture, my mother, my grandmother, and Aunt Elsa had decided we should hold a Passover seder on the eve of our departure. For this occasion, two giant candelabra would be brought in from the living room, and it was decided that the old sculptured candles should be used as well. No point in giving them away. Aunt Elsa wanted to clean house, to remove all traces of bread, as Jews traditionally do in preparation for Passover. But with the suitcases all over the place and everything upside down, nobody was eager to undertake such a task, and the idea was abandoned. "Then why have a seder?" she asked with embittered sarcasm. "Be glad we're having one at all," replied my father. I watched her fume. "If that's going to be your attitude, let's *not* have one, see if I care." "Now don't get all worked up over a silly seder, Elsa. Please!"

My mother and my grandmother began pleading with him, and for a good portion of the afternoon, busy embassies shuttled back and forth between Aunt Elsa's room and my father's study. Finally, he said he had to go out but would be back for dinner. That was his way of conceding. Abdou, who knew exactly what to prepare for the seder, needed no further inducements and immediately began boiling the eggs and preparing the cheese-and-potato *buñuelos*.

Meanwhile, Aunt Elsa began imploring me to help read the Haggadah that evening. Each time I refused, she would remind me that it was the last time this dining room would ever see a seder and that I should read in memory of Uncle Nessim. "His seat will stay empty unless somebody reads." Again I refused. "Are you ashamed of being Jewish? Is that it? What kind of Jews are we, then?" she kept asking. "The kind who don't celebrate leaving Egypt when it's the last thing they want to do," I said. "But that's so childish. We've never not had a seder. Your mother will be crushed. Is that what you want?" "What I want is to have no part of it. I don't want to cross the Red Sea. And I don't want to be in Jerusalem next year. As far as I'm concerned, all of this is just worship of repetition and nothing more." And I stormed out of the room, extremely pleased with my *bon mot*. "But it's our last evening in Egypt," she said, as though that would change my mind.

For all my resistance, however, I decided to wear one of my new ties, a blazer, and a newly made pair of pointed black shoes. My mother, who joined me in the living room around half past seven, was wearing a dark-blue dress and her favorite jewelry. In the next room, I could hear the two sisters putting the final touches to the table, stowing away the unused silverware, which Abdou had just polished. Then my grandmother came in, making a face that meant Aunt Elsa was truly impossible. "It's always what she wants, never what others want." She sat down, inspected her skirt absentmindedly, spreading its pleats, then began searching through the bowl of peanuts until she found a roasted almond. We looked outside and in the window caught our own reflections. Three more characters, I thought, and we'll be ready for Pirandello.

Aunt Elsa walked in, dressed in purple lace that dated back at least three generations. She seemed to notice that I had decided to wear a tie. "Much better than those trousers with the snaps on them," she said, throwing her sister a significant glance. We decided to have vermouth, and Aunt Elsa said she would smoke. My mother also smoked. Then, gradually, as always happened during such gatherings, the sisters began to reminisce. Aunt Elsa told us about the little icon shop she had kept in Lourdes before the Second World War. She had sold such large quantities of religious objects to Christian pilgrims that no one would have guessed she was Jewish. But then, at Passover, not knowing where to buy unleavened bread, she had gone to a local baker and inquired about the various qualities of flour he used in his shop, claiming her husband had a terrible ulcer and needed special bread. The man said he did not understand what she wanted, and Elsa, distraught, continued to ask about a very light type of bread, maybe even unleavened bread, if such a thing existed. The man replied that surely there was an epidemic spreading around Lourdes, for many were suffering from similar gastric disorders and had been coming to his shop for the past few days asking the same question. "Many?" she asked. "Many, many," he replied, smiling, then whispered, "*Bonne pâque*, happy Passover," and sold her the unleavened bread.

"*Se non è vero, è ben trovato*, if it isn't true, you've made it up well," said my father, who had just walked in. "So, are we all ready?" "Yes, we were waiting for you," said my mother, "did you want some scotch?" "No, already had some."

Then, as we made toward the dining room, I saw that my father's right cheek was covered with pink, livid streaks, like nail scratches. My grandmother immediately pinched her cheek when she saw his face but said nothing. My mother too cast stealthy glances in his direction but was silent.

"So what exactly is it you want us to do now?" he asked Aunt Elsa, mildly scoffing at the ceremonial air she adopted on these occasions.

"I want you to read," she said, indicating Uncle Nessim's seat. My mother stood up and showed him where to start, pained and shaking her head silently the more she looked at his face. He began to recite in French, without irony, without flourishes, even meekly. But as soon as he began to feel comfortable with the text, he started to fumble, reading the instructions out loud, then correcting himself, or skipping lines unintentionally only to find himself reading the same line twice. At one point, wishing to facilitate his task, my grandmother said, "Skip that portion." He read some more and she interrupted again. "Skip that too."

"No," said Elsa, "either we read everything or nothing at all." An argument was about to erupt. "Where is Nessim now that we need him," said Elsa with that doleful tone in her voice that explained her success at Lourdes. "As far away from you as he can be," muttered my father under his breath, which immediately made me giggle. My mother, catching my attempt to stifle a laugh, began to smile; she knew exactly what my father had said though she had not heard it. My father, too, was infected by the giggling, which he smothered as best as he could, until my grandmother caught sight of him, which sent her laughing uncontrollably. No one had any idea what to do, what to read, or when to stop. "Some Jews we are," said Aunt Elsa, who had also started to laugh and whose eyes were tearing. "Shall we eat, then?" asked my father. "Good idea," I said. "But we've only just begun," protested Aunt Elsa, recovering her composure. "It's the very last time. How could you? We'll never be together again, I can just feel it." She was on the verge of tears, but my grandmother warned her that she, too, would start crying if we kept on like this. "This is the last year," said Elsa, reaching out and touching my hand. "It's just that I can remember so many seders held in this very room, for fifty years, year after year after year. And I'll tell you something," she said, turning to my father. "Had I known fifty years ago that it would end like this, had I known I'd be among the last in this room, with everyone buried or gone away, it would have been better to die, better to have died back then than to be left alone like this." "Calm yourself, Elsica," said my father, "otherwise we'll all be in mourning here."

At that point, Abdou walked in and, approaching my father, said there was someone on the telephone asking for him. "Tell them we are praying," said my father. "But sir—" He seemed troubled and began to speak softly. "So?" "She said she wanted to apologize." No one said anything. "Tell her not now." "Very well."

We heard the hurried patter of Abdou's steps up the corridor, heard him pick up the receiver and mumble something. Then, with relief, we heard him hang up and go back into the kitchen. It meant she had not insisted or argued. It meant he would be with us tonight. "Shall we eat, then?" said my mother. "Good idea," I repeated. "Yes, I'm starving," said Aunt Elsa. "An angel you married," murmured my grandmother to my father.

After dinner, everyone moved into the smaller living room, and, as was her habit on special gatherings, Aunt Elsa asked my father to play the record she loved so much. It was a very old recording by the Busch Quartet, and Aunt Elsa always kept it in her room, fearing someone might ruin it. I had noticed it earlier in the day lying next to the radio. It meant she had been planning the music all along. "Here," she said, gingerly removing the warped record from its blanched dust jacket with her arthritic fingers. It was Beethoven's "Song of Thanksgiving." Everyone sat down, and the adagio started.

The old 78 hissed, the static louder than the music, though no one seemed to notice, for my grandmother began humming, softly, with a plangent, faraway whine in her voice, and my father shut his eyes, and Aunt Elsa began shaking her head in rapt wonder, as she did sometimes when tasting Swiss chocolate purchased on the black market, as if to say, "How could anyone have created such beauty?"

And there, I thought, was my entire world: the two old ones writhing in a silent stupor, my father probably wishing he was elsewhere, and my mother, whose thoughts, as she leafed through a French fashion magazine, were everywhere and nowhere, but mostly on her husband, who knew that she would say nothing that evening and would probably let the matter pass quietly and never speak of it again.

I motioned to my mother that I was going out for a walk. She nodded. Without saying anything, my father put his hand in his pocket and slipped me a few bills.

Outside, Rue Delta was brimming with people. It was the first night of Ramadan and the guns marking the end of the fast had gone off three hours earlier. There was unusual bustle and clamor, with people gathered in groups, standing in the way of traffic, making things noisier and livelier still, the scent of holiday pastries and fried treats filling the air. I looked up at our building: on our floor, all the lights were out except for Abdou's and those in the living room. Such weak lights, and so scant in comparison to the gaudy, colored bulbs that hung from all the lampposts and trees—as if the electricity in our home were being sapped and might die out at any moment. It was an Old World, old-people's light.

As I neared the seafront, the night air grew cooler, saltier, freed from the din of lights and the milling crowd. Traffic became sparse, and whenever cars stopped for the traffic signal, everything grew still: then, only the waves could be heard, thudding in the dark, spraying the air along the darkened Corniche with a thin mist that hung upon the night, dousing the streetlights and the signposts and the distant floodlights by the guns of Petrou, spreading a light clammy film upon the pebbled stone wall overlooking the city's coastline. Quietly, an empty bus splashed along the road, trailing murky stains of light on the gleaming pavement. From somewhere, in scattered snatches, came the faint lilt of music, perhaps from one of those dance halls where students used to flock at night. Or maybe just a muted radio somewhere on the beach nearby, where abandoned nets gave off a pungent smell of seaweed and fish.

At the corner of the street, from a sidewalk stall, came the smell of fresh dough and of angel-hair being fried on top of a large copper stand—a common sight throughout the city every Ramadan. People would fold the pancakes and stuff them with almonds, syrup, and raisins. The vendor caught me eyeing the cakes that were neatly spread on a black tray. He smiled and said, "*Etfaddal*, help yourself."

I thought of Aunt Elsa's chiding eyes. "But it's Pesach," I imagined her saying. My grandmother would disapprove too— eating food fried by Arabs on the street, unconscionable. The Egyptian didn't want any money. "It's for you," he said, handing me the delicacy on a torn sheet of newspaper.

I wished him a good evening and took the soggy pancake out onto the seafront. There, heaving myself up on the stone wall, I sat with my back to the city, facing the sea, holding the delicacy I was about to devour. Abdou would have called this a real *mazag*, accompanying the word, as all Egyptians do, with a gesture of the hand—a flattened palm brought to the side of the head—signifying blissful plenitude and the prolonged, cultivated consumption of everyday pleasures.

Facing the night, I looked out at the stars and thought to myself, over there is Spain, then France, to the right Italy, and, straight ahead, the land of Solon and Pericles. The world is timeless and boundless, and I thought of all the shipwrecked, homeless mariners who had strayed to this very land and for years had tinkered away at their damaged boats, praying for a wind, only to grow soft and reluctant when their time came.

I stared at the flicker of little fishing boats far out in the offing, always there at night, and watched a group of children scampering about on the beach below, waving little Ramadan lanterns, the girls wearing loud pink-and-fuchsia dresses, locking hands as they wove themselves into the dark again, followed by another group of child revelers who were flocking along the jetty past the sand dunes, some even waving up to me from below. I waved back with a familiar gesture of street fellowship and wiped the light spray that had moistened my face.

And suddenly I knew, as I touched the damp, grainy surface of the seawall, that I would always remember this night, that in years to come I would remember sitting here, swept with confused longing as I listened to the water lapping the giant boulders beneath the promenade and watched the children head toward the shore in a winding, lambent procession. I wanted to come back tomorrow night, and the night after, and the one after that as well, sensing that what made leaving so fiercely painful was the knowledge that there would never be another night like this, that I would never eat soggy cakes along the coast road in the evening, not this year or any other year, nor feel the baffling, sudden beauty of that moment when, if only for an instant, I had caught myself longing for a city I never knew I loved.

Exactly a year from now, I vowed, I would sit outside at

night wherever I was, somewhere in Europe, or in America, and turn my face to Egypt, as Moslems do when they pray and face Mecca, and remember this very night, and how I had thought these things and made this vow. You're beginning to sound like Elsa and her silly seders, I said to myself, mimicking my father's humor.

On my way home I thought of what the others were doing. I wanted to walk in, find the smaller living room still lit, the Beethoven still playing, with Abdou still clearing the dining room, and, on closing the front door, suddenly hear someone say, "We were just waiting for you, we're thinking of going to the Royal." "But we've already seen that film," I would say. "What difference does it make. We'll see it again."

And before we had time to argue, we would all rush downstairs, where my father would be waiting in a car that was no longer really ours, and, feeling the slight chill of a late April night, would huddle together with the windows shut, bicker as usual about who got to sit where, rub our hands, turn the radio to a French broadcast, and then speed to the Corniche, thinking that all this was as it always was, that nothing ever really changed, that the people enjoying their first stroll on the Corniche after fasting, or the woman selling tickets at the Royal, or the man who would watch our car in the side alley outside the theater, or our neighbors across the hall, or the drizzle that was sure to greet us after the movie at midnight would never, ever know, nor ever guess, that this was our last night in Alexandria.

TAMIM ANSARY
Afghanistan

Tamim Ansary (1948–) was born in the capital city of Kabul in Afghanistan to a Pashtun Afghan father, Amanuddin, and an American-Finnish woman, Terttu. Identified as an "American" by his classmates, Ansary was part of a large, close-knit clan and grew up as a Muslim in a comfortable bicultural household. His father had studied in the U.S. through the support of the royal family and was later the dean of the College of Literature at Kabul University, while his mother taught English at a girls' school. At the suggestion of an American friend, Tamim applied for and won a scholarship to Colorado Rocky Mountain High School in Fort Collins, Colorado, and then left Afghanistan in 1964, at age sixteen, with his mother and siblings. After graduating high school and college, he went on to become a senior editor of educational publications and an author.

Between 1953 and the 1970s, only 230 Afghans are estimated to have immigrated to the U.S. to become citizens, but it's debatable whether the Ansarys should be considered a part of this group. As Tamim explains, according to the Afghan government, he and his siblings were Afghan by birth through their father, but they could assert U.S. citizenship through their mother. Immigration from Afghanistan to the U.S. would dramatically increase in the wake of the Soviet invasion in 1980, resulting in a steady annual stream of up to four thousand immigrants through the decade, leading to an estimated forty-five thousand to seventy-five thousand refugees by 1990. A second wave of immigration to the U.S. began in 1996 with Afghans fleeing the Taliban, an increase halted in 2001 following the 9/11 attacks.

In the wake of those attacks, many Afghan immigrants experienced discrimination and felt isolated. Ansary was moved to try to put the situation into context for "anyone who [would] listen." An e-mail sent to friends on September 12 denounced Osama bin Laden and the Taliban before going on to distinguish them from the majority of impoverished Afghans. The message went viral, and he was soon being called on by media outlets to "interpret the Islamic world for the West." Ansary's timely, well-received memoir, West of Kabul, East of New York *(2002), charts his family's history in Afghanistan, his formative years in the U.S., along with his sobering 1980 trip through Islamic countries and his experiences surrounding 9/11. Ansary continues to work as an editor, in addition to directing the San Francisco Writers Workshop. In this excerpt from the prologue of his memoir, Ansary recalls the "volcanic moment" that changed his life.*

Excerpt from

West of Kabul, East of New York

— 2002 —

For many long years, my siblings and I thought we were the only Afghans in America. When I introduced myself to people, they'd say, "Interesting name. Where are you from?" When I said Afghanistan, I could feel myself changing, not unpleasantly, into a curiosity. Few knew where Afghanistan was, and some were amazed to learn it existed at all. Once, in a college gym class, a coach found my free-throw shooting form humorous.

"Where have you been all your life," he guffawed, *"Afghanistan?"* When I said yes, he was taken aback: he thought Afghanistan was just an expression, like ultima Thule, meaning "off the map."

The Soviet invasion put Afghanistan on the map, but it didn't last. By the summer of 2001, a new acquaintance could say to me, "Afghanistan, huh? I never would have guessed you're from Africa."

That all changed on September 11, 2001. Suddenly, everywhere I went, strangers were talking about Kandahar and Kunduz and Mazar-i-Sharif. On September 12, the abrupt notoriety of Afghanistan triggered a volcanic moment in my own small life.

I was driving around San Francisco that day, listening to talk radio. My mind was chattering to itself about errands and deadlines, generating mental static to screen me off from my underlying emotions, the turmoil and dread. On the radio, a woman caller was making a tearful, ineffective case against going to war over the terrorist attacks in New York and Washington. The talk-show host derided her. A man called in to say that the enemy was not just Afghanistan but people like that previous caller as well. The talk-show host said thoughtfully, "You're making a lot of sense, sir."

The next caller elaborated on what should be done to Afghanistan: "Nuke that place. Those people have to learn. Put a fence around it! Cut them off from medicine! From food! Make those people starve!"

More than thirty-five years had passed since I had seen Afghanistan, but the ghosts were still inside me, and as I listened to that apoplectically enraged talk on the radio, those ghosts stirred to life. I saw my grandmother K'koh, elfin soul of the Ansary family. Oh, she died long ago, but in my mind she died again that day, as I pictured the rainfall of bombs that would be coming. And I saw my father, the man who wouldn't, or couldn't, leave when the Soviets put the country in a clamp. He was long gone, too, but if he'd lived, he would be in Kabul now, an eighty-three-year-old man, in rags on the streets, his ribs showing, one of the many who would be starving when the fence was flung up around our land.

I didn't begrudge those callers their rage, but I felt a bewilderment deeper than shock. No one seemed to know how pitifully harmless Afghans were, strong contenders for the Poorest People on Earth award, overrun by the world's most hardened criminals, and now, it seemed, marked out to suffer for the crimes of their torturers.

I wanted to call that talk show, but when I came home, I felt too shy. I'd never spoken to the media at any level. So I went downstairs to my office and wrote an e-mail to a few of my friends. I poured out to them what I would have said to the public if I could have mustered the courage to call that talk show. The moment I clicked on SEND, I felt infinitesimally better.

Later that day, some of the people on my list asked if they could pass my note on to their friends, and I said, "Sure," thinking, Wow, with luck, I might reach fifty or sixty people.

That night, I logged on to my server and found a hundred e-mails in my in-box, mostly from strangers responding to the message I'd hammered out earlier. It boggled my mind. The power of the Internet! I had reached . . . hundreds.

The next day, I realized something bigger was rising under me. At noon I got a call from my old friend Nick Allen, whom I hadn't seen in fifteen years. Somehow, he'd received the e-mail and had felt moved to track me down and say hi.

An hour later, I heard from Erik Nalder, the son of an American engineer, whom I had last seen in Afghanistan thirty-eight years ago. He'd received my e-mail—I couldn't imagine how—and had felt moved to track me down and say hi.

Then the phone rang again. A caller from Chicago. A hesitant voice. "My name is Charles Sherman. . . ." Did I know this guy? "I got your e-mail. . . ." I couldn't place him. "You don't know me," he said.

"Then how did you get my number?"

"I looked you up on the Internet—anyone can get your number. . . . I just wanted to tell you that . . . your e-mail made a lot of sense to me."

I thanked him and hung up, but my heart was pounding. Strangers were reading my e-mail, and anyone could get my phone number. What if the next caller said, "Hi, I'm with the Taliban"? What if Al Qaeda knocked on the door? How long before some hysterical racist sent a brick through my window?

I wanted to cancel my e-mail. "I've reached enough people, thank you; that will be all." But it was too late. I couldn't withdraw the e-mail. I couldn't issue corrections, amendments, or follow-ups. My e-mail spread like a virus throughout the United States and across the world. My e-mail accounts overflowed with responses, and the servers had to start deleting messages I had not read. Radio stations started calling—then newspapers—then TV. By the fourth day, I found myself putting *World News Tonight* on hold to take a call from Oprah's people—inconceivable! I have no idea how many people received the e-mail ultimately. A radio station in South Africa claimed it reached 250,000 people in that country alone. Worldwide, I have to guess, it reached millions—within a week.

What had I written? I wondered. Why the response? I barely had time to ponder these bewildering questions. The media seized on me as a pundit. The questions came at me like hornets pouring out of a nest, and all I could do was swing at them. From those first few insane weeks, I only remember Charlie Rose's skeptical face looming toward me with the question, "But Tamim . . . can you really compare the Taliban to *Nazis*?"

I tried to tell him about that guy I'd met in Turkey, the one in the pin-striped suit who had wanted to convert me to his brand of Islam, and the horror that had filled me as I read his literature afterward, but my long-winded digression wasn't appropriate for that or any TV show. I stumbled out of the studio, my mind reeling. What *did* I mean? The words I had used in that e-mail were so brutal. The Taliban, I had written, are a

CULT
of IGNORANT
PSYCHOTICS.
When you think *BIN LADEN,* think
HITLER.

I never would have used such language if I'd thought millions of people were listening. I'm sure I would have measured my language more carefully. But in that case, probably no one would have listened. And had I misspoken? Would I now renounce my words? I decided the answer was no.

Two weeks later, my cousin's wife, Shafiqa, called to tell me there was going to be a memorial service for Ahmed Shah Massoud that night, complete with speeches, videotapes, posters, and more speeches. I should come.

Massoud was the last credible anti-Taliban leader in Afghanistan, the man who put together the Northern Alliance, a towering figure, assassinated by Arab suicide bombers two days before the attacks on the World Trade Center. I admired Massoud, and his assassination disheartened me, but I was just too spent to go to his memorial service. "I need to rest," I pleaded.

Shafiqa was silent for a moment. Then she said, "Listen, Tamim, we are all proud of what you have done. You have written a letter. That's good. But Massoud slept with only a stone for a pillow for twenty-three years. He scarcely knew the names of his children, because he would not set down the burden of liberating our country. I think he was tired at times, too. I think you should be at his memorial service."

I hung my head in shame and said I would be there.

The following week, a representative of the Northern Alliance phoned me. "You have the ear of the American media. You know how to say things. We know what things must be said. Let us work together. From now on, you must be the spokesman."

"The spokesman? For what? For whom?"

"For our cause. For our country."

I could feel my ears shutting down and my eyes looking for the back door. Was Afghanistan really my country?

Dear reader, let me pause to introduce myself properly. Yes, I was born and raised in Afghanistan, and I know Islam intimately, from the inside, in my very soul. Yes, I learned to say my prayers from my Afghan grandmother; yes, I know the flavor of sundown on the first day of Ramadan, when you're on the porch with the people you love, waiting for the cannon that will mark the moment when a white thread can no longer be distinguished from a black one and you can put the day's first sweet date in your mouth.

But my mother was American, and not just any American, but a secular one to the max, and a feminist back when there hardly *was* such a thing—the daughter of an immigrant labor agitator in Chicago who would have been a Communist if only he could have accepted orders from anyone but his own conscience. And I moved to America at age sixteen, and graduated from Reed College, and grew my hair down to my waist, and missed Woodstock by minutes, and revered Bob Dylan back when his voice still worked. I made a career in educational publishing, and if you have children, they have probably used some product I have edited or written. I am an American.

How could I be an adequate spokesman for Afghanistan or for Muslims?

"Look, I have nothing to tell people but my own small story," I told the fellow from the Northern Alliance. "Maybe I can help Americans see that Afghans are just human beings like anyone else. That's about all I can do."

"That is important, too," he said, his voice softened by anxiety and despair.

In the weeks that followed, however, the media kept punching through to me, and I kept answering their questions. It turned out that I did have plenty to say about Afghanistan, Islam, and fundamentalism, because I have been pondering these issues all my life—the dissonance between the world I am living in now and the world I left behind, a world that is lost to me. And as I kept talking, it struck me that I was not the only one who had lost a world. There was a lot of loss going around. Perhaps it wasn't really nostalgia for the seventh century that was fueling all this militancy. Perhaps it was nostalgia for a world that existed much more recently, traces of which still linger in the social memory of the Islamic world. Lots of people have parents, or grandparents, or at least great-grandparents who grew up in that world. Some people even know that world personally, because they were born in it. I am one of those people. . . .

My friend Roger Fritz went to a private high school in Colorado called CRMS—Colorado Rocky Mountain School—but he spent summer vacations with his family, which had moved to Lashkargah. In the summer of 1963, he told me that CRMS would give me a scholarship if I wrote to them. "They'd even pay your way to America," he said. "They did that for a couple of boys from Africa." It was a throwaway comment on his part, but it lodged in my brain like a worm.

I had big plans that summer. The swimming pool was back

in operation and I hoped to better my record of swimming forty continuous laps. I had started on this project when the bombshell dropped.

The king seized power.

From whom does an absolute monarch seize power? Well, Zahir Shah (King Zahir) had been a figurehead ever since he was nineteen, when the assassination of his father put him on the throne. Normally, his adult uncles would have eliminated him and then fought among themselves, but the Mohammedzai uncles broke the pattern. They put the prince on the throne and took turns running the country as prime minister. Various royal relatives held all other top posts in the government. This civilized autocracy gave Afghanistan forty years of stability. King Zahir, formerly the prince, got to live in a palace, ride in a Rolls-Royce, and take vacations in Italy. But he did not get to order troops into battle, set policy vis-à-vis Pakistan, or go eyeball-to-eyeball with the Soviet ambassador.

When the last uncle died, the king's cousin Daoud took charge, and this must have chafed. The king was getting on toward fifty, and no doubt he wanted to be a real king at last. And then Daoud screwed up. He forced a macho showdown with Pakistan over a border dispute—and lost. When he backed down, Afghanistan lost face. This gave Zahir Shah an opening.

The king moved swiftly to fire his cousin and all the rest of his relatives. He announced that he was launching Afghanistan on a path to democracy. He convened a committee of "wise men" (including my uncle Najmuddin) to draft a new constitution, and they came up with a document that *prohibited*—strong language!—any member of the royal family from holding any cabinet-level post in government. Henceforth, only commoners could hold these posts.

In 1963, the king accepted this constitution, which then became the law of the land. Commoners like Dr. Kayeum and my father had been groomed to administer the country. Now they were being invited to step up and rule it. The Western-educated technocrats began jockeying for power.

My father did not get in on the jockeying. He was in the United States on government business at the time, and his best friend did not save him a seat at the show. The scrambling must have been intense, and Kayeum no doubt had his hands full securing his own seat. Nonetheless, when my father returned to Afghanistan and discovered that all his friends had moved up and he was an unemployed has-been, he felt betrayed.

His "best friend," Dr. Abdul Kayeum, was now Minister of Interior. In Afghanistan (as in most Third World countries), this ministry did not concern itself with recreation and parks. It was in charge of keeping the "interior" under control. It mirrored the foreign portfolio. The minister appointed governors, operated the police force, and conducted diplomacy with the ever-dangerous tribes. A comparable office in the United States would run the state governments, the National Guard, and the FBI. On paper, then, Kayeum was roughly the fifth-most-powerful man in Afghanistan.

Kayeum promised to get my father a post in the Ministry of Interior, and he did, a few months later, but not the post my father expected—that of deputy minister. My father got a job one rung lower down, director of administration or some such.

His government-issue car served as a visible emblem of his fall. Cabinet ministers and their deputies each got a Mercedes. We got a clunky cast-iron Soviet-made Volga. We were Volga-class officials now. It could have been worse. We could have gotten a Moscovitz, the Soviet version of a Ford Escort. Or no car at all. Or we could have fallen out of government service altogether, back into Neolithic Afghanistan.

But I could only see what we weren't. My teenage years in Afghanistan were dominated by the shame of my father's fall, even though in truth he was not such a failure. He was four tiers down from ruling the country, maybe five. What did I want of him—that he lead a coup d'état? I don't know.

My father's appointment meant we had to move back to Kabul. Our quasi-American life in Lashkargah was over. My mother was depressed. We children were depressed. At the last of several going-away parties, Rona cast off all pretense of doling out her favors equally and chose Matt, clinging to him during the last dance. I was not jealous. It was Matt I loved—our camaraderie, our trips to the island, our explorations of the ruined city, our swimming competitions at the pool. Competing for Rona was just an element in our great friendship, now ending.

We returned to the family compound with the nine-foot walls. It seemed so much smaller now, prisonlike. I enrolled in a Kabul high school, the one situated next to the Royal Palace. Most of the upper-class families sent their sons there—the various branches of the royal family and those commoners who had risen to the level of cabinet minister. Among them, I felt humiliated because we had sunk to Volga-class status.

Istiqlal was the second-oldest school in Afghanistan and still in its original plant, a standard Afghan compound: a ring of rooms surrounding a courtyard hidden from the public eye. The classrooms smelled of mold and must, and the floors were of worn, uneven brick. Each of the Kabul high schools had been built by a different Western country—two by the United States, one by Germany, and this one, Istiqlal, by France.

All the scientific and technical classes at Istiqlal—math, physics, chemistry, and the like—were taught by Frenchmen, in French. Another new language! I studied nothing but French for six months. Only then could I attend regular Istiqlal classes. We sat in the familiar rows of two-person desks. My seatmate, Humayun, was fond of sexual innuendo and often tried teasingly to feel me up. Once, he pulled his homework out of his notebook clumsily and a chunk tore out of the middle. When I suggested that the teacher might not like this, he winked at me and said, "I'll just tell him, 'But Teacher-sir, every one of God's creatures has a hole.'" I had to laugh in disbelief that he'd found a way to put a sexual slant on even this trivial situation.

That year, the government decided to follow up on the Lashkargah experiment and move toward coeducation in the Kabul schools. Our school was chosen as the testing ground. Again they started slowly, with just two girls. One was the daughter of a Madame Shukoor, a French woman married to an Afghan. The other was good old Rona Kayeum again. There they sat, in our classroom at Istiqlal, wearing the regulation outfit: black dress, black stockings, white head scarf, gloves, the works.

In all the months those girls were in my class, only once did I hear words exchanged between them and any boy. I remember the occasion clearly. The French–Afghan girl (I don't remember her name) approached a clump of boys and said, "Does anyone have a pencil I can use?"

A pencil, for God's sake! Of all things for her to request! But there was no eruption of sexual humor. Although I'm sure these boys knew nothing of the episode in Lashkargah, they knew not to treat intergender stuff in the public realm lightly. Not in that era, not in Afghanistan. With great ceremony and utmost tact, my seatmate, Mr. Sexual Innuendo himself, walked up the aisle to the front of the room and placed a pencil on the arm of a chair, where she could pick it up after he had sat down again.

Such was coeducation in Afghanistan. But here's the thing. When I got home, I'd go over to the Kayeums'; they lived down the block from us again. Rona and I would discuss the day at school, laugh at the religion teacher. I'd tell her who was who among the boys: We were friends, and with a sexual tingle.

Two systems. The mind cannot contain both as legitimate. That's my testimony. When you're in two worlds so different, your mind is forced to say that one is legitimate and the other is a crock.

My mind chose the American ethos as legitimate. Why? Because it promised more fun? I don't know. I do know, however, that on this issue of sex, Afghanistan and I parted ways. And parting ways on this, we parted ways on everything. I'll go out on a limb and say that I think it is on this issue of sex and the relationship between the sexes that Islam and the West have parted ways, and parting ways on this, have parted ways on everything.

One day, application forms arrived from CRMS. I went out to the backyard and gazed at jagged mountains far away. Growing up, I had dreamed of living alone in the mountains when I came of age. It amounted to a spiritual yearning—an intense desire to be part of all that naked beauty. Now, the idea of going to America had that same quality—that same intensity and sweetness, that same "Is this actually possible?" feel. Could I, Tamim Ansary, son of a Volga-class Afghan official, actually live in America someday? I just couldn't tell.

Nervously, I filled out the application. As it happened, my parents were already busy working out a way to send my sister Rebecca to college in the United States. They'd found an option in Kentucky, at a college called Berea, which would basically be free if she could get in.

When I told my parents about my CRMS scheme, they thrummed with hope. After twenty years in Afghanistan, my mother wanted to return to America. And that whole business with the Volga-class job had left my father angry and embittered. He was ready to consider a move. My parents told me that if I could get a scholarship to CRMS, they'd somehow rustle up the airfare.

The day the letter of acceptance arrived from CRMS, I told Humayun I was going to America on a high school scholarship. He stood up in math class that day and announced the news to the whole class. The teacher, a Frenchman famous for slapping misbehaving students with a limp hand—the boys said it felt like a sack of boneless meat—just stared at me and said, *"Très bien. Bonne chance."*

Another few months would pass before I left for America, but after that day, the classes, the boys, the courtyard, the willow trees, the soccer games, the homosexual innuendos, all grew curiously fantastic, as if Afghanistan was losing its reality for me while I was still in the middle of it.

Sometime in those last days, Madame Shukoor invited our family to a party. We'd never had much truck with French-Afghans, but we recognized them to be part of that charmed otherworld, the West. The Kayeums were invited, too, and so were about a dozen other Afghan–European families. After dinner, one room was cleared of furniture, and we young people danced to rock 'n' roll records. Madame Shukoor's daughter was wearing a red cashmere sweater and a skirt that ended at her knees, leaving her legs bare. All that school year, I had seen her only out of the corner of my eye, garbed in bat black and covered with a head shawl. Never had I forgotten myself so utterly as to meet her eyes. Now suddenly she was a vibrant, hot-blooded female; we were dancing and trading repartee; she was letting me hold her close during slow numbers. It wasn't lust that I felt; it was passionate romantic love. Needless to say, I never set eyes on her again.

Late one night, a Mr. Green from the American embassy knocked on the door of our compound. My father let him in. He hurried furtively across the yard and to the house, a blond man in a long khaki coat. He was carrying a bulky briefcase. We pulled shut the burlap curtains in the living room, turned off the lights, and lit candles so no one could peep in at us. Then he opened the briefcase and produced the dangerous document hidden within: the U.S. Constitution.

My mother, it turned out, had discovered she was still an American citizen. She had never lost her citizenship, because she had never renounced it. And when we kids were born, she had gone to the U.S. embassy and quietly registered our births, never really knowing why. As a result, however, we could now be U.S. citizens, too, just by swearing an oath.

Mr. Green set the Constitution on the dining room table; we raised our hands in the candlelight and swore to uphold the laws of the United States. Then he handed us our passports. I felt like one of those peasants in the fairy tales who discover that they are actually princes who were given away at birth to protect them from some evil spell. Now that we had come of age, we could claim our rightful inheritance. We were Americans after all!

My father was there, but he didn't get a passport, of course, because he certainly wasn't an American citizen, but I didn't think we were leaving him behind. I assumed he would be staying in Kabul only long enough to tie up the loose ends of his affairs. Then he would follow us to America, where we would all be together as a family again.

And later, in America, when people asked if my parents were separated, I always said no, except for the fact that she was in America and he in Kabul. After our departure, my father's fortunes turned around in Afghanistan. He jumped to the Mercedes level of government official by receiving the post he coveted, Deputy Minister of Interior. But he gave it up and followed us to America. He took the very junior position of press attaché at the Afghan embassy in Washington, D.C., a job far beneath his age and status, in order to live with us.

The job didn't even last a whole year, however. The government in Kabul went through some upheaval, and a faction unfriendly to my father came to power. They stripped him of his job by abolishing his position. I was away at school when this happened, but my brother was home. And I learned many years later that when my father broke the news about his job at the dinner table, my brother burst out crying. He was only nine or so, but he knew what this meant. He knew it meant that my father was going to leave us, and that our family, so recently joined together, would be torn asunder.

And that's just what happened. The Kabul government ordered my father to come home, whereupon he faced a decision. Should he obey his orders or stay in America with us? His American option was to apply for a position as professor of Persian literature in an American university. All summer, he kicked around the apartment morosely, doing crossword puzzles and trying to decide. I had no sympathy for his anguish. I had just finished my junior year at Colorado Rocky Mountain School and was busy exploring college options. Big school or little? Urban or small-town locale? Classical education or one of those free-form new schools springing up? Now, those were some tough decisions, in my opinion.

My father's situation struck me as a no-brainer. A college professor—what a great life! What was the problem?

Only later did I realize that my father was not fundamentally agonizing over his job prospects. In his mid-forties by then, he felt a dreadful finality about the choice. If he went back, he might never get out again: He would lose us. If he stayed, he might never be allowed into Afghanistan again: He would lose his larger family, his brothers, the clan—that greater self to which an Afghan belongs by birthright.

In the end, he chose the larger family. Without them, I think, he felt he wouldn't exist. I was away at school when he took off, so I never did say good-bye to my father, and I certainly didn't say it or even think it the night Mr. Green gave us our passports.

• • •

I never said a real good-bye to my relatives in Afghanistan, either, because we weren't supposed to be leaving forever. The
Afghan government didn't consider us to be Americans. To
them, we were Afghans, since our father was an Afghan and
since we children were born in Afghanistan. Officially, therefore, we would be returning at some point. My father completed
the paperwork and bribed the necessary bureaucrats to get us
Afghan passports.

We arrived at the airport with our American passports hidden in our baggage. At the gate, we showed our Afghan passports and travel documents. Even the other Ansarys thought that
my sister and I were going abroad to study and that my mother
and eight-year-old brother were coming along just to get us settled. Our departure from Afghanistan was actually a defection—
an escape. The plane took off and I watched the terminal
receding below. About leaving Afghanistan, I felt nothing. I
only felt sorry to be separated from that girl in the red cashmere
sweater. I fell asleep fantasizing that we would meet again someday in the United States . . . where we could date. . . .

The next thing I knew, we were landing in Tehran and our
journey to the West had truly begun. Soon I would be relieved
of the discomforts of a divided self, free to roam the world as just
one person: Tamim Ansary, American guy.

H. B. CAVALCANTI

Brazil

H. B. (Keo) Cavalcanti (1956–) was born in northeast Brazil, the son of Brazilian Protestants, a significant minority in this widely Catholic country. His forebears had converted to Protestantism in the nineteenth century, under the influence of ministers from the American South. The Protestant clergy had come to Brazil to attend to the spiritual needs of refugees from the Confederacy, who found themselves more at home with the racial stratification there than they were with Reconstruction. Cavalcanti grew up with a deep fascination for U.S. culture, especially its music, and most especially its Southern folkways. In Brazil, he took bachelor's degrees: first in theology and then in law, before he traveled to the U.S. to pursue his graduate education. His first postgraduate degree was in social work (from the Southern Baptist Theological Seminary in Louisville), but he soon transferred his interest to sociology and earned his doctorate at Vanderbilt. Cavalcanti taught at the University of Richmond and, for the bulk of his career, at James Madison University, where he is now a professor emeritus.

Almost Home: A Brazilian American's Reflections on Faith, Culture, and Immigration *(2012) is unique among the autobiographies on which this collection is based, primarily because it is written by a scholar looking at his career as an individual immigrant tale as well as a general case study. Interwoven with episodes of Cavalcanti's life are his meditations and explanations, drawn from his long career studying the sociology of immigration. He shows, for example, how the immigrant experience from South America is particularly conditioned by living under military dictatorships and the adjustments these immigrants must make when they find themselves living beyond a police state. He also shows how his career fits a significant immigration pattern of immigrants who come to the U.S. for its superior training in sciences and technology (foreign-born students compose anywhere between 33 percent and 60 percent of doctorates in these fields) and then find employment in the U.S. upon the completion of their studies.*

As a sociologist, Cavalcanti can also analyze how immigrants, from all over, make sense of their new environments. He draws our attention to how his life models the immigrant experience as a "cultural hybrid," meaning those immigrants, more and more populous in a global society, who embrace two cultures, the home and the host societies, and do not see the necessity or allure of forsaking one for the other. Instead, such binationals seek to flourish in both worlds, enjoying the richness of both cultures. In the nineteenth century, such a vision would have been much more difficult to sustain, but modern travel and communication actually encourage such hybridism. What for immigrants of the past was a source of anxiety and conflict can now be a life-enhancing, animating wholeness.

Excerpt from

Almost Home

— 2012 —

Long and Winding Road

If migration benefits both migrant and host country, why aren't more outsiders moving to the United States? The answer is simple—given the large volume of applicants, even when done by the book, immigration and naturalization are slow and cumbersome processes. All travelers to the United States need an entry visa to come legally into the country. The types of entry visa range from family reunification to studying to opening a business to being a temporary worker or even a refugee. Once here, of course, the next step is to obtain a legal permanent resident visa, a green card. Green-card holders are allowed to work, to travel abroad, to own property on U.S. soil, and they can eventually request American citizenship.

But the immigration logjams start at the entry visa point. By 2004 the total backlog for entry visa applications to the United States stood at 4.7 million petitions. Meanwhile, family reunification visas that year were capped at 480,000, employment visas at 140,000, and the White House set the limit for refugees at 70,000. It is not hard to see why the logjam keeps growing. The funneling effect starts at the entry level. Once here, immigrants come up against further backlogs. By law only 140,000 green cards are issued annually. So the backlog for green-card requests is equally staggering, with a waiting period that runs up to five years or more. By one estimate there are currently 615,000 people waiting for their green cards. Then you have the backlog for citizenship, too. Some 1.4 million green-card holders sought to become U.S. citizens in 2007, double the number of requests for 2006.

As you clear each logjam, be prepared to pay a series of hefty fees to change your immigration status. The application for employment authorization costs $340. The fee for a green card is now about $930, with an $80 separate fee for collection of fingerprints and associated biometric data. The final step, the application for naturalization, costs $595. Those fees are expected to go up soon. If you are an employer, sponsoring an immigrant could cost you from $3,000 to $5,000 in fees. But if his green card is delayed for six years or more, the employer has to apply for extensions. Of course, the fees do not include the immigrant's own legal expenses. Successful immigration cases, managed by competent immigration attorneys, can range anywhere from $5,000 to $20,000.

Obviously, the logjams and time delays complicate the immigration and naturalization processes, exacting quite a toll on those waiting for a status change. I entered the United States in 1981 on a student visa (F-1), planning to finish my MDiv and PhD programs at the Southern Baptist Theological Seminary and return to Recife for a career in theological education, possibly ministry. Upon completing my MDiv, I discovered that the mission board sponsoring my U.S. studies was altering our agreement. I was told to return to Brazil for two years prior to requesting a renewed sponsorship for the PhD. Not willing to postpone my doctoral studies, I decided to transfer to a secular university.

When Vanderbilt University accepted me into the PhD program, my immigration status changed to that of a visiting scholar (H-1 visa). That visa allowed me to work on campus for a maximum of twenty hours a week. The campus job paid my bills except for large-scale expenses (you pray you won't get sick or need hospitalization, or that the car will not break down, etc.). But I never dared to travel abroad from 1983 to 1994, since there were no guarantees that my Certificate of Eligibility for Non-Immigrant Student Status (I-20) would be renewed. The inability to go home was an added hardship causing me to miss a number of critical events in the life of my extended family. I missed the funerals for my father, my grandparents, and my aunt. When Dad passed away, I had my green card but could not get the appropriate paperwork done in time to go pay my final respects.

There were missed joyous occasions as well. I missed my brothers' graduations and weddings. I missed the births of my nephew and my cousins' children. Each time my family moved into a new home, I missed the housewarming parties. Each time

they took a new job or started a business, I missed the appropriate celebrations. Family reunions were not frequent, thus ever
more precious. I missed them all. Waiting for a green card or a
final naturalization ceremony makes for a lonely exile. True, life
here gets better, you finish school, you get a good job, you start
your career, but at the cost of being unavailable to your loved
ones back home. I dedicated my PhD dissertation to my nanny,
but I was not there to pay my final respects to her, a woman who
was such an important part of my childhood.

My path to a green card came through teaching at a community college during my dissertation-writing days. That school
became my job sponsor with the Immigration and Naturalization Services. To hire me, they had to prove to the American
government that they could not find any qualified Americans
who could do my future job. Thankfully I had enough graduate
credits in counseling, philosophy, ethics, and sociology to make
me a unique candidate for the position they advertised. Nevertheless, what was supposed to have been a thirty-six-day process
took four years to complete. By the time the green card was issued I was already on my way to a tenure-track job in Virginia.

After clearing all the hurdles in my green-card application,
I bumped into one further step. Foreign students who complete
graduate studies in the United States are expected, due to international agreements between the United States and their countries, to spend two years back home prior to accepting an
American job. This has to do with preventing brain drain, with
keeping the United States from "stealing" highly qualified
workers from other nations. Never mind that the Brazilian government did not contribute a dime toward my graduate education. Never mind that they had offered me no jobs had I
returned. I still had to request a waiver from the Brazilian authorities in order to finalize the green-card process.

Since there is a five-year waiting period before green-card
holders can petition the American government for naturaliza-

tion, it took me a decade to finally become an American citizen. After my son was born in Tennessee, I had decided to stay in the United States, and that led to the community college job offer. The school applied for my green card in 1989. It arrived in 1993. But I would not become a U.S. citizen until 1999, literally ten years after my initial application. In my case, doing everything by the book meant that I would spend those ten years of my life in suspense, waiting to find out whether my American stay was temporary or permanent. And that did not include the previous eight years I had spent in graduate school on student visas.

Requiring someone to put his life on hold for ten years is a hardship. Looking back now, I realize that I risked a lot. The consequences would have been severe had I not gotten the green card and become naturalized. Professionally, it would have meant going back to Brazil to restart my academic career after spending those ten years in the United States. Starting again in Brazil at the age of forty-three would have been difficult to say the least. My son was born in 1986. By the time I became an American citizen, he was an eighth grader and the United States had been the only home he had ever known. By then I had been divorced for two years. Thankfully, his Brazilian mother got her green card through my employment application. That way she did not have to return to Brazil while I stayed here with our son.

The irony is that I consider my personal immigration and naturalization experience as one of the most successful I have known. At no time was I required by American immigration authorities to leave the country and restart the process with the American Embassy back in my homeland. At no time was I deported or denied re-entry for overstaying my visa (something I took great pains to avoid). At no time did I breach my legal welcome, or was forced to go underground due to missing documentation or misunderstanding between my immigration attorney and the U.S. authorities. Despite the fact that U.S. immigration authorities lost all the original documents I sub-

mitted to them three times, documents difficult to produce in a
pre-digital-era Brazil, I still managed to get through the whole
thing without major disruptions.

I can't imagine what the process must be like for immigrants who come to the United States in other visa categories.
The backlog for those who migrate through the Family Reunification Act, for instance, has reached approximately 4 million
applicants in 2010. The average wait for a sibling of a Filipino
American to be issued an entry visa is twenty years. The delays
for business immigrants, guest workers, or those seeking asylum
as political refugees is quite lengthy as well. As Judy Golub, the
spokeswoman for the American Immigration Lawyers Association, put it, "Legal permanent residents often wait up to twenty
years to reunite with their spouses and children." To her, "Such
long separations make no sense in our pro-family nation and
reflect poorly on us."

One thing is certain. Migration is not for the faint of heart.

Becoming an Alien

Those of us who, in the words of Somerset Maugham, go "far
and wide in the search for something permanent," fail to realize
something crucial in our quest. Simply settling in a new land
does not a native make. Our drive to seek the familiar abroad
and our sense of comfort upon arriving at our new destination
delay our perception that our hosts may not be welcoming us
with open arms. Though we may feel that we belong to this new
place, the feeling may not be reciprocal. Though familiar with
our new country, we may still be seen as outsiders. It took me a
while to discover that. Language fluency, American manner-
isms, and awareness of local etiquette do smooth social relations.
And time in-country aids our seizing of local ways. But none of

that accomplishes tribal inclusion. All along, there remains an invisible line, which cannot be easily crossed. We live among them, but are still not of them.

Newcomers to the land, we might not see the barrier at first. After a few mishaps, we grow wise in sensing its boundaries. In a way, that is the dark side of Somerset Maugham's wise quote. We may be home in the new place, but we settle amid alien scenes, and we live among folks we may never fully know. Tragically, the longer we are here, the less our loved ones in our country of origin will understand us. They remain forlorn with our departure and eventual transformation. And our new relations will constantly measure our performance in their culture by their own standards. Thus, the price of "coming home" is to remain strangers—to our homeland folks and to our hosts in the new country.

Very few migration studies explore this duality of strangeness. But we immigrants know it well. It comes up whenever we gather, at work or leisure. We are constantly reminded of what it takes to navigate both worlds. We know which parts of us are missing when we visit home, and which are missing as we return to our new nation. We identify with certain things local residents of one place or the other do, and dislike others. We dwell in that netherworld created by the cherry-picking of elements from disparate cultures. Our identities always carry this mix of traits that are appreciated by both, and also traits that make us strangers to either group. Wherever we immigrants are, we share the same sense of wonder and frustration with the way we fit our surroundings.

We ponder what it must be like to be fully home in a single world. The questions multiply—why are certain virtues more cherished by one society than another? Are there any truly universal tastes? What social expectations are non-negotiable in a given society; which are flexible? Why? What social markers attest to one's "native status"? If so, why are natives unaware of their own markers? Things that seem so obvious to us easily escape folks who fully inhabit a single culture. For them, their way of life is just "the way things are." They are blessed with a healthy dose of ethnocentrism, that marvelous belief that their society's ways are superior to those of others.

Ethnocentrism is critical to group survival. The deeper one believes in the merits of her own society, the more she has a stake in preserving it. So, ethnocentrism fosters group solidarity. Without it, social cohesion (and social order) might collapse. In that sense, a nation's values represent the ultimate commitment its citizens make to each other as a group. Their norms set the baseline for appropriate and inappropriate behavior among its members, and for belonging or not to that particular community. Those who grow up in that group pick those norms up as part of their "natural" world. And their adherence to those standards engenders among them a deep sense of commonality, of group loyalty.

Ethnocentrism is formed over time, of course. In its daily dealings, a community generates the values and norms it needs to organize or smooth in-group relations and interactions. Children born to that community acquire those ways as they become fully functional members of the group. To group members, their behavior is the only appropriate way to live. "Insiders" don't distance themselves much from their group standards, lest they incur the group's penalties for deviating from "normal" behavior. This is why ethnocentrism leads group members to use their shared values as a yardstick by which to judge outsiders—people who do not follow or fit in their ways. Learning to recognize outsiders is important, because it helps members of the group reaffirm its boundaries, acknowledge its common identifiers.

Ethnocentrism works as the internal glue of a community. But it does little to prepare natives to positively appreciate or engage with the ways of other cultures. Ethnocentrism can smooth relationships within a group, but not as easily relationships between groups. As a result, members of a group develop cultural blinders as they gaze upon the ways of outsiders. Their ethnocentric approach to culture keeps them from realizing the relative nature of their customs, of their value judgments. They don't immediately assume that what they hold dear is simply a collective statement of preference. Instead, the question becomes, "the way we do things is the right way—who would not want to be like us?"

Since all communities have unique histories, their histories create different ways to address unique local problems. The value judgments of a given group simply represent the way it chooses to handle certain aspects of its common life. Other societies may find equally acceptable but distinct ways to reach the same goals, but the members of a given group are not aware of that. For instance—not every culture practices monogamy, not every culture raises children inside nuclear families, and not every culture recognizes kinship on both the mother's and father's side. And yet children in all those societies grow up fully acclimated to their ways and continue to perpetuate their values and norms without any major social disruption.

For group members, however, their norms and ways of life are not an option. They are the ultimate markers that set the insider apart from the alien in a given culture. Those of us who have lived in more than one society know that norms or values are not fixed. Monocultural folks are not so quick to buy that. So, learning to adapt to a host culture means understanding what it prizes and why. For outsiders, this adds a "layer," a second lens with which they now must perceive or interpret their new world.

But unlike a child born in that culture, we know we are adopting it. We know ours is an optional, intentional act on our part. We must learn to reason differently about the way we do things; we must develop different aspirations. Becoming ethnocentric in a new culture is a demanding process—one that feels very natural if you grew up in that community, but very artificial if you are picking it up later in life. And between those two cultural layers lies our tribal exclusion. Somehow, natives can tell when our adopted behavior falls short of the mark, when it comes across a bit artificial. They know it does not come naturally to us to act like them. So living abroad means engaging in constant rehearsals, in constant practice at being like people of our adopted country.

Furthermore, what makes learning a new culture even more difficult is that often the values prized by folks in a particular country reflect deep, contradictory social undercurrents. For instance, immigrants learn that Americans prize individualism even as we watch them work really hard to fit in, to conform at the same time—be it at work, in the neighborhood, or at the club. A nation's values are not necessarily logically ordered. They betray the group's internal conflicts, tensions, fissures. The values may contribute to the group's survival, but that does not assure their ultimate congruence. For those coming from the outside, that nuanced reading of an alien culture takes time, sensitivity, and a deep desire to belong.

Pledging Allegiance

If you are my age and grew up in Latin America, you are probably unfamiliar with the Anglo-Saxon need to swear public oaths. Pledge-making was part of our private lives, of course; but not public oaths, and never as an outward display of patriotism. We learned our national anthems in grade school, perhaps the state anthem, and a few assorted civic hymns. We lined up every morning at the school patio for the hoisting of the flag. And we pulled for our countries during international games and tournaments. But pledging allegiance was never part of our cultural vocabulary. We simply were our country's citizens, period. There was no choice but to ally ourselves with our own tribe. To us, pledging allegiance made no sense, since everything we did was immersed in our Brazilian-ness, Chilean-ness, Uruguayan-ness. Allegiance was implicit.

Only as a teenager in New Mexico did I discover the Anglo-Saxon need to swear public oaths. A foreign exchange student, I was confronted with the school ritual of the pledge of allegiance since the pledge was a constant presence in school activities. At first, the ritual felt very odd, very alien to me. That any natural-born citizen would be required to swear an oath of loyalty to his own country seemed a bit of overkill. But I could tell that those around me took it seriously. As a hallowed practice, the pledge was done willfully and without reservation (many times out of sheer force of habit). Only later, as a trained sociologist, would I dwell more carefully on the need for public displays of tribal allegiance. Back in New Mexico, the thought of pledging allegiance to one's own country seemed excessive.

Who else could my classmates pledge allegiance to? I wondered. Mexico? Canada? Born here, they knew no other way of life; they had lived in no other culture. Who could they be loyal to other than the only place they had ever known? And the more I learned about the pledge itself, the more puzzled I became. That it was written in 1892 by Francis Bellamy, a Baptist minister and Christian Socialist, to foster patriotism among readers of a popular children's magazine made little sense. The hallmark of the Baptist faith in the European Continent had been the separation of church and state, especially the freedom from oath-swearing! Why would a Baptist minister in the New World be so concerned with children's loyalty to their own country?

This is what I mean by cultural blinder. Something that makes perfect sense to a native is quite befuddling to the outsider. To a Latin American, who witnessed waves of military regimes break their promises to citizens, oath-swearing was simply meaningless. It cost nothing to mouth off words. It reminded me of what Dietrich Bonhoeffer, the German theologian, called "cheap grace," a promise devoid of any sacrifice. No self-discipline was required, no follow-through. The promise itself was the end goal. Nothing further was asked of those who swore it. By comparison, for us in Latin America, the point of living right seemed to be the faithful discharge of one's duties, not the pledging of it.

But if you grew up in an Anglo-Saxon culture, public oath-swearing was simply part of your larger civic life. Even British monarchs swore a coronation oath upon ascending to the throne, promising to govern their subjects according to the laws and customs of the land. Parliament passed the Coronation Oath in 1688, but an older version was already in use in 1660. British kings demanded the same swearing of their subjects. The Oath of Supremacy established by King Henry VIII in 1534, repealed by Queen Mary I, and re-established by Queen Elizabeth I in 1559, was required of anyone taking public or church office. The subject had to swear allegiance to the monarch as "Supreme Governor of the Church of England." Later on, the same oath was required of members of Parliament and those attending English universities. Failure to comply could lead to indictment for treason, as Sir Thomas More, the Roman Catholic counselor to King Henry VIII, discovered. He was tried and executed in 1535 on that account.

Clearly, the practice of public oaths transferred to the British colonies in the New World. To this day, an oath of office is still a common observance in the United States at all levels of government. Presidents, members of Congress, and Supreme Court justices are all sworn in at the beginning of their terms in office. That carries through to the state and local levels as well. Every citizen who registers to vote in Vermont is required to swear a Voter's Oath before a notary public. Vermont established the practice in its 1777 constitution. So, there is something to public pledging among people of Anglo-Saxon descent that almost rises to the level of the holy, something akin to civil religion.

Back in New Mexico, I never knew what to do as the occasion arose to pledge allegiance. On the one hand, I was not a citizen. Those around me knew that quite well. On the other, the pressure to conform was intense. Nothing feels more isolating than to be caught in a public ceremony as the only nonconformist. When everyone around you stood up and recited the oath, you had no choice but to follow them. Yet, what a strange experience it was, to pledge allegiance to another homeland at the tender age of fifteen. Part of me knew this was only a formality, a cherished rite of an alien culture. But there was something terribly amiss in the exercise. The rights and privileges covered by the oath did not apply to me. That may have been my first exercise in tribal exclusion.

Public oaths in the Anglo-Saxon world are meant to divide, to sift, to make visible distinct categories. When King Henry VIII demanded an Oath of Supremacy from his subjects, he used it to screen out the Roman Catholics in his kingdom. The oath bestowed advantages to some, and dispensed—in Sir Thomas More's case—deadly consequences to others. In the United States, the oath of office segregates the office holders from the rest of us. In Vermont, since 1777, it sets apart those who are eligible and willing to vote from those who are not. In the Anglo-Saxon world, oaths preserve the tribal boundaries of restricted communities. Thus, I should not have been surprised that the final step in my naturalization process would be the swearing an oath of allegiance to the United States at a public ceremony in an American court.

In fact, oath day is supposed to be the festive part of naturalization. Local papers and TV stations drop by the courthouse to cover the proceedings, while the Daughters of the American Revolution festoon the court chambers in civic motif to welcome the new citizens. Some ceremonies are even scheduled for important civic holidays, like July 4. Or they take place in hallowed locales like Independence Hall in Philadelphia or Mount Vernon, Washington's home in Virginia. This is the country welcoming brand-new citizens, so the red carpet is rolled out at last. As the final step to becoming an American, the oath carries tremendous symbolic meaning. But its demands make for quite a somber day for those of us who must swear it, for it separates us permanently from our birthplace and loved ones back home. Before an immigration judge, we swear the following:

> I hereby declare, on oath, that I absolutely and entirely renounce and abjure all allegiance and fidelity to any foreign prince, potentate, state or sovereignty, of whom or which I have heretofore been a subject or citizen; that I will support and defend the Constitution and laws of the United States of America against all enemies, foreign and domestic; that I will bear true faith and allegiance to the same; that I will bear arms on behalf of the United States when required by the law; that I will perform noncombatant service in the armed forces of the United States when required by the law; that I will perform work of national importance under civilian direction when required by the law; and that I take this obligation freely without any mental reservation or purpose of evasion; so help me God.

All of us who swore the oath that day had no problem supporting and defending the U.S. Constitution or the laws of the country. Nor did we have problems with bearing faith and allegiance to them. The pacifists among us might have struggled with the notion of bearing arms to defend our adopted nation, but the noncombatant service option would have assuaged them.

I do not think that any of us pledged the oath with mental reservation or purpose of evasion. After all, we chose to become Americans; no one forced us. It was the first part of the oath that weighed heavily on our minds. Publicly, in front of representatives of our adopted community, we were asked to absolutely renounce our homelands, to forfeit all allegiance to our birthplace, and to turn our backs on the home where we were raised.

This was not an easy promise to make, and no one I know did so with a light heart. Of course, we were glad to have become American citizens. Many of us had waited decades for the ceremony. Our friends honored us with their support at the occasion. But something very dear was given up that day. As immigrants, we understood the need for such an oath. We understood that we could not serve two masters. We understood that we had to start our citizenship in a new nation unencumbered by former loyalties. But the choice is neither easy nor joyful. The Daughters of the American Revolution present at our ceremony failed to comprehend that deep sadness, focusing instead on our bright future ahead. But we said goodbye to our past that day in such a public and irrevocable fashion.

Ironically, after I became a U.S. citizen, I was informed by the Brazilian Embassy that Brazil's constitution had been changed to recognize dual citizenship. It was now possible, at least on the Brazilian side, for me to remain a citizen of both countries. "But should you prefer to keep only your American citizenship you will have to request from the Brazilian government the divestment of your rights as a Brazilian citizen," instructed the embassy website. So, it turns out that my country of birth allows me to fully forsake it, but only in a public statement, one that has to be published in the official acts of the Brazilian Congress. Even Latin American countries now have ways to segregate their former citizens.

A "Hyphenated" American

Not long after my naturalization ceremony one of my Anglo professor friends asked in half-jest, "How does it feel to be a Hispanic-American now?" Despite living in the U.S. for eighteen years and teaching about race and ethnicity regularly, I was not prepared for the "joke." Only then did the importance of ethnic boundaries finally dawn on me. In my new homeland, I was not simply to be an American. I had to be a "hyphenated" one. Never had I felt with such clarity the full force of the ethnic divide. In return, I mentioned something self-deprecating and stumbled back to my office. But the remark eventually prompted me to start a line of research on immigration studies. I needed to find out who else shared my ethnic niche. What other folks were assigned the same label?

So I turned the experience of exclusion into a professional project—a five-year study of Latinos in the greater Richmond area, as far as I know the first survey research of Latinos in Virginia. Looking back now, I realize the research was my way of coping with being culturally pigeonholed. In truth, my family came from Italy to Brazil, bypassing the whole Spaniard heritage. But in the United States, for all intents and purposes, I was Hispanic. That is the tiresome thing about migrating—that ever-present feeling that you will never reach home. You swear allegiance to a host country only to find out that your Zion remains quite elusive, a receding horizon at best. Sure, there are places for people like me in this country, that is, with our own kind and long history of exclusion.

The niche was there all along, lurking. Studying Latinos in Richmond fleshed out, experientially, its dynamics—the construction of "safe" American cultural ghettoes. As part of the immigrant experience, they shelter minorities in a solidarity and dignity of their own, while keeping them simultaneously apart from the dominant group. In other words, hyphenation means always dealing with feeling "almost there." In a sense, no matter how long you live in the place, how well-integrated you become, you are still an outsider. There is no solace for that kind of parsing out. One puts up with it, but it is not a chosen manner of living.

Nevertheless, among other Latinos in the greater Richmond area, I found a rich tribe of sorts. We hailed from many countries. We had diverse tastes. But here we were, lumped together under one large cultural umbrella, one easily recognizable by the dominant group. So we danced together, shared joys and sorrows, and tried to make the best out of the situation. Our kids attended the same schools. We shared a few neighborhoods in the area. There were ethnic associations that sponsored soccer leagues and cultural events. We tried to create a pan-ethnic identity as part of the effort to integrate ourselves into this patchwork society.

Traditionally, citizenship was established by birth (*jus sanguinis*) or soil (*jus soli*). *Jus sanguinis* is the "right of blood." It is an inheritance—as citizens of a nation, your parents bestow their same citizenship upon you. *Jus soli* refers to citizenship from place of birth, or "right of soil." Those born in a territory are by right its citizens. Most countries, in fact, use a mix of the two as criteria for legal citizenship. My son, born in the United States, is an American citizen by *jus soli* and a Brazilian citizen by *jus sanguinis*. In modern times *jus matrimonii,* citizenship by marriage, has become another common tool of incorporation, just as with naturalization—which allows one to choose his own nationality.

In medieval days, a person's political identity was determined by the lord he served. The connection between lord and subject was permanent. One could not simply choose to relocate to other lands. Vestiges of that legal straightjacket are still found today in failed communist countries like North Korea or Cuba.

But in modern times, nationality is more portable. It represents someone's legal tie to the state insofar as it concerns the rights and privileges appertaining to citizenship—the freedom to reside permanently in a given country, the right to work, to vote, and to run for office. Of course, along with it come the duties of citizenship—serving in the country's armed forces, paying taxes, performing jury duty, and the like. That it is possible nowadays to obtain those rights from a place not of one's birth is the real novelty. . . .

Family, the Latino Way

If preserving family connections is hard for the average American, for immigrants the lack of family ties is a fact of life. My kid's relatives on both mother's and father's sides lived some 4,200 miles away. There was no going home for Thanksgiving or Christmas. We sent pictures and videos, keeping the grandparents abreast of Gui's victories. But the reality was he did not grow up around them. He saw them twice on Brazilian vacations that lasted a little less than a summer. It is hard to build a sense of extended family for a child so far removed from every living kin beyond his parents. But my mother's questioning points to a loaded meaning of family. Families are everything to Latin Americans, so it behooves her to ask the question.

In Latin America, extended families are far more important and more controlling than the average U.S. family. By comparison, members of American families enjoy far more freedom and privacy. For Latin Americans the family unit, its well-being, and its honor represent the very glue that holds everyone together, the basis for our individual and collective identities. No matter where you were born in the region, your family's interests came first, never your own. We lived for our families, not the other way around. That message was constantly reinforced for my generation as we were growing up. Family commitment came first and was non-negotiable in all matters of life.

There is reason for such loyalty. In a region of weak political institutions and corrupt economic structures, your family is your ultimate shield. Your family alone protects you from the outside world and takes care of you when you need help. But you have to do your part; you have to be loyal to kin. Your family mediated all conflicts, internal or external. If any two of us were having a problem with each other the matter became a group concern. Family members stepped in to resolve it, reminding the warring parties of their mutual responsibility and pushing them to make up. Solidarity was always the norm, always the expectation (ironically, when Brazilians migrate that sense of solidarity seems to weaken).

Unlike the typical post–World War II American family, Latin American kinship reached far beyond the nuclear unit. Our families were multigenerational—grandparents, children, and grandchildren sometimes lived under the same roof. They also stretched horizontally, reaching blood and marriage relatives to the second and third degree. Finally, family ties even included folks related by informal adoption (it is not unusual in the region for a family to take in children whose parents are going through tough times and cannot provide for them) or by godparenting.

Godparenting—*compadrazco* in Spanish, *apadrinhamento* in Portuguese—is a Catholic ritual kinship, extended to people not legally your kin. Godparenting bonds unrelated families, by creating religious ties of mutual obligation. Your godparents provided lifelong mentoring and the kind of moral instruction most Americans expect only from parents.

Of course, life in an extended family of this sort offers no sense of privacy. To put it mildly, your business is everybody's business. There is little to no individual liberty. Your well-being concerns all those who surround you. Everyone has an opinion of how you should best live your life. Relatives meddle avidly in your studies, who you should date or marry (sometimes the two are not necessarily the same), who you should befriend and why, and which careers were most appropriate for someone of your family lineage. The last item is critical, because in Brazilian culture, your family lineage locates you within a system of privileges that sorts out the "well-bred" from their social "inferiors."

A rank-based society, with far less social mobility than the United States, Brazil has often allowed the powerful to enjoy benefits those below them could never hope to gain. We truly lacked the American egalitarian ethos. Political and economic perks were clearly tied to family heritage, and, of course, to class and race. Brazilian elites (almost always white or light-skinned) expected special treatment from those they outranked (mostly brown, black, or poor white). So your family was also the foremost source of status and esteem. Therefore its hold on us never abated. Our personal needs remained aligned with our family's interests, our decisions made within those parameters.

Family loyalty carried into the smallest details of everyday life. For instance, unlike American college students, Brazilians never leave to pursue their studies. Few Brazilian universities have dorms. You remain with your parents until the day you marry, and then settle within a short distance from them. In adulthood, you are expected at your parents' (or grandparents') home for weekly family meals, for celebrations, and for regular interaction. The family continues to play a role in all major decisions of your life, impacting your personal choices and aspirations to the day they die. Only as a foreign exchange student in New Mexico was I able to marvel at the whole construct from the outside. My "adopted" American siblings enjoyed a freedom to pursue their own interests that I could only envy.

On a curious note, the Latin American family pattern tends to be stronger among Catholics than Protestants. Within the

Catholic communal worldview, one's loyalty is tied to the well-being of the larger group. So, there is no need to strike out on your own, to leave your mark, to seek your place in the world away from the close scrutiny of relatives. This is a culture that predates the individualism of modern capitalist societies. Among the children of Calvinist merchants in Northern Europe, for example, individual fame and fortune were expected in all manner of enterprise. As a result, Protestant individualism trickled down to family matters. Their Iberian counterparts, on the other hand, even those who roamed far away as seafarers, did so for their families, their church, and their Catholic kings.

Nevertheless, given the prevalence of Catholicism in Brazilian culture, Brazilian Protestant families are not as individualistic as their American counterparts either. When I was growing up, my mother followed the more communal Catholic pattern, while my father leaned toward the individualism brought by Protestant missionaries. He waxed eloquently about the merits of the self-made man, of the entrepreneur. His universe was filled by books from Dale Carnegie and Henry Ford, pushing the Horatio Alger rags-to-riches myth to the max. That, of course, makes for a confusing childhood. My father approved of my early efforts to discover the world on my own, while my mother mourned my independent streak.

As a teenager I spent every summer at youth conferences and camps (common here in the United States, not so much in Brazil those days). Of four siblings, I was the one who chose to participate in a foreign exchange program, away from the family's support network. To this day I'm the one who settled the farthest away geographically. With few exceptions everybody else, despite our Protestant leanings, stayed home. It befuddled my relatives that I seldom consulted them for anything, that I always solved problems on my own. I chose my hobbies and extracurricular activities. They were not consulted when I picked a college or a wife, topics usually requiring a great deal of input in most Brazilian families. My father never understood why I took up theology instead of business. He imagined his eldest son a captain of industry someday.

Sometimes it was hard to be so independent. But personal freedom certainly defined my growing up and set me apart from siblings and peers. Emotionally, this mixture of Protestant and Catholic affections still complicates my life as an immigrant. I cherish my independent life in the United States, but there is a sadness that hangs over my chats with family back in Brazil. My noted absence is a constant source of disappointment for them. None of my relatives can fathom why I remain abroad, especially now that I have reached a certain level of stability in my professional career. None see the point of a life away from the homeland. And none appreciates my need for personal liberty or privacy.

So in my interactions with folks back home they find me reticent, "distant." They wonder why I do not require, or seek, the same kind of intimacy and busybody connections that are so essential to their well-being. They long to keep me updated on the smallest details of their lives and expect me to do the same in return. When that fails, the sense of loss is rekindled in their voices. Perhaps I was always a bit removed, I want to say, while reminding them of my independent youth. Perhaps this individual streak has been part of my life all along. But clearly, they seem to notice it more these days.

"Congratulations, It's a Boy"

My countercultural sense of independence was only shaken up by the advent of parenthood. As a child I could always count on my parents and adult relatives to empower my flights of fancy. They supported my interests and praised my accomplishments.

What I did not realize then was that my carefree disposition was made possible by their careful and constant watch. In their selflessness, they cleaned up my mistakes and quietly contributed to my successes. I claimed all the credit, of course. But there was always a safety net; I just never took the time to see it. Until my own son was born. Having a baby abroad, away from my entire family, quickly became downright exhausting and scary. His mother and I were his only family, with no help from relatives.

When I was born, my parents had the constant aid of grandparents, aunts, and great-aunts. As my son came into the world, he had his mom and me as his entire support system. As Brazilians, my wife and I were worried about raising a son without relatives. In fact, his birth exposed our lack of connections in the United States. For the first two years of his life we did not go out in the evening because we did not know any babysitters. Our few friends were either college students or coworkers who happened to be single or childless. We lacked a support network for parenting tips, or shared duties, and other issues like finding a dentist or a pediatrician. We met a couple at the Lamaze class, but they were busy professionals, pressed for time.

For two Brazilian immigrants, having a child in the United States raises the question of operating as a nuclear family. Prior to Gui's arrival we were simply a couple whose extended families happened to live elsewhere. We remained our families' children, with no responsibility for creating our own family traditions. We traveled, enjoyed life abroad, and studied. Nothing pushed us to rethink our family unit as Gui did. All of a sudden, every child-related holiday begged for a new family tradition. Of course, living in a foreign country, our family traditions were built around "borrowed" holidays, since we celebrated what other families in the neighborhood were celebrating. We kept track of American rather than Brazilian holidays.

In the process, we ended up raising a very American son,

in a very American family unit. His childhood was unlike our own. Halloweens were huge at the Cavalcanti residence, though Brazilians do not celebrate Halloween. Gui loved the costumes, the trick-or-treat rounds. Neither his mom nor I had the heart to tell him we had never celebrated Halloween until he came along. Christmas meant decorating the Christmas tree, his treasured ritual. But we did not grow up with Christmas trees, carols, or snow. Christmas came at the height of summer in Brazil. Instead of Rudolph and Santa Claus we had beach picnics and street festivals at night. The Easter Bunny and the traditional egg hunt were a huge part of our son's calendar, though Easter was not celebrated that way in South America either.

The absence of a large Brazilian expatriate community made it hard for us to observe Brazilian holidays at home. To this day our son has no idea what a real Brazilian Carnival is like. He never learned the *Frêvo*, the most typical of Recife's Carnival dances. He never celebrated St. John's and St. Peter's Days eating corn-based country food and square dancing around the neighborhood, like his mother and I did when we were growing up. He never learned the mellow rhythms of a *Ciranda*, the gentle fishermen's round dance from my hometown, one that beautifully highlights their way of life.

But there was no way to raise a Brazilian kid by ourselves in the United States. And so much had changed about parenting since our childhood days! Our kid was part of the American millennial baby boom. So he rode the wealth of activities that businesses and community agencies created for his cohort. For instance, his mother and I did not grow up around public libraries. Back in Brazil, there were no public library branches in our respective neighborhoods. But Gui's weekly visits to the Tuckahoe Public Library were a huge part of his growing up. After-school activities and summer camps were unlike anything his parents ever experienced as kids. We grew up self-entertained, surrounded by siblings and cousins. He grew up shuttled instead.

I have the feeling that our childhood was more leisured, more spontaneous. It had to be. Our extended families were a moving feast. As parents of a kid in the millennial generation we did not have that luxury. Not even our language survived the pressures of suburban American life. The initial plan was to speak Portuguese at home and English elsewhere, so as to raise a bilingual child. That lasted till he started day care. Then he simply refused to speak Portuguese. So I quickly switched to all-English-all-the-time. His poor mother waged a losing battle to keep Portuguese alive, despite his insistence on replying in English. When he did speak in Portuguese, he had a curious southern accent that he never showed in English.

To be sure, all immigrant parents face the issue of language loss. As the first generation, they struggle to acculturate into a new language and new customs. But the second generation, the American-born generation, is fluent in English and often answers their parents' remarks in their mother tongue with English replies. Our case was not so different from that of other immigrant parents. In fact, it is not unusual for English to become the language spoken at home. Moreover, large-scale studies of immigrant children show that few remain truly bilingual. Portes and Rumbaut found that only 28 percent of their sample was fully bilingual by the time of high school graduation.

How to explain this American life of our kid to relatives back home? Our parents expected frequent reports. Siblings were curious about Gui's latest doings. And cousins bugged our immediate families for news from America. We reported on what we could. But our families had no frame of reference for our "small" (by Brazilian standards) suburban nuclear lifestyle. We sent photos and videos, but they lacked the cultural translation. All in all, there remained a persistent gap in our ability to explain how our little nuclear family deviated from the traditional Brazilian standards.

School Days

Another thing we did not realize, prior to having a child in the United States, was that American schools would need to find the right ethnic pigeonhole for Gui as part of his education. As a professor, I had taught sociology of education multiple times, lecturing benignly on the virtues of multicultural classrooms. As a parent I discovered that by honoring my kid's Brazilian identity, the school accentuated his difference, making it far more visible. In doing so, it turned him into an outsider in his classmates' eyes. The last thing my son needed was to be an outsider.

For someone who preached respect for cultural diversity in the classroom, that was a tough lesson to swallow. But what I had failed to realize was that family membership deeply defines a child's ethnic identity in America. Schools are perhaps the first governmental agencies to classify our children on the basis of an official ethnicity. Gui spoke fluent English without any accent. In every way that mattered he was a thoroughly American child. Nevertheless, his parents' ethnicity became the ultimate criterion for his cataloging at school. Sadly, immigrant children, whose social markers ascribe them a minority status in school, spend their days seeking to normalize their condition, to rejoin the larger crowd. The need to be "normal" makes them spend a great deal of time and energy mimicking the modal responses of the dominant group.

The irony is that my son did not know his home culture was foreign. We spoke Portuguese and dabbled in Brazilian food from time to time, but he had no way of comparing that to anything else. Given the somewhat segregated residential pattern of American cities, most children do not fully realize the stereotypes attached to their ethnicity until they reach school age. Once they become aware of them, they work hard to "blend in." They compare themselves with those around, sorting out similarity and dissimilarity, especially in relation to their reference groups. Pressure from peers and parents creates an impossible tug-of-war throwing competing loyalties against each other, contributing to the kid's sense of marginality.

By going to school, Gui finally encountered his foreign condition. All of a sudden, my son became painfully aware that our home culture had a label, and that label placed him squarely on the outside, looking in. Following the pattern of other immigrant children, Gui tried desperately to "normalize" his identity. Since *Guilherme* means *William* in Portuguese, he insisted that his classmates call him Will. But he was bullied repeatedly during second grade on account of his weird-sounding surname. Eventually the principal agreed to transfer him to a smaller school. There, he finally made lifelong friends among kids of other ethnic minorities and those who were part of the dominant group.

A unique part of Gui's struggle had to do with the issue of multiple identities, something that is commonly experienced by American minorities. When immigrants first arrive in the United States they are still wedded to their nationalities. As they settle down, those nationalities undergo a transformation. They become ethnicities. Eventually those ethnicities end up grouped into a larger umbrella. Let's say a Vietnamese refugee enters the United States. She will first be seen as an outsider, only to later be described as Vietnamese American as she becomes naturalized. Down the road her identity will be further conflated into the larger category of Asian American. This process happens continuously as the American society adds new ethnic groups to its composition.

In Gui's case he had to juggle "Brazilian," "Brazilian American," and "Latino." The more he tried to look like everyone else, the more he struggled with the Brazilian side of his identity, the more the larger society limited his options due to his parents' ethnic categories. He spent his entire childhood trying to belong. By the time he reached high school he refused to be boxed into the condition of Brazilian American, or the ultimate pan-ethnic category of Latino. In their study of immigrant children, Portes and Rumbaut found that over 53 percent of them identified themselves as American or "Other" American in 1992, but only 34 percent did so three years later.

The struggle followed Gui to college. When he was exploring his college options, he was offered full scholarships to two top engineering undergraduate schools in Massachusetts. One school made the mistake of awarding him what would be their first Latino scholarship. The other gave him the regular, run-of-the-mill full ride. Needless to say, Gui chose the latter, partly on the basis of getting that all-American merit scholarship. His father's lectures on the importance of opening doors to other Latinos were of no avail. And to this day he refuses to be boxed in. Mind you, he is proud of his heritage—he speaks Portuguese and has taken Italian in school. He is not ashamed of who he is. But he wishes to honor it on his own terms.

One thing we failed to realize as "ethnic" parents was that once school started, our son's loyalty to us and our Brazilian home would be seriously tested by his classmates. Loyalty to family of origin only heightened his outsider status in their eyes, whereas loyalty to things American would improve his chances of becoming an insider. So, Gui sided with his peers. By the end of high school, his loyalty to his parents' culture was almost nonexistent. He opened up to the promises of the dominant culture but did so at our expense. Considering the other choices available to immigrant children—to stick to their ethnicity or hopelessly try to straddle both—Gui's option made sense.

Andrew Fuligni, Gwendelyn Rivera, and April Leininger, in their study of ethnic identity among teenagers, found that teens in Gui's generation attending urban schools had cast their lot with their ethnic side—perhaps because their schools had larger minority populations, perhaps because they had stronger minority markers. Nevertheless, those who chose the ethnic route had a stronger sense of ethnic identity as teenagers and felt a stronger sense of obligation toward family. They were more likely to take their parents' wishes into account in their decision making. And their loyalty to family became an asset during adolescence. Following the Latin American mold, in their adult years, these students were more likely to assist parents and siblings than those who left their ethnicity behind.

The interesting thing is that those adolescents did not necessarily feel more emotionally close to their parents. Rather, they felt a deeper sense of belonging to their unique ethnic group. Loyalty to group defined them above and beyond what their classmates might say. That kind of family attachment is common among immigrants from Latin America. Comparing children of immigrants from the Americas, Europe, Asia, the Middle East, and Canada, Portes and Rumbaut found Latin American nationalities to have the most cohesive families and the lowest levels of parent-child conflict. Most Latino groups had the lowest proportions of kids who reported being embarrassed by their parents.

Nevertheless, they also found that those children's successful acculturation weakened their family cohesion, leading toward a more individualistic orientation. Needless to say, that happened to our son. Rather than choosing his Brazilian side, Gui went on to adopt his classmates' culture, growing up in ways his parents could never have imagined as Brazilians. To us, love of family and loyalty to kin were essential ingredients in a healthy upbringing. We could not imagine not needing or wanting our parents' friendship when we were growing up. That kind of expressive bonding was critical to our sense of well-being. They affirmed us with their ties—their love was an emotional asset helping us navigate adolescence.

Our son never felt as strong a need for our company. Mind you, he didn't dislike us. He never rejected our instruction, nor doubted our care or concern for his well-being. But there was something a little more American about him, something that pushed him to strike out on his own. As any suburban American kid, Gui piled up laurels in a highly successful academic career, all spent in magnet schools from second grade on. He was active in school clubs, busy with school projects, and seemed to enjoy the opportunities that came his way. His college career was equally successful. These days he owns his own business in Boston. He just never needed the Brazilian closeness we grew up with.

Much like his peers of other nationalities, Gui showed high levels of self-esteem and independence throughout middle and high school. That is not unusual among children of immigrants. Nearly 58 percent of Portes and Rumbaut's total sample had high self-esteem scores. In follow-up surveys from junior high to high school, their level of self-esteem jumped ten percentage points. But that does come at a cost. Sadly, much like his ethnic peers, Gui also experienced bouts of depressive symptoms. In fact, in Portes and Rumbaut's sample, the depressive scores of children of immigrants remained stable from junior high to high school.

Our case clearly represents the paradox of immigrant parenting. Gui's successful acculturation was purchased at the expense of close family ties. When his mother and I were growing up in Brazil, closeness to family was foundational. Our son, on the other hand, took on the cultural traits of his suburban American generation. And like them, he grew up with a healthy sense of entitlement, a sense that parents existed solely to provide the needed resources for setting out on their own. I imagine that for Gui, the parent-child relationship was never a mutual giving and receiving. He knew he had a solid home base and knew he could count on us to support his efforts. Once he took off, however, there was no looking back.

I take comfort that Gui's choice, from the point of view of

acculturation, was not altogether a bad one. The prospects for the average children of immigrants in the United States these days are rather grim. First of all, they struggle with invisibility. In 2007 about 16.4 million children—more than one in five children in America—had at least one immigrant parent. I doubt the average American would be familiar with that statistic. Moreover, that number had doubled since 1990, with the share of immigrant American children jumping from 13 to 23 percent of the population. They also struggle to fit in, lacking the cultural capital to fully integrate into the American economy or to avoid discrimination as my son did.

More than half of those children were of Hispanic heritage, though only 17 percent had parents from Central and South America or the Spanish-speaking Caribbean. Many faced serious obstacles trying to make it in the States. Their parents lacked legal status or citizenship, as well as access to public services for their children and families. A good number lived in linguistic isolation—19 percent of those aged five to seventeen had limited English proficiency; one or both parents of the 61 percent had limited English-language skills as well. A quarter of the parents lacked a high school degree. Some 82 percent of the children lived in large families with limited resources—51 percent had family incomes twice the poverty level, while 22 percent were poor.

The children of Brazilian immigrants in the United States face similar difficulties. Like Gui, they make their parents more committed to a future in this country. But studies of Brazilian teenagers in America show that they tend to reproduce the career path (i.e., menial jobs) of their parents. Sadly, for them, schooling is not a path to social mobility. The fact that the parents are engaged in multiple dead-end, low-wage jobs means that schooling becomes secondary to survival. The children need to work to help with the household budget. And the parents' long hours give them little time to oversee the children's schooling. For them education is a means to learn English, but not much more. So very few of their children move up the occupational ladder.

What we find, when we take a closer look at the lives of these children, is a process of segmented assimilation. Not all immigrants find full integration into American society, nor do they experience similar kinds of social mobility. Race and ethnicity, social class, labor market demands, and the context of the receiving nation affect immigrant access to resources and a successful pathway to integration. Immigrant children who attend better schools and whose parents have more human capital will experience assimilation in the same fashion as did the children of European immigrants during the first half of the twentieth century. Immigrant children whose parents' race or low socioeconomic status places them in disadvantaged settings face the same limitations of other American working-class minorities, with the same reduced opportunities.

Parents and peers can have a profound effect on the aspirations and expectations of immigrant children. Since aspirations and academic performance are strongly correlated, children who do well and attend better schools will take advantage of this country's best educational opportunities. Their parents' level of human capital will assure that they will acquire the needed social skills to be successful in their endeavors. By contrast, the children of immigrants who enter the labor force at the bottom are more likely to reproduce their parents' status. They will learn the language and culture better than the parents ever will, but will still face serious difficulties climbing up America's social ladder.

FIROOZEH DUMAS

Iran

Firoozeh Dumas (1965–) was born in the oil-rich coastal town of Abadan in eastern Iran. Her father, Kazem, then an engineer with the National Iranian Oil Company (NIOC), was a consultant for an American firm and in 1972 moved his family to Whittier, California, for a two-year assignment. After briefly returning to Iran, Kazem was next sent to the affluent, ethnically homogenous city of Newport Beach, where Dumas spent her childhood. For Kazem, the decision to remain in the U.S. was difficult, but the onset of the Iranian Revolution and the government's suspension of building new refineries put him out of work and led him to pursue a career in the U.S. Prior to the Iranian Revolution in 1979, immigration to the U.S. was quite low (some thirteen thousand between 1970 and 1974). Following the Tehran hostage crisis, immigration became much more difficult, yet the number of Iranians moving to the U.S. rose exponentially, with more than fifty-six thousand between 1980 and 1984. The U.S. continues to be a favored destination of the Iranian diaspora, with more than half of that population living in California.

As an ethnic immigrant, Dumas regarded her given names as identifying her foreignness, and at the age of twelve, she chose to adopt a more assimilated name. The author's excitement at transforming into "Julie," albeit a simple thing, is echoed by other immigrants who also take on new names. As Firoozeh, she was marked as an immigrant, but as Julie she becomes more seemingly American, an extremely important distinction, especially given the discrimination the family faced during the crisis of 1979 and 1980.

Dumas attended the University of California at Berkeley as an art

history major and still makes her home in northern California. A finalist
for the Pen/USA Award for creative nonfiction and the Thurber Prize for
humor, Funny in Farsi *(2003) took its initial shape in stories she wrote*
as gifts for her three children. Following the success of her first memoir
came another book of anecdotes about assimilation, Laughing Without
an Accent *(2009).*

Excerpt from

Funny in Farsi

— 2003 —

In 1977, the Shah and his wife were scheduled to come to
America to meet the newly elected president, Jimmy Carter.
Very few Iranians lived in America then, and those of us who
did were invited to go to Washington, D.C., to welcome the
Shah. The Iranian government would cover all expenses.

My father accepted the invitation. My brothers reacted
with a few choice words.

"Are you completely crazy?"

"Haven't you heard about the anti-Shah demonstrators?"

"You'll definitely get beaten up."

"Don't go."

My brothers clearly did not understand the lure of the
phrase "all-expense-paid trip."

A few weeks later, drinking fresh-squeezed orange juice in
our first-class seats, my parents and I looked forward to our first

visit to the nation's capital. During our three-night stay, we were supposed to show up at two events welcoming the Shah. The rest of the time was our own. My father had promised to take me to at least one museum. My mother looked forward to seeing the famous sights.

We arrived at our hotel to find the lobby full of Iranians. Unaccustomed to seeing so many of our fellow countrymen in one place, my parents started mingling feverishly, discovering friends of friends and long-forgotten colleagues. As we went to find our room, we felt like a bunch of kids on a field trip.

A fruit basket would have been nice, but instead we found that a flyer had been slipped under the door.

> Dear Brainwashed Cowards,
>
> You are nothing but puppets of the corrupt Shah. We will teach you a lesson you will never forget. Death to the Shah. Death to you.

My father crumpled the flyer and threw it away. "Let's find out where they're having the dinner buffet," he said.

The next day, half a dozen buses lined up in front of our hotel to take us to the lawn across from the White House. We were given Iranian flags and told to wave them at the Shah's arrival. Moments before we left, a man boarded our bus and introduced himself as a lawyer working for the Iranian government. "In case anybody attacks you," he told us, "please try to take his picture. This would be most useful."

We arrived at the White House to find a group of masked demonstrators carrying signs denouncing the Shah and his government. "Don't worry," my father assured me, "they're on the *other* side of the street."

Opposite the demonstrators, scaffolding had been built for the Shah's supporters. Speakers took turns giving speeches on the glories of Iran. To my delight, I found that the lawn had been strewn with miniature Iranian flags. "Help me find thirty of them," I asked my parents. "I'm going to hand them out in Miss Crocket's social studies class."

My mother and I headed toward the back of the lawn, while my father went to the front to look for more flags. A few minutes later, we heard my father say, "Look how many I found!" He held up his bounty. But his voice was drowned out by the twenty-one-gun salute announcing the arrival of the Shah's limousine. People started to cheer, but the cheering wasn't entirely cheerful. The demonstrators had crossed the road. They were stampeding toward us waving sticks with nails driven into them. People were screaming and running. Instead of Iranian flags, the lawn was suddenly covered with bloody and injured Iranians. My parents and I ran and ran and ran.

We found an empty bus and, not caring about its destination, climbed on board.

"I'm sorry, folks," the bus driver drawled, "y'all are gonna hafta get off this bus, 'cuz it's outta service and I'm on break."

Across the street, we found a police officer on horseback. "Excuse me," I said, "we're afraid we're going to get beaten up. Could you please help us get back to our hotel?"

Perhaps this officer had joined the police force because of the handsome uniforms or perhaps he wanted a job that let him ride a horse. He looked at us and said, "Sorry, that's not my job."

Spotting another bus, we boarded it immediately. "Do you have tickets?" the driver asked.

"How much are they?"

We paid twenty-one dollars and took our seats just as the bus started to leave. We had no idea where we were going. A recorded narration began.

"Our next stop is the Lincoln Memorial, built in honor of Abraham Lincoln, the sixteenth president of the United States. On the north wall of this majestic memorial, you will see the words of the Gettysburg Address: 'Four score and seven years ago our fathers brought forth . . .'"

Three hours, four monuments, and one cab ride later, we arrived at our hotel. The lobby was filled with bandaged survivors exchanging horror stories. At the sight of all the wounded, my father turned to my mother and me and said, "Don't mention we went on a tour. It's going to look bad that we were having fun while everyone else was suffering." Before I could tell my father that the tour had *not* been fun, he was accosted by a friend, whose arm was now in a sling.

"Where have you three been the whole time? We were getting ready to call the hospitals."

"Well," my father sighed, "we had to walk back."

Like a story written in installments, a second flyer awaited us in our room.

Dear Brainwashed Cowards,

We are going to blow you up.

Even the prospect of the dinner buffet was no longer enough to keep us in the nation's capital. "That's it," my father announced. "We're leaving."

Six hours later, we found ourselves in the coach section of a crowded airplane, sitting in three different rows. We were thrilled to be headed home.

As the airplane took off, my father turned around and shouted from four rows ahead of me, "That really wasn't that bad. Firoozeh, you know how you like historical places? Well, we saw a bunch."

He continued, "Of course, I do have one regret."

"What's that?" I yelled back.

"I shouldn't have dropped all the flags. I'm sure I had enough for your whole class."

"That's okay," I replied. "We can always go back."

• • •

A t the age of seventeen, my father began working for NIOC, the National Iranian Oil Company, as a student employee. He worked his way up the corporate ladder and eventually became a senior project manager. His lifetime of experience with oil refineries brought us to America, where he worked as a representative of NIOC, supervising American contractors in the design of an oil refinery in Isfahan. After thirty-three years of working with the same company, my father never doubted the security of his future.

But with the Iranian Revolution, my father's world turned upside down. The building of more refineries in Iran was halted and overnight my father's expertise was no longer needed. Although NIOC offered him other positions in Iran, none was within his field of interest. With much dismay, he requested and was reluctantly granted early retirement. My father was confident in his abilities to find a job in the United States.

Within a couple of weeks, he found an engineering position with an American company. As he was settling into his new job, a group of Americans in Tehran were taken hostage in the American embassy. My father was laid off.

Every evening, we sat in front of the television and watched the news for updates on the hostage situation. For 444 nights, we waited. With each passing day, palpable hatred grew among many Americans, hatred not just of the hostage takers but of all Iranians. The media didn't help. We opened our local paper one day to the screaming headline "Iranian Robs Grocery Store." Iran has as many fruits and nuts as the next country, but it seemed as if every lowlife who happened to be Iranian was now getting his fifteen minutes of fame.

Vendors started selling T-shirts and bumper stickers that said "Iranians Go Home" and "Wanted: Iranians, for Target Practice." Crimes against Iranians increased. People would hear my mother's thick accent and ask us, "Where are you from?" They weren't looking for a recipe for stuffed grape leaves. Many Iranians suddenly became Turkish, Russian, or French.

To add to my family's collective anxiety, my father's pension from Iran was cut off. The Iranian government told him that from now on, if he wanted his hard-earned retirement pay, he would have to go to Iran to collect it. Even worse, with the turmoil in Iran, the value of my father's pension dropped to the point of worthlessness.

At fifty-eight, my father found himself unemployed and with no prospects. Nobody wanted to hire an Iranian. My father returned to Iran to sell all our belongings. Within three weeks, he sold our house for a tenth of its previous value. A colleague bought our fourteen room-size Persian rugs for $1,300—and sold one of them for $15,000 a few months later.

Perhaps the greatest irony in the wave of Iranian-hating was that Iranians, as a group, are among the most educated and successful immigrants in this country. Our work ethic and obsession with education make us almost ideal citizens. Nobody asked our opinion of whether the hostages should be taken, and yet every single Iranian in America was paying the price. One kid throws a spitball and the whole class gets detention.

For my father to be treated like a second-class citizen truly stung. If there were ever a poster child for immigration, it would be Kazem. Perhaps nothing speaks louder than his obsession with voting.

When I became an American citizen, in college, my father called to ask whether I was planning to vote in the upcoming election. "If I have time," I answered. My father then told me that perhaps I did not deserve to be a citizen. Any immigrant who comes to this country and becomes a citizen and doesn't vote, according to him, should just go back.

"What about American citizens who are born here and don't vote?" I asked, egging him on.

"They need to be sent for six months to a nondemocratic country. Then they'll vote," he replied.

I told my father that his "Ship 'Em Abroad" program didn't sound too democratic to me, that perhaps included in the freedoms in this country is the freedom to be apathetic.

He hung up on me.

I voted.

But that wasn't the end of it. After every election, my father called me to ask me whom I had voted for. After several such phone calls, we realized that our votes simply negate each other. We stand on opposite sides of all issues. I have since learned not to share any information with my father, instead reminding him that the voting process is confidential, which explains why there are booths instead of, say, people just raising their hands in a public voting hall so that someone like my father can tell them they're wrong.

"Well," he always huffs, "you always vote for the wrong people anyway. Thank God for your mother."

My mother's voting ritual is a whole other story. She, like most Americans, doesn't fully comprehend the American political system. I'm convinced that the average American would have an easier time naming Elizabeth Taylor's ex-husbands than, say, his or her congressional leaders. To complicate matters, my mother does not understand English well enough to learn more, which is where my father comes in.

As soon as my father receives his voting pamphlet in the mail, he sits on the sofa, pen in hand, and reads it cover to cover. He underlines, he circles, he writes in the margins. If he doesn't know how to vote on an issue, he looks for an endorsement by firemen or police officers. In my father's world, firemen and police officers wear white cowboy hats. If the local firefighters' union thinks it's a good idea to raise taxes to build more tap dance studios, then so does my father.

Once my father decides how to vote on all the issues, he

then practices democracy with a dash of dictatorship thrown in for good measure. He tells my mother how *she* should vote. My mother rarely questions my father's choices, and when she does, he answers her with one of his typical opinions: "Anybody with a brain can tell that's a no vote." (Chances are I voted yes.)

In 1980, however, despite my father's staunch devotion to freedom and fairness, he was still a foreigner with an accent, an accent that after the Iranian Revolution was associated with all things bad. He was treated like someone who should just pack up and go. But go where?

After selling our possessions in Iran, Kazem returned to America and started, yet again, looking for a job. Now, though, he no longer applied to American companies. He eventually applied for a job with a large oil company in Saudi Arabia. This entailed relocating, but we had no choice: by now, my parents had cut up all our credit cards, and our modest savings were disappearing quickly. After weeks of interviews and negotiations, he was offered an executive position and the contract was ready to sign. My father was hopeful for the first time since being laid off. Before signing the final papers, the lawyer asked for his passport, a requirement for any overseas job. At the sight of the Iranian passport, the lawyer turned pale and said, "I am so sorry, but the government of Saudi Arabia does not accept Iranians at this time. We thought you were an Arab."

My father resumed his job search. In *The Wall Street Journal*, he spotted an ad for an executive position with a Nigerian oil company. He immediately applied and was hired within two weeks. With its high salary and unlimited expansion potential, this job almost seemed too good to be true.

My father's first assignment was to go to New Jersey and negotiate the purchase of an oil refinery for $400 million. Once that was done, he was sent to Texas to purchase another refinery. He was thrilled to be using his expertise again.

After returning from his assignments, my father discovered

that his first and only paycheck had bounced. He was told that there had been a small delay with funds being wired from Nigeria and that his second paycheck would cover the first. He had no option but to keep working.

A few days later, he came to the office to discover a swarm of journalists looking for information on a hot new breaking story. Apparently, the owner of the company was a con man who had already been deported from the United States once but had returned under an assumed name. My father packed his office supplies and left.

The hostages were finally freed. Besides them and their families, no one was happier than the Iranians living in America.

Shortly after their release, my father found a job with an American company, working as a senior engineer. His salary was half what it had been before the revolution, but he was nonetheless extremely grateful to wake up and go to work every day.

Throughout his job ordeal, my father never complained. He remained an Iranian who loved his native country but who also believed in American ideals. He only said how sad it was that people so easily hate an entire population simply because of the actions of a few. And what a waste it is to hate, he always said. What a waste.

REYNA GRANDE

Mexico

Reyna Grande (1975–) is the second of three children born to a poor family in Iguala, Guerrero, in southern Mexico. In 1977, her father, Natalio, went north to the U.S. to earn enough money to pursue his dream of building a house in their hometown. Natalio's case was fairly typical. He crossed the border alone as an undocumented worker, only later sending for his wife, Juana, while Reyna and her siblings, suffering malnutrition and illness, remained in their grandmother's care. Later, Natalio returned to take his children with him to the U.S., nearly leaving nine-year-old Reyna behind due to the dangers of a desert journey. After two unsuccessful attempts, the family arrived in the predominantly Latino neighborhood of Highland Park in Los Angeles.

Mexican immigration to the U.S. has fluctuated based on each country's political and economic circumstances, a history quite complex, to say the least. For example, the labor-poor U.S. encouraged Mexican immigration during WWI and again during and after WWII but forcibly repatriated Mexican immigrants during the Great Depression. There has also been a steady flow of illegal immigration to the U.S., driven by economic and political difficulties in Mexico, combined with greater economic opportunity in the U.S., that U.S. employers dependent on cheap labor have abetted. Moreover, there is a circular migratory pattern wherein Mexican immigrants, legal and illegal, work for months or years in the U.S. (often sending money home) before returning to Mexico with their earnings.

Grande's father was a mercurial disciplinarian, demanding academic excellence and repeatedly threatening to return the children to their mother, from whom he had separated. Following the U.S. Immigration and Re-

form Act of 1986, the Grandes became legal permanent residents. Amid the intense homesickness and family turmoil of her youth, Grande found solace in reading and creative writing. Grande attended Pasadena City College and completed a bachelor's in creative writing from the University of California at Santa Cruz before taking an MFA from Antioch University.

Written in order to "shed light on the complexities of immigration and how immigration affected my entire family in both positive and negative ways," Grande's very well-received coming-of-age memoir The Distance Between Us *(2012) was dedicated to her father and all of the DREAMers, the undocumented youth with whose plight she easily identified. An award-winning novelist, Grande teaches creative writing at the University of California at Los Angeles Extension.*

Excerpt from

The Distance Between Us

—— 2012 ——

One sunny day in May of 1985, when I was four months away from turning ten, my cousin Félix showed up at Abuelita Chinta's house and said, "Your father is going to call you in an hour. He wants to talk to you."

He turned around and ran off, and it took us a moment to recover from the shock. By the time we could speak, Félix was already hurrying across the bridge and turning the corner to head to the main road.

"Papi is going to call?" Carlos asked, and then the question turned into something else when he shouted, "Papi is going to call!"

We laughed and danced around in a circle. "Papi is going to call. Papi is going to call."

"But what are we doing? We don't have much time, let's go!" Mago said. Since Abuelita Chinta wasn't home to give us bus money, we had no choice but to walk to Abuela Evila's. My heart beat so hard against my chest, it hurt. I couldn't believe Papi was going to call. I couldn't believe that soon I would hear his voice.

Is he finally coming home? I wondered. We walked along the pereférico, passing a mango grove and a sugarcane field. Finally, after forty-five minutes, we came to the entrance of my grandmother's neighborhood, La Guadalupe. I glanced up the hill at the familiar church towers. We stopped to rest by Don Rubén's house, which by then had been turned into a liquor store. The walls were white and a huge Corona bottle was painted on one side. I felt so sad to look at that little house, which was no longer a house but a place for drunks like Tío Crece.

"Come on," Mago said. She wiped her forehead and then picked up Betty. Carlos and I ran after her. Since I didn't want to be the last one to Abuela Evila's house, I ran as fast as I could, but my side hurt and my throat was dry and my head was burning from too much sun. Then I thought of Papi, and I picked up my pace again. I could kiss Juan Gabriel. It seemed that the lyrics of his song had finally touched a chord in Papi. Thank goodness Mago had thought of using them in the letters she had written to him not only in December, but in the past few months as well.

Abuela Evila's house finally came into view.

"What should we tell him?" Mago said as we stood outside our grandmother's gate. There was so much to tell him, but how much time would we have before Abuela Evila snatched the phone from us?

"Let's just tell him we miss him," Carlos said. "I think he has something he wants to tell us, don't you think? Or why would he be calling us, after all this time?"

We knocked on the gate and waited. Then Élida came out and smirked. She glanced at us and shook her head. "You could have at least changed out of those rags," she said. "Look at you, you look like beggars."

"So what?" Mago said. "It's not like he's going to see us like this."

Then my cousin Félix poked his head out the kitchen doorway and laughed. He whispered something to Élida, and then Élida laughed, too. We walked past them and went into the living room. I wondered what could be so funny.

Nobody had to tell me who the man sitting on the couch was. I thought about the eight-by-ten-inch photo I had placed on my grandmother's altar. He had put on weight. He wore glasses now. Instead of black-and-white, he was in color, and I could see that his skin *was* the color of rain-soaked earth. There he was, the Man Behind the Glass, in the flesh.

"Go say hello to your father." Tía Emperatriz came up from behind us and pushed us toward him. I didn't want to go. All I wanted was to run away, run back to Abuelita Chinta's house, far away from him. I didn't want to see that look on his face. All those years staring at his photo, wishing that his eyes were not looking to the left but instead were looking at me. All those years wishing to be *seen* by him. And here he was, looking at me, but not really seeing me. He couldn't see past the tangled hair, the dirt on my face, my tattered clothes. He couldn't see the girl who had longed so much for this moment, to finally meet her father.

I knew he was ashamed by what he saw. What a cruel joke Félix played on us by not telling us the truth! If he had, we would have bathed and changed our clothes before going to my grandmother's house. Instead, I had to stand before the father I hadn't seen in almost eight years, looking like a beggar. I touched my hair, and I knew it was matted and oily. When was the last time I bathed? I wondered if he could see the lice that at that very moment were running around on my scalp. I had an overwhelming urge to scratch, and I bit my lips and tried not to move.

Papi hugged Mago, Betty, and Carlos and then called me over. I had no choice but to go to him. He hugged me too briefly, too hesitantly, the way one would hug an acquaintance's child, as if out of obligation. Looking back on it now, I understand how awkward it must have been for him as well. We were strangers to him, too.

He introduced us to the woman standing by his side, whom I hadn't noticed until then. My eyes were focused on him, only him.

"This is Mila," he said.

I looked at the woman who had broken up my family. I wanted to yell at her, to say something mean, but I couldn't think of anything to say. Instead, I compared her to my mother. She wore her wavy black hair in a stylish cut, whereas Mami, ever since she returned from El Otro Lado, had worn hers short, like a boy, but permed into tight curls, and dyed a rusty red. Mila was light-skinned and wore makeup in soft colors such as peaches and browns, unlike Mami's dark blues, purples, and hot pinks that didn't go well with her olive skin.

The woman was wearing white pants and a pink blouse, and white sandals with straps. Mami was always wearing flowery dresses like the kind Abuelita Chinta wore. I suddenly wished to see Mami wearing a pretty pair of white pants. I wished that the woman before me didn't look younger than my mother, even though she was five years older. I wished her skin wasn't so light and smooth looking, so different from my mother's sunburned face lined with wrinkles.

I wanted to kick myself for thinking those thoughts. I was

betraying my mother. I told myself I should hate that woman, not admire her clothes or makeup or pretty skin.

"I'm starving," Papi said. "Let's eat."

He gave Tía Emperatriz money, and she went to buy a pot of menudo at the nearest food stand. Out of the suitcases, he took out three dolls, one for me, one for Mago, and one for Betty. They were life-size baby dolls with blue eyes that closed when they were laid down, and opened when stood up. I buried my face in my doll's hair and smelled the scent of plastic, the smell of a new toy. He gave us girls a couple of dresses and Carlos got jeans and three shirts. This time, he had gotten our size right. He looked at our feet. I put one foot behind the other, ashamed of my old sandals. He said he hadn't known what our shoe size was, so he hadn't brought us any. He promised to buy us new shoes the next day.

We played with our new dolls. Mago, who was going on fourteen and claimed to be too old for baby dolls, was more than happy to play with Betty and me, just to spite Élida. Papi didn't give Élida anything, and part of me was glad. Now she knew how we had felt when her mother had visited from El Otro Lado and didn't give us a single present. But part of me wanted Papi to be different than Tía María Félix. I wanted him to be kinder to his niece.

Soon evening came and he still hadn't told us why he was there. I waited for him to tell us that he missed us. I waited for him to say he was sorry for being gone for so long. I watched him sitting on the patio with his new woman, laughing at something she said. I felt the sting of jealousy burning sharp like a scorpion sting, and I thought of Mami. Just briefly, I understood how she had felt. For a moment, I understood her anger.

We spent the night at Abuela Evila's house. In the morning Papi shaved Carlos's hair to get rid of the lice. He even gave him a bath, as if my brother were a little kid, but he said Carlos was in need of a good scrubbing. He took us girls to the hair salon and told the hairstylist to cut our hair short. I wanted to protest. I wanted to tell him no. But when I looked at him, I was afraid he would disappear if I angered him. I was afraid he might leave again and never come back. So I sat still and closed my eyes when I heard the hissing of the scissors. I cried silent tears about losing my hair once again.

"Look at all the lice," the hairstylist said to her coworkers. Papi picked up a copy of the newspaper on the seat next to him and hid behind it. Mago sat with Betty on her lap, waiting. When the hairstylist was done with me, it was Betty's turn. She cried and kept moving her head and Mago had to hold her still. When the hairstylist was done with Betty and asked Mago to sit down, Papi said, "Not her." I looked at Mago, and I was so angry I could spit at her. On our way home we stopped at the pharmacy and Papi bought special lice shampoo and made us wash our hair with it as soon as we got home.

"You didn't have to cut my hair," I said.

"It'll grow back, Chata. Don't worry." My anger disappeared immediately at hearing Papi call me by the special nickname he had given me when I was little.

Later, he inspected the house he had built for us. We were surprised to see it almost finished; it just needed the windowpanes installed. As we walked from room to room, we told him how we'd helped to build this house by carrying the gravel and the mortar buckets and bricks. "Which is going to be your room?" Mago asked him. Papi didn't say anything.

In the evening, when Papi reached into his suitcase to grab his pajamas, he found a big surprise. A dozen baby scorpions and their mother came tumbling out to the floor when he took out his pajama pants. I screamed and jumped onto the couch. He stepped on the scorpions and killed them.

"You could've been stung," Mila said, glancing around the

floor to make sure he had killed all the scorpions, and then she added, "How soon do you think we can go home?"

Go home? I wondered. *But this* is *his home.*

As if reading my thoughts, Mago said, "Our house is finished now. He doesn't need to leave again." She turned to him and said, "Right, Papi? You're staying now, aren't you?"

Papi looked at Mila and then at us. "Let's talk about it later. ¿Está bien?"

"Why don't you tell them now, Natalio? Tell them you aren't staying," Mila said.

"All right," he said. He sat us down on the couch and said, "Well, you see, kids, I've decided I can't come back here. Even though the house is finished, there are no jobs here. If I come back, we'll still live in this miserable poverty, ¿entienden?"

"But the house is finished, Papi. We'll be safe there," I said.

"We don't eat much," Carlos said. "You wouldn't need to make a lot of money to feed us. Mago already has a job at the train station. I could get a job, too. I'm old enough."

"No!" Papi said. "You need to go to school. All of you need to stay in school, you hear? Negra, what is this about you working already?"

Mago stayed quiet. He looked at her, waiting for her to say something. Finally, Mago stood up and said, "Abuela Evila was right all along. Excuses, that's all you have to give us. Excuses as to why you can't come back." She ran out of the living room crying.

The next day, Papi told us he would be leaving in a few days. Mila would be flying back because she was a naturalized U.S. citizen. Since he had no papers, he would hire a coyote to take him across the border.

"I'm not coming back here," he said to us. "I have a new life in El Otro Lado. I don't want to give up that life, but I know it isn't fair for you not to have a father. I thought your mother was taking care of you, but now I see that she isn't. I don't have enough money to take all of you with me. I can take only one of you."

Tears gathered in my eyes because I didn't want to hear what he was going to say next. I knew who he had chosen.

"I'm going to take Mago with me. She's the oldest, and she won't have as much trouble running across the border with me."

"You can't take her," I said. "You can't take her."

"Why not?" he asked.

"Because she's all I have."

Mago put an arm around me. I held on tight. I had survived being left by my father. I had lived through my mother's constant comings and goings. But if Mago left me, I didn't think I could survive. I looked at him, and I wished he had not come back. I wished he had stayed where he was. I wished he were just a photograph hanging on the wall. I would've preferred that to losing my sister. Why did he have to come back, only to leave again, and not just that, but take away the only person who truly loved me?

"And what about me, Papi?" Carlos said. "I can run really fast. Just ask my friends. They can never catch me when we play soccer. I'd leave la migra in the dust! Take me with you, Papi."

Papi put his hand on Carlos's shoulder. "You're right, Carnal. You could probably manage the crossing as well as Mago. I'll take you with me. But you, Chata, I cannot."

"How could you split us up?" I asked Papi. "How could you take them away?"

"I don't want to separate you," he said, bending down to look at me. "I will come back for you, Chata. I promise that as soon as I have some money I will come back for you."

I shook my head, unable to believe him. "The last time you left, you were gone eight years, Papi," I said.

Papi looked down and didn't say anything.

• • •

We returned to Abuelita Chinta's house that evening because
Papi didn't want us to miss school.

"You'll still be here tomorrow, won't you?" Mago asked.
We were afraid that while we were gone, he would pack up and
leave, never to return again.

"Of course I will, Negra," he said.

At school my classmates wanted to know all about him.
They asked painful questions I didn't want to answer. "Is he finally moving back here?" they asked. "Or is he taking you with
him?"

I didn't want to tell them the truth. I didn't want to admit
that Papi didn't want me. He only wanted my sister and my
brother. So I started to lie. "Yes, my papi is taking me to El Otro
Lado with him. Goodbye, my friends. I will miss you." I could
see the look of envy in their eyes.

"You're so lucky Reyna," they said to me. By the end of the
school day, I was starting to believe the lies myself. But then I
was suddenly afraid. When my classmates found out I wasn't
going anywhere, they would make fun of me so much I knew I
would die of shame because they would never let me forget that
my father had not wanted me. Like my mother, I was afraid of
people knowing that I had failed.

After school, when we got to Abuela Evila's house, Papi and
Mila were sitting on the patio with my grandmother. He called
us over, and I was the first to rush to his side.

"Papi, you have to take me back to El Otro Lado with
you," I said.

"Why is that?"

"Because I told my friends you would, and I have said
goodbye to all of them! I'll die of shame if they know that I lied,
Papi. Please take me with you."

He laughed. Mila didn't laugh. She glared at me.

"She's a stubborn one, isn't she?" Mila said.

"You leave her here with me, Natalio, and I will teach her some manners," Abuela Evila said. "This girl needs to learn that bad things come to women who don't know their place."

Mila looked furiously at my grandmother. Abuela Evila had not liked the fact that in the days Papi and Mila had been there, not once had Mila offered to help with the cooking or to wash the dishes. After the meals were over, she usually stood up, along with Papi, and left the kitchen to go sit on the patio or watch TV.

"It's different for women in the U.S.," Mila said. "Over there, women aren't treated like servants."

"I won't go with you if you don't take Reyna," Mago said. "I mean it." I looked at my sister's face, and on it I saw the conflict inside her. I knew she was dying to go. More than anyone, it had been she who had yearned for him all those years. But destiny had also made her become my little mother, and unlike my mother, Mago's maternal instincts won over her need to save herself. "I'm serious, Papi," she said.

"M-me, too," Carlos said, halfheartedly.

Papi reached his hand out to me, and I took it. "You really want to go live with me?"

"Sí, Papi. Please take me with you."

"All right, then in that case, I will take all my children back with me."

"But, but where in the world are you going to get the money?" Mila said.

"We'll borrow it," he said. "Beg everyone we know."

Papi said he would need money to pay a smuggler for the four of us—me, Carlos, Mago, and him. Betty could fly back with Mila since she was a U.S. citizen. For a brief moment, I felt the familiar jealousy I'd felt when I had first heard of my American sister. Being born in the U.S. was a privilege I wished I had

had. That way, I wouldn't need to sneak across the border like a thief. I thought about the time Mago, Carlos, and I had tried to steal mangoes from El Cuervo's grove, and how frightened I had been of his gun. I felt a shiver run through me.

"Will they shoot at us?" I asked as we listened to Papi talk about the crossing, the people called la migra. I could hear the fear in his voice.

"No, Chata, no. No one will shoot at us," he said as he sat me on his lap. "Don't be afraid." But I saw the way he glanced at Mila before hiding his face in his beer.

The next day, Mago and I went to give Mami the news. Papi didn't want to talk to her himself, claiming that Mago might have a better chance of convincing her to let us go. He knew Mami had not forgiven him for what he'd done. At the sight of him, who knows what might have happened. As it was, Mago and I had a hard time convincing her to let us go. Fortunately, Tío Gary had come to Abuelita Chinta's house just in time to talk some sense into my mother. He said, "You aren't taking care of them, Juana, why deny them the chance to go to El Otro Lado? Besides, our mother is too old to be taking care of your kids. Let them go, Juana. It's for the best. Don't deny them the opportunity to have a better life."

"Fine," Mami said. "If they want to leave with him, so be it." She turned to look at us and said, "Tell your father that he can't have Betty."

My father was furious. "That's why I couldn't be with her anymore," he said when Mago had delivered Mami's message. "She has never had a good vision of the future." He turned around and looked at us. "I know I promised not to separate you, but if your mother won't hand over Betty's birth certificate, I won't be able to take her. She's too little to run across the border."

Mago was holding Betty's hand. Papi reached his arms out

and put Betty in his lap. "You hear that, mija? Your mother is keeping you from me."

Betty had just turned four in March. Like me, she had no memory of him and this was why, as he held her in his arms, she squirmed away and returned to our side. "I want my mami," she said.

"You see what your mother has done to me?" Papi said. "She has robbed me of my youngest child. There are laws in the U.S. I could have gone to court, filed for custody. I would have had rights. Instead, your mother took off like a thief and came back here, stealing her from me. And now look, my own daughter doesn't even know me."

"You tried to shoot her, Papi," Carlos said. "Mami was scared."

Papi laughed. "She overreacted. I wasn't going to shoot her. And whatever happened to that man was an accident. An accident."

"If you had just listened to your mother, this wouldn't have happened," Abuela Evila chimed in. "I told you she was not good enough for you, Natalio. I told you she would be trouble. But you didn't listen."

"I will go talk to her one more time," Mago said, standing up. "If we're going with you, we can't leave our little sister behind."

Mago and I went to Mami's work. We walked into the record shop and saw Mami dusting the counter while dancing to a cumbia. We stood there and watched her, and I knew that this was a different side to Mami she didn't allow us to see. There she was smiling, dancing, singing, things I hadn't seen her do ever since El Otro Lado had taken her away. I thought that part of Mami was gone. But then I knew that it was there, except not when she was with us.

Mami turned and saw us standing there at the entrance of the store.

"You startled me!" she said, clutching her chest. She rushed to the stereo and turned down the volume.

"Mami, we want you to let Betty come with us," Mago said as she pulled me into the store with her. "We can't leave her behind."

"Well, as you've always said, Betty is my daughter, not yours, so I get to decide her fate," Mami said.

"Why would you separate us like that?"

Mami took a deep breath. "Mago, I don't want to fight with you. If your father wants to take you with him, then you should go. Going to El Otro Lado is a good opportunity, for you, for your brother, for Reyna."

"So, why won't you let us take Betty, too?" I asked.

Mami looked away and didn't answer. Later, I would come to realize that her decision had come from stubbornness. Pride. If she had allowed my father to have Betty, it would have meant that he had won.

"Come on, Nena, let's go," Mago said. We went out into the busy street, and I turned to look behind me. Mami stood there at the door of the record shop and waved goodbye. Too soon, I couldn't see her anymore through the crowd of people rushing down the sidewalk. In my head I could still hear the song Mami was listening to. I could still see her dancing in the record shop, her lips curved into a smile. I pulled my hand from Mago's and stopped walking. *What if I stay? Could Mami be that woman, the one in the record shop, when she was with me? Could she finally start being the mother she was before she left? Maybe she could, maybe she would, but if I leave, then I'll never know.*

"Nena, you coming or what?" Mago said as she stood there holding out her hand to me. I turned to look at Mago, and at the sight of her I knew I could not survive being separated from her. Back then, she had still been *my* Mago. Hers was the first face I saw when I woke up and the last when I fell asleep. How could

I think of staying, when knowing that if I did, I would lose the one person who had always stood beside me?

I ran to take my sister's hand, choosing not to follow the crumbs back to my mother.

I thought of Mami dancing in the record shop, and I promised myself that was how I would always think of her, and I would try to forget that other mother, the one who left and left and left.

Our first two attempts across the border were failures. Even now I blame myself. I was not used to walking and running so much and so fast. To make things worse, I had woken up with a toothache on the morning of our first attempt, and my father didn't have anything to give me for the pain. Around noon I began to get a fever, and the pain became unbearable. My father ended up carrying me on his back, but still, it wasn't long before a cloud of dust rose in the distance, and before we knew it a truck was heading our way. We rushed into the bushes, but the truck pulled over and border patrol agents got out and told us to come out from our hiding places. We were sent back to Tijuana.

The second time we tried to cross, we had the same bad luck. Again, I couldn't keep up with the rest of them, and the heat of the sun's rays beating down on my head gave me a headache. Once, when we sat down to rest, I walked away to relieve myself in the bushes and found a man lying not too far from me. I thought he was asleep, but when I got closer to him, I saw the flies buzzing over him and the big bump on his forehead.

I screamed for help. Papi arrived first, followed by the coyote, and then Carlos and Mago. Papi told Mago to shut me up before la migra heard me.

"Is he dead?" I asked Mago as she took me away. "Is he dead?"

"He's sleeping, Nena. He's just sleeping," she said.

We got caught shortly thereafter, and I was glad because I couldn't get that dead man out of my head.

I am grateful now that back then I was too young to fully grasp the extent of the danger we were in. I am glad I did not know about the thousands of immigrants who had died before my crossing and who have been dying ever since.

After getting sent back twice, Papi said, "This is the last time, mijos." He sent us off to bed even though it was only two o'clock in the afternoon. But that night we were attempting our third—and final—border crossing, and Papi said we needed to rest as much as possible. We would be running through the night.

Papi lay down on the floor beside our bed and said, "If we don't make it this time, I'm going to have to send you back. And I will send you to my mother, since your own mother isn't doing a decent job of caring for you kids."

"No, Papi, please!" I said. The thought of going back to Abuela Evila's house filled me with dread. But I knew it was my fault. If I hadn't gotten sick the first time, we probably would have made it. If I had walked faster, run faster, not complained about the heat or my hunger, or hadn't constantly asked for water, maybe then we would have made it. If my molar hadn't been hurting me so much and had I not whined about the pain, maybe then we could have made it.

"I'm sorry, mijos. I'm going to lose my job if I miss any more days." He said he didn't have the money to keep paying for food and the motel. He had barely been able to borrow the money for the coyote to take us across the border, and there was almost no money left. Some of it had also been spent on our trip, which had been a very uncomfortable two-day bus ride where we had suffered from endless motion sickness. I don't remember how many times my siblings and I threw up.

"Don't make us go back there again," Mago said in a voice so soft I didn't think he'd heard her. But after a minute or two, Papi finally looked at us. I grabbed Mago's and Carlos's hands and squeezed them. I thought about going back to Abuela Evila's house, back to being an unwanted, parentless child, back to waiting, always waiting, to hear from Papi so far away in El Otro Lado.

He sighed and said, "This will be our last time. If we don't make it, you're going back. Now, go to sleep. You will need all your strength tonight."

But I couldn't sleep. I thought about the past seven days and how quickly they had passed. I thought about Mami, little Betty, my grandmother, and I couldn't help feeling torn about our situation. I was so happy that my father had not left me behind, but I was also sad about leaving my little sister. I felt as if we had abandoned her. The day we left for the bus station she had cried as we walked away. Abuelita Chinta had cried, too. I stopped at the canal to wave goodbye to them and part of me wanted to tell Papi I had changed my mind, that I *did* want to stay. But then I thought about Mago, and I knew I couldn't be without her. And I wanted to have a father. *Why does it have to be so hard?* I had to leave my mother, my little sister, my grandmother—so that I could have a father. But even that was in jeopardy. If we didn't cross that third time, I would lose him.

Please God, give me wings.

Papi woke us up at sunset, and we took a bus to the meeting point where the coyote was waiting for us. We crossed the dirt path, slipped under the hole in the fence, and immersed ourselves in the darkness that had quickly fallen around us. "Remember," Papi said, "this is the last time." He followed the coyote. We followed our father in single file: Mago, me, and Carlos at the end. We walked along a small path, the thin moon curved into a smile, and I thought that if the moon was smiling at us, it must be a good sign. Far in the distance, I saw two red lights, like evil eyes. I shivered.

"They're just antennas," the coyote said when Carlos asked about the lights.

I thought about the church pilgrimages we had taken with Abuelita Chinta a couple of times. *If I once made it through nine days of walking, surely I could make it now, couldn't I?* But hard as I tried, I couldn't lie to myself. This journey was similar to the pilgrimages because we were walking through bushes and hills, but I hadn't been afraid back then. At this moment, every muscle in my body was tense. Every noise, like the chirping of crickets, the wind rustling the branches of the bushes, the sound of our labored breathing, frightened me. I thought those sounds were coming from la migra. I thought that somewhere in the endless darkness, la migra was there, ready to capture us and send us back to Tijuana, and ultimately, back to Abuela Evila's house.

I kept my eyes on Mago's back as I sang the songs from the pilgrimage in my head. I thought about Abuelita Chinta, her gap-toothed smile, and I felt a pang of sadness just thinking about the fact that with every step I took, I was getting farther and farther away from her, Mami, and little Betty.

"Reyna, apúrate!" my father hissed. I sprinted to catch up to the group. I didn't even notice that Carlos had passed me.

At first, it sounded like a kitten purring. Then the sound got louder, and the coyote yelled, "¡Córranle!" In the darkness, I saw him take off without us. My father grabbed my hand and ran, too. I couldn't keep up with his long strides, and I fell flat on my face. He scooped me up and ran with me in his arms. Mago and Carlos followed close behind.

A light shone in the distance, and the purring got louder.

"What's happening, Papi?" Mago asked.

"Helicopter."

Carlos tripped on a rock, but Papi kept on running and didn't wait for him to get up. "Wait, Papi!" I said, but Papi was like a frightened animal. He scampered through the bushes trying to find a place to hide.

"Get down!" the coyote yelled from somewhere in the darkness. Papi immediately dropped to the ground, and we became lizards, rubbing our bellies against the cold, damp earth, trying to find a place to hide. Pebbles dug into my knees. I couldn't see Carlos in the darkness, and I cried and told Papi to wait, but he pushed me into a little cave created by overgrown bushes. Mago and I sat by Papi's side, and he held on to us tight while we listened to the roaring of the helicopter right above us.

The beams of the searchlight cut through the branches of the bushes. I yanked my foot back when a beam of light fell on my shoe. I wondered if the people in the helicopter had seen my foot. I tried to hold my breath, thinking that even the smallest sound could give us away. *Please God, don't let them see us. Please God, let us arrive safely to El Otro Lado. I want to live in that perfect place. I want to have a father. I want to have a family.*

Finally, after what felt like hours, the helicopter left. We could hear the chirping of the crickets once more, the howling of a coyote in the distance, and then we tensed up when we heard the sound of branches breaking.

Papi poked his head out of the cave and sighed in relief. "I'm sorry, Carnal." We came out, and Carlos and the smuggler were standing outside our cave. Carlos smiled, proud of himself for not getting us caught.

"You should have seen him crawl under the bushes," the smuggler said. "He's a real iguana, this one."

When we finally got across the border to a place called Chula Vista, we headed to the house of the second smuggler, the man in charge of driving us to Los Angeles. We got there early in the morning.

My father got in the passenger side of the car, and my siblings and I sat in the back. The smuggler, who was called El Güero, told us to lie down and stay out of sight. Papi said that even though we had succeeded in crossing, the danger was not over yet. We could easily get pulled over by la migra on our way to Los Angeles. So Mago and I lay down on the backseat like spoons and Carlos had to lie on the floor. My stomach growled. We had gone the whole night without food.

As we drove from Chula Vista to Los Angeles, I wished I could get up and see what El Otro Lado looked like. I wanted to see with my own eyes the beautiful place where I would be living from then on. I started to get motion sickness, and the only thing we could look at was the roof of the car, which wasn't very interesting. Then Carlos threw up and for the rest of the trip the car stank of vomit. Finally the smuggler said we could get up for just a minute, to stretch, and what amazed me the most were the palm trees. I had never seen so many palm trees, and there they were, on either side of the freeway whizzing by. The freeway was amazing, so enormous compared to the tiny dirt roads in my colonia. And the cars were clean and shiny, so different from the rusty old cars back home. I wanted the smuggler to slow down. I'd never been in a car that traveled so fast, and I knew that in a few seconds I would have to lie back down again. I wanted to take everything in. The last thing I saw when El Güero said to lie down was a pair of golden arches, and I wondered what they were.

"Can't we stop to get some hamburgers for my kids?" Papi asked the smuggler.

I'd never eaten a hamburger before, but I heard this was what people in El Otro Lado liked to eat. My stomach rumbled in anticipation.

El Güero shook his head. "Too risky."

He took out a bag from the glove compartment. I saw him put his hand in the bag and then put something in his mouth. He opened the window and spat. He did that several times, and my curiosity grew more and more, but I was too embarrassed to lean closer to see what he was eating. He must have remembered we were hungry because he said, "You kids want some?"

Mago said, "What is it?"

"Sunflower seeds." He rolled down the window and spat again.

Mago, Carlos, and I looked at one another. Sunflower seeds? Here we were, coming to the richest country in the world, and this man was eating bird food? In my town, I had never, in my whole nine years, seen anyone eat bird food before. I would have preferred one of those hamburgers.

"They're almost like pumpkin seeds," Papi said, urging us to take some.

To my amazement, Mago reached out her hand. She grabbed the bag El Güero gave her and then put a pile of seeds into Carlos's and my cupped hands. She took some for herself and gave the bag back to El Güero.

"Look, there's the exit to Disneyland," El Güero said, pointing out the window. Then he remembered that we couldn't see anything because we were still lying down. "You can get up now," he said. "I think we're safe now."

Mami had mentioned Disneyland and how sad she was that she never got to go while she was here. I hoped one day we would get to see it. I hoped one day I would get to do everything people said you could do in El Otro Lado, like speak English. We sat up and got ready to eat our sunflower seeds. I let Mago go first. She put the seeds in her mouth and chewed them. When she swallowed, she started to choke.

"You're supposed to remove the shell," El Güero said. "I forgot to tell you that."

I put a seed in my mouth and did what El Güero said to do,

to crack the shell with my teeth and eat only the kernel inside. I wondered if it was my hunger, but those sunflower seeds tasted delicious. I sucked the salt off the shells before cracking them and eating the inside. My first breakfast in the United States was bird food.

Not too long after, Papi pointed to the tallest buildings I'd ever seen and said that was downtown Los Angeles. I thought about the map Mago had once showed me. I remembered that little dot labeled Los Angeles. It suddenly hit me that Mami and I had switched places, but the distance between us was just as big as it had been three years before.

"How far are we from home?" I asked Papi. "From Iguala."

"Home?" Papi said. "This is your home now, Chata."

I could hear the anger in Papi's voice, and I wished I could tell him that even though this was my home now, my umbilical cord was buried in Iguala.

The smuggler said, "Guerrero is about two thousand miles or so from here."

Two thousand miles was the distance between us and Mami. Between me and the place I had been born. Between me and my childhood, however painful it had been. I turned to look behind me as the car sped on. Mami had once said she didn't want me to forget where I came from.

"I promise I'll never forget," I said under my breath. We exited the freeway and arrived at our new home.

LE LY HAYSLIP

Vietnam

Le Ly Hayslip (1949–) was born to a family of Vietnamese farmers in the small village of Ky La, now known as Xa Hao Qui, near the city of Da Nang. During the escalating tensions between North and South Vietnam, the adolescent Hayslip worked as a lookout for the communist Vietcong, actions that led to her arrest and torture by the South Vietnamese. After her release, the Vietcong considered Hayslip untrustworthy and sentenced her to death, but she escaped after the two soldiers assigned the task chose to rape her instead. Fleeing to Saigon, where she could work alongside her mother as a housekeeper, Hayslip became pregnant by her employer, which left her, at sixteen, "an unwed mother supporting [her] family on Danang's black market." In 1969, in an effort to escape the war, Hayslip married and had a son with Ed Munro, a middle-aged American civilian. She arrived in San Diego the following year.

Following the years of U.S. military involvement in Vietnam, President Gerald Ford authorized the immigration of 125,000 South Vietnamese refugees, a group overwhelmingly composed of the elite and those with close ties to the American military. Smaller waves continued to arrive between 1976 and 1978. Amid deteriorating conditions in Vietnam, and its emerging hostilities with China and Cambodia, the U.S. then expanded its refugee program, taking in more than 225,000 Vietnamese between 1979 and 1981.

Despite her having arrived nearly a decade earlier, Hayslip's experiences in the U.S. mirror those of largely uneducated and rural Vietnamese refugees. And she found that she was as disadvantaged as later immi-

grants, though she could still rely on her husband and his extended family
to assist her acculturation. After her husband died in 1973, his family
continued to support Le Ly until she married her second husband, Dennis
Hayslip, with whom she would have a third child. A few years after his
death in 1982, Hayslip founded East Meets West, a nongovernmental
organization aimed at assisting disadvantaged people in South and South-
east Asia. Later, she would focus her humanitarian efforts in Vietnam
with the Global Village Foundation.

Hayslip's immensely successful first memoir, When Heaven and
Earth Changed Places (1989), which depicted the Vietnam War from
the perspective of the rural population, was later adapted into a feature
film by Oliver Stone. Her second memoir, Child of War, Woman of
Peace (1993), focuses on Hayslip's subsequent arrival in the U.S. In
addition to portraying the author's negotiation of cultural differences, the
memoir shows how her early humanitarian efforts helped her to overcome
the horror of her wartime experiences. Hayslip's foundations have significantly expanded since their inception, and she has been recognized by the
California State Assembly for her work.

In the following passage, the author is on her first grocery-shopping
trip in the U.S. Near the end of this disorienting experience, Hayslip
confronts a male clerk's thinly veiled hatred. This encounter causes her
to reflect on her own participation in the war and the guilt she feels for
surviving.

Excerpt from

Child of War, Woman of Peace

— 1993 —

Anyway, my string-tied pants and stern moral upbringing were barriers to more than sex. The only dress I had on arrival in America was an *ao dai*, the traditional long-paneled tunic worn by Vietnamese ladies since ancient times. On my first Saturday (shopping day in America), I would find out that dressing up in a way that was right in my old country was very wrong in my new one.

In Vietnam, we had two kinds of shopping: *dao pho mua sam*, which is "dress up and go to town"; and *di cho*, which is to buy food in the local market. So when Ed said, "Get dressed, we're going to get groceries," I assumed he meant we were going to the neighborhood fish market.

"I am dressed," I answered, pointing to my black pajamas— the kind I had worn to the village market all my life.

"Not that!" Ed almost choked. "People will think you're lazy or sick. Put on pants or a dress. You know, something you'd wear outside."

Ed's huffy tone left me confused and a little insulted. Although I was young, I wasn't stupid or without experience. I knew my *ao dai* would leave me overdressed for haggling with fish peddlers, but with my lousy record of mistakes, I figured it was better to be safe than sorry.

Although I was dressed and perfumed for a night on the town, everyone else was dressed for the beach—or bedroom.

"Look at that girl!" I whispered to Ed as we approached the local Safeway. Her big breasts bounced around inside a spongy tube top. Ed had already noticed. Behind her came another woman in high, creased shorts that showed things her doctor would be ashamed to see. I was scandalized and grateful I had left my innocent kids at home with Leatha and Erma. These housewives and schoolgirls were more provocative than anything I had seen outside the sleaziest nightclubs in Danang. In my country, a polite woman hid her body out of consideration for society (what man could work with such distractions?) as well as self-respect. If we felt free to dress like tramps, the men around us would feel free to behave like bums. In a war zone, temptation was the same as provocation.

"So, you don't like my pajamas, eh?" I poked Ed in the ribs. "Maybe next time I shop in my underwear!" The spirits guarding Safeway, obviously pleased at my proper attire, opened the door with unseen hands.

That's when I noticed: American markets don't smell like markets at all. Everything is canned, packaged, wrapped in cellophane, and hidden in boxes where, instead of seeing and smelling the fruit or vegetable or meat or whatever, you get a pretty picture of what the seller wants you to think the product looks like. You pay so much money for a pretty picture! Everything in the supermarket reeked of Freon or cleanser or corrugated cardboard boxes. How was I to tell if my husband's steak and potatoes—hidden behind plastic and frost in a refrigerator too cold to touch—was fit to eat? And the produce counters weren't much better. Everything was air-conditioned or on crushed ice. I felt as if I were visiting a "fruit hotel" rather than picking out tomorrow's dinner. It was all so strange that my stomach began to hurt. Ed mistook my pained expression for amazement.

"So—what do you think of our big American supermarkets?" he asked proudly, steering our huge metal cart down the aisle. "Pretty impressive, huh?"

"Oh, there are too many choices!" I replied, trying to find

something nice to say. "And the wagon they give you is very nice," which was true enough. I was used to shopping day by day, not for a week of groceries at a time.

Ed stopped in the middle of a rainbow of packages.

"Here now," he said, adjusting his glasses like a professor, "you always say we don't eat enough rice—what do you think of this?"

He waved his hand along the shelf. From the pictures on the labels, all the boxes contained rice, although I had no idea what distinguished one kind from another. Of course, I *had* complained (in the nicest way possible) that I sorely missed my daily bowl of rice. The Munros were a steak and potatoes family and liked thick sandwiches of bread and meat for lunch instead of the greens and rice and noodle soup even wealthy Orientals preferred.

In the village, we had a dozen names for rice depending on its stage of preparation. Generally, we had three kinds of finished rice: *tam* rice, or bran rice, which was fit only for animals and beggars; brown (or "autumn"—*gao mua*) rice, which most of us ate every day; and sweet rice, called *xoi*—the white kind served at ceremonies, on holidays, or sacrificed to our ancestors. Here, Americans ate Spanish rice, fried rice, converted rice, steamed rice, wild rice, paella rice, rice pilaf, risotto rice, and dozens more I couldn't pronounce. Ed must've thought I had been a poor rice farmer, because I couldn't tell the difference. Finally, I grabbed a nice-looking box.

"Great," Ed said. "What kind did you get?"

Timidly, I showed him.

"Uncle Ben's?" he said. "Why Uncle Ben's?"

"The label," I tapped it like a smart American shopper. "I want number-one rice for family, right? So, this brand called 'Uncle Ben.' Vietnamese call trusted friend 'Uncle,' right? Like 'Uncle Ho' for Ho Chi Minh? So, Uncle Ben must be very good rice—trusted very much by all Americans, right?"

Ed laughed again and shook his head. I began filling the cart with Uncle Ben's but Ed stopped me after a few boxes.

"Whoa—hold on!" he said. "We aren't feeding the whole neighborhood!"

I was still battling old reflexes—to clean out American goods for resale on the black market. Our credo had been: Stash, hoard, and survive. It was also customary in the Orient to buy rice in hundred-kilo bags, not tiny boxes printed like colorful storybooks. As things turned out, it wasn't the kind of rice I thought it was after all, and Leatha let me spoil a batch before stepping in to show me how converted rice was cooked. She, too, must've thought I was a terrible farmer as well as an incompetent wife. Imagine—an Asian woman who can't cook rice!

When we went to the checkout counter, the male clerk, seeing my *ao dai*, gave me a nasty stare. It was an expression I had seen before—mostly from Vietnamese in Danang who disapproved of my American boyfriends—but here it was something more. The clerk was too young to have been in the service, but he had the warrior's look: hate and fear and sorrow all mixed. Maybe he had a brother or father killed in my country. Maybe he was just one of the many Americans I would meet who were so fed up with the war that they hated anyone who reminded them of it.

Still, this was his country, not mine, so I lowered my eyes. I tried to make myself look humble and even smaller, which was easy next to my big American husband.

Like many in my village, I never really hated American soldiers. We resented them for invading our country, of course, but we didn't take it personally. As a rule, they weren't mean to us for meanness' sake—like the Moroccans or Koreans, or the Japanese in World War II. Americans' funny racial differences—big noses and round eyes on long faces—were objects of amusement and sometimes fear, but seldom hate. As a result, I was surprised to see those embers glowing in the eyes of this angry young clerk.

Even worse, *I* began to take it personally. I thought I must look funny or was standing or gesturing in some way that gave offense. I tried to summon up the guilt I often felt for planting jungle booby traps as a twelve-year-old conscript for the Viet Cong. What had once seemed right and necessary now seemed cruel and useless. Had I actually helped to wound or maim this young man's brother? Had I led his hapless father into a Viet Cong ambush? Today, the breezy, bustling Americans around me seemed no more threatening than a load of tourists. War and "real life" were now as opposite as night and day. War guilt, I had learned, was partly the chagrin you feel for outliving a crisis that once consumed you. One does not strike a match where there is no darkness, although one may still be afraid of the dark.

So I tried to play the role this young man gave me, but I could not. What alarmed me most was the racial anger that popped up inside me like the flame on a GI's lighter. People can reason about anything they have the power to change, like their attitude or their clothes, but when condemned for their race they react like cornered rats. I longed for my father's spirit to cool me, as it had so often those last years in Vietnam. *"Con o dau—ong ba theo do,"* he used to say, assuring me that wherever his children wandered, our ancestors would surely go to comfort and protect us. But how could they find me so far from home? More than a stranger in a strange new land, I was becoming a stranger to myself. I didn't like that feeling one bit.

The clerk rang everything up and Ed didn't haggle about price or freshness, and when the boy told us how much we owed, I almost fell over. Ed, however, wasn't fazed. Instead of handing out cash, he simply wrote the amount on a slip of paper, which he signed and tore out of a book.

"What's that?" I asked.

"A check. I'm paying for our groceries. Surely you've seen somebody write a check!"

"Of course!" I sniffed. I didn't want to appear ignorant in front of the surly cashier.

"Well, maybe our American checks are different," Ed said softly as the clerk copied down more numbers from some cards Ed showed him. "You see, the store gives the check to our bank, which gives them money for us."

No money for food! I was astonished, *Just a paper check! No wonder Americans eat so much!* And no wonder wealthy Vietnamese were the only people in my country to use banks. That's how the rich got rich—because the banks paid all their bills! It also explained why Ed guarded his checkbook the way I guarded my kids. Checks were better than money!

Over the next few weeks, I met many more of Ed's friends and relatives. Usually, I served them tea Vietnamese style, offering the cup with both hands and bowing slightly when they took it. Word must have gotten around, because sometimes they would clap after my "performance." Each visitor would congratulate Ed on his beautiful young wife—as if I were a new TV set or lawn mower—ask me how I liked America, then begin talking to Ed as if I weren't there. True, my English wasn't the best, but I understood a lot and was willing to learn more. For some reason they always asked me questions through Ed—although he spoke no Vietnamese—and I was assumed to be incapable of anything except pouring tea, looking pretty, and caring for my children, who were greeted with a mix of amusement and distaste. "Cute kids," I would hear them say, "but such urchins—especially the one that isn't Ed's." Did they think I didn't have ears?

During these long conversations, I often wondered what these "wise" Americans really knew about life and living, let alone death and survival. How many of them had their world split in two—saw brother fight brother with bullets, bombs, and bayonets? How many had their homes invaded by strange-looking, strange-smelling giants? Had to hide in leech-filled swamps or were tortured with snakes and electricity for information they didn't have? How many sent wives and husbands and brothers and sisters out to work in the morning only to have their pieces come back in a basket? What had their cozy houses and bulging refrigerators and big, fast cars and noisy TV sets really taught them about the world: about back-breaking labor, bone-grinding poverty, and death's edge starvation? Could they imagine their sons and husbands, so peaceful and happy in civilian life, coming into my village and making old men and women beg for their lives? *"Xin ong dung giet toi!"*—"Please, sir, don't kill me!"—was our standard greeting for the American boys in uniform who came our way.

We once watched a TV war correspondent interview a young GI in front of a burning village.

"Do you think your operation was successful?" the journalist asked.

"Yeah, we burned down a lot of Charlie's homes and destroyed the village—really killed a lot of gooks!" the soot-faced young man said with a big grin.

I could only imagine the wailing villagers, unseen by the camera and Ed's relatives. How successful had the "operation" been for them? Did anyone realize how many lifetimes we villagers crammed into our first twenty years on earth? *Tre chua qua, gia da den*—Before youth has left, old age has come! Did Ed's relatives realize what an old lady looked back at them through the tear-moistened eyes of Ed's "lovely young bride"?

When I started crying like this—"for no reason at all," Ed would say after the visitors had gone—I felt more foolish than ever. "The poor dear is homesick," Leatha would say, just out of hearing. "She misses her mother," and that was true enough. "She's just a spoiled crybaby," young Kathy would add, going off to her own lovely house and young husband. Erma would sniff into her coffee mug after glancing around to see if I was near, and say things like, Not that she lifts a finger to help out. She leaves long black hairs around the house and those poor children would *starve* if I didn't fix them a proper meal. Nothing but rice and noodles—how can they live on that? And she never socializes with our guests, have you noticed? Just bows and bats her eyes, then goes into her dream world. Lord knows what she thinks about—probably all the things Ed's going to buy her. He's going through his second childhood, all right, and he's found the perfect playmate!

To tell the truth, I didn't feel like much of a playmate, or even much of a wife or mother. Because Ed enjoyed telling the story of how we met—on a Danang street corner through a girlfriend of mine who used to be a hooker—his family concluded I had been a streetwalker. Even in their more charitable moods, they seemed sure I'd married Ed for his money and a life of ease in America. They couldn't conceive of mere survival as a motive, with gratitude, not greed, the consequence.

I tried to solve their problem with my hair, which now flowed like a waterfall down to my waist, by lopping it off with kitchen scissors—short, like a Chinese rice-bowl haircut. I redoubled my efforts to impress both Leatha and Erma in the only way I knew—by working harder and longer than anyone, but even this tactic only widened the gap between us. When I tried to wash clothes by hand, Erma chided me for not using the automatic washer and dryer. When I scrubbed the floor on my knees, Leatha chuckled at my stupidity and told me to use the mop. When I cooked good fish and rice, they turned up their noses and wondered why I was starving "my boys" of old-fashioned meat and potatoes. When I picked up my kids and carried them around, even when they weren't crying—handling them the way all kids need to be handled if they are to learn love and affection—Leatha pointed to the playpen and said, "Leave them alone, or they'll never become independent!" In a land of instant gratification and miracle conveniences, apparently, there was no room for a spontaneous show of love through the labor of one's heart and hands.

On top of it all, whenever the women took me shopping, the only sizes I could wear were in the children's department, so the kids and I bought our clothes together. I felt more like a foster child than an honorable daughter-in-law with a family of my own.

After a few weeks of this, I began to hate myself as the useless teenager everyone supposed me to be. I hated my hair for being Oriental black, not European brown or blond or silver. I hated my body for being Vietnamese puny and not Polish plump or German hardy or big-boobed and long-legged like the glossy American girls Ed ogled on the sidewalk.

For that matter, being married to "my father" made me feel even more like a child, which was how I responded as a wife, and I hated myself for that. Unable to communicate with anyone in any of the ways I knew, I felt alone, like a stone at the bottom of the sea.

As much as I hated the war, I began to miss Vietnam very much—not for the dangerous and depressing life I used to live, but for the home and family I remembered as a child. The more I tried to make such a family here, the more I ached for the one I had left behind. I waited like a puppy for the American mail carrier, hoping for a letter or postcard from my family. At sunset, I would sit in Leatha's yard and sing to the bloodred sun—in the direction of my absent mother—but the palms of Southern California were not magical sau dau trees, and my soul did not flower in the dirt beneath my feet.

Worst of all was when we gathered after dinner for an evening of TV, which in those days always began with war news from Vietnam—the U.S. invasion of Cambodia and the Kent State massacre that had followed.

"Look at those awful people!" Erma would say when stories about "Viet Cong atrocities" filled the screen. To her and Larry, the enemy had one face. Ed and Leatha, like me, just sat in silence, speaking only when Jimmy's playing got too loud or little Tommy began to cry. I understood the newscasters, and the pictures spoke for themselves. But where the Munros saw faceless Orientals fleeing burning villages, tied up as prisoners, or as rag dolls in a roadside trench (even innocent villagers were "VC" or "Charlie"), I saw my brother Bon Nghe, who fought twenty-five years for the North; my mother's nephew, who was a lieutenant for the South; my sister Lan, who hustled drinks to Americans in Danang; and my sister Hai, who shared sleepless nights with my mother in our family bunker at Ky La. I saw floating on the smoke of battle the soul of my dead brother, Sau Ban, victim of an American land mine, and the spirit of my father, who drank acid to avoid involving me again with Viet Cong terrorists. I saw in those tiny electronic lines, as I saw in my dreams, the ghosts of a hundred relatives, family friends, and playmates who died fighting for this side or that, or merely trying to survive.

When the news changed to a story about a little girl who fell into a well, however, the whole room filled with compassion. In the Vietnam newsreel, children and women and old people had been blown to bits and everyone just yawned, because they were *the enemy*—bad guys on a real-life "cops and robbers" show. Now that one little girl-in-the-well made my in-laws weep bitter tears: because she was *one of them*. I wanted to tell these kind, well-meaning, but ignorant people the truth about my war, their war—*our* war—that my brothers and sisters and that poor trapped little girl were really all one family.

But I didn't know the words, even in Vietnamese.

After striking out in his local job search, Ed finally decided to accept a contract with his old employer in a place called Utah.

Ed decided we would visit Yellowstone Park before he reported to work. Erma said it would be a great chance for me to see the country, but I think she and Kathy were secretly pleased to see me leave. When it came time to plan our trip, I was not surprised when they volunteered to keep Tommy in order to make our travels easier. I didn't like the idea of leaving one of my boys with near-strangers, but their affection for Tommy seemed genuine and they were his blood relations. With a strained smile, I agreed.

On the appointed day, we packed the car and pulled out of the driveway. The last thing I saw was Kathy grinning on the curb, holding my little boy like a prize and waving his tiny arm as we drove away.

"Oh, turn off the waterworks!" Ed said gruffly, trying to cheer me up. "Tommy will have a wonderful time. The girls will treat him like he was their own."

I cried even harder.

Within hours of leaving San Diego, though, I had other things to think about: big, desolate America had swallowed us up. The horizon jumped back and I felt smaller and more insignificant than ever. If Vietnam were a delicate teacup, America—with its craggy peaks and endless, dusty plains—was a gigantic banquet platter, inviting hungry immigrants from all over the world to come and sup, to indulge their appetite for a better life. Still, immigrants like me don't arrive with our dreams full-blown. Rather, it seems, we expand our hopes to fit this country's vast horizons.

When our car radio went fuzzy, I sang all the songs I knew (in Vietnamese, of course—Ed couldn't understand a word) and realized that for the first time in five years I could shout anything I wanted—about the damned Viet Cong or greedy Republicans or backbreaking paddy work, or ridicule American soldiers—and not get into trouble. In America, I was as big as my voice and I liked that feeling a lot.

When we were still driving at sunset, however, I began to get nervous. In Vietnam, driving after dark in the middle of nowhere was a quick ticket to your next life. Even if you escaped the land mines and enemy patrols, you could easily be ambushed by what we Vietnamese called "cowboys": renegade Republican soldiers or big-city gangsters who robbed and killed anyone who traveled unescorted—crimes usually blamed on the Viet Cong. Although my head reassured me that the war was thousands of miles away, my heart told me to play it safe.

"You drive down middle," I said, nudging Ed's arm. I knew mines were usually seeded on the shoulder of the road and that cowboys often rolled boulders down from narrow passes to stop a car. I supposed that was why smart Americans painted yellow guide lines in the middle of their highways.

"Don't be silly," Ed replied. "You want us to get killed?"

We chased our headlights into the deepening night and I only felt worse and worse. Finally, a car pulled up to pass.

"Good," I blurted out as the vehicle—our convoy—roared by on the left. "Keep up with him! Don't let him get away!" The sight of those big taillights ahead of us in the vast American wilderness was immensely comforting and I didn't want to lose it.

"What?" Ed laughed. "You're crazy! He must be going ninety!"

I clamped my lips over gritted teeth and didn't say another word. Fortunately, our next stop was at a place that was famous for its lights.

Ed's sons, Ron and Ed Jr., had just left the navy and lived in Las Vegas. I assumed a family reunion would be the main reason for our visit—what else could you do in the middle of a desert?

I soon found out.

We arrived about midnight, but the streets were as bright as day. All I could think of was Saigon, which had the same effect on me when I arrived there as a teenager a half-dozen years before. We were inside a giant jukebox, with the tunes of a thousand upside-down lives spinning all around us: sailors five hundred miles from the sea; husbands looking for girlfriends and wives looking for lovers; poor people dreaming of riches and rich people terrified of losing whatever they had.

Ed told me a joke about a man who "struck it rich" in Las Vegas, arriving in a ten-thousand-dollar Cadillac and leaving in a forty-thousand-dollar bus! I knew we were not among the people arriving rich, despite our comfortable (and by Vietnamese standards, lavish) lifestyle, when Ed told me to look for a motel. I pointed to the first building I saw, a towering high-rise with uniformed doormen, and he said, "No, a *mo*tel, not a hotel."

More American word tricks. "Okay," I asked, "what is difference between hotel and motel?"

"About fifty bucks a night," Ed replied, and laughed his big-daddy laugh.

Finally, he spotted a place he liked and we checked in. It was too late to call Ed's sons, so I suggested we go to bed. Ed would hear nothing of it.

"You don't come to Las Vegas to sleep!" he exclaimed, astonished at my latest stupid idea. "I'll call a babysitter so we can go gamble."

Gambling I understood; but calling for someone to sit on my baby was something else. My worry showed on my face.

"You know," Ed explained, "a person to look after Jimmy."

"You mean Ron and Kim?"

"No, a *babysitter.*"

"You mean a friend you know in Las Vegas?"

"Nope. You just call the front desk and they send someone up, like room service. Watch."

He picked up the phone and a few minutes later a teenager in high-spun hair, miniskirt, and bracelets appeared at our door. My mouth dropped open. No way was I going to leave my child with a stranger, let alone a girl young enough to need a nanny herself. Besides, when it came to strangers, I'd heard rumors about Asian children being kidnapped for sale on the black market—and my beautiful little Jimmy had all the best features of his race. *No way, Charlie!* We had escaped cowboys on the highway and I wasn't about to press my luck. Ed could go gamble if he wanted to; I would stay with my baby.

Five minutes later, on our way to the casino, Ed explained how he hadn't brought a pretty wife to Las Vegas just to wander around like a bachelor. Frowning, sleepy, and miserable, I followed him into a giant room that looked like a *cho*, a frenzied Vietnamese meat and vegetable market.

"Here's ten bucks," Ed said, slipping a bill into my hand. "Turn it into a million."

I stared at the money as Ed disappeared into a canyon of one-armed bandits. As well-off as we were, Ed rarely gave me cash for anything; he either bought it at my suggestion, gave me a check, or used one of several plastic cards. The first thing I thought of was how much ten dollars in "green" money would buy in Danang: a week's worth of food for me, my mother, and Jimmy; or enough PX goods to breed five times that amount on the suburban black market.

I also recalled how many Vietnamese men had a special weakness for gambling, so it was not something daughters and wives approved of. In the village, whenever we kids passed a man whose habit had harmed his family, we softly sang, *"Co bac bac thang ban; cua nha ban het ra than an may"*—"Gambling is the uncle of the poor and miserable; bet your house and lose your belongings, win a new job as a beggar!" We didn't sing it to be mean, but to show the man we cared about his family. Anyway, despairing of my husband's order, I changed the whole thing into nickels, which had a comforting heft, and began depositing them into the slots like a child feeding goats at the zoo.

Fortunately, Ed wasn't much of a gambler either. I felt a

little better when I returned a few dollars a couple of hours later. The Chinese say "where there is no gain, the loss is obvious," and we Vietnamese know the opposite is true as well.

To my great relief, Jimmy survived being sat on by his rock-and-roll nanny, and the next day's visit with Ed's sons went well. Being Vietnam veterans, they understood not only some of what I had gone through, but what both veterans and Vietnamese were still going through in America: the "baby killer" sneers for them and the smoldering "VC Commie" looks for me. We all had regained the ability to see each other as people instead of shooting-gallery targets, and I felt a little sad for ever having accepted war as a way of life. I would later find out that this strange, out-of-body feeling of disconnectedness from life and helpless shame over the past was what many U.S. vets called guilt. I could hear it crackle in the voices of Ed's sons and see its shadow in their eyes. In this respect, encountering a Vietnam vet (soldier or civilian, it didn't matter), whether he hated, respected, or just tolerated me, was like finding a long-lost cousin. A distant cousin may dislike you, but you are united by a bond of blood. For many Vietnamese and Americans alike, the blood bond of battle was stronger than the blood tie of birth. We were all orphans of the same shattered dream.

In Utah, the job Ed had been promised fell through, so after another night in a motel we drove straight on to Yellowstone. I was secretly pleased we didn't stay in Utah. The Indian name must've meant "rocks and dirt"! I felt more at home once we had climbed into the mountains. The superhighway narrowed to more Vietnamese proportions and the view beyond the windows turned cool and green. Eventually, we passed patches of funny white dust—like China Beach!—by the road, then more and more of it, piled even on the rocks.

"What on earth is that?" I asked Ed, rolling up my window. The air had turned frosty like a draft from Erma's freezer.

Ed laughed his famous laugh and I knew I was about to get another lesson on America. "Don't you know what that is? That's *snow*! You know—frozen water!"

I knew Ed was kidding, because frozen water was ice cubes. Nobody would go to the trouble of freezing water, then grinding it up and dumping it all over the ground for miles and miles, especially where nobody lived.

Ed saw my doubtful expression and pulled the car off the road. He grabbed Jimmy like a sack of potatoes and plunked him down in the nearest patch of white. Jimmy started to laugh, then cry, then laugh again. I knelt and put my hand in the snow. It crunched like cotton candy and was very, *very* cold.

"Ow!" I pulled my hand back. "It burn! Where does it come from?"

"The sky," Ed said cryptically.

More American magic. I glanced upward, half expecting a freezerload of ice cubes to tumble down on my head. It was strange to feel cold in a green forest—another American contradiction: a freezing jungle.

Farther down the road, we parked with other tourists and Ed led us from the car. I walked, bundled up like an Eskimo, to the edge of a boiling pond. I cried out and jumped back.

Ed, in shirtsleeves, holding Jimmy's hand, asked, "What's wrong?"

"My god! It's *hell*! I see pictures!"

Buddhists, like Christians, believe in the heaven and hell vividly explained to them as children. One difference is that Vietnamese think virtually nobody makes it to heaven whereas Western saints admit almost everyone if they repent before they die. Unlike Christians, though, we Buddhists must atone for the sins of many former lives, not just our current incarnation, so a simple deathbed confession won't do the job.

For example, if I spent my life accumulating wealth and never helped the poor, I might return in my next life as a beggar until I learned the rule of charity. Even good souls have to spend ninety days in limbo before they're assigned a future. It's not that the cosmic god is cruel, just practical. Consequently, his holy men on earth talk mostly about hell because that's where their congregation is likely to wind up. As a Buddhist, I knew from what I had already been through in my short life that I must be atoning for a lot of bad karma.

That day, I remembered especially one book a monk gave me when I was young. It showed ordinary people with the heads of beasts. One man had the head of a water buffalo and another looked like a terrible devil. The buffalo-man, they said, had been cruel to animals, and the witch-headed fellow had had evil thoughts when he was alive, so these were their punishments in hell. The idea that these pictures were really clever symbols meaning something else—that "bullheaded" and "malicious" thinking could create a hellish life—never occurred to us. The notion that a bad act in life would lead to retribution in kind after death, though, made us little kids really sit up and take notice.

The worst picture, I thought, was one of a beautiful woman hanging upside down over a boiling pond, tormented by demons. The devils were sawing off parts of her body and throwing them into molten lava—the punishment for someone who cheats on her husband. The idea of body parts writhing like skewered worms made me sick with horror. A village elder, of course, might have seen in the picture a symbol of how broken vows can "dismember" a family, but such thinking was for monks and wise men, not little kids. Because I was ashamed of many things I had done in Vietnam and was now questioning my new marriage in America, I teetered on the edge of that boiling pond like a woman poked by demons.

"Be careful"—Ed steadied me with a hand— "people have fallen in there and died."

"I don't want to see this," I blurted out, shivering and confused, and ran back to the car.

I heard Ed tell Jimmy in a fatherly voice, "That's okay. Mama's just tired. We'll go see something more fun."

We drove farther into the mountains with the heat on full blast for my benefit—past wedges of snow plowed against the curvy highway. After a while we came to another smoking lake that Ed thought would cheer me up. But when we pulled up to this smoking lake, surrounded by mist and shadows and looking very much like the home of the Buddhist's *Mang Xa* snake—a fire-breathing monster—I refused to get out. "You go ahead," I told Ed. "Show Jimmy the sights. I'm too cold to walk around."

"Okay," Ed said. "We're just going to climb the bridge. We'll be back in a jiffy."

I didn't know how long a jiffy was, but it was long enough to do a lot of worrying. As they were about to disappear from the foggy windshield, I saw something that confirmed everything I had suspected about the United States.

From the edge of the forest, a lone stag approached the lake, antlers bobbing above its shoulders. In the face of such terror—before the very gates of hell—the deer was proud, calm, and strong. I knew then that America really *was* as magical as I had heard—that the mystical things I had been taught as a child were true. To Buddhists, the deer is a symbol of goodness, purity, and peace. When their antlers are prepared *nai to*—cut as buds and ground into a potion—they are said to cure illness and extend life, like the unicorn horns of Western myth. Even more startling, in one of our stories of a great smoking lake, the Buddha himself crossed a bridge and was confronted by the serpent. Instead of crying and trying to run away like other people, the Buddha reached out and quenched the flames with his compassion. Now, in the middle of this hell on earth, I had seen with my own eyes the symbol of purity come down to quench his thirst at the lake of evil. This was no coincidence—and was possibly an omen for me. In a land where ponds boil and ice falls from the sky, my son had walked the *Mang Xa* lake and been kissed by the Buddha deer. Good and evil lie down together and peace blooms like the buds of enchanted antlers. *This* was why Americans revered this holy place. This was what America is all about!

When Ed and Jimmy came back with rosy cheeks and smoky breath, I gave them each a big hug and asked Ed when we were going to eat. I was starving now and ready for anything from the great American banquet.

ALEKSANDAR HEMON
Bosnia

Acclaimed fiction writer and essayist Aleksandar Hemon (1964–) was born in Sarajevo, Bosnia and Herzegovina, then a part of socialist Yugoslavia. The son of an engineer and a schoolteacher, Hemon enjoyed a middle-class lifestyle in Bosnia's capital until he was drafted into the army at nineteen. Afterward, Hemon attended the University of Sarajevo, majoring in great literature; upon graduating, he worked as a journalist and cultural editor for a local magazine, which proved especially challenging in the shifting world of post-Yugoslavia. Despondent over the effects of the Bosnian War, Hemon eagerly accepted an invitation from the United States Information Agency and watched from Chicago as the horrors of that violence unfolded.

While Sarajevo was under the longest siege in modern history, Hemon's father advised him to remain in Chicago since the family was preparing to flee, so Hemon applied for political asylum. Working various low-wage jobs, Hemon strived to replicate in Chicago the "personal infrastructure" he previously enjoyed in Sarajevo. Eventually, he enrolled in graduate school at Northwestern, where he began to write in English and publish in literary journals and some well-known periodicals. His two books of stories, The Question of Bruno *(2001) and* Love and Obstacles *(2009), and two very successful novels,* Nowhere Man *(2002) and* The Lazarus Project *(2008), all draw from his experiences as a Sarajevan and ultimately as an immigrant. Hemon has won several prestigious prizes, among them a Guggenheim Fellowship and a MacArthur Award. He currently lives in Chicago and regularly publishes in* The New Yorker *in addition to editing his annual* Best European Fiction *series.*

The Book of My Lives is a series of essays that follow Hemon from his childhood in Bosnia to his success as a writer in the U.S. Conflicted over his decision to remain in the U.S. while Sarajevo was under siege, Hemon moved from the Ukrainian Village area of Chicago to the North Side neighborhood of Edgewater, where he gradually assimilated among the new Bosnian refugees (some forty thousand fled between 1992 and 1995). Prior to this wave of immigration, there was not a substantial Bosnian population in the U.S., and as a result, Bosnians tended to settle in Croatian ethnic enclaves and large urban areas like Chicago, the most popular U.S. destination, where they could rely on community support while waiting to reunite with their families. This sense of leading two lives, says Hemon, is a "self-othering" fundamental to the immigrant experience: "Displacement results in a tenuous relationship with the past, with the self that used to exist and operate in a different place, where the qualities that constituted us were in no need of negotiation. . . . You are forced to negotiate the conditions of your selfhood under perpetually changing existential circumstances. The displaced person strives for narrative stability—here is my story!—by way of systematic nostalgia."

Excerpt from

The Book of My Lives

— 2013 —

In the spring of 1997, I flew from Chicago, where I was living, to Sarajevo, where I was born. This was my first return to Sarajevo since the war in Bosnia and Herzegovina had ended a year and a half before. I'd left a few months before the siege of the city started. I had no family there (my parents and my sister now lived in Canada), except for teta-Jozefina, whom I thought of as my grandmother. When my parents had moved to Sarajevo after graduating from college in 1963, they'd rented a room in the apartment of Jozefina and her husband, Martin, in the part of town called Marin dvor. In that rented room I was conceived, and it was where I lived for the first two years of my life. Teta-Jozefina and čika-Martin, who had two teenage children at the time, treated me as their own grandchild—to this day, my mother believes that they spoiled me for life. For a couple of years after we'd moved out to a different part of Sarajevo, I had to be taken back to Marin dvor to visit them every single day. And until the war shattered our common life, we spent each Christmas at teta-Jozefina and čika-Martin's. Every year, we followed the same ritual: the same elaborately caloric dishes crowding the big table, the same tongue-burning Herzegovinian wine, the same people telling the same jokes and stories, including the one featuring the toddler version of me running up and down the hallway butt-naked before my nightly bath.

Čika-Martin died of a stroke toward the end of the siege, so in 1997 teta-Jozefina was living alone. I stayed with her upon my return, in the room (and, possibly, the very bed) where I'd commenced my exhaustingly messy existence. Its walls were pockmarked by shrapnel and bullets—the apartment had been directly in the sight line of a Serb sniper across the river. Teta-Jozefina was a devout Catholic, but she somehow managed to believe in essential human goodness, despite all the abundant evidence to the contrary surrounding her. She felt that the sniper was essentially a good man because during the siege, she said, he had often shot over her and her husband's heads to warn them that he was watching and that they shouldn't move so carelessly in their own apartment.

In my first few days back in Sarajevo, I did little but listen to teta-Jozefina's harrowing and humbling stories of the siege, including a detailed rendition of her husband's death (where he had sat, what he had said, how he had slumped), and wander around the city. I was trying to reconcile the new Sarajevo with the 1992 version I'd left for America. It wasn't easy for me to comprehend how the siege had transformed the city, because the transformation wasn't as simple as one thing becoming another. Everything was fantastically different from what I'd known and everything was fantastically the same as before. Our old room (and, possibly, bed) was the same; the buildings stood in the same places; the bridges crossed the river at the same points; the streets followed the same obscure yet familiar logic; the layout of the city was unaltered. But the room had been marred by siege scars; the buildings had been mutilated by shells and shrapnel showers, or reduced to crumbling walls; the river had been the front line, so some of the bridges were destroyed and much in their vicinity was leveled; the streets were fractured by mortar-shell marks—lines radiating from a little crater at the point of impact—which an art group had filled out with red paint and which the people of Sarajevo now, incredibly, called "roses."

I revisited all my favorite spots in the city center, then roamed the narrow streets high up in the hills, beyond which lay a verdant world of unmapped minefields. I randomly entered building hallways and basements, just to smell them: in addition to the familiar scent of leather suitcases, old magazines, and damp coal dust, there was the smell of hard life and sewage— during the siege, people had taken shelter from the shelling in their basements. I idled in coffee shops, drinking coffee that tasted unlike what I remembered from before the war—it was like burnt corn now. As a Bosnian in Chicago, I'd experienced one form of displacement, but this was another: I was displaced in a place that had been mine. In Sarajevo, everything around me was familiar to the point of pain and entirely uncanny and distant.

One day I was strolling, aimlessly and anxiously, down the street whose prewar name had been Ulica JNA (The Yugoslav People's Army Street) and now was Ulica Branilaca Sarajeva (The Defenders of Sarajevo Street). As I walked past what had been called, in the heady times of socialism—which now seemed positively prehistoric—the Workers' University (Radnički univerzitet), something made me turn and look over my shoulder into its cavernous entranceway. The turn was not of my own volition: it was my body that spun my head back, while my mind went on for a few steps. Impeding impatient pedestrian traffic, I stood puzzled before the late Workers' University until I realized what had made me look back: the Workers' University used to house a movie theater (it had shut down a couple of years before the war), and whenever I'd walked by in those days, I'd looked at the display cases where the posters and show times were exhibited. From the lightless shafts of corporal memory, my body had recalled the action of turning to see what was playing. It had been trained to react to urban stimulation in the form of a new movie poster, and it still remembered, the fucker, the way it remembered how to swim when thrown into deep water. Following that involuntary revolution, my mind was flooded with a banal, if Proustian, memory: once upon a time in Sarajevo, at the Workers' University, I'd watched Sergio Leone's *Once upon a Time in America*, and now I recalled the pungent smell of the disinfectant that was used to clean the floors of the cinema; I recalled peeling myself off the sticky fake-leather seats; I recalled the rattle of the parting curtain.

I'd left Sarajevo for America on January 24, 1992. I had no way of knowing at the time that I'd return to my hometown only as an irreversibly displaced visitor. I was twenty-seven (and a half) and had never lived anywhere else, nor had any desire to do so. I'd spent the few years before the trip working as a journalist in what was known, in socialist, peacetime Yugoslavia, as the "youth press" (*omladinska štampa*), generally less constrained than the mainstream press, reared in the pressure chamber of Tito's one-party state. My last paid job was for *Naši dani*, where I edited the culture pages. (Before the war, the domain of *culture* seemed to offer a haven from the increasingly hateful world of politics. Now, when I hear the word *culture*, I pull out the quote commonly attributed to Hermann Göring: "When I hear the word *culture*, I reach for my revolver.") I wrote film reviews but was far better known for my column "Sarajevo Republika." The name was intended as an allusion to the Mediterranean Renaissance city-states—Dubrovnik or Venice—as well as to the slogan "*Kosovo republika*," which had been sprayed on Kosovo walls by the "irredentists," who demanded that Kosovo be given the status of a republic in the federal Yugoslavia; given full sovereignty, that is, in place of its status as an "autonomous province" of Serbia. In other words, I was a militant Sarajevan. I set out in my column to assert Sarajevo's uniqueness, the inherent sovereignty of its spirit, reproducing and extolling its urban mythology in a prose arrogantly thick with abstruse Sarajevo slang. The first column I ever published was about an *ašćinica*—a traditional Bosnian storefront restaurant, serving cooked (as opposed to grilled) food—which had been run by a local family, the Hadžibajrićs, for a hundred and fifty years or so. One of the urban legends about the Hadžibajrićs claimed that, back in the seventies, during the shooting of the movie *The Battle of Sutjeska*, a state-produced Second World War spectacle, starring Richard Burton as Tito, a Yugoslav People's Army helicopter was frequently deployed to the set deep in the mountains of eastern Bosnia, to transport the Hadžibajrićs' *buredžici* (meat pies in sour cream) for Elizabeth Taylor's gastronomic enjoyment. To this day, many of us are proud of the possibility that some of the fat in Purple Eyes's ass came from Sarajevo.

The columns that followed were about the philosophy of Sarajevo's baroque slang; about the myriad time-wasting strate-

gies I believed were essential for urban-mythology (re)produc-
tion, and which I executed daily in innumerable *kafanas*; about
bingo venues, frequented by habitual losers, bottom-feeders, and
young urbanites in pursuit of coolness credentials. One of the
columns was about the main pedestrian thoroughfare in the heart
of the city—Vase Miskina Street (known as Ferhadija since the
fluttering fall of socialism)—which stretched from downtown to
the old town. I referred to it as the city artery, because many
Sarajevans promenaded along it at least twice a day, keeping the
urban circulation going. If you spent enough time drinking coffee at one of the many *kafanas* along Vase Miskina, the whole city
would eventually parade past you. In the early nineties, street
peddlers stationed themselves along the street, pushing the
penny-cheap detritus of the wrecked workers' state: sewing-ma-
chine needles, screwdrivers, and Russian–Serbo-Croat diction-
aries. These days, it is all Third World–capitalism junk: pirated
DVDs, made-in-China plastic toys, herbal remedies and miraculous sexual enhancers.

Fancying myself a street-savvy columnist, I raked the city
for material, absorbing details and generating ideas. I don't know
if I would've used the word back then, but now I'm prone to
reimagining my young self as one of Baudelaire's flaneurs, as
someone who wanted to be everywhere and nowhere in particular, for whom wandering in the city was the main means of
communication with it. Sarajevo was—and still is—a small
town, viscous with stories and history, brimming with people I
knew and loved, all of whom I could monitor from a well-
chosen *kafana* perch or by patrolling the streets. As I surveyed
the estuaries of Vase Miskina or the obscure, narrow streets
creeping up the hills, complete paragraphs flooded my brain; not
infrequently, and mysteriously, a simple lust would possess my
body. The city laid itself down for me; wandering stimulated
my body as well as my mind. It probably didn't hurt that my
daily caffeine intake bordered on stroke-inducing—what wine

and opium must've been for Baudelaire, coffee and cigarettes were for me.

As I would in 1997, I entered buildings just to smell their hallways. I studied the edges of stone stairs blunted by the many soles that had rubbed against them over the past century or two. I spent time at the Željo soccer stadium, deserted on a gameless day, eavesdropping on the pensioners—the retirees who were lifelong season-ticket holders—as they strolled within its walls in nostalgic circles, discussing the heartrending losses and unlikely victories of the past. I returned to places I'd known my whole life so that I could experience them differently and capture details that had been blurred by excessive familiarity. I collected sensations and faces, smells and sights, fully internalizing Sarajevo's architecture and physiognomies. I gradually became aware that my interiority was inseparable from my exteriority. Physically and metaphysically, I was *placed*. If my friends spotted me on a side street looking up at the high friezes typical of Austro-Hungarian architecture, or lingering on a lonely park bench, watching dogs fetch and couples make out—the kind of behavior that might have seemed worrisome—they just assumed that I was working on a column. Most likely, I was.

Despite my grand plans, I ended up writing only six or seven "Sarajevo Republika" columns before *Naši dani* ran its course out of money. The magazine's dissolution was inconspicuous within the ongoing dissolution of Yugoslavia. In the summer of 1991, incidents in the neighboring Croatia developed into a full-fledged fast-spreading war while rumors persisted that the army was secretly transferring troops and weapons to the parts of Bosnia with a majority Serb population. *Oslobodjenje*, the Sarajevo daily paper, got hold of a military plan outlining troop redeployment in Bosnia and Herzegovina that clearly suggested the imminence of war, even though the army firmly denied the plan.

The army spokespeople weren't the only ones denying the

blatant likelihood of war—the urbanites of Sarajevo were also intent on ignoring the obvious, if for different reasons. In the summer of 1991 parties, sex, and drugs were abundant; the laughter was hysterical; the streets seemed packed day and night. In the seductive glow of inevitable catastrophe, the city appeared more beautiful than ever. By early September, however, the complicated operations of denial were hopelessly winding down. When I wandered the city, I found myself speculating with troubling frequency as to which buildings would provide good sniper positions. Even as I envisioned myself ducking under fire, I took those visions to be simply paranoid symptoms of the stress induced by the ubiquitous warmongering politics. I understand now that I was imagining *incidents*, as it was hard for me to imagine *war* in all its force, much the way a young person can imagine the symptoms of an illness but find it hard to imagine death: life seems so continuously, intensely, and undeniably present.

Nowadays in Sarajevo, death is all too easy to imagine and is continuously, undeniably present, but back then the city—a beautiful, immortal thing, an indestructible republic of urban spirit—was fully alive both inside and outside me. Its indelible sensory dimension, its concreteness, seemed to defy the abstractions of war. I have learned since then that war is the most concrete thing there can be, a fantastic reality that levels both interiority and exteriority into the flatness of a crushed soul.

One day in the early summer of 1991, I went to the American Cultural Center in Sarajevo for the interview that was supposed to determine my suitability for the International Visitors Program, a cultural exchange run by the now defunct United States Information Agency—which I hoped was a spy outfit whose employees went undercover as culture lovers. Even being considered for an invitation to America was flattering, of course, because you had to be deaf, dumb, blind, and comatose to avoid

American culture in the Sarajevo of my youth. By the time I
graduated from high school, in 1983, my favorite movie of all
time was Coppola's *Apocalypse Now.* I worshipped Patti Smith,
Talking Heads, and Television, and CBGB was to me what Jerusalem must be to a devout believer. I often imitated Holden
Caulfield's diction (in translation) and once manipulated my un-
witting father into buying a Bukowski book for my birthday. By
the time I graduated from college, in 1990, I could act out with
my sister chunks of dialogue (mispronounced) from *His Girl
Friday.* I'd get angry at people who couldn't recognize the genius
of Brian De Palma. I could recite Public Enemy's angry invec-
tives, and was up to my ears in Sonic Youth and Swans. I piously
read American short-story anthologies, available in translation,
in which Barth and Barthelme reigned. I hadn't really read
Barth's famous essay, but I thought that the notion of the literature of exhaustion was very cool. I wrote an essay on Bret Easton
Ellis and corporate capitalism.

I met the man in charge of the center, chitted and chatted
about this and that (mainly that), and then went home. I didn't
think that my visit to America would ever come to pass, nor had
I noticed the man actually evaluating me. Despite my fondness
for American culture, I didn't care all that much. Even if I
thought it would be fun to Kerouac about in America for a
while, I had no particular desire to leave Sarajevo. I loved my
city; I intended to tell stories about it to my children and my
grandchildren, to grow old and die there. Around that time, I
was having a passionate on-and-off relationship with a young
woman who was working hard to get out of Sarajevo and move
abroad because, she said, she felt that she didn't belong there.
"It's not about where you belong, it's about what belongs to
you," I told her, possibly quoting from some movie or another.
I was twenty-seven (and a half) and Sarajevo belonged to me.

I'd pretty much forgotten about my summer chitchat when,

in early December, I received a call from the American Cultural Center inviting me for a monthlong visit to the United States. By that time I was exhausted by the onslaught of warmongering, and I accepted the invitation. I thought that being away would provide some relief. I planned to travel around the States for a month, then, before returning to Sarajevo, visit an old friend in Chicago. I landed at O'Hare on March 14, 1992. I remember that day as vast, clear, and sunny. On my way in from the airport I saw for the first time the skyline of Chicago—an enormous, distant, geometrical city, less emerald than dark against the blue firmament.

By this time, the Yugoslav People's Army's troops were fully deployed all over Bosnia, following the previously denied plan; Serbian paramilitaries were crazy-busy slaughtering; there were random barricades and shootings on the streets of Sarajevo. In early April, a peaceful demonstration in front of the Bosnian Parliament building was targeted by Karadžić's snipers. Two women were killed on the Vrbanja Bridge, a hundred yards or so from teta-Jozefina's apartment, quite conceivably by the same good sniper who later maculated the walls in the room of my conception. On the outskirts of the city, in the hills above, the war was already mature and raging, but in the heart of Sarajevo people still seemed to think that it would somehow stop before it reached them. To my worried inquiries from Chicago, my mother would respond, "There is already less shooting than yesterday"—as though war were a spring shower.

My father, however, advised me to stay away. Nothing good was going to happen at home, he said. I was supposed to fly back from Chicago on May 1, and as things got progressively worse in Sarajevo, I was torn between guilt and fear for my parents' and friends' lives, kept awake by worries about my previously unimagined and presently unimaginable future in America. I wrangled with my conscience: if you were the author of a column entitled "Sarajevo Republika," then it was perhaps your duty to go back and defend your city and its spirit from annihilation.

Much of that wrangling I did while incessantly roaming Chicago, as though I could simply walk off my moral anxiety. I'd pick a movie that I wanted to see—both for distraction and out of my old habits as a film reviewer—then locate, with my friend's help, a theater that was showing it. From Ukrainian Village, the neighborhood where I was staying, I'd take public transportation to buy a ticket a couple of hours before the show and then I'd wander in concentric circles around the movie theater. My first journey was to the Esquire (now no longer a movie venue) on Oak Street, in the affluent Gold Coast neighborhood— the Esquire was my Plymouth Rock. The movie was Michael Apted's *Thunderheart*, in which Val Kilmer played an FBI agent of Native American background who pursues a case to a reservation, which somehow forces him to come to terms with his past and heritage. I remember the movie being as bad as it now sounds, though I don't remember many details. Nor do I remember much of my first Gold Coast roam, because it has become indistinguishable from all the other ones, the way the first day of school is subsumed in the entirety of your educational experience.

I subsequently journeyed to movie theaters all over Chicago and walked in circles around them. I saw more bad movies in so-called bad neighborhoods, where, the movies notwithstanding, nothing bad ever happened to me. There was always plenty of space for walking, as few cared to crowd the streets in those parts of Chicago. When I had no money for the movies— my main source of income was the card game Preference, which I had taught my friend and his buddies to play—I would explore the cinema-free areas of Wicker Park, Bucktown, or Humboldt Park (Saul Bellow's childhood neighborhood), which was adjacent to Ukrainian Village and, I was warned, gang-infested.

I couldn't quit. A tormented flaneur, I kept walking, my Achilles tendons sore, my head in the clouds of fear and longing for Sarajevo, until I finally reconciled myself to the idea of staying. On May 1, I didn't fly home. On May 2, the roads out of the city were blocked; the last train (with my parents on it) departed; the longest siege in modern history began. In Chicago, I submitted my application for political asylum. The rest is the rest of my life.

In my ambulatory expeditions, I became acquainted with Chicago, but I didn't *know* the city. The need to know it in my body, to locate myself in the world, wasn't satisfied; I was metaphysically ailing, because I didn't yet know how to *be* in Chicago. The American city was organized fundamentally differently from Sarajevo. (A few years later I would find a Bellow quote that perfectly encapsulated my feeling of the city at the time: "Chicago was nowhere. It had no setting. It was something released into American space.") Where the urban landscapes of Sarajevo had been populated with familiar faces, with shared and shareable experiences, the Chicago I was trying to comprehend was dark with the matter of pursued anonymity.

In Sarajevo, you possessed a personal infrastructure: your *kafana*, your barber, your butcher; the streets where people recognized you, the space that identified you; the landmarks of your life (the spot where you fell playing soccer and broke your arm, the corner where you waited to meet the first of the many loves of your life, the bench where you kissed her first). Because anonymity was well-nigh impossible and privacy literally incomprehensible (there is no word for "privacy" in Bosnian), your fellow Sarajevans knew you as well as you knew them. The borders between interiority and exteriority were practically nonexistent. If you somehow vanished, your fellow citizens could have collectively reconstructed you from their collective memory and the gossip accrued over the years. Your sense of who you were, your deepest identity, was determined by your position in a human network, whose physical corollary was the architecture of the city. Chicago, on the other hand, was built not for people to come together but for them to be safely apart. Size, power, and the need for privacy seemed to be the dominant dimensions of its architecture. Vast as it is, Chicago ignored the distinctions between freedom and isolation, between independence and selfishness, between privacy and loneliness. In this city, I had no human network within which I could place myself; my Sarajevo, the city that had existed inside me and was still there, was subject to siege and destruction. My displacement was metaphysical to the precisely same extent to which it was physical. But I couldn't live nowhere; I wanted from Chicago what I'd got from Sarajevo: a geography of the soul.

More walking was needed, as was, even more pressingly, reasonably gainful employment. Nothing in my experience had taught me how to get a job in America. Neither De Palma's oeuvre nor the literature of exhaustion contained any pointers about getting urgently needed work. After a few illegal, below-minimum-wage jobs, some of which required me to furnish someone else's Social Security number (fuck you, Arizona!), I received my work permit and entered the crowded minimum-wage labor market. For restaurant managers and people in temp agencies looking for bouncers and bartenders, I created a vast and partly false universe of my previous life, at the center of which was a familiarity with all things American. They couldn't care less; it took me a few weeks to learn that (a) rambling about American movies could not even get you a most penurious job; and (b) when they say "We'll call you!" they don't really mean it.

My first legal job was canvassing door-to-door for Greenpeace, an organization inherently welcoming to misfits. When I first called the Greenpeace office to inquire, I didn't even know what the job was, what the word *canvassing* meant. Naturally, I was terrified of talking to Americans on their doorsteps, what

with my insufficient English, devoid of articles and thickly con-
taminated with a foreign accent, but I craved the ambulatory
freedom between the doors. So, in the early summer of 1992, I
found myself canvassing in the proudly indistinguishable, dull
western suburbs (Schaumburg, Naperville); in the wealthy
North Shore ones (Wilmette, Winnetka, Lake Forest), with
their hospital-size houses and herds of cars in palatial garages; in
the southern working-class ones (Blue Island, Park Forest),
where people invited me into their homes and offered me stale
Twinkies. Soon I learned to assess the annual income and political leanings of the household based on the look of the lawn,
the magazines in the mailbox, and the makes of the family ve-
hicles (Volvo meant liberal). I enabled myself to endure questions about Bosnia and Yugoslavia and their nonexistent relation
to the nonexistent Czechoslovakia. I grinned through lectures
on the spirituality of *Star Trek* and confirmed, calmly, that, yes,
I had been exposed in Sarajevo to the wonders of pizza and television. I smiled at a young man who implored me to understand
how broke he was, as he had just bought a Porsche. I had lemonade at the home of a soft-spoken Catholic priest and his
young, gorgeous boyfriend, who was bored and tipsy. I sought
shelter with a couple who had a beautiful Alphonse Mucha print
on the wall, after their neighbor had shown me his gun and his
willingness to use it. I discussed helmet laws with a herd of pot-
bellied balding bikers, some of them veterans who believed that
what they had fought for in Vietnam was the freedom to spill
their brains on the freeways of America. I witnessed African
American fellow canvassers being repeatedly stopped by the police protecting their quaint suburban domain.

My favorite turf was, predictably, in the city: Pullman,
Beverly, Lakeview, and then the Parks—Hyde, Lincoln, Rogers.
Little by little, I began to sort out the geography of Chicagoland,
assembling a street map in my mind, building by building, door
by door. Occasionally, I took my time before canvassing and

slacked off in a local diner, struggling to enjoy the burnt-corn taste of American coffee, monitoring the foot traffic, the corner drug trade, the friendly ladies. Every once in a while, I skipped work entirely and just walked and walked in the neighborhood assigned to me. I was a low-wage, immigrant flaneur.

At the same time, I was obsessively following TV reports from the besieged Sarajevo, trying to identify people and places on the screen, to assess from afar the extent of the devastation. Toward the end of May, I watched the footage of a massacre on Vase Miskina, where a Serb shell hit a bread line, killing scores of Sarajevans. I attempted to identify the people on the screen—writhing in a puddle of rose-red blood, their legs torn off, their faces distorted with shock—but I couldn't. I had a hard time recognizing the place as well. The street I'd thought I owned, and had frivolously dubbed the city artery, was now awash in the actual arterial blood of those I'd left behind, and all I could do was watch the looping thirty-second stories on *Headline News*.

Even from Chicago, I could guess at the magnitude of my hometown's transformation. The street that connected my neighborhood (Socijalno) with downtown was rechristened Sniper Alley. The Željo stadium, where I'd eavesdropped on the pensioners, was now controlled by the Serbs, its wooden stands burned down. The little bakery in Kovači that produced the best *somun* (leavened pita bread) in town, and therefore in the world, was also burned down. The Museum of the 1984 Winter Olympic Games, housed in a beautiful Austro-Hungarian building of no strategic value whatsoever, was shelled (and is still a ruin). The pseudo-Moorish National Library was shelled; along with its hundreds of thousands of books, it burned down.

In December 1994, I briefly volunteered at the International Human Rights Law Institute of DePaul University's College of Law, where evidence of possible war crimes in Bosnia was being collected. By then, I'd quit canvassing and enrolled in graduate school at Northwestern, and I desperately needed another job, so I showed up at the institute's downtown office, hoping that they would give me one. There was no way for my prospective employers to know who I was or had been—I could easily have been a spy—so they offered me what they thought were simple volunteer tasks. At first, I did some data input for the concentration-camp database, where every testimony or mention of a camp was filed. But eventually I was given a stack of photos of destroyed and damaged buildings in Sarajevo, as yet unidentified, and asked to note their locations. Many of the buildings photographed were roofless, hole-ridden, or burned, their windows blown out. There were few people in those pictures, but what I was doing felt very much like identifying corpses. Now and then I could recall the street or even the exact address; sometimes the buildings were so familiar they seemed unreal. There was, for example, the building at the corner of Danijela Ozme and Kralja Tomislava, across from which I used to wait for Renata, my high school girlfriend, to come down from Džidžikovac. Back then, there was a supermarket on the ground floor of the building, where I'd buy candy or cigarettes when she was late, which was always. I'd known that building for years. It had stood in its place solid, indelible. I'd never devoted any thought to it until I saw its picture in Chicago. In the photograph, the building was hollow, disemboweled by a shell, which had evidently fallen through the roof and dropped down a few floors. The supermarket now existed only in the flooded storage space of my memory.

There were also buildings that I recognized but could not exactly place. And then there were the ones that were wholly unknown to me—I couldn't even figure out what part of town they might have been in. I have learned since then that you don't need to know every part of a city to own the whole of it, but in that office in downtown Chicago it terrified me to think that there was some part of Sarajevo I didn't know and probably never would, as it was now disintegrating, like a cardboard stage set, in the rain of shells. If my mind and my city were the same thing, then I was losing my mind. Converting Chicago into my personal space became not just metaphysically essential but psychiatrically urgent as well.

In the spring of 1993, after a year or so of living in Ukrainian Village, I moved to a lakeside neighborhood called Edgewater, on Chicago's North Side. I rented a tiny studio in a building called Artists in Residence, in which various lonely and not exactly successful artists resided. The AiR provided a loose sense of community within the city's anonymity; it offered a rehearsal space for musicians, dancers, and actors, as well as a public computer for those of us who harbored writerly hopes. The building manager's implausibly appropriate name was Art.

Back then, Edgewater was where one went to acquire cheap—and bad—heroin. I'd been warned that it was a rough neighborhood, but what I saw there were varieties of despair that exactly matched my own. One day I stood on Winthrop Avenue looking up at the top of a building on whose ledge a young woman sat deliberating whether to kill herself, while a couple of guys down on the street kept shouting, "Jump!" They did so out of sheer asshole malice, of course, but at the time their suggestion seemed to me a reasonable resolution to the continuous problem we call life.

I was still working as a canvasser for Greenpeace, walking different city neighborhoods and suburbs every day, already becoming far too familiar with many of them. But every night I came back to the Edgewater studio I could call my own, where I was beginning to develop a set of ritualistic, comforting practices. Before sleep, I'd listen to a demented monologue delivered by a chemically stimulated corner loiterer, occasionally muffled by the soothing sound of trains clattering past on the El tracks. In the morning, drinking coffee, I'd watch from my window the people waiting at the Granville El stop, recognizing the regulars. I'd occasionally splurge on breakfast at a Shoney's on Broadway (now long gone) that offered a $2.99 all-you-can-eat deal to the likes of me and the drooling residents of a nursing home on Winthrop, who would arrive en masse, holding hands like schoolchildren. At Gino's North, where there was only one beer on tap and where many an artist got shitfaced, I'd watch the victorious Bulls' games, high-fiving only the select company of those who were not too drunk to lift their elbows off the bar. I'd spend weekends playing chess at a Rogers Park coffee shop, next to a movie theater. I often played with an old Assyrian named Peter, who, whenever he put me in an indefensible position and I offered to resign, would crack the same joke: "Can I have that in writing?" But there was no writing coming from me. Deeply displaced, I could write neither in Bosnian nor in English.

Little by little, people in Edgewater began to recognize me; I started greeting them on the street. Over time, I acquired a barber and a butcher and a movie theater and a coffee shop with a steady set of colorful characters—which were, as I'd learned in Sarajevo, the necessary knots in any personal urban network. I discovered that the process of transforming an American city into a space you could call your own required starting in a particular neighborhood. Soon I began to claim Edgewater as mine; I became a local. It was there that I understood what Nelson Algren meant when he wrote that loving Chicago was like loving a woman with a broken nose—I fell in love with the broken noses of Edgewater. On the AiR's ancient communal Mac, I typed my first attempts at stories in English.

Therefore it was of utmost significance that Edgewater turned out to be the neighborhood where shiploads of Bosnians escaping the war ended up in the spring of 1994. I experienced a shock of recognition one day when I looked out my window and saw a family strolling down the street—where few ever walked, except in pursuit of heroin—in an unmistakably Bosnian formation: the eldest male member leading the way, at a slow, aimless pace, hands on their butts, all of them slouching, as though burdened by a weighty load of worries. Before long, the neighborhood was dense with Bosnians. Contrary to the local customs, they took evening walks, the anxiety of displacement clear in their step; in large, silent groups, they drank coffee at a lakeside Turkish café (thereby converting it into a proper *kafana*), a dark cloud of war trauma and cigarette smoke hovering over them; their children played on the street, oblivious to the drug business conducted on the corner. I could monitor them now from my window, from the *kafana*, on the street. It was as if they had come looking for me in Edgewater.

In February 1997, a couple of months before my first return to Sarajevo, Veba came to Chicago for a visit; I hadn't seen him since my departure. For the first few days, I listened to his stories of life under siege, the stories of horrible transformation the war had forced upon the besieged. I was still living at the AiR. Despite the February cold, Veba wanted to see where my life was taking place, so we wandered around Edgewater: to the Shoney's, the chess café, the *kafana* on the now-iced-over lake. He got a haircut at my barber's; we bought meat at my butcher's. I told him my Edgewater stories: about the young woman on the ledge, about the Bosnian family walking in formation, about Peter the Assyrian.

Then we ventured out of Edgewater to visit Ukrainian Village, and I showed him where I'd lived; I took him to the Burger King where I'd fattened myself into American shape while listening to old Ukes discussing Ukrainian politics over sixty-nine-cent coffee—I used to call them the Knights of the Burger King. We wandered around the Gold Coast, spotting a Matisse in some rich person's apartment, nicely positioned so that it could be seen from the street; we saw a movie at the Esquire. We visited the Water Tower and I spoke about the great

Chicago fire. We had a drink at the Green Mill, where Al Capone used to imbibe martinis, and where every giant of jazz, from Louis Armstrong to Charlie Mingus, had performed. I showed him where the St. Valentine's Day massacre had taken place: the garage was long gone, but the urban myth had it that dogs still growled when walking past, as they could smell the blood.

Showing Veba around, telling him the stories of Chicago and of my life in Edgewater, I realized that my immigrant interior had begun to merge with the American exterior. Large parts of Chicago had entered me and settled there; I fully owned those parts now. I saw Chicago through the eyes of Sarajevo and the two cities now created a complicated internal landscape in which stories could be generated. When I came back from my first visit to Sarajevo, in the spring of 1997, the Chicago I came back to belonged to me. Returning from home, I returned home.

DR. ROSE IHEDIGBO

Nigeria

Dr. Rose Ihedigbo (1952–) was born in the village of Umudu in the southeastern Nigerian state of Abia to a working-class family who valued education. A Christian Igbo, she was eight when Nigeria declared its independence in 1960 and fifteen when the largely Igbo eastern region of the country, Biafra, tried to secede as a result of ethnic cleansing in the Hausa-dominated northern region. The brutal hostilities and pervasive starvation in the Nigerian Civil War (1967–1970), also known as the Biafran War, caused more than two million deaths.

In the war's aftermath, many Nigerians sought assistance from recently arrived missionary groups, and it is at that time that Rose met her husband, Apollos, a college-trained teacher whose career was halted by the war. The deeply religious pair remained in Nigeria, working with church groups while continuing their educations until 1979, when Apollos moved to western New York to attend Houghton College, a school affiliated with the Wesleyan Church. Rose and their three children joined him the following year.

As a fairly young nation, Nigeria has a relatively short history of immigration to the U.S. A primary driving factor has been educational opportunity, especially because a college degree was understood to provide access to government positions. Indeed, prior to the Biafran War, many ethnic groups sought to sponsor Nigerian students' educations at their own expense. Immigration totals for this time period, however, do not account for Nigerians on student and other temporary visas. Nearly nine thousand Nigerians arrived as students between 1971 and 1980, while another thirty-five thousand in the ensuing decade either received green cards or secured permanent residence by applying for amnesty via the Immigration Reform and Control Act of 1986.

Upon Rose and her children's arrival at Houghton, the family moved into a small apartment and relied on the moral and financial support of the church community as well as that of other Nigerian immigrants. The young, religiously devout parents eschewed secular recreations and happily secluded themselves within this community until moving to South Deerfield, Massachusetts, so that Apollos could attend graduate school at the University of Massachusetts in nearby Amherst. The growing Ihedigbo family endured financial hardship but remained committed to pursuing education; after a short time at Greenfield Community College, Rose joined Apollos on the UMass campus, where she took her bachelor's, master's, and PhD, all in early-childhood education. In 1999, Apollos and Rose established the Nigerian-American Technical and Agricultural College (NATAC) in Umuahia, the capital city of the state of Abai. Although Apollos died two years after opening the school, NATAC remains active, enabling lower-income families to receive affordable educations. In addition to cofounding NATAC, Rose Ihedigbo was also a former reviewer of Head Start programs and now works as an early-childhood-education consultant.

The full title of her memoir, Sandals in the Snow: A True Story of One African Family's Journey to Achieving the American Dream, *sums up the tone and purpose of the memoir. Mixing narrative and interview, the author calls on her family's collective memory to recount their early years in the U.S. In the first excerpt, "Signs of a Brighter Future: Life in the Suburbs of Amherst," Ihedigbo describes the significance of homeownership, which symbolizes successful acculturation and upward mobility. The second excerpt describes the family's various ways of maintaining cultural ties via an extended Nigerian community, along with the parents' measured responses to the children's exposure to U.S. customs.*

Excerpt from

Sandals in the Snow

— 2013 —

The house at 29 Tamarack Drive in Amherst, Massachusetts, housed many of the earliest memories of the Ihedigbo children. This gray house with hints of blue was a two-story paradise in a new subdivision for the family that previously lived in the UMass university apartments. On the day the Nigerian family moved into the neighborhood, the day they carefully transported the meager goods that they had collected while they resided on the UMass campus, the house had four bedrooms and a gravel driveway. However, these were the Ihedigbos whose leader Apollos was always improving, always advancing, always growing.

"The day we moved into our house on Tamarack Drive," Onyii recalls, "when we drove up to it, I remember feeling like 'Wow! We're like really middle class now! We're really normal now!' Not only were we the first Africans to move into this all-white neighborhood, we were the first blacks. I had my own room in a suburban neighborhood—I felt so special! This was the day I started feeling normal because prior to this, my brothers and I had always felt different or out of place. We all struggled with it at some level, but this move changed things for us."

Emeka also remembers the significance of purchasing a house like 29 Tamarack Drive. "The house on Tamarack was the embodiment of the American dream! After living in apartments for so many years, we finally owned our own home! Being able to say, 'Hey, this is ours!' was a significant moment for us."

• • •

Apollos nestled on his favorite spot on the family's comfortable sofa with his youngest son, James, at his side, casually enjoying the evening television network lineup. As he was giving his commentary on the last scene of the show before the commercial break, he stopped in midsentence at what he saw.

"Who needs a professional painter when you've got *this*! With the wave of one hand, you have one full coat of paint on the walls, and then you can get back to your weekend!" The commercial showed one of the most beautiful sights a do-it-yourselfer could ever hope for.

"Finish your painting in record time, all with the fast and easy flick of a wrist!" The commercial went on to show a high-pressure spray-painting machine whose ease and efficiency appeared to turn several days' worth of painting into only hours. It was amazing to this elder Nigerian who was not one to want everything that he saw, but who—when he saw something he really wanted—had to have it, especially if it was for the family.

"We're getting *that*!" Apollos exclaimed! James, who knew that he would inevitably be a part of the painting crew, concurred; however, he noted there were things that arose after the fact that had not been considered.

"The commercial failed to mention how you had to plug your ears because the machine was *so* incredibly loud and so messy that it didn't even make sense! Dad made us get up on a ladder and made us paint away. It took us three weeks to get done, when it would have taken a contractor only one week to do. Fortunately, Dad gave in and let a professional builder come to do the driveway." Apollos and his built-in labor force would go on to complete many do-it-yourself projects, and though the outcome was not always necessarily as precise as a professional contractor would have it, they got the job done.

"When we moved into the house, it had four bedrooms

and a gravel driveway," recalls James. "By the time we moved out, it had seven bedrooms, a paved driveway, and it was completely repainted. It looked like a new house, and we did just about everything ourselves. After all, when you have four boys living in your house, you have an instant paint crew!" The Ihedigbos, as with everything they engaged in, started with the small and humble and put in the work to turn the house into their own beautiful masterpiece that was the envy of their neighbors—the typical Nigerian way.

Perhaps the biggest deal surrounding their move into the new home was the fact that all of the boys did not have to share one bedroom. "I would share with either David or James," Emeka explains, "and my other two brothers would share a room—but this did not last. Bedrooms changed with allegiances. We quickly turned into factions. I would partner up with James to go against the other two in whatever silly disagreement we would have. Then the next week, it was, 'You're not my roommate anymore!' and the rotation would begin again. It was like musical chairs!"

If the house at 29 Tamarack Drive suggested "normal American family," the purchase of the family's first minivan solidified it. "The minivan was created for us!" son Emeka says.

"One day, my dad said, 'I'm going to get a car for us.' He came back with a Dodge Caravan with a turbo engine in it! I was like, 'Dad! Where did you *find* this thing?'"

The family gained much use out of the minivan all over town and up and down the road when they went to visit aunts and uncles, attend conferences, or take family trips. As soon as one of the kids was old enough to drive, he was put behind the wheel to chauffeur the rest of the crew to its destination.

Wanting to experience the true power of the minivan's turbo action, when the rest of the family would be asleep, the driver, always one of the boys, would inch the speed up higher and higher to see what the engine was made of. Emeka could personally testify that it did 110 mph like a dream. The van also impressed the muscle cars in the next lane; making eye contact with the driver of a Mustang, the boy would give the van a little power that invited the Mustang driver to open up his own engine, and the two would be on their way, racing at top speeds down the highway. When they happily woke upon arrival at their destination, the rest of the Ihedigbos always wondered why their road trips always seemed so short.

Though the Ihedigbo children did not have much in the way of the gadgets, toys, and accoutrements that are designed to entertain passive, sedentary young people today, they manufactured plenty of fun on their own.

When David, Nate, Emeka, and James hopped on their bikes riding throughout the neighborhood seeking their next adventure, smiling as those without a care in the world, they weaved in and out, up and down the neighborhood streets, jumping curbs, popping wheelies, and waving at their friends who longingly peered out at them, noses pressed against the glass of the front window that looked onto the street. Boys who were their parents' only son grew green with envy at the fact that anytime the Ihedigbo boys were ready to play, they had an instant team of two-on-two basketball, an instant offensive and defensive play line for a football game, or an instant bicycle gang, harmless as they were, but nonetheless a gang of boys who knew, understood, and looked out for one another.

The Ihedigbo bike gang was not without its shenanigans though. As with all groups, there were challenges to be experienced among its members; where there are boys involved, there will be "situations" that incite the emotions and push them to the edge. Every child remembers his first bike and the bike that he loves most. The image of that bike—in most cases, a child's only means of transportation to the pockets of fun around the neighborhood—never leaves the memory, no matter how old we become, and the image of the beloved bike becomes even more heightened when this critical piece of machinery is lost. James experienced one such encounter.

"My mother bought me a brand-new ten-speed bike, the racing-style kind with the elephant handlebars and the skinny tires. Man, I loved that bike! One day, I left the bike outside because I'd planned to go to my friend's house in a little bit. I went into the house to do something, and when I came back, my bike was gone! I was in a panic! I asked my brothers where it was, and my brother Emeka told me that he'd taken my bike and left it at the bus stop and that someone had stolen it! I was so mad at Emeka! In our neighborhood, you walked or rode your bike everywhere, so not having my bike meant that I was stuck!"

The journey to the National Football League (NFL) fame that James enjoys today began when he was only six years old. One day, Rose was driving around town, running one of the many errands that occupy the time of any mother of a large family, when James peered out the window at two groups of little kids dressed in uniforms with large shoulder pads hitting each other. "I said, 'Mom, I want to do that! I want to play *that* game!'" James recalls of the day he was bitten by the football bug. Rose, always one to encourage her children to try new things, discussed the idea with Apollos and then promptly signed her youngest son up to play Pop Warner pee wee football.

"Before then," James explains, "I didn't really play with my brothers because I was too small. After I started playing pee wee ball with my pads, I got more skills and confidence. We would have backyard football games on the weekends where all of the kids in the neighborhood would come to our house and play."

In the backyard of the Ihedigbo home, boys, young and old, would gather to play all out, full-blown tackle football with no pads. "It's where I got my toughness from," James recollects proudly.

David remembers the backyard football games that he and his brothers played with the rest of the boys in the neighborhood fondly. They were surrounded by a number of immigrant families and were always able to coax them into playing at a moment's notice. This was no easy backyard league—not for the faint of heart. It was fast and it was free, but it was rough!

"Our type of play was very rough. There were no pads involved, although we played in fearless competition like we were fully padded, so it was really intense. On that field, we weren't just boys in the neighborhood, we would picture ourselves actually playing in the NFL. You were your favorite player wearing your favorite team's uniform. I was always Ed Reed from the Baltimore Ravens, and James was always Brian Dawkins. We played football for real, with a lot of one-on-one matchups and lots of serious drives."

Emeka also remembers these gridiron games in his family's backyard. "We played violent tackle football like we saw them play on TV—not flag football—with no pads. It's a wonder that none of us got paralyzed or killed!"

As Rose stood inside of her kitchen preparing yam flour for the evening meal, peering out of the curtained window at what seemed like scores of neighborhood boys in her yard, she was all at once concerned and relieved. Her concern came because of the fact that her boys were right outside being hit, pummeled, and pounded as they tried to compete and win the game. There were boys of all sizes out there, big and small, old and young, and she constantly prayed that no one would get seriously hurt. Her relief came as a result of her children finding something to do that they seemed to love so passionately.

The backyard games would start during the daytime and last for hours, the players barely recognizing the fact that the sun had gone down and the streetlights had come on. She would step outside of the door and make the announcement they all knew was inevitable.

"Okay, boys, next touchdown wins the game, and then it's over! It's late . . . time to come in the house!" she would call out as they would all groan in unison, "Awwww, Mom!"

Pee wee football represented the official beginning of James's love for the game, and this game that the child loved was teaching him some valuable lessons about himself. One of the first observations he made of himself as a player, besides recognizing that he happened to be *really* good at this game, was, "I never wanted to quit the game. I had to show my brothers and the other kids that I was tough enough to play, so I wouldn't let anything stop me, no matter how much it hurt."

While organized football gave James an opportunity for exposure, it was the backyard football league, however, that made him tough. "He took a lot of beatings because he was usually the smallest one on the field," explains his brother David.

After a few years, Emeka, David, and Nate finally allowed little James, who was now nine years old, a spot on the team in their backyard league. In doing so, his brothers soon discovered something incredibly unique about him as they watched him play—something special. Emeka tells the story of this first time he noticed this distinction in his baby brother.

"One day, we were one man down. Almost like clock-work, James said, 'I'll play!' We were big guys, so we said, 'Nah, you're too small, James!' But James insisted. 'Let me play!' he kept saying, so we let him in the game. Right off the bat, he was good. We would throw the ball, and he would catch it, and then someone would tackle him as hard as they could. He was laying there, decimated. Crying. Sobbing. We expected him to get up and go away. Instead, he would get up still sobbing and line up for the next play! We gave him a few moments—still not finished crying. We'd call the snap and hike the ball . . . and he'd *still* be sobbing! But he was *still good*! We knew this guy was going to be a professional. Those backyard games taught him how to be able to take punishment and dole it out. Now he's one of the hardest-hitting players in the NFL."

In every neighborhood's backyard football league, there is a legendary story—one that every boy in the neighborhood remembers, whether he witnessed it firsthand or not. After all, it is a legend, and it is worthy of telling again and again because of some exceptional feat or accomplishment on the field that defied logic or reason. The legendary story surrounding the Ihedigbo backyard football league just happened to be one of their youngest brother, James Ihedigbo, and it is one best told from eyewitness accounts.

"I'll never forget that day," David explains with eyes shining. "It was a really big play that would determine the game. On one side of our house, there was a wooden fence that came up about waist high. On the other side, there was no fence, so you could run your routes deeper. My brother threw to James a real deep route, and it was like everybody held their breath at the same time because you could see the ball just hanging in the air. James ran into the fence, through the wooden fence, broke the fence, but still caught the ball! Here was this little kid with this huge strength! All everybody could do was gather around him and ask over and over, 'How did you catch that *ball*? How could you have *caught* that ball?' It was amazing. James had fence marks all over his chest, and you could tell he was in a lot of pain, but we won. James never complained, he didn't have anything to say except, 'We won the game!' This was competition at its best and showed that James would do whatever it took to get to the next level and shine. That is a quality that has never left him from high school all the way through to the NFL. . . ."

The sometimes harsh and uncomfortable realities of being an "other" in society made the need for fellowship among their own cultural group a necessity—necessary for social, emotional, and mental health. The sense of acceptance and belonging that the Nigerian community offered in the midst of a larger society that was not always so accepting made it that much more valuable.

Apollos and Rose knew how necessary it was to keep their children connected to their roots, especially since their offspring lived most of their lives in a school context that silently demanded their conformity in order to be accepted. Hence, Nigerian gatherings were a must, as they provided a sense of culture and connection that it was impossible for the children to otherwise receive in the suburbs.

The children themselves looked forward to these gatherings as well, as they were great fun. James recalls some of his fondest memories in heading to these Nigerian affairs. "We always looked forward to it," he remembers with a smile. "It was a great time with great food, and lots of aunties, uncles, cousins, and music. They were so festive, and it felt good because we got to see people that we didn't get to see on a regular basis. It was like being around hundreds of family members, and it was no different from a family reunion. Times like these provided me with something that I didn't get from the culture on the Amherst front—a sense of acceptance and connectedness."

Just by virtue of enjoying an American education, the children of an immigrant family will be exposed to various values and practices that fall outside of what is traditionally accepted in their un-Westernized homes.

"We were a very tight family with very strict parents and very strong biblical beliefs," Nate explains of his early childhood. "The kids at school and the American kids who lived in the apartment complex were just . . . different. They introduced us to things that we did not know about, we were just seeing kids act like this for the first time because we didn't act that way as Nigerians," he recalls. "For example, when I was in the first grade, the neighborhood boys got their hands on a Polaroid camera, which my brothers and I had never seen before, and they started doing dumb stuff like taking pictures of their butts and doing other nasty stuff with the camera. We were mortified just witnessing that kind of behavior. We would have *never* thought of doing things like that!"

Further, the Ihedigbo children could easily be marked as "others" when it came to the way they treated their elders and how their level of respect for those older than they were differed from that of their classmates. In the home, they respected their parents greatly, politely relating to them, paying deference to them and recognizing that they were the leaders and authoritarians of the household. Simply put, Mom and Dad were in charge. Their neighborhood friends, on the other hand, especially the white ones, would not hesitate to talk back disrespectfully to their parents, rebel against their instructions, and throw fits when they did not get their way. In those households, the boys observed, it was unclear who was in charge!

Emeka, Nate, David, and James would marvel when they witnessed such things as this at the homes of their neighborhood friends. As young as they were, it seemed to them that those households lacked something very important, though they could not put their finger on it at the time. Observing the dramatic difference of what they experienced at home versus their friends' houses, they decided that the missing elements were fear and accountability.

Here, there was no fear of consequences and no accountability. The American kids that surrounded them knew that if their mother or father got out of line, all the kid would have to do was pick up the phone and call the Department of Child Protective Services and Mom and Dad would have to suffer the consequences. As a result, instead of the kids having a fear of the parents, the parents had a fear of their children, which led them on most occasions to acquiesce to the child's demands. The same lack of fear, respect, and reverence for consequences led to their friends acting irreverently throughout the neighborhood and at school.

As James and David made a visit to the mall, for example, they witnessed a young white child yelling at his mother in the store as he held up an expensive pair of basketball shoes.

"I want *this* pair of shoes, Mom! I *swear*, Mom, why are you so *dumb*? Why don't you listen to me and get me what I *want*?" the child yelled loudly. Embarrassed and humiliated, the red-faced mother tried to soothe and calm her "spirited" child down.

The brothers looked at one another in amazement, each ensuring that the other had just witnessed what would have gotten them knocked out in their own culture.

"Did you *see* that?" James asked with a smile of disbelief.

To this, David answered, "Yes! I wish I *would* try to swear at my mom! It would be the first *and* the very last time!" They both laughed, knowing it was true. Such behavior would never be tolerated in their community. It was here that they marked another cultural difference: Nigerian children understood what it took for their parents to get where they were, so they valued whatever their parents could afford for them.

The American model of family that surrounded them seemed so off kilter to the Ihedigbo boys! In their own home, as well as in the homes of their Nigerian cousins, the situation was quite the opposite.

David explains, "In America, the family system seems to have been thrown out of the window. There were times when I was growing up when I was scared of not only getting a beating from my mom but my uncle and aunt. Any uncle or aunt who saw me do something wrong had the power to put me back in line. They don't have that in American culture. If a kid gets out of line and is punished, he will call the authorities. There is *no way* that would happen in a Nigerian family. The moms and dads would never let it happen!"

David goes on to describe the process of the "It Takes a Village to Raise a Child" discipline that is characteristic of the Nigerian community. "At Nigerian functions, I've seen kids act up and get slapped by someone *else's* parents. 'What are you doing?' they would ask the kid. Then the kid would not talk back. Instead, he would just say, 'I'm sorry. I shouldn't have been doing that.' But that's not the end of it. The kid would go and tell his own parents what happened and why he got slapped so that he wouldn't get into even more trouble when the report got back to his mom and dad. They would discipline him for what he had done too, saying, 'You've been taught better than that. Why would you do such a thing?' In Nigerian culture, you learned from your mistakes, you were not resentful about the discipline, and you definitely didn't even think about calling child services. We understood that if you did not act up, you would not get reprimanded. Everything was cause and effect."

Additionally, the Ihedigbos extended this respect for their elders outside of their household, as their parents had trained them to do. While their friends, again the mainstream white ones, would not hesitate to call an adult by his or her first name, the Ihedigbo children were accustomed to calling adults within their community uncle or auntie. They would be mortified to ever attempt to call a Nigerian adult, or any adult for that matter, by a first name.

Another clear differentiation between the Ihedigbos and their American counterparts was one that the children picked up on almost immediately: the spirit of entitlement. For some reason, they observed, their neighborhood and school friends felt that others owed them something—a second chance, an easier option, an extension of a deadline, the right to enjoy a certain privilege without putting in the work, the acceptance of an excuse, a free pass, or whatever it is they were demanding at the time.

The Ihedigbos, on the other hand, had been trained up all their lives with a different mentality: no one owes you anything, so whatever you want, you must work hard to obtain yourself. They were grateful that their parents had ingrained this way of thinking into their young minds and wondered how long their American counterparts would go in life before they understood that the world did not owe them a thing.

Because he was a natural athlete, James did not limit himself to playing football; he also ventured out to play lacrosse. However, his high school lacrosse career was short-lived. "The kids who played lacrosse were kind of preppy, suburban, all-American players. Though I grew up in the suburbs as well, their attitude of self-righteousness, self-importance, and over-privilege turned me off. I wasn't raised that way, so although I was cool with them, I didn't fit in, so I quit the team."

Being an African in Massachusetts is like being a black panther walking in the snow; blending into such surroundings is no easy feat. Such was the case for the Ihedigbo children, who had to navigate a context that is challenging enough for even the most "typical" of American child. Negotiating the rules of friendship, boyfriends and girlfriends, making good grades, what to wear, where to sit in the lunchroom, keeping up with the cool kids, and staying out of harm's way by avoiding the bullies are difficult enough without having to face the challenge of being the most obvious outsider of the entire group.

As Africans, the Ihedigbo children were used to being different. Nowhere was this notion truer than in the way they dressed. Their clothing was different. They did not wear the flashy name-brand clothing that set the class boundaries of cool, popular, and unpopular within the trendy, upscale Massachusetts schools they attended. The kids at school wore brands like Polo, Izod, and Liz Claiborne; however, the Ihedigbo kids wore "clothes," just clothes. While the kids at school wore Nike and Puma sneakers, the Ihedigbos wore "shoes," just shoes—Survival Center shoes.

The differences in external appearance that marked this unique Nigerian family also showed forth in their cultural expressions, particularly Rose's way of ethnically styling Onyii's hair. Not everyone in Onyii's non-diverse school was fond of Rose's painstakingly elaborate techniques of fashioning her daughter's hair and sending her into a sea of curious, merciless white kindergarteners at Marks Meadow Elementary School.

"One time," Onyii explains, "my mom spent the whole night putting my hair in plaits—the kind that are wrapped really tight with thread and that stick out so you can shape and mold them any way you want. Because they were tight, my head hurt *so* badly. 'What is that on your hair? Why does your hair look like that?' all the kids would ask as they reached out to touch it, mocking me. I was really embarrassed and went crying to my teacher to ask her if I could take the plaits out. She and I took them out together, and when I got home, my mom was soooo mad! She kept asking, 'Why would you take them out, Onyii? Why would you *do* that?'"

"It really broke my heart to hear that the other kids were teasing my child because they did not understand her hair," Rose explains, reflecting on the ordeal with a shake of the head. "Onyii was traumatized and bullied by her classmates who repeatedly called her names and made her cry over her hair. I was shocked that the teacher let this go on so many times! I went to the teacher time after time to meet with her—just about my daughter's *hair*! Each time I went, I demanded that the teacher do something about the problem, and each time, she would say that she would talk with the students, though nothing ever really changed."

Sometimes our pain is so real, so palpable, and so utterly inconceivable in life that we maintain some remnant or keepsake of it to remind ourselves in the future about the magnitude of the heartbreaking experiences we have overcome. The reason for our saving these mementos varies as widely as the broad spectrum of experiences that we encounter. Perhaps we keep them as evidence of pain that was so agonizing that without such evidence, those to whom we tell the story would never believe it happened. Perhaps we hold on to them in anticipation of the opportunity to reflect upon them later in life and celebrate ourselves for our diligence and determination to overcome life's obstacles. Perhaps we hold on to them to test the diminishing emotional impact that the experiences related to these tokens have on our lives over the years. Regardless of why we guard them so closely, these mementos matter to us and fill a need that only we ourselves can define. Such is the case in a letter written to Onyii (Debbie) by one of her elementary school classmates kept in a safe place by her mother, Rose. Reading the letter today still elicits raw emotion in the heart of a protective mother who saw the very image of her proud Nigerian self reflected in her daughter.

Debbie,

My friends don't like your kind! Beacaus [sic] you don't have any nice clowhs [sic]. And your [sic] in 3rd grade and, my friends and I are all in 4th! And your [sic] not my kind! And I know much more than you and if you tell on me that will just pruve [sic] that you're a baby, and it will just mack [sic] things whours [sic]. So if you just shut your mouth nouthing will happen [sic]. But if you tell, I will kill you!!

—*Karen X.*
P.S. DON'T Tell!!!!!!

"Things did not change until we left that school and went to a different one when Onyii was in fourth grade," Rose recalls. "To this day, I do not know why those students did not understand her or her hair and why they bullied her for it."

The move of their daughter from Marks Meadow Elementary School to Fort River Elementary School resulted in a much better environment for young Onyii. While some might have viewed the change as giving in to the hostile Western society that surrounded them, for Rose it was quite the opposite. The change was for her daughter's safety, but she never felt the pressure to change her daughter's Nigerian hairstyles.

"I insisted on helping my daughter understand why she was wearing her hair this way, and I taught her to ignore the bullies that did not understand why she wore her hair this way," Rose reveals proudly. "I never felt the pressure to conform to what they were doing contrary to my African culture. As a result, Onyii continued to grow and mature, she learned how to avoid the bullies, and she became stronger in defending herself!" For Rose, a Nigerian in America, there would be no compromise—no defeat.

Though not as dramatic, the Ihedigbo boys had their own challenges in making their way through a very white, very unexposed school system. "I remember being in elementary school where the kids called me African booty scratcher," Emeka explains. "Then one day, I was just sitting there at my desk, and a little white girl came up to me and said, 'Hey, can I touch your hair?' I said no, but she reached out and started rubbing it anyway. She turned to her friends and said, 'It feels like a rug!' I felt more like a specimen than a human being. They were so culturally different, and the transition was tough."

Fortunately, by the time he'd entered high school, James, the youngest of the Ihedigbo clan, had an advantage. James had seen his four older siblings take on the assimilation battles of being "the African in the school," a fact that automatically made them different than the school's population norm. However, James had another advantage working in his favor: he was quite successful at sports, so students wanted to be around him.

"People wanted to be around me and to be my friend because being good at sports made me one of the cool kids. Because I was an athlete, people just accepted me for who I was, regardless of where my family was from, and I accepted them as well," he explains.

It was not only that which was seen on the exterior that differentiated the Nigerian children from their American counterparts; it was the unique way they smelled.

Onyii recalls, "When I was seven or eight years old, kids used to whisper and say that I and my brothers smelled. I would ask, 'What do you mean?' We never noticed a smell. The kids would say, 'You don't wear deodorant!' and we didn't, so there was nothing I could say to that. But I didn't know that we *smelled bad* until they told me. To us, we just smelled like Nigerians. Nigerians have always had a natural smell."

Even though the "Nigerian smell" was not an issue for the Ihedigbos, it was clearly an issue for their non-Nigerian guests.

"We always had a fear of people coming over to our house because they were not used to our smell. When I was in junior high, my friend Susie came over to the house, and after that one time, she never wanted to come back to our house again. She said our house smelled different. After that day, I became supersensitive to smell. Today, I smell things all the time, and if I smell anything in my house, I do not want people to come over. I instantly want odors eliminated as soon as I smell them. It's so bad now that my husband thinks I have a disorder!"

After being enlightened on the impact that she and her brothers' malodorous state was having on their social standing among the other kids in school, this made some—though not all of the children—want to wear deodorant. However, the request to wear deodorant could easily be mistaken as one's desire to be less Nigerian and more American, and knowing this, Onyii broached the topic delicately with her father. It wasn't as much of a challenge as she thought it would be.

"I was standing around with my dad in the health and beauty section of K-Mart one day, and I decided to ask, 'Dad, why don't we wear deodorant?' My dad simply shrugged and said, 'I don't know.' I asked, 'Can I get some?' He said, 'Sure.' And that was that. I picked up a pretty pink and white bottle of Suave deodorant that day and never looked back."

Onyii, the eldest, was accustomed to being the trendsetter in the family. In the same way that she was first to adopt the American standard of using deodorant, she was also the first to incorporate the use of shampoo in her beauty regimen.

"We always used to use bar soap on our hair. I remember seeing a shampoo commercial once and asked my mom why we didn't use shampoo. Her reply was, 'It's all the same thing. Shampoo is the same as Irish Spring!' After I insisted, we got shampoo and were using it by the time I got to high school."

The ways of life that made the Ihedigbos different from those around them did not always occur behind the four walls of a local Nigerian home. In fact, anyone watching the family closely would catch nuances of behaviors that were telltale signs that this family was a bit different than the typical Massachusetts family. One such incident occurred when the children's maternal grandmother herself, Helen, traveled to Massachusetts from Nigeria for a visit. Grandmother knew that she was different— she openly acknowledged it—but this did not bother her, for she simply did not care. As with any older person, she knew exactly who she was and what she wanted to do and no one would stop her.

The family station wagon rolled slowly up to the First Baptist Church in Amherst. The children, faces shiny and clothes neatly pressed, filed out of the car in an orderly fashion in the parking lot, their shiny hand-me-down shoes reflecting the light of the warm summer sun. Rose proudly looked her children over, as was her custom every Sunday morning, to ensure that all gently worn shirts were tucked, all pants were securely belted, all faces were shiny and clean.

As was the children's custom every Sunday morning, they walked in a calm and orderly fashion towards the door of the church, eager to see their friends. On this particular Sunday, Grandmother Helen was a part of the processional into the church. As they made their way from the car to the church door, Rose proudly introduced her mother to her other friends who were also arriving in the parking lot.

"Please meet my mother. Mother, meet my friends." The introductions continued as the children stood around and greeted their own friends.

In a moment, however, things changed as the children saw something that stopped them dead in their tracks. In the middle of a parking-lot introduction to one of Rose's fellow church members, Grandmother, who wore a *wrappa* (a large, colorful piece of African cloth wrapped around the body and tucked in at the waist), spread her legs apart and relieved herself on the ground—in a very deliberate, conspicuous fashion! What their grandmother had done was impossible to not notice, and her grandchildren Nate, James, Emeka, David, and Onyii were eyewitnesses—horrified ones! They'd heard the sound of the water hitting the cool paved asphalt before they saw it, and then they turned to watch in utter amazement as their grandmother peed on the ground right next to a car—standing straight up and without concern or fear of any critique of onlookers!

"Oh no! Grandmother's peeing in the parking lot!" they whispered with guarded embarrassment, shock, and horror as they nudged one another in disbelief.

"Grandmother, what did you *do*?" Nate questioned as he turned towards his family's matriarch, eyes wide as saucers at what he'd just witnessed and hoping none outside the family had seen such a thing.

"I relieved myself," she answered nonchalantly. "I had to

relieve myself, so I relieved myself," she explained unapologetically. With that, she proudly lifted her head and proceeded to walk in stately fashion through the front doors of the church and into worship leaving her little puddle behind!

Sometimes it was the Ihedigbos themselves that marked the fact that they were different from their surroundings, and other times, as in the case of Grandma's visit to church, it was others. Another such case is a story that the family recalls with laughter about Uncle Smarts, an uncle that lived with the family while they lived in the university apartments at UMass.

There was clearly a commotion going on outside of the apartment window. An uncharacteristic amount of loud voices and laughter summoned several of the Ihedigbos out of their rest and into the bright, warm outdoors. As they stepped outside, they caught sight of a man moving as fast as a cheetah, running through the grassy courtyard in an all-out sprint.

"Eh! Eh! Eh!" he called out excitedly to his family that now stood by as he tried to run and point at the same time towards thick, brushy squirrels running for their dear lives. "Good meats! Good meats! Eh! Good meats!"

"Oh no! What is he *doing*?" one of the Ihedigbo boys asked, expressing the shared horror and embarrassment of his siblings.

The squirrels darted up the first trees they could find, sensing that their predator meant business. All around, people laughed at Uncle Smarts, who chased after the innocent creatures in pursuit of "good meats." While they laughed, the Ihedigbo youngsters could only shake their heads and return to their apartment, where they were safe from ridicule and sheltered from being so different. In fact, in a self-protective effort, they began to refer to their Uncle Smarts as Uncle Dumb so that others would not associate them with their uncle—and that they would not think that the Ihedigbos ate squirrel.

• • •

Of course, squirrel was not on the menu at the Ihedigbo house; however, the foods they ate were different from that which sat on the tables of the homes surrounding them. Early on when the kids were younger, their mother cooked up an abundance of Nigerian food like palm oil, *egusi* soup, stews, rice, yams, and traditional West African fare, only occasionally tossing in American delicacies like spaghetti and hot dogs for the children.

As they grew older, and especially as the kids learned to cook for themselves, the menu migrated towards more American cuisine like chicken wings, hamburgers, and the like. Though all of the siblings learned to cook, Onyii was the first to learn, and Rose trained her children well in making the Nigerian staples. However, when their mother and father were away and Onyii had to cook dinner for her brothers, their assimilated tastes demanded selections from the American side of the menu, and she complied.

Even today when the family gets together, instead of going to a restaurant, someone will run to the store to pick up some ingredients, and together they will prepare a feast in the kitchen. While Emeka is the professional in the restaurant industry and loves preparing his unusual chef selections, each Ihedigbo has his or her specialty: James makes chicken wings, David makes lasagna, Nate makes rice and stew, and Onyii makes macaroni and cheese.

Other differentiating elements, like the difficulty of writing the last name "Ihedigbo," an exercise which often caused the children to run late or miss out on recess because they had not finished writing their names like their shorter and simpler-surnamed counterparts, helped to set the Ihedigbos apart as the "others" in the community. While they could do nothing about their last name, by the time Onyii and Emeka reached high school, they decided to go by their more American middle

names of "Debbie" (for Deborah) and "Joseph" respectively.
These names were much more culturally friendly in the city of
Amherst. They would not pick up their Igbo names again until
after they had graduated from high school.

The Ihedigbo kids further understood the extent of their
differences when their neighborhood friends would ask, "What
did your mom and dad just say?" Not meaning any slight to
Rose and Apollos, their friends found it difficult to understand
their parents' thick Nigerian accents when they came over to the
Ihedigbo house for a visit. It could not be mistaken that the
Ihedigbos were special in so many ways.

OKSANA MARAFIOTI

Russia

The diasporic Roma have been persecuted and enslaved for centuries, surviving numerous nations' attempts to remove or exterminate them, including sterilization efforts in the Czech Republic and Slovakia and the genocide perpetrated by the Nazis and the Ustaše (Croatian Revolutionary Movement), known by Romani as the Porajmos. Oksana Marafioti (1975–) was born in Riga, Latvia, to an Armenian mother, Nora, and a Russian Romani father, Valerio, who performed in a traveling music ensemble run by the author's paternal grandfather. The family was subject to ethnic discrimination during their travels, none affecting Oksana more than the death of her boyfriend during a Roma rights demonstration in Romania. Despite their success and middle-class status, Marafioti's parents decided to immigrate to the U.S. to give their daughters better opportunities as well as to fulfill Valerio's dream of playing with B. B. King, the famous blues musician.

Marafioti's Armenian uncle, already living in the U.S., sent the family the requisite paperwork but omitted the sponsorship document, a gesture that the Marafioti family understood as reflecting their relative's disdain for their Roma background. Nevertheless, Nora Marafioti spent years networking and paying bribes to expedite their emigration, which she accomplished just before the collapse of the USSR in 1991.

The family arrived in Los Angeles when Oksana was fifteen years old, and their Armenian relatives begrudgingly hosted them until her father left the family to continue an affair with a woman whose own immigration he planned on sponsoring. For Marafioti's cousins, this situation reinforced their negative stereotypes of Roma people, and they hastily moved the Marafiotis into a dilapidated apartment complex nearby. At Hollywood High as an ESL student, Oksana had difficulties negotiating the cultural demands of her parents and new stepmother while trying to become "a real American." A classically trained pianist, she eventually transferred to the Performing Arts Magnet School and then, upon graduating, attended a film crew training program at the University of Nevada at Las Vegas.

American Gypsy *focuses on Marafioti's childhood in the USSR and the years following her family's immigration. In "The Curbs of Beverly Hills," Oksana describes her family's first intimate interaction with gadjee (non-Roma); and sympathy among immigrants, regardless of ethnicity or nationality, becomes a dominant theme, with members of previously arrived groups often helping the recently arrived.*

Excerpt from

American Gypsy

—— 2012 ——

I once heard a rumor about immigrants who, unable to read English, had mistaken cat food for canned tuna. That unwelcome image was wedged in my mind as Mom and I stepped through the sliding doors of the local supermarket on our first official shopping trip alone. When we moved out of Uncle's, the Russian Immigrant Outreach Program brought us groceries, but their services ended after a month or so.

"First things first," Mom said as we pushed our cart down

the bright aisles. "We need butter." Her black pumps echoed against the canyon of freezers stuffed with food. She wore a gray dress with intricately carved silver buttons down the front. With her freshly curled and styled hair, she looked like a Mediterranean Jane Seymour. When she'd spent an hour dressing up, I had complained, worried we'd draw too much attention. I was right. People stared, not only because of her opera-ready makeup, but also because she shouted in Russian to me as if we were miles apart. The heels and the crimson nails weren't too bad. We came from a culture where outside excursions meant people would be checking you out, forming opinions behind your back. You absolutely had to look your best. God forbid you went to the downstairs bakery in your sweats and slippers; eventually the neighborhood would learn of your poverty. Party invitations would be withdrawn and rumors of mental illness would circulate.

It was the volume of my mother's voice that drove me to pretend I didn't know her that day. For the first time, I was ashamed of my language.

"Do you see butter, Oksana?" Mom bellowed.

Anybody familiar with Eastern European cooking practices will understand the value of good butter. If you don't use a stick of the stuff in your recipe, you're either a miser or a lousy cook.

We had found the dairy section, and with it, our first dilemma: too many varieties. Butter, according to *Merriam-Webster*, is a solid edible emulsion obtained from cream by churning. How many different ways of churning are there? How many kinds of cream?

I missed the days when I'd walk up to our local market's dairy counter, ask the brightly lipsticked Elena Leonidovna for a kilo of butter, and be on my way.

"Oksana. What does this mean?"

I squinted at a beige tub Mom pointed to, studying it with the curiosity of an archaeologist. "'Fat-free.' I don't think that's good."

"Why not? What does this 'fat-free' mean?"

I envisioned a golden cloud of creamy mass floating in the sparkling sky, blobs of fat swirling around it in fancy-free abandon. "It means it has way too much fat. Fat has complete freedom. It has taken over this butter."

"Oh . . . then we don't want it."

In the produce aisle I almost forgot about my mother's vocalizations. I had never seen so much food in one place, not to mention so many off-season fruits and vegetables. The neat rows of unreasonably large strawberries and glossy apples made me think they must've come from a factory instead of a farm.

We couldn't splurge with the thirty dollars we had allotted for food that week, so we bought potatoes, bread, bologna, cheese, milk, and pasta. I did get the strawberries, but Mom drew the line at the apples, which she said smelled like candle wax. It took a good two hours, but in the end, we left with a sense of great accomplishment. And that night Roxy and I sifted sugar over our tasteless strawberry giants while I told tales of the market: not just a market but a *supermarket*.

The next task made me a bit more nervous: paying the rent. The landlady, Rosa Torres, lived downstairs in a unit tucked into the corner of the courtyard. Mom had officially elected me as her interpreter, though I could say little more than "My name is Oksana, I am fifteen years old."

At age twelve, with help from my tattered Russian-English dictionary, I had started writing songs with English lyrics. I performed this one at a school concert.

> *Today, me not to think of in the past.*
> *Stars to burn how fires.*
> *Them show to me way*
> *To fairy-tale valley full happiness.*

Only when I came to America did I laugh at those lyrics. Hurriedly I'd acquired a used Russian-English dictionary from one of the workers at the Russian Immigrant Outreach Program to replace the one my dad had taken when he left. Every day I opened to a random page and scanned the words, saying them out loud, trying them on for size. The ones I found especially beautiful I wrote down in my journal. "Transparent" was the first, then "shenanigans." I'd stand in front of a mirror and have conversations with myself in a language that still felt like a pair of new shoes. Or I'd repeat things I heard on TV, memorizing phrases like "buy one, get one half off." In front of that mirror I interviewed Madonna. In public I stuttered while buying milk.

"You know plenty of English, Oksana," Mom said as I knocked on the landlady's door, hoping for no answer. "At your age I spoke Russian with barely an accent." Russian was the official language of the USSR, but you could tell which of the fifteen republics a person came from by their accent when they spoke it.

I haphazardly pieced together all the useful words I could think of, and forgot them the instant the door opened.

"Jes?" Rosa smiled at me above the door chain. Her bleached hair shrieked next to her dark, pockmarked skin.

"Hello. We pay rent. Please. Thank you."

"Come. I'll give ju a receipt." Her apartment, rich with dark furniture against very pink walls, smelled strongly of beans, onions, and spices I didn't recognize.

We carefully counted out the money on top of Rosa's polished dining-room table: $450. But we didn't leave right away. One hour passed, another, and the three of us . . . talked. A true conversation. Rosa, an immigrant herself, had come from Mexico with her husband and daughter, Maria, six years before. Like Mom, she was now divorced. As it turned out, Maria and Roxy had met only days after we moved in and had without hesitation become best friends. And it wasn't long before our two broken families became very close.

Once Rosa saw the inside of our apartment she began to visit regularly. Almost every day, she walked up the stairs carrying a shiny toaster, or a chair, or some curtains for the bedroom windows.

Mom kept refusing the gifts, uncomfortable with the idea of taking handouts—especially since back in Russia, she'd been the one handing them out.

"*Mija*. This stuff is free and ju need it."

"Free?" I asked.

"Rich people gets rid of things. Good things. They leave them on street in front of their houses."

"To throw away?"

"Jes. But dose are good things: furniture, clothes. Expensive. I go to Beverly Hills and pick up for my garage sales."

That weekend Rosa talked Mom into going to Beverly Hills with her. Roxy, Maria, and I piled into the back of Rosa's purple 1978 Buick Regal, with Mom and Rosa in the front. We drove past unremarkable houses, but as the neighborhoods changed, those houses blossomed.

"Maybe my George lives here," Roxy said, staring out the window in fascination.

"Or not," I said.

"You're such a grump, Oksana. We should ask somebody."

We stopped at our first curb, where cardboard boxes overflowed with clothes and vibrant fake flowers. Rosa kept the car running. She tossed the boxes in the trunk and jumped back in, driving away quickly.

"It is okay to take them?" I asked. The process felt too much like stealing.

"Is fine. They jes don't like to see us do it." While Rosa stuffed the car with merchandise, I admired the grandeur of the impeccable lawns and the plentitude of Mercedes-Benzes. This, I thought, was the America I'd expected. Unfortunately, I was scavenging from its garbage.

We went to Beverly Hills regularly, raking in carloads of stuff Rosa later sold. Each time her Buick passed the Beverly Hills sign, we entered a universe most people glimpsed only on TV. On both sides of the spotless streets, beautiful palms swayed their model-thin necks. The houses lay scattered about like multicolored beads. Everything here glimmered with that special, extra-golden sunshine. And for the few hours a week we spent ragpicking, we, too, got to bathe in its rays.

D ad called our apartment a week before Christmas. Several months had passed since the last time we'd heard from him, and during that silence I'd tried to make sense of his actions. What did Roxy and I do to make it so easy for him to abandon us? Why did he never try to help?

Roxy had picked up the phone first, and we took turns talking to him in hushed voices while glancing in the direction of the kitchen, where Mom was battling with her hand-cranked meat grinder.

"You girls okay?" he asked in Russian. "How's school?"

I cupped the phone with the palm of my hand. "Everything's fine." He didn't need to know that although Roxy had been going to Marshall Elementary for the past month, I had refused to enroll in the local high school. "Where are you?" I asked.

"Are you coming home?" Roxy interrupted, sticking her face into the receiver and fighting to grab it as I pushed her away.

I hadn't asked him that question because I knew better.

When I'd heard him tell Mom that he loved her that night in Moscow, I'd believed he'd always live by those words. Yet he'd walked away from us as if our family had been a temporary arrangement. Some part of me wanted him back, but the stubborn me refused to let him know that.

"I'm sorry I didn't call you on your birthday," he said.

I wanted to tell him how he had ruined it for me. "No big deal," I said.

I'd turned sixteen a month earlier, in October. Mom had made brownies from a box. We'd never heard of brownies before, and she wanted to surprise me with an authentic American dessert. She'd ended up burning the mix into the pan. After dinner we scraped the remains off the sides. They tasted like dried fertilizer, and my birthday wish was never to have to eat brownies again.

Dad cleared his throat. "Is your mother there?"

I turned to check and found Mom drilling holes in me with her eyes. "Who is that?" she asked, but the question sounded more like "It better not be who I think it is."

Roxy jumped up and down in the middle of the living room. "It's Papa. It's Papa!"

Mom flew out of the kitchen, hair bouncing. She yanked the phone out of my hand, ordering us to leave the room, and shut the door.

Roxy and I ran to the bedroom and then listened with our ears pressed against the wall.

Growing up, I suffered from what I now call a split nationality disorder, never quite sure if I was Romani or Armenian. I was an impostor; a half-breed trapped between two vibrant cultures, never allowed a choice without guilt. My parents' breakup was feeling eerily familiar. I didn't know whose side to be on, and they made sure I couldn't choose both.

After some customary bickering my parents finally came to

an agreement on the subject that was the reason for Dad's call: the holidays. The winter season ranked high for both sides of my family, and even the worst rivalries were often temporarily put off to celebrate it. Roxy and I would spend Christmas with Dad, and New Year's at home with Mom. A truce, however shaky.

The following day, Dad picked us up in a dark blue van with pictures of howling wolves on its sides. No surprise there. When I was nine, he'd painted eyelashes around the head-lights of our Volkswagen Beetle and a tail in the back. Mom had refused to get in when she saw what he had done, but I'd thrown my arms around it and called it Sipsik, after my favorite stuffed toy.

It felt like years instead of months since I'd last seen Dad. He wore a leather jacket and pants, and had dyed his long hair to cover the gray. We managed a clumsy hug. Dad was never big on affection. Also, neither of us knew how broken families were sup-posed to act. Roxy, as always, had too much energy to be awk-ward. She jumped into Dad's arms and gave him two sloppy kisses on each cheek. "Papa, can I show you my George Michael book?" She reached out and grabbed a handful of Dad's ZZ Top beard.

Divorce was the new "empowered," or so my mother had been trying to convince me. But the moment I saw him, it be-came clear that we'd been lying to ourselves. I was glad to see him and mad at myself for being glad. On the way to his West Hollywood house, Dad made conversation as if nothing weird had happened, and even though I felt betrayed by his actions, I was happy to have him back.

"Girls, I have great news," he said. "I've got a few gigs booked for next year. What do you think of that, eh? Your old dad, back on top."

"You bought new equipment?" I asked.

"Not yet," he said, and I knew I shouldn't have asked that question. He grew quiet, shaking his head. "Remember my

Gibson? Now, that was an instrument to befriend the Devil for. No other guitar had such a juicy sound, like a ripe watermelon in July. Scored it off a Finnish tennis player."

"I know, Dad." A twinge of sadness made me want to wrap my arms around his neck. Before leaving Russia, Dad had sold everything except for his father's guitar. He had moped around for days as if he'd lost his entire family. And now he had, by his own choice.

He slapped a hand on the wheel. "No matter. I found a way to make extra cash. It's a premium idea. If everything goes well, we'll be rich by spring. I had a dream."

Here we go again, I thought. Dreams were my family's version of the *Farmer's Almanac*.

Every morning in Moscow, after Dad had dragged his feet into our kitchen, his hair Einstein-wild, he'd sit at the kitchen table, sigh, and complain about his insomnia, and then proceed to tell Mom about his dreams.

"I'm a spider," he once said. "Inside that new restaurant on Arbatskaya. And I'm biting my legs off. Then I see Elvis. He's a spider, too, except instead of legs he has guitars. And he's calling me to follow him onstage. Now, what do you think it means?"

"You should cancel that gig," Mom said, and then added as an afterthought, "Thank God you didn't listen to Elvis." Everyone knew that if you followed the dead in a dream, you'd soon perish.

There in the van, I didn't know what to say. Both my parents had hatched their share of ingenious plans that often backfired. Like the time Dad convinced Mom to sell homemade *oladushki* (pancakes) on the side of the Medvedkovo metro station. At first Mom laughed. "Why would people pay extra for our *oladushki* when they can make their own?" "For convenience," Dad said. We learned that Russians still preferred their own pancakes to those of strangers.

For this reason I didn't ask about Dad's latest scheme or the dream that had inspired it. Better not to encourage him, I thought. Roxy, on the other hand, began to list dozens of luxury items she would need Dad to buy with his millions. Even at a young age she knew that every courtship must begin with toys. Surely George Michael would not be able to resist a pink fairy bicycle with a matching helmet.

Immaculate houses lined both sides of Dad's street. This neighborhood was a galaxy away from ours.

"It's no Beverly Hills," Dad said, "but it's all I can afford right now."

On the outside, the house had a flat-roofed Spanish design, but once you stepped across the threshold, it resembled the interior of a traditional Romani wagon. Richly hued rugs swallowed every inch of the floor, some even continuing up the walls and to the ceiling. Everywhere I looked, I found yet more rugs and wall hangings. It would be very difficult for one to get hurt surrounded by so much wool. Red-and-gold shades predominated; there were burgundy-framed pictures, red statues of Hindu men on top of gold-colored elephants, and a number of bright-red pieces of furniture. I tried not to stare at the garish decor, but my eyes would not obey as they attempted to find a moment of peace.

Dad hadn't decorated on his own. One thing he couldn't stand was ethnic or folksy art on his walls. "Modern" was his motto. Our Moscow house had images of British flags painted on the bathroom walls, Miles Davis above the fireplace, and Japanese concubines in the kitchen. He had a style all his own. All signs pointed to one thing—my father's mistress was in the house—and before I had time to imagine myself charging at her with fists on the ready like a cocksure Irishman, she floated into the room to greet us.

"Girls, welcome. I am so happy you are here! Sit. Sit now, and I will make tea." Her dress sparkled like a Vegas showgirl's. Threaded heavily with sequins, it fell to her feet. Golden hoop earrings clinked through a mass of long black wavy hair. When she grinned, two golden teeth winked out of her mouth. She hugged Roxy and me zealously, an assortment of golden brace-lets jingling on her wrists.

People often comment on Gypsies' obsession with gold. Sometimes you can pick out Romani by the amount of jewelry they wear. This habit comes from a time when the wandering caravans didn't possess the freedom to settle anyplace long enough to grow roots, so wagons, forests, and riverbanks became their homes. But the wagons were often vandalized by outsiders, most of the forests belonged to uncharitable nobles, and the rivers were as unpredictable as the towns around them. The Romani learned to trust no one. They developed a tradition of carrying their wealth in the safest place they found—on themselves.

"How did you get here?" I blurted out, not expecting to see Olga, our old family acquaintance from Moscow, in my fa-ther's living room.

She flashed a diamond ring, and grinned. "We're married."

"What?" Roxy and I shouted in unison. This was the woman my father had gone back to Russia for? Olga was eigh-teen years Dad's junior, and besides the fact that she was not our mother, her reputation didn't stand out as exemplary. Olga was one of those Romani women whom tourists are warned about before their overseas trips; the kind *we* were warned about by Grandpa Andrei all our lives. She told fortunes for a living and would do anything to rid people of their money short of actually digging in their pockets. You'd never find her losing sleep over an unpaid bill or planning for retirement. If she had money enough to invite twenty guests for dinner, she would, even if it meant that she would have to eat cheese sandwiches for the rest of the month. Many of my Romani relatives considered her at-titude too risky for modern times. But Olga always said, "You can't plan life." A street-reared Romani, she'd come from a family that practiced but one motto: "Survive the day by all means necessary and start over tomorrow."

Although Olga danced fairly well, my grandfather had refused to have her in his shows, claiming she reinforced the stereotypes he'd worked to eradicate. So how did my father end up married to her?

It was about five years after my parents' divorce that I learned their affair had gone on for years before our move to the States. When Mom found out, just months before coming to America, Dad promised to stop seeing Olga. Turned out he'd been planning to bring her over all along and had waited until after the move to ditch us and send Olga a tourist visa. The marriage my mother was hoping to save was the furthest thing from his mind. Of course Olga had no intention of going back to Russia, but long-term resident visas were almost impossible to get. With a tourist visa Olga had a chance to come to America and get lost in the system.

My own father, an adulterer. In the past, every time Mom had accused Dad of sleeping around, I hadn't wanted to believe it. But the reality, I knew, was that many women thought of him as a catch. He was not only good-looking but also rich (at least in terms of Soviet-era Russians) by way of his parents.

Sitting around the kitchen table, Dad, Roxy, Olga, and I were soon drinking black tea together as if this were the natural order of things. On the outside, I was doing my best impression of a girl with manners. On the inside, I was a hunter with a fresh kill. I was dragging Olga by her hair out of the kitchen, across the scratchy living-room carpet, into the front yard, where I could skin her with my curved dagger. This Oksana was uncharacteristically ruthless, and I almost felt remorse until my mother's face came to mind. For Mom I was ready not only to mount Olga's head above a fireplace but to do so with Dad watching.

Olga had arrived in Los Angeles a few weeks earlier but had already come to the conclusion that Hollywood was a place with broken hearts galore. Plenty of immigrants meant great business potential. The woman never changed her ways—you could drop her in the middle of the Bible Belt, and she would not only find a way out but inevitably make cash doing so.

"I have already placed an ad in the local Russian paper," she told us through a cloud of Marlboro smoke. "'Famous Gypsy fortune-teller Olga, with extraordinary abilities to predict the future, will help you in your quest for happiness. Call, and see your troubles fly away.'"

"It's coming out next week. It'll be premium," Dad added, sitting between us and her at the head of the table. He bit into an open-faced salami sandwich, a trail of bread crumbs in his beard. Then he smiled at Olga. "You did a great job, my little sparrow."

They exchanged sweet looks. I was speechless and a little sick to my stomach. My father had never spoken a word of lovey-doveyness before.

"Ah, I can't wait to begin," Olga said.

I wasn't sure if she was exuding such enthusiasm for our father's benefit or ours. I had heard that she lived and breathed everything occult, as much at ease channeling spirits as she was shopping for shoes.

"But it's the holidays," I protested.

"Exactly. The best time for hooking the shunned, the desperate, the hopeful, and all the rest of the assholes who want miracles for pennies. Plus, the nights are more favorable for séances around Christmas and New Year's—you know that."

"But you were going to start playing again, Dad. You said you were buying equipment."

He shrugged. "Too many musicians in L.A. We're like rats scampering after a crumb of cheese. Remember my plan? This is it. I've got three gigs booked in February, and I need my instruments before that. But I can see already that no matter how many gigs you have, you can't make a decent living playing *gadjen* weddings in L.A. In this city, you need serious money to survive."

"But, Dad . . ." I said, still uncomfortable with the idea of Olga's psychic business. In the Soviet Union, practicing occultism or paganism was against the law.

Occultism might have persisted more in Russia than in the rest of Europe because we never truly experienced the Renaissance or the Enlightenment. If it weren't for Peter the Great introducing French culture to his country, ordering his ministers to shave off their "heathen beards" to appear more civilized, Russia might not have discovered progress for centuries to come. But Russians are stubborn people. Two hundred years after Peter, many still followed their ancestors' traditions steeped in thousands of years of superstition. Some believed in both Christianity and paganism, the practice called *dvoeverie* (two faiths), and I first encountered it when I was thirteen. Mom used to go to this ancient woman for readings, and if I insisted enough, she'd take me along.

Agrefina lived in a *derevnia*, a small hamlet, two hours north of Moscow. She was an oracle of sorts, a seer, but she never read for money. Mom brought her sacks of groceries one could find only in large cities. Toblerone chocolate bars were Agrefina's favorite. She'd cut them into chunks and share them with me.

I remember first seeing her house and thinking that I'd stepped into a fairy tale. It was made of logs, with a rooster-topped ridgepole on the roof and ornamental woodwork around the windowsills and doorframes. I thought they were for looks until Agrefina explained they were symbols of protection. The most important was a circular carving with a six-petaled rose in the middle, called *gromovoi znak*, or the thunder sign. It belonged to Rod, a pagan god of light and creation. Inside the house, a candle burned next to an icon of Jesus set high on a shelf. A large hand-carved cross hung over the threshold, and from it dangled a number of talismans in the form of gems and dried-herb sachets.

Having never seen anything like it, I asked Agrefina about the cross. She patted my head and replied, "The Lord minds not how we pray so long as we mean it."

I'd immediately drawn my own version of *gromovoi znak* in my journal. People like Agrefina fascinated me. Like Romani, they adapted to changing reality while retaining their beliefs. But what Olga had in mind had little to do with tradition and a lot with making money.

I didn't want Dad to be a part of it, especially not with Olga, whose Devil tarot depicted menacing figures with impish eyes. But she'd hooked him on the idea, and I could tell by the animation in his voice that he couldn't be persuaded to give it up. At least not by me. Maybe not even by his own father, who'd always been against divination.

Many Roma found Grandpa Andrei's attitude strange, particularly since his own mother, Baba Varya, had been a notorious magicker who performed spells in addition to being a healer and a midwife.

The very first thing I remember hearing about Baba Varya was that she was a giantess. The second, everyone was afraid of her. But according to the stories I'd collected over the years, she wasn't always a witch. She'd led a rather normal life as the wife of a farmer. They had three children who all helped tend the family plot. But one day her husband died unexpectedly and everything changed.

Grandpa Andrei said that after that, his mother withdrew from life for a very long time. She wasn't able to tend the land on her own and spent her time in a roomful of black-magic books. She started doing spells for the townsfolk, barely making enough money to support the family. Eventually they lost the

land. All three kids left school to work, but they never lived as
well as they had when their father was alive. All the stories after
this painted Baba Varya as a *vedma* (black witch).

But then I heard this from Aunt Laura: during World War
II Grandpa Andrei went to prison in Siberia for faking food-
ration tickets for his Roma band; the Communists didn't consider Gypsies to be model citizens yet, and the rations were
issued first to those loyal to the Red Party. The sentence was ten
years. Grandpa and a couple of inmates attempted escape from
their labor camp in Gulak, but got lost in the tundra for days. By
the time the authorities found them, Grandpa had developed
gangrene in his frostbitten toes, and the prison doctor gave him
no more than a couple of months before his feet would have to
be amputated. Grandpa sent Baba Varya a letter. At this time,
Baba Varya traveled with various caravans and only the Roma
knew her whereabouts. They used something they called *Tzi-
ganskaya pochta*, or Roma mail, to contact one another. Even
those Roma who didn't travel in caravans visited with relatives
throughout the year. It wasn't unusual for grandparents to stay
at each of their kid's houses for months, and the local Roma
were always aware if someone new showed up in town. The
mail was passed from hand to hand without the need for postal
service. That's why Grandpa's letter was addressed to:

Varya Nikolaevna,
In care of the Roma at the central Kiev marketplace

Baba Varya immediately set off for Siberia, carrying a jar of
homemade ointment, and once at the prison, she bribed the
infirmary medic to allow her entrance. Grandma Ksenia claimed
that the jar's contents were pure black magic, made from puppy
fat, but it could have been a simple folk remedy. No one knows
for sure. Black magic or not, Baba Varya saved her son.

Still, Grandpa Andrei had constantly lectured his employees about the harm that practicing occultism could do to their reputation as legitimate artists. Society didn't know the difference between gifted practitioners and scam artists. Once, he found out about Dad's spirit-channeling sessions; Dad defended his actions by claiming that he had the "gift" to help him lift the family curse. They got into a terrible fight over it and didn't speak for almost a year.

And now Olga had rekindled my father's fascination with everything occult.

"Girls, I know that the business will do well. I have seen it. Besides, your father is too old for the stage," Olga said, a sly glint narrowing her heavily penciled eyes. "Isn't that so, my honey-lambshank?"

Roxy's face lit up. "He's, like, Santa's age! It's true."

Olga winked at Dad. "Hey, Valerio? Those picks getting too heavy for you?"

Dad dropped his sandwich on the table with an indignant frown. "Who's old? Me? Your dipshit ex-husband is old, that's who! If I have to, I can wrestle a bear."

"Lucky for us there are no bears in Hollywood for you to terrorize."

Okay. So they acted like they had been cozily married for years; so what? I smiled politely, not completely sold on this show of domestic incivility.

"Oh, come on," Olga said, catching the lukewarm set of my lips. "I'm kidding. Your dad is a great musician. I'll bet you right now he'll soon be playing until his fingers fall off. I only think we can make more money by doing this on the side."

"Yeah, right," I said. "Nobody's going to pay you for reading their palms. This is America."

"So what? Everybody wants to believe something else controls their lives. That way, we don't have to feel responsible for what happens to us."

"But you can't lie to people to make them feel better."

"Who said anything about lying? I tell them what they want to hear. Like a head doctor, no? But instead of giving people pills, I have them sprinkle dirt in their husband's shoes and pray he will stop cheating."

"Dirt does not have superpowers," I said.

"No, but faith does."

ANCHEE MIN
China

Acclaimed novelist and memoirist Anchee Min (1957–) was born in Shanghai, China. As Mao's Great Proletarian Cultural Revolution was winding down, the fanatical student Red Guards, of which Min was one, were sent to work in the countryside to get "a real education" among the proletariat. At a collective farm near the East China Sea, Min was discovered at the age of seventeen by Madame Mao's talent scouts, and she became an actor in propaganda films produced by the Shanghai Film Studio.

Following Mao's death in 1976, many of the perceived shortcomings of his rule were attributed to Madame Mao, who was labeled a counter-revolutionary. Min and other performers became known as "Madame Mao's trash," and her status was reduced to being a "borrowed laborer." Joan Chen, an actress and friend from the Shanghai Film Studio, helped Min apply to universities in the United States as a means of escaping Communist China.

Despite revisions to immigration laws and the changing definition of what constituted China as a political entity, Chinese immigration totals nearly doubled each decade from 1960 through 1980 (from 237,292 to 812,178), with the bulk of immigrants being students and professionals. Although Min had neither extensive art training nor the requisite English competency, in 1984 she was accepted at the Chicago Institute of Art as a modernist painter and persuaded immigration officials of her potential as an international student.

When the Institute discovered that Min's English was insufficient, she was sent to the University of Illinois at Chicago for ESL, where she first began writing about her life for her English class. These early writings focused on her youth in China and would later be compiled into her first memoir, Red Azalea, *a* New York Times *bestseller that has been published in multiple countries. Twenty years later, she published her second memoir,* The Cooked Seed.

In many immigrant memoirs, education emerges as a primary means of acculturation, but for Min and others it is also the means by which they achieve immigration. Coming to the U.S. as a student requires the intrepid immigrant to face the financial and emotional challenges of immigration alone. The following excerpt depicts Min's initial experiences at the Institute of Art and how two female friends try to introduce her to U.S. culture. Unbeknownst to Min, her two eager friends have very different ideas about America, which leads to Min's first brush with U.S. race relations.

Excerpt from

The Cooked Seed

— 2013 —

I had never met my cousin, my aunt's son. I was told by my aunt that he would pick me up from the airport in Chicago. I held the paper with his name on it above my head as I exited the terminal. We met but were unable to communicate. I spoke Mandarin and he Cantonese. He was kind enough to allow me to temporarily stay at his student apartment. I promised my aunt that I'd leave as soon as possible.

The foreign-student adviser at the School of the Art Institute of Chicago was upset. I had lied about my "language skills" on the application form. In the "Please describe the level of your English" section, I had marked "Excellent." I confessed that I was guilty, and that I was willing to accept the punishment.

I was sent to the intensive tutorial class held at the University of Illinois Circle Campus. The program cost five hundred dollars. I already felt the weight of my debt and regretted having to borrow more from my aunt. It was painful for me to pay for the university's dormitory. I would have preferred to live on the streets.

I was given a tour of the school and the city of Chicago. I tried to read the street signs and memorize bus numbers and routes. But all I could hear was the soundtrack of a Chinese opera as I bent my head back to admire the Sears Tower.

When asked what type of roommate I'd prefer, I had replied, "Anyone who speaks English, and who doesn't mind my silence."

This was how I met Takisha, my first American friend.

The dorm room was way too luxurious for me. My first thought after entering the room was: I need to look elsewhere for a cheaper place to live.

Chicago's winter was brutal, but the room was heated. It had a window facing a tree. The hallway was freshly painted, and the shared bathrooms were spacious. That hot water was available twenty-four hours a day was incredible. I felt like a princess, because for the first time in my life I would get to sleep on a mattress. Each roommate had her own desk and closet. I was tormented by the amount I was paying for this. I found myself checking out the garbage Dumpster every time I walked by. I didn't need a mattress. I'd be fine sleeping on concrete.

I heard laughter and a loud knock on the door followed by the sound of a key turning. The door opened and a dark-skinned person entered.

An African freedom fighter, I thought. Takisha looked exactly like the girl I grew up seeing on a Communist propaganda poster calling for the Proletarians of the World to Unite.

Takisha enthralled me. She was a breathing sculpture with chocolate-colored skin and large, fig-shaped eyes. She had a wide nose and pink lips. She had the whitest teeth I had ever seen. Her hair was a ball of frizzy curls in the shape of a tall cake. She was about my height, five foot five.

I realized that Takisha was a cripple. She limped from side to side as she walked. It amazed me that she didn't act like a handicapped person. In China cripples would act timid and scared because they would be subjected to disrespect and vicious bullying. Takisha laughed loudly and freely.

I didn't expect Takisha to treat me like an old friend, which made me feel wonderful and grateful.

"I am Takisha," she said, opening her arms. "I am eighteen, and I am from Alabama."

My English escaped me. All I could do was smile.

"Oh, gosh, is it A.Q., An-Qu, or An-Qui?" Takisha giggled. "Oh, I'm so sorry. Forgive me if I don't pronounce your name correctly."

I tried to figure out what she was saying. I took out my dictionary and said to her, "English. Help."

"Where are you from?" Takisha asked, gesturing with her arms. "East, west, south, or north?"

I opened my *English 900 Sentences* book. "I name are . . . my name is . . ."

"I see, so you don't speak English." Takisha smiled broadly. "It's okay. No problem. Now follow me. Where . . . are . . . you . . . from? Where, watch my mouth, wh . . . *ere* . . ." She pointed her hand at me. "Don't look at your book. Look at me. Now tell me your home. Home. Do you understand? Home? Papa, mama, milk, dog. Do you understand what I mean?"

"No understand—"

"Hey, listen carefully!" Takisha pointed at herself. "Home Alabama."

I pointed at her. "Your home."

"That's right! My home, Alabama. Now tell me yours. Your home."

"Home? Do you mean h-o-m-e?"

Takisha laughed. "I mean your motherland—"

Yes, I knew the word *motherland*. It was one of the few slogans in English taught in China in 1972 during the visit of the American president Nixon. "I love my motherland" was taught along with "Long live Chairman Mao," "Long live the Communist Party of China," and "Albania is a great socialist country."

"Motherland is China," I said.

"Oh, you talk!"

"China, Papa, Mama, is China."

"You're from China! How wonderful! I want you to tell me all about China."

"Me English poor."

"You'll learn."

Takisha wanted to know how I had enjoyed America so far. I wished that I could have told her that I enjoyed air-conditioned rooms. I loved the flow of warm water from the faucet, I enjoyed sitting on a toilet, and of course the big moving room—the elevator. I loved the American city nights with the streets and buildings all ablaze. I couldn't imagine the cost of electricity, though. Most of all I enjoyed Takisha, the way she accepted me without reservation.

Takisha wanted to know what had brought me to America, and what life was like for me in China. With the help of my dictionary, I composed and wrote down my answer: "It was like you are hung, your neck bone is breaking, but death doesn't arrive."

"What?" Takisha frowned.

• • •

Takisha wrote words for me to look up in my dictionary. This was how I discovered that she was studying to become a doctor. I asked what motivated her to study medicine. She replied that she wanted to find a cure for her mother, who was severely diabetic.

"My mother is in bad shape," Takisha said. "You know what 'bad shape' means? Her doctor wants to cut off her legs. I said no way. I will not let anybody cut off my mother's legs. 'You will keep your legs,' I told my mother. 'I will be your doctor.'"

As I looked for words to express my admiration, I heard a ringing sound and saw that the room had a telephone. Takisha picked up the phone. "Excuse me, it's my mother!"

"My roommate IQ is from China," I heard Takisha say. "Hey, IQ, my mother says hello to you. Hey, wait a minute. Oops, her name is not IQ. It's A.Q. A . . . An . . . Qui . . . Oh, never mind, I'm sorry. How do I pronounce your name again? Ah-Choo? Ah-Chi? Ann? What? Oh, I see, An like Ann. Chee like cheese. Ann-Cheese. That should do it. I got it. Ann-Cheese, without the 's'! Did I get it right this time? What? A-n. Not A-n-n. An-c-hee. Oh, one more try. Okay, Anchee. Is it Anchee? Yes, I got it! Anchee!"

I turned to my *English 900 Sentences* while Takisha continued on the phone. It was hard to concentrate with the noise. I left the room and went to sit on the floor in the hallway. I buried myself in the book for hours on end. What confused me the most about English was its sentence structure, which was completely different from Chinese. For example, "You are not a thief," a policeman might ask. "You didn't steal, did you?"

In English, one would answer, "No, I didn't." But in Chinese, you must answer yes, meaning, "You are correct, I didn't steal." But it would be wrong in English if I said, "Yes, I didn't steal."

I also had great difficulty with *on, in, the, am, was, are*, and *were*. I could never figure out where and when to use them. *Have been, has been*, and *had been* also gave me trouble.

"Good night, Ann Chee," Takisha said, turning the light off on her side. I covered my lamp with my jacket and the room was instantly dark and quiet. I was tired and wished that I could go to sleep, but I knew I couldn't waste any time.

The next morning, the sound of a door slamming jolted me awake. It was followed by Takisha's loud voice: "Oh, I am *soooooo* sorry!"

This would be my alarm clock from now on. Takisha had a habit of slamming the door and then saying, "Oh, I am *soooooo* sorry!"

It was still dark outside after Takisha took her shower. She was drying herself with a towel in front of me. She didn't seem to be concerned about revealing her naked body in front of a stranger.

I left the dorm as soon as Takisha did. The day's task I had set for myself was to go to downtown Chicago. I planned to look for a job waitressing or dishwashing. I would knock on the doors of Chinese restaurants.

The tall buildings in Chicago were fantastic in my eyes. I didn't feel real walking between them. I was reminded how far I had come from home, that my feet were truly on American soil. I remembered the news clip depicting America's poor as I walked past the Chicago city hall, where a small group of people was picketing. It was as if I had stepped into the same TV scene, except it was not black-and-white.

I was surprised by how fancy the post office was. A large American flag hung above its entrance. I wanted to take a picture of myself under that flag and mail it home. My parents were worried about me. My letter to them would take three weeks to arrive in China.

I found a sign that read CHINESE RESTAURANT on Michigan Avenue and let myself in.

A lady greeted me asking, "How many?"

I put on my best smile and replied politely in Chinese, "Do you need a waitress or a dishwasher?"

The lady looked disappointed. She shook her head and waved me away.

I tried another restaurant and received the same response. I kept on. The begging part was the most difficult. I told myself that I must learn to get used to it.

I went as far as my legs could carry me. By the end of the day, I was tired and starving. I had visited every Chinese restaurant in downtown Chicago, but without luck. The one Chinese carry-out-only restaurant owner who had a help-wanted sign in his window said to me, "No English, no job."

On the sidewalk I was blocked by a fat lady who looked like a wrestler. She wore a dirty, grease-covered, brown knee-length coat. Holding a cardboard sign, she approached me. A strong scent of cheap perfume came from her messy orange hair. She spoke to me, but I couldn't understand.

"Sorry me no English," I apologized.

She flashed the sign in front of my face and stuck out her hand. "Spare some change?"

I took out my dictionary and looked up the words on her sign, HUNGRY & HOMELESS.

I said to her, "Yes English, yes job!"

The students in my English class came from all over the world. Since I had trouble pronouncing and memorizing their names, I tried to memorize their faces. It was not easy because black people looked alike, as did the whites and Hispanics. My classmates told me that they had a similar problem—to them Oriental people all looked the same.

A man from Italy with dark wavy hair sat on my right, and a beautiful high-nosed girl on my left was from Greece. With a lot of hand motions and make-believe words, we tried to communicate. Unfortunately, nobody understood anybody.

Our teachers were Americans. One was heavyset with curly blonde hair and the other slender with short dark-brown hair. I made it easier for myself by calling one Light Head and the other Dark Head. I secretly gave names to my classmates. I called the Italian man Michelangelo and the Greek girl Goddess Helena. I called another Middle Eastern–looking man Ali Baba, and a Russian Comrade Lenin.

What fascinated me was not the way the teachers taught, but what they taught. For example, the textbook featured a world that seemed unreal to me. It described an American small town where all the residents could vote and the people decided whether to give permission to a developer to build a shopping mall near the town square. Besides the town's mayor, there were also other elected officials.

Where I came from, everyone was considered "a bolt on the Communist machine." Unless you wanted to be arrested and spend the rest of your life in a prison or labor camp, you wouldn't ever voice your opinion against the authorities. I asked if the world described in the textbook was an accurate reflection of American reality. The teacher, Dark Head, turned to me and said, "Pretty much."

I didn't want to be too hard on my teachers, but I did want my money's worth. I was unsatisfied by the speed of the teaching. The teachers didn't press for results and allowed the class to run at its own pace. They assigned little homework, and only a few students turned in the work that was assigned. The teachers were okay with that, as if they didn't care. I seemed to be the only one who really drilled at the grammar.

Miss Light Head suffered a cold for several days. She carried a box that looked as if it had toilet paper in it. She called it "tissues." She kept sneezing. It made me want to laugh when I saw her cover her nose with toilet paper.

Each time she would blow her nose she would say two words: "Excuse me." I wondered why. There was nothing to be excused for—you couldn't help it when you sneezed.

In China, in order to ask to be excused, you had to commit a crime, such as wipe your behind with newsprint that had Mao's portrait on it, as my mother had once done accidentally. My mother didn't mean disrespect. She wasn't plotting an anti-Mao event. She was simply out of toilet paper and used the newspaper instead. It was hard to avoid Mao, whose portrait was printed on every page.

I found "excuse me" very useful. It was almost like saying hello. You would say it not only when you sneezed, but also when you entered a building, joined a line, walked past someone, or stepped off a train. I started to practice saying "Excuse me."

Then I couldn't stop saying it. "Excuse me," I said to the man who opened the door for me. "Excuse me," I said to the school janitor. People gave me the friendliest looks when I said "Excuse me." I loved saying "Excuse me."

I didn't mind Miss Light Head's "excuse me," but I did mind that she let the students do the teaching. She seemed exhausted by her sneezing and excuse me's. She sat in front of her desk, and the language cripples took over the class. I didn't pay to listen to the cripples!

Michelangelo loved to express himself in class. He had a thick Italian accent and would take forever to complete one sentence. Although I enjoyed his good looks, I couldn't understand much of what he was saying. What he said didn't sound like English to me.

The Greek Goddess Helena spoke with a thick accent, too. She told the class that she had just celebrated her twentieth birth-

day. "Happy birthday" was about the only English we under-
stood from her. She threw up her arms and tried to interrupt the
Italian. They got into a fight. Eventually they quit speaking
English and went with their native tongues.

People started to drift away. Comrade Lenin excused himself to get coffee while Ali Baba took his smoke break. A Frenchman said to a Korean girl who sat in front of him, "I love you! I
love you! I love you!" like a parrot. A Hispanic woman wrapped
in a bright-colored shawl started a heated conversation with a
black man dressed in yellow patterned cloth like an African
tribal chief. She told him that the trick to mastering English was
to sing it, and she was sure it was something he would do well
since he was from Africa.

The black man in the yellow patterned cloth explained that
he was not from an African tribe. He had been born in Germany
and grew up in France. The woman ignored him and kept going
on about singing English until he started to yell at her in French.
A Polish man with a thick beard told an Egyptian man who had
an even bigger beard, "English is ah . . . aard vark!"

I was appointed to partner with a short Asian man named
Suzuki. We were supposed to figure out where the other was
from.

"Japan?" I said, and he nodded.

"China?" he said, and I nodded, and that was it. We sat in
silence and wasted our time waiting for the others to finish.

During the last week of the class, the teacher came out of
her sneezing spell. She smiled warmly for the first time and took
control of the class. "We're going to play a game called Pass on
the Story," she announced. She whispered into the ear of a student who repeated the story to the next student.

When it was my turn, I listened with full concentration,
but I had a hard time understanding the accent of the Greek
Goddess Helena. I did my best to guess. The only word I understood was *ox*.

I was supposed to pass on the story to Michelangelo. Since I didn't get the full story, I decided to add my own version. I whispered into Michelangelo's ear a story about China's national hero, known as the People's Ox.

"He died pulling his rickety cart toward Communism," I said into his ear.

Michelangelo nodded as if he understood, and then he turned to the student next to him.

After the circle was completed, our teacher announced that her original story was lost.

I was excited about an ad I found in a free newspaper. The description read, "No skill necessary." With the help of my dictionary and Takisha, I came to understand that the job was to be part of an "experimental drug trial."

Takisha said that she wouldn't do it if she were me. "You will be used as a human guinea pig, a human rat—know what I mean? The drug will do damage to your vital organs."

"But it pays a hundred and eighty dollars per week!" I argued.

"Oh, money, Anchee, so you sell yourself! That's absolutely a bad idea!"

Anything that would help me pay my debt is a good idea, I thought.

Taking the subway to the northwest side of Chicago, I located the address I'd found in the newspaper. I didn't call ahead because I didn't want to reveal that I didn't speak English.

I was received by a middle-aged lady. She sat among stacks of papers piled high against her wall. After I filled out her form with my name and address, she read from a piece of paper, which I assumed was about the drug. The lady had a high-pitched child's voice. I nodded at the end of her sentences. I replied "Okay" to her "Okay?"

After she finished, she pulled out a box from an overhead shelf and presented me with a package filled with bottled pills. She told me when to take the pills and provided me with a booklet of forms on which I was to record my daily dosage of the drug.

"We'll be in touch." She smiled. "You'll receive the payment in the mail."

I got up and bowed slightly. "Thank you and good-bye."

"Wait, Miss Min, I need you to sign the contract here."

"No need, no need," I said quickly as I began to collect my stuff.

"I am afraid you have to, Miss Min."

"What is it?"

"It's the conditions and terms."

"I'll sign."

"You must read it first."

"I don't read English. I'll sign. I sign now."

The lady withdrew the paper. She stared at me suspiciously. It was too late when I realized my mistake. Before I could get out the door, the lady jumped from her desk. She grabbed my arm and took away the package of bottles.

"Please," I begged. "I need the money."

The lady pointed at the door. "Leave, now."

Kate was my next-door neighbor at the dorm. Her beauty reminded me of Esmeralda. With her makeup on, she looked like a cover girl out of a fashion magazine. When she spoke to Takisha in the hallway, I listened. Although I could understand very little, I enjoyed their conversation. I got busy with my dictionary as they talked.

Kate had the brightest eyes and a worry-free smile. Her manner was trusting and childlike. She didn't look like she had suffered any hardship in life. Kate was a little taller than Takisha and me. She loved to say to me, "Let's hang out, Anchee."

My dictionary showed me the meaning of *hang* and *out*, but not "hang out." So I asked Kate to explain what it meant. Like Takisha, Kate was not bothered that I was a language cripple. She didn't mind explaining and repeating until I got the meaning.

"Where . . . are . . . you . . . going?" she would say to me, for example. When I failed to understand, she would pick up my dictionary, locate the page, and point out the word for me. She introduced me to other people in the dorm. Now I was fluent in "My name is Anchee, spelled 'An-Qi,' and I am from China."

I noticed that Kate and others never said, "How do you do?"

Instead they greeted each other with "What's up, dude?" I told Kate that I couldn't find "What's up, dude?" in my dictionary, or in *English 900 Sentences*.

She laughed. "It's a silly expression, a fun way of saying the same thing."

From then on I changed my greeting from "How do you do?" to "What's up, dude?"

Takisha was unhappy about my visiting Kate. She tried to convince me that something was *wrong* with Kate. "She is rich," Takisha said. "Her parents must have a lot of money, or she wouldn't be able to afford a room all to herself." The other evidence of Kate being rich, according to Takisha, was that she owned a TV.

I wanted to explain to Takisha that I hung out with Kate because it gave me a chance to practice English. I knew how boring I was to Kate. It was like trying to have a conversation with a baby. I wouldn't want to spend time with anyone who spoke infant Chinese. I felt guilty about taking advantage of Kate. Takisha voiced her thoughts and views, but she was not interested in anything I had to say. My baby English didn't help either. In a way, Kate had become my best friend in the dorm.

I asked Kate, "What does 'goof around' mean?" She laughed and told me that it meant to have a good time.

I asked, "What are you supposed to do when you goof around?"

Kate laughed again and said, "Nothing!"

I took notes and wrote down the phrases I learned from Kate.

"You are funny, Anchee Min, do you know that?" Kate said.

"What does 'funny' mean?"

The afternoon turned into evening. I sat in Kate's room looking up words in my dictionary while she worked on her homework. I asked Kate what a real American classroom looked like and if she, by any chance, could show me.

"That's easy," Kate said. "Come with me to my business-marketing class tomorrow morning."

I became excited. "Are you sure I wouldn't be intruding? Will I upset your professor since I am not a student?"

"Nobody will notice you," Kate replied. "It's a lecture. It takes place in a hall with hundreds of people."

"Lecture? Will I get caught for not speaking English?"

"Well, pretend you do speak English."

I followed Kate to the cafeteria because I was curious about what kind of food she ate. She sat down with a plate of what she called "salad." This was the first salad I'd seen that was not made of potatoes. To a mainland Chinese, *salad* meant Russian food, which was basically potato. Kate told me that Americans didn't have a strict rule about what constituted a salad. "It could be a mix of lettuce with chopped cucumbers, carrots, onions and nuts, leafy greens, and, of course, potatoes. Basically, anything you want."

I couldn't help but laugh when I watched Kate eat. She chewed like a rabbit as she ate the raw leaves. "Are there salads in Chinese food?" Kate asked.

"No," I replied. "In China it's dangerous to eat raw greens. One can get diseases like malaria."

"So you cook everything?"

"Yes, mostly."

"Here, please share my salad." Kate gave me a fork. "This will be your first American experience. I insist."

In order to speed up learning English, I bought a used nine-inch TV set. The only shows I could follow were *Sesame Street* and *Mister Rogers' Neighborhood*. I had never seen anything like them in China. I fell in love with the gentle Mr. Rogers. Every day I would learn new phrases from him; for example, he would say "Good to go" as he finished tying his shoes. TV commercials became my lessons, too. My favorites were McDonald's and 1-800-Empire Carpet. Later I would get sick of them. I found myself improving so much so quickly that I decided to withdraw from the English tutorial class to save money.

An hour hanging out with Kate proved to be the most effective. I felt like I was walking out of the darkness and into the light. I began to understand bits of people's conversations. I also found myself less afraid. I saw a young man by the elevator. I remembered that he was Kate's friend Steve. When I returned to Kate, I told her, "I saw Steve in the refrigerator."

It took Kate a moment to realize what I meant. "Oh, you mean you saw Steve in the elevator?" The similar-ending sounds *-rator* and *-vator* confused me. When Steve came to visit the next time, Kate joked, "Hey, Steve, what were you doing in the refrigerator? My friend Anchee saw you there. Yep, she saw you in the refrigerator. What do you mean, no? Wait, hey, Anchee, is this the guy you saw in the refrigerator?"

• • •

I didn't realize the trouble I'd created until I heard a loud banging on the door. I was with Kate in her room. Kate got up and
opened her door. It was Takisha, and she was visibly upset. She
refused to step in when Kate invited her. Takisha leaned against
the doorframe and said to me, "What are you doing here, Miss
Anchee? Let me remind you that you have your own room and
your own roommate."

I smiled and said, "I am hanging out with Kate."

"I can see that," Takisha said.

"I am practicing English," I told Takisha.

"It's time to return to your own room," Takisha responded.

I said good-bye to Kate and followed Takisha back to our
room. Locking the door, Takisha motioned for me to sit down
on my bed. "We have to talk," she said. She went to sit on her
bed facing me.

"Thank you for coming back with me," Takisha began.

"You are welcome."

"May I have your attention?" Takisha asked. "Full attention, understand? I want you to listen."

"Attention, yes. You talk, me listen."

"I am going to share with you a piece of American history,
which I don't think you are aware of," Takisha said. "Know
what I mean?"

I nodded. "Know what you mean."

Takisha wrote down the word *slave* for me to look up in my
dictionary. She waited patiently until I located the word.

"I'd like you to understand that we, the black people of
America, used to be slaves."

"My dictionary says *slave* means *proletarians*," I responded.

"That's right! Slaves are proletarians!"

"Unite the world's proletarians!" I recited. "It's Mao's slogan."

"Mao who?"

"Mao Zedong, the founding father of the Communist Party of China."

I was shocked that Takisha had no idea who Mao was. I asked if she knew a famous African black who claimed to be the leader of the black slaves of the world, and who came to China in the late 1960s to study guerrilla warfare. Takisha shook her head.

I got busy with my dictionary. It took a long time to find the words I needed. Takisha looked restless. "The black slave leader wanted to meet Mao in person but was refused," I finally told Takisha. "In China, Mao was God. Mao was 'the reddest sun in the universe.' We worshipped Mao. A quarter of the population on earth. See what I mean? Over a billion people! How could anybody, like that African black, schedule a meeting with God?"

"So what happened?"

"Well, the black slave leader took the initiative," I continued. "To demonstrate his affection for Mao, he pinned a Mao button on his bare chest, took a picture of his bleeding chest and sent the picture to China's authorities."

"Did it work?"

"You bet!"

"But it's terrible!" Takisha cried.

"I couldn't pin a Mao button on my bare chest," I said, "although I loved Mao, too! Anyway, the Communist Party officials liked the story so much that they insisted it be told at schools across the nation. That was how I learned about it. The story convinced us that our leader Chairman Mao was popular in the world."

"Did the black guy get to meet Mao in the end?"

"It was said that Mao was so moved that he received the black slave leader inside his home in the Forbidden City."

Takisha had a hard time making me understand that there were differences between African blacks and American blacks.

"You all fight for the same freedom, don't you? In China, we consider all blacks our comrades in arms. We were afraid of whites and considered them enemies until recently. There were a few exceptions of course. One was the American journalist named Edgar Snow, and the other a Canadian Communist physician, Norman Bethune. Both of them came to China and devoted their lives to our revolution."

I asked Takisha to identify America's friends and foes. "Mao had said that such identification was critical to winning a revolution." I waited for Takisha's response, but she blinked her eyes and gave me a confused look.

"For example, China is friends with North Korea, Albania, and Vietnam," I said. "Russia used to be our friend, but since the Russians betrayed us, we dropped them."

Takisha said that the only famous black leader she knew and admired was Dr. Martin Luther King.

"I know Martin Luther King!" I said.

Takisha became excited. "Tell me, please, how did you know our King?"

"He was in China's school textbooks," I replied.

"Chinese school textbooks? Are you kidding me?"

"Mao wrote an article supporting Dr. Martin Luther King after he was murdered. Mao protested on behalf of the world's proletarians. Mao said that Dr. King's death showed that American society was an evil one."

"It is," Takisha echoed.

"Believe it or not, Takisha, I grew up shouting, 'Down with American imperialism!' but I didn't know where America was located."

"That's weird," Takisha said, looking at me.

"What does *weird* mean?"

"Well, *weird* means . . . 'weird.'" Takisha laughed. "Oh, I'm sorry—I was just teasing you. *Weird* is kind of like *strange*, okay?"

"Okay. Thank you."

"You are welcome." Takisha smiled. "Anyway . . ."

"What does *anyway* mean?"

"Oh, shoot, not again."

Daylight faded and the room became dark. I sat upright and listened to Takisha. I waited for her to stop. I wanted to ask Takisha if Dr. King had achieved his dream.

Takisha told me that her ancestors were slaves. I was confused by the tenses of Takisha's sentences.

Did the *re* sound in *they're* mean "are" or "were"?

While Takisha paused to catch her breath, I interrupted. "Are you a slave?"

"I am not a slave, but—"

I waited.

"Well, it's too complicated to explain."

"Try, Takisha, would you? I want to learn."

"I can't talk to you," Takisha said. Strangely, her voice sounded tear-filled.

"I am sorry, I mean no offense, Takisha. Talk to me, and educate me."

"You wouldn't understand."

"I shall understand if you talk to me. I'll write the words down. My dictionary is good. I can comprehend you."

"Listen, you'd never understand what it is like to be owned. You were never owned and never will be."

I knew what it was like to be owned. In fact, I didn't know what it was like *not* to be owned. The Communist Party of China and Mao never declared their ownership, yet every person in China knew that one never owned oneself. One was not allowed to do what one liked. Disobeying Mao and the Party meant hell and punishment.

Takisha was too provoked to come out of her own world. Words flowed out of her mouth like water from a broken pipe.

I concluded that Takisha might not be a slave, but her family members in Alabama might be. It would explain the anger Takisha had. She couldn't bear that I hung out with a white person like Kate. If being friends with Kate hurt Takisha, I was willing to stop. What I couldn't understand was the fact that Takisha was a medical student at this university.

Takisha told me that she was granted a "full scholarship" to study to be a doctor. I asked her who offered the scholarship, and she replied, "The government."

I asked who ran the government, whites or blacks.

"People of all colors," was Takisha's reply.

I found myself thinking: *I'd love to be a slave so that I could be given a full scholarship to study to become a medical doctor.*

In tears Takisha described how her ancestors were sold, beaten, hanged, and burned when they tempted to escape. I wondered what that had to do with Kate.

I interrupted Takisha. I told her that when I was living in China, I was not allowed to see a doctor when sick. I was not allowed to leave the labor camp when my spinal cord was injured. I had no weekends nor holidays. I was not allowed to pursue an education. The price for dating a boy at the labor camp would be humiliation, punishment, and torture.

"Have you heard of the Chinese saying 'Killing a hen to shock the monkeys'? It was the tactic the proletarian government adopted to keep us in place."

I described to Takisha what it was like to witness the revolution. The poor and lower classes took over the government. It was truly the People's Democracy. Within weeks, China's economy shut down completely. Factories, schools, hospitals, and other public service buildings became ghost towns. Even in remote villages, peasants quit farming to join the rebellion.

Being illiterate became glorious. It was exciting to challenge China's five-thousand-year-old tradition. Peasants took over hospital operating tables. They believed that anybody could perform a doctor's job. All one needed was to stock his mind with Mao quotations.

It didn't take long for factions to form. Rallies to consolidate greater power were held in stadiums, which often ended in bloody battles. Every day there were funerals in Shanghai. The city's walls filled up with photos of "new martyrs."

"My parents warned us to stay off the streets because people who had access to large trucks were looting weapons from military compounds. We could hear gunshots in the middle of the night." I told Takisha about the day a group of Red Guards from Beijing came to my house. "They received a tip from our downstairs neighbor saying that we were capitalists and had money. The Red Guards started to loot, but they quit in a few minutes."

"Why?" Takisha asked.

"They discovered that we were so poor that there was nothing to loot. Our downstairs neighbor had always been jealous of us for having a larger space than theirs. Eventually our neighbor drove us out of our home."

"Are there good things about poor people being in control of their power?" Takisha asked. "Did their life improve?"

"I wouldn't say so. Most people had to get up before dawn to go to the market," I replied. "We had to stand in long lines to buy food. People became irritable and violent after standing in lines for hours in heat or snow only to be told to go home because everything was sold out. I fought with other kids over rotten cabbages and potatoes. Some people simply turned into thieves."

I told Takisha that my parents sent us to my grandparents on my father's side in the summer. The village town was located in Jiangsu province by the Yangtze River. We thought we would escape the Red Guards, but no, they were there, too. When we arrived, a denunciation rally was being held against my grandpa, who lay on his bed suffering from a stroke. The Red Guards couldn't get any response out of the old man. My grandpa was a retired schoolmaster. The Red Guards were mad at my grandma, because she wouldn't cooperate either. She was deaf and mute. She had bound feet and was barely able to walk. She couldn't tell the difference between the new and the old society.

SHOBA NARAYAN
India

Shoba Narayan (1968–) was born to a Hindu family of the Brahmin caste in Coimbatore, India. They enjoyed a comfortable life in a suburb of Madras, where Shoba, like many Indian Hindu children, attended Christian schools. As a student at India's Women's Christian College (WCC) studying psychology, Narayan was accepted to its sister college, Mount Holyoke, as a Foreign Fellow. Proud of their daughter's accomplishment, her parents allowed her to go, even though they feared she might start a family in the U.S. and remain. At twenty, Narayan arrived in South Hadley, Massachusetts, to begin a year's visit.

Indian immigration increased significantly following the passage of the Immigration and Nationality Act of 1965. The overwhelmingly urban and educated second wave of Indian immigrants, an estimated hundred thousand between 1965 and 1975, adapted quickly to life in the U.S. Since 1965, nearly 40 percent of Indians entering the country do so through student or exchange-visitor visas, with most pursuing graduate degrees, after which they frequently secure work and permanent residence. As a result of large-scale Indian immigration between 1990 and 2000, the ethnic population grew 113 percent, while the total U.S. population increased only 13 percent.

Narayan was "eager to lose" herself within Mount Holyoke's "expansive embrace" and pursued coursework in both journalism and the arts. She appreciated the small-town charm of South Hadley, and the college students eagerly introduced her to U.S. culture. After a year, Narayan returned to India to complete her psychology degree at WCC. She also agreed to an arranged marriage to Ram, a Western-educated financial *consultant with whom she returned to the U.S., where Narayan soon took a master's degree in journalism from Columbia University.*

"The God of Small Feasts" (2000), Narayan's essay about the role of food in convincing her parents to permit her to keep her fellowship, won the James Beard Foundation's M. F. K. Fisher Award for distinguished culinary writing. Food remains central in Monsoon Diary: A Memoir with Recipes *(2004), the source of the following excerpts. Narayan's second memoir,* Return to India *(2012), continues with the author's difficult decision to repatriate to India with her husband and children. Having written for numerous publications in the past, Narayan is currently a columnist for* Mint Lounge, *an Indian business daily, and* The National, *a newspaper in the United Arab Emirates.*

Excerpt from

Monsoon Diary

— 2004 —

The sun was setting when the plane landed at Bradley International Airport in Connecticut. Clutching my suitcase and handbag, I came out of baggage claim, shivering slightly from the cold and my own nervousness. It had been a long journey and my first international one: Madras, Bombay, onward to Paris, before clearing customs in New York's JFK Airport. Then a terrifying ride on the airport shuttle—watching for pickpockets, muggers, and drug addicts—to New York's domestic airport, La

Guardia, and finally Bradley, where I was met by a smiling, spectacled girl who introduced herself as Quatrina Hosain.

Within minutes we were on our way. I tried to pay attention to the newness of my surroundings but felt tired and groggy. It was dark when we reached Dickinson House, where all the Foreign Fellows lived. Inside, Seema, an Indian girl who had just arrived from Boston, was in hysterics. She had been allotted a room on the ground floor and wanted no part of it. Anyone could break the window and enter her room, she said. Apparently, stories about America's muggers were not confined to just my family.

Harriet, the head resident of Dickinson House, was clearly distressed. An elderly woman with a platinum coif, she was not used to volatile displays of emotion so early in acquaintance. When I walked in, she saw a solution. Would I switch rooms with Seema?

I didn't especially want to live on the ground floor, but a lifetime of proving myself equal to any boy prevented me from saying that I was just as scared. So I mutely nodded assent and Harriet almost hugged me.

My room was spacious, comfortably equipped with a bed, writing table, lamps, armchair, and a closet for my clothes. The college even supplied my pristine white bed linen. All I needed was a warm nightgown. It was September and my cotton clothes were already proving inadequate for the nip in the air.

Before retiring for the night, I peered through the window into the darkness outside. All my childhood fears about monsters and intruders surfaced, in spite of Harriet's assurances that nobody could open the window from outside. I lay in bed, leaving the lights on just in case.

As a Foreign Fellow, I was given carte blanche to study whatever I wanted for one year. I signed up for all those subjects that I had been interested in but never had the opportunity to pursue: piano lessons, theater, modern dance, music composition, and journalism.

At twenty, I was a tabula rasa, eager to learn. And South Hadley, although I didn't realize it then, was a safe place to begin my exploration. It was the quintessential New England town, with undulating roads, steepled churches, white picket fences, Colonial homes with sloping roofs, and little traffic. After imagining America as a vast, noisy metropolis, I found South Hadley, with its tiny Main Street dotted with a single bank, post office, restaurant, and general store, a pleasant surprise.

Everything was new: a falling leaf with flaming colors; pennies, nickels, dimes, and dollars; a bagel, with a hole in the center; cold spells in September. The cleaning lady who drove a Cadillac, unlike Ayah, who came by foot. Vegetables in boxes with nary a soul to haggle; cold cereal instead of warm *idlis* in the morning. Strangers smiled and said hello. Nobody littered, spit, or cursed.

I got up every morning and went to nearby Rockefeller Hall for breakfast, since my own dorm didn't have a dining room. There was a dizzying array of food: softly folded omelettes that I spiced up with Tabasco sauce; breads, round and square; pastries sprinkled with sugar, called doughnuts, even though they didn't have nuts. Waffles, French toast, pancakes, a bounty of sauces, cereal boxes with cartoon characters on the side, fruits that I didn't recognize, creams and cheeses, milk of various fat percentages. I would stand in front of the counter, overwhelmed by the choices.

Harried servers tossed questions at me: did I want it toasted or untoasted, with or without syrup, orange or apple juice, coffee or decaf, skim or regular? When I blinked uncomprehendingly, the people in line behind me shifted from one foot to the other. I could hear the sighs and feel the impatience. I was used to my mother plunking a plate in front of me and ordering me to eat. I was not used to choosing something and having it lead to yet another choice. I was not used to thinking about food in such a specific fashion.

I told my breakfast mates that I wasn't used to eating sweet food—jams, jellies, and syrup—so early in the morning. When I added that a main component of my morning meal was a spicy *dosa* with chili powder, they looked shocked. A Japanese student added that she ate rice and salty miso for breakfast. It was perhaps my first lesson in globalism.

One month into the program, I met my host family. Incoming foreign students were assigned to American families who had volunteered to help us adjust to America and serve as surrogate parents. Mine were Mary and Doug Guyette, who lived in neighboring West Springfield, and their two daughters, Margie and Kathy. They were my window into family life as I attempted to piece together the jigsaw puzzle that was America.

On a chilly October evening Mary picked me up at my dorm and took me out to dinner at a fancy Northampton restaurant along with her teenage daughter Kathy. When she noticed that I was throwing my garbage into a cardboard box, she quietly equipped my room with a wastebasket, table lamp, and a few other essentials that I didn't realize were essential. Two weeks later she drove me to a giant, sprawling shopping mall, the likes of which I had never seen before, and bought me my first Elizabeth Arden makeup box, a glittering pink-and-gold confection with eye shadows, mascara, lipsticks, and foundation.

When I told my mother about it during our monthly phone calls, she was delighted. "A girl needs makeup and you won't wear any," she said. "I'm glad someone is taking you in hand."

A middle-aged woman with kindly eyes, Mary held a part-time job and was very involved in her church. Her husband, Doug, worked at a bank and drove an impressively large Cadillac. Occasionally he would pick me up on Friday evening and drive me to their house for the weekend. Their elder daughter,

Margie, was away in the Peace Corps, while Kathy, lanky and reserved, was in high school.

We would have supper together: salad, bread, rice and beans for me, chicken for them, a fruit tart of some sort, and coffee afterward. At first the conversation was stilted and awkward. They were too polite to probe, and I was intimidated by their accents. I had hundreds of questions—which came first, fork or spoon? how many dates did it take to "go steady"? which trees changed color in the fall? what subjects did Kathy study in high school?—but I concentrated merely on making sense when I did speak.

It was at Mary and Doug's house that I got my first glimpse of American family life, the soap and suds of it, the gentle grace of setting a table with fork and knife rather than baldly eating with our hands as we did back home; the carpet and ruffled curtains; and "my" bedroom upstairs, which smelled of linen and rose potpourri.

I loved my classes. Most of the subjects I chose were fantasies come true rather than a natural progression of my studies. I signed up for music composition without knowing how to read or write Western music and having listened to it only rarely. I didn't play an instrument. I was a music imbecile with lofty aspirations. Allen Bonde, the professor, wasn't insulted when I told him that I had only trained in Indian classical music. He didn't kick me out of class like I expected him to. Instead, he told me to record my compositions and offered to transcribe them for me.

I sought out one of the piano rooms in the music building and improvised, experiencing for the first time the thrill of creation. When my piano skills didn't keep pace with the tunes in my head, I hummed them into a tape recorder. In class, while the rest of the students demonstrated their homework compositions through flying fingers and sheet music, I simply turned on the boom box.

Claire, a fellow student, took pity on me and transcribed my improvisations into organized sheet music with notes that moved up or down according to the rise and fall of my voice. I wandered the halls of the music department trying to decipher the various instrument sounds coming from within closed doors and figure out which one was suitable for a particular section. Occasionally, when I didn't recognize an instrument, I barged in and asked the surprised musician what she was playing. When she gave me the name of the composition—Mozart's Sonata in D Major or whatever—I shook my head. "No, I meant the name of the instrument," I muttered, embarrassed by my ignorance.

At the end of the term there was a recital of all our compositions complete with a program sheet. My piece had four instruments: piano, violin, cello, and flute. It was probably amateurish and middling, but it was mine. Gloriously, totally mine.

My theater class was just as exciting. Something was always in production—Alan Ayckbourn, *Medea*, O'Neill, and Shakespeare in rapid but disconnected progression during my term.

I was put to work on the sets. The set designer, a bearded salt-of-the-earth man named John, countered the air of high drama elsewhere in the building with his dour humor. On my first day, he handed me a chain saw with the injunction "Don't cut your fingers off."

I was pleasantly surprised by his confidence in my abilities. While my parents or teachers in India had never denied me something just because I was a girl, I had to work hard to gain their trust.

Not so at Mount Holyoke. The professors displayed their faith in our abilities without a hint of condescension. They weren't foolhardy. John stood by me while I gingerly held the chain saw, he heard me gasp when I turned it on, my body vibrating like Morse code in reaction, and watched through narrow eyes as I aimed it on a piece of wood and slowly, deliberately, cut a jagged line. I turned off the machine, exhilarated by its power.

The chain saw was just the beginning. I discovered that I loved power tools and was constantly at the "shop" begging John to teach me how to use the sanders and polishers, screw and staple guns, chisels, ratchets, and wrenches. I memorized the various sizes of drill bits and saw blades and learned to estimate the thickness of wood without a tape.

A few weeks later I found myself striding into the shop and wielding a rotary hammer with careful confidence. I glanced at myself in a mirror as I stood there in my paint-streaked apron, helmet, goggles, gloves, and earmuffs, bent double over a thudding machine that was half my size and shrouded by a cloud of dust and wood chips. I looked like a space alien. I felt like Superman. Or rather, Superwoman.

I was deliriously excited by the novelty of it all, so wildly enthusiastic and eager to learn that nobody had the heart to turn me down, to say no.

At Mount Holyoke I was offered a world without context, and I approached it like a child, unfettered by the American stereotypes that I have since learned. When a woman told me that she lived in Hollywood and summered in Cannes, I didn't know enough to differentiate her from the work-study student who had graduated from the Bronx High School of Science. I didn't know that plaid skirts were preppy and batik prints bohemian. I was deprived of all the clues that I normally used to typecast people.

I couldn't tell if the women around me were rich, poor, or middle-class, if the clothes they wore were fashionable or gauche, if their accents were crude or sophisticated. In India I could slot a person into a stereotype within a few minutes, just by her name, the way she talked, and what she wore. At Mount Holyoke I couldn't even tell if a girl was pretty or not. My ideas of beauty were different from theirs. When I showed my American friends some of my family photographs, they didn't think that the "beauty" of our family—a fair cousin with an oval face and long hair—was actually beautiful. Instead, they gushed over another cousin with asymmetric dark features and cascading curly hair.

As a result, I brought no prejudice to my interactions. I simply didn't know enough. I couldn't read between the lines or see beyond their smiles. While my ignorance prevented me from penetrating the façades of the American girls I met, it also prevented me from indulging in what had been the bane of my teenage existence in India: comparing myself with others. In India I was constantly comparing myself with my peers and feeling inadequate, embarrassed, or superior. At Mount Holyoke I was simply me. Not me, the middle-class Madrasi who went to the fashionable Women's Christian College; not me, the daughter, granddaughter, sister, and niece, but just me, Shoba the student.

I was enamored of America's newness, eager to lose myself within its expansive embrace. I wanted to suck it all in. At dinnertime I would approach total strangers without qualms and ask to sit at their table. These women (Mount Holyoke emphasized the fact that we were women, not girls) were probably too dumbstruck to refuse, and if they threw out any hints for me to get up and leave, I didn't recognize them. It was over these long lunches and dinners that I made friends and learned about the country.

I met a lot of people—at Rotary lunches and campus dinners, at receptions and in the dining room. People took me into their homes, their churches, and their offices. Over roasted marshmallows at an Amherst home, I learned about Thanksgiving, Halloween, and other American holidays. In between chanting "Go, Red Sox!" at a baseball game in Boston, I eavesdropped on a discussion about Michael Dukakis, the state's gov-

ernor who was running for president. I learned that when people
greeted me by saying, "Hi! How are you?" the correct response
was not to elaborate on how I actually felt but to toss it right
back at them with a "Fine. How are you?"

They were a proud people, these New Englanders, and I
envied their Yankee directness, unencumbered by eons of tradition. They were also curious and asked a lot of questions. As the
months passed these questions took on a predictable pattern. One
that popped up within five minutes of any encounter, be it at a
bar, in a corridor, or at a luncheon, was "Where are you from?"
I didn't mind answering that I was from India, but I disliked the
way India became the sole topic of conversation after that. Some
international students loved talking about their countries. I
didn't. I didn't care for the caste system, I didn't know enough to
talk about Indian politics, I resented having to defend my country's poverty, and I was insulted when people asked if Indians
rode on elephants. Over time I grew to hate the well-meaning
friendly question "Where are you from?"

As long as I was in small-town America, I realized, I was
no longer just a person. I was a representative of my country. It
was a daunting realization and an enormous burden.

I started working in the kitchen at the Rockefeller cafeteria to
make some money. Tom, the head chef, was a demanding man
but a good teacher, A ruddy, volatile New Yorker, he was humorous or bad-tempered depending on the time of day. When
I checked in at 9:00 A.M. the whole kitchen was relaxed as we
prepped for lunch. Tom taught me how to chop vegetables for
the salad. He had a particular palate and insisted that we do
things his way. Mashed potatoes had to be coarse rather than
creamy so that you could feel a potato or two in your mouth.
Clear consommé with julienned vegetables was better than
blended soup with no distinguishable flavor. The salad bar had
to be set up in a logical fashion. "Why do you put the celery

before the croutons, huh?" Tom would bark. "It isn't alphabetical; it's logical. Do people pile on croutons after celery?"

Even though he was an equal-opportunity taskmaster—everyone in the kitchen had to do everything—Tom let me stay away from the meat, knowing my aversion to the sight of blood-lined beef or fish with beady eyes. But when I mentioned that I was willing to deal with any meat item that I didn't recognize as a particular animal, he had me flipping burgers. On burger days—always popular—Claire and I stood beside each other, flipping a dozen hamburgers at a time, spurred by Tom's incessant shouts of "Keep 'em coming!" Claire was a musical wizard who could transcribe my hummed tunes into musical compositions, but I proved to be more adept at flipping, something that I took great pride in.

As the clock inched toward the lunch hour, Tom's temper mounted. Besides the salad bar, lunch included a hot entrée, a side, and a vegetarian alternative. This was not an overcooked, underspiced, never chopped clump of vegetables that masqueraded as a vegetarian dish. Mount Holyoke had hearty, flavorful fare from around the world, and I dug into the food with gusto. Pastas, pizza, enchiladas, falafel, potato pierogis, and vegetable fried rice. I tried them all.

I couldn't bring myself to eat meat, and the fact that Claire described a hamburger as tasting like "chewing gum" didn't help either. I learned to love cheese and tolerate eggs, and I didn't eat anything that moved. But I always returned to Indian food. While the foreign flavors teased my palate, I needed Indian food to ground me. When all else failed, I would sit in my dorm room late at night, mix some rice with yogurt and a dash of salt, and gobble it down.

Yogurt rice is the classic end to an Indian feast. After eating spicy curries, Indians like to finish up with a simple, bland, soothing mixture of creamy yogurt and plain white rice. I had eaten this dish countless times growing up in India, and at

Mount Holyoke it became my salvation, my weekly comfort food.

Sometimes, I would take some chopped tomatoes, onions, and cucumber from the salad bar, ask Tom for some ginger, green chiles, and a sprinkling of curry powder, and retreat into my room with a tub of plain yogurt and cooked white rice. I would mix it up and indulge in my secret treat, sitting cross-legged on my dorm bed and thinking about Uma, trapped in the blue-lit underworld.

On moonlit nights, my uncle took us children to the roof and told us stories. Our favorite was the Blue Light story in which the ten-year-old heroine, Uma, was trapped in a blue-lit underworld populated by goblins and gremlins. We sat in a circle, wide-eyed, jaws agape, as my uncle described how Uma made yet another desperate attempt to claw her way out of the underworld and join our world above. Halfway through the story, my grandmother would come upstairs with a large pot of yogurt rice. She would roll it into bite-sized balls, spoon a dollop of *inji* curry on top, and press it into our palms. We would absently pop the balls into our mouth, engrossed by the monsters, gremlins, and bad guys who foiled Uma's escape plans. The Blue Light story never ended. We simply grew up. . . .

I took on other campus jobs. I babysat for the French professor, worked in the greenhouse for a couple of afternoons just to feel the heat of my hometown. I begged and cajoled alumni into donating money for the college during a massive fund-raising phonathon. On many nights I worked at the dorm's reception desk, or bell desk as it was called.

In between asking visitors to sign in and answering the telephone, I decided to finish a play that I had started writing while at WCC. I was deluded enough to send it in as an entry for the Five College Theater Workshop held at Smith College, and flabbergasted when it was accepted.

For three days, five of us playwrights and several volunteer actors and actresses practiced our craft under the watchful eye of Kathleen Tolan, a New York playwright-in-residence. Two actors and two actresses read parts from my play, thrilling me by reciting the lines I had written—and also showing me how soppy some of them were. In a frenzy, I wrote and rewrote the play, which Kathleen ended up directing.

At the end of the workshop the five plays were performed in a small but packed auditorium for three nights. I had written what I thought was a melodramatic tragedy, similar to the Indian movies I watched as a child. The scenes were heavy with symbolism and nostalgia, the lines full of sadness and longing. I was shocked to see the audience laughing throughout the performance. They thought the lines were over-the-top, the characters larger than life. They thought it was satire.

I was beginning to realize that my critical faculties were rather underdeveloped.

On Fridays the dorms hosted dozens of parties. Mount Holyoke is part of a five-college consortium that includes Amherst, Hampshire, and Smith Colleges and University of Massachusetts at Amherst. We could take classes in any of these schools, and their students could come to ours. This cross-pollination worked, especially on weekends.

Friday nights found me in the room of my friend Natasha, a dance major from my modern dance class. Tall and statuesque with curly auburn hair and speckled green eyes, Natasha was popular. A succession of men came to pay homage to her, waiting in the lobby while she got dressed. I would sit in her room munching popcorn and watching her smudge gloss over her lips and line her eyes carefully. After an hour of primping she would stand in front of the mirror and pout coquettishly.

Natasha always invited me to go with her, but I refused, not wanting to be the third wheel in a couple. Then one day her date stood her up and a furious Natasha insisted that I accompany her to a frat party.

We took the Five-College free bus to Amherst, Natasha in her short sequined skirt and me in my tight black pants. Music blared from every house on Frat Row; cars honked as people dropped off dates and angled for a parking space. Natasha and I skipped up the stairs. It was so crowded we could hardly get in. There was beer everywhere, in kegs, on the floor, in half-finished bottles. Cigarette smoke swirled lazily up to the ceiling. The music was deafening.

Natasha confidently pushed through, shouting out hello to a Robert here, a Greg there, dodging old boyfriends and meeting new ones. From a keg in the corner she poured some beer into a plastic glass and handed it to me with the injunction "Sip." The frothy yellow liquid tasted liked yeast and grain water. I tried some more.

"Don't leave me," I said, clutching Natasha's arm, intimidated by the ruddy faces with wide, plastered smiles.

Suddenly, screams erupted in the backyard. Natasha and I elbowed our way to a window. A group of men were emptying kegs of beer into a large hot tub. Someone pumped up the music. Men carried women and threw them into the beer-filled tub. It felt like a mob was about to go on a rampage. I was terrified.

Greg, Natasha's old boyfriend, lurched toward us. Goofy and good-natured, he had endeared himself to me by his realistic imitation of an Indian accent. He was one of Natasha's ex-boyfriends whom I actually liked.

"Ladies! Your turn," he said, grinning.

As we screamed in protest, Greg dragged us toward the hot

tub and pushed us in. I sat there, shaking my head like a spaniel, surrounded by strange men and women, all of whom were laughing like banshees. Somebody retched; everyone scampered out. Shivering, I stood in a corner, looking for Natasha. She had disappeared.

There were more screams, this time from inside the house. Curiosity overcoming caution, I elbowed my way back in and stood mesmerized at the sight of a long line of freshmen swallowing dead goldfish as an initiation rite into the fraternity, while their "brothers" thumped fists and shouted words that were Greek to me. Once I realized that I wouldn't get assaulted, I exhaled and let my shoulders down. I looked at an attractive man standing nearby and smiled. The night was getting interesting.

It was at Mount Holyoke that I encountered feminism for the first time. I remember clearing my throat one evening after dinner and asking the others around the cafeteria table what I thought was a naive, innocuous question: "So what exactly is this feminism that everyone talks about?"

I was not prepared for the torrential response from the Frances Perkins Scholars—older women who'd come back to finish their education. Feminism was about inequality, they said. It was about women getting paid sixty cents for every dollar that a man made. Feminism was about choices and freedom. It was not having to play games, not having to defer to a man even though you were smarter than he was.

The ideas and concepts were new to me, but they made sense. I came from a society in which women deferred to men in public but ruled the roost in private. This was the first time I was hearing that described as a "game" that women should not have to play. However, what stayed with me long after that evening ended was the anger I felt coming from these older women. I couldn't help comparing Beverly, Anne, and Ellen with the women in my family.

While my mother didn't have the anger and resentment that was simmering in these women, she wasn't as free as they were either. She was tethered by rules and tradition, and limited by her own vision of herself. She wouldn't dream of wearing the stylish, tight clothes that Beverly wore, even though they were the same age. She would sniff at Anne's enthusiasm and Ellen's loud laugh. She would say that they ought to act their age.

But my mother had done many things in her life, just like these women. She had my father's support, for sure, but she also had the confidence to undertake new ventures. Would she have opened a beauty parlor against my father's wishes? Probably not. Did that mean that she was suppressed? Was it better to question and overthrow the system as these women did or to navigate within its confines like my mother had done? Which made a woman happier, being single and independent or being married and confined? I didn't have an answer. Indeed, it was the first time I was even asking those questions.

The contradictions between my two cultures—one that I was born into and one that I adopted—were enormous. India's fatalism was in direct contrast to the flux I felt in America. Everyone was moving, searching, asking for more. People were changing spouses, changing jobs, changing homes, changing sexes. It seemed like the more choices people had, the more they searched for something else, something new, something different.

I went many places on weekends. Kim Kusterlak, who was in my theater class, drove me to her home just outside Boston. When Kim announced that I was vegetarian, her father, bald, jolly, and Turkish, rubbed his hands with glee. "I will make you my favorite dish," he said. "Cabbage dolma." I helped him mince carrots, onions, and other vegetables and watched him stuff the dolma. Kim's mother, a fashion designer, sat at the kitchen table, sketching designs and smoking a cigarette. "Don't tuck your shirt into your pants, dear," she told me in a husky voice laden with drink and smoke. "You are short-waisted and it doesn't suit you."

Susan Smith, my kitchen coworker, took me to her home, set amidst a sprawling wooded estate. Susan informed me that it was owned by the Whitney family, her voice suggesting that they were somehow very important. Susan's father was the groundskeeper and manager. We ice-skated on the lake on the property, or rather, Susan ice-skated and I careened, mostly on all fours. We built a fire and drank port, while her father, a ribald Englishman, regaled us with stories of his youth. Susan took me to tea at the owner's mansion. We wore skirts and sat side by side eating thin finger sandwiches off dainty china, while the matriarch quizzed Susan about her studies, which the family was funding.

My Greek dorm mate took me to her home in Cape Cod one weekend, where her large, boisterous family feasted on a buffet dinner. Maria's brothers boasted about the size of the fish they had caught and suggestively eyed me through dark eyes rimmed with thick lashes. I tasted rice wrapped in grape leaves, eggplant moussaka, and a fragrant, fresh Greek salad with crumbly feta, juicy olives, and crisp romaine lettuce. It was the first time I tasted Greek salad, and I loved the combination of flavors immediately.

Claire Wilson, who transcribed my music, invited me to her home in Woodstock, Connecticut, for Thanksgiving. Her father picked us up on Thanksgiving Day and drove us to their large Colonial house. Relatives with names like Winthrop and Muffy asked me polite questions about India. Crystal decanters tinkled by the fireplace as the men helped themselves to drinks and discussed golf, politics, taxes, and horses but never one another. In spite of their welcoming warmth, I was acutely aware that I was the only nonwhite person in the whole house and ended up in the warm, spacious kitchen, trying to make myself useful.

"Here, my dear," said Mrs. Wilson, handing me a brush. "You dip the brush into this paste and baste the turkey like so."

I watched her baste the bird with practiced strokes, trying not to turn away or wrinkle my nose. Being Hindu and vegetarian, I had never touched a turkey before. But Mrs. Wilson's kind face and eager smile prevented me from demurring. She was trying so hard to include me, to make me feel part of her family and the Thanksgiving holiday, that I didn't have the heart to tell her that I felt queasy, not thankful, at the opportunity to baste. So baste I did, taking care not to touch any part of the dead turkey with my fingers.

Perfectly coiffed women wearing smart, sensible clothes bustled around, laying out the crystal, china, and silver on the antique cherry dining table that seated fifteen. Silver swans held place cards, and a large silver rabbit in the center of the table displayed the menu that had never changed since the "Pilgrims landed in Boston," according to Claire. Classical music played in the background. Everything was so refined compared with my family's feasts in India, where a hot, chaotic kitchen with sweaty, harassed cooks turned out vast quantities of food; where relatives insulted one another, abused the servants, or went off in a huff never to return.

By the time we sat down to dinner at three o'clock, the men were tipsy, the women were piqued, and I was famished. I devoured the mashed potatoes, stuffing, and wild rice that Mrs. Wilson had set aside for me, and ate generous slices of every pie on the table.

The days sped by, each bringing a new discovery. November turned to December. The dorms served roasted marshmallows by the fire along with hot chocolate for the nightly "Milk and Cookies" ritual. The Vespers Choir gave their annual concert in the chapel followed by a reception with warm chestnuts and spicy apple cider.

As Ellen and I walked back to Dickinson House, it began snowing. Plump, feathery flakes lightened the gray sky and frosted the earth. It was the first time I had seen snow. Ellen and I held out our hands and twirled around. We lifted our faces and laughed out loud. I slid a snowflake to the tip of my fingers and tasted it. It tasted like iced cotton candy. It tasted like winter in a puff. It tasted like magic.

"This is why New Englanders come home for the holidays," said Ellen. "Because you can't duplicate a white Christmas anywhere else in America."

Natasha and I took the train to her home in Madison, Wisconsin, for Christmas. Her father was a soft-spoken college professor who reminded me of my own dad. Her mother, tall and statuesque, looked like Natasha a few decades older. On Christmas Eve we stood in her warm kitchen, brushed melted butter on phyllo sheets for a rich cheese strudel, and mixed noodles, eggs, and raisins into a fragrant kugel, scented with vanilla essence and cinnamon.

Mary and Doug had me over several times during the course of the semester and gave me a sweater for Christmas. I gave them a cassette tape I had made of all my music compositions.

For New Year's, I was back in South Hadley, where icy needles bristled off the trees. Mary Jacob, the dean of international students, whose reassuring voice I sought many a time during my early days at Mount Holyoke, invited several international students to her house for a party. Ayesha, a girl from Pakistan, and I hatched a plan to do a radio show each week, with music and guests from different countries. Since WMHC 91.5 FM was a very local radio station, we had no problems convincing the station manager that such a show was necessary, given the burgeoning international population.

On Thursday nights Ayesha and I carried bags of warm

buttered popcorn and mugs of hot chocolate from our dorms to
the radio station at the edge of campus. We wrapped ourselves
in turquoise and aquamarine Pashmina shawls, surrounded ourselves with colored beads and silken bedspreads reminiscent of
an Eastern pasha, and sat within the cozy confines of the recording studio. We had many guests. Niloufer, the daughter of a
Turkish diplomat, played mournful music and shared recipe secrets from the Topkapi Café, which her family owned. Carlos,
who attended Hampshire College, introduced us to Mexican
rhythms and taught me to make salsa *picante*, which I replicated
on days when the kitchen served bland food. Reza, an Iranian
consultant who took part-time courses at U. Mass, "just to meet
girls," instantly guaranteed himself repeat-guest status by bringing a gilt-wrapped box full of the most delicious Iranian pista-
chios, salted almonds, and dried fruits. Emilie, my next-door
neighbor from Camaroon, brought her friend Elizabeth from
Ethiopia; they wiggled their hips in time to the hypnotic drum-
beats with a precision and speed that awed us. Todd, an English
painter, drank lots of wine and denounced English cuisine. Polish professors and Russian poets engaged in fits of nostalgia.
Thai scientists, Vietnamese musicians, and Indian philosophers
felt bouts of homesickness as we played music from their home
countries.

Just before school reopened in late January, Claire invited me to
go with her to New York City. Her parents had arranged for us
to stay in the apartment of old friends of theirs who were visiting
Europe. In exchange for three nights at a two-bedroom apartment on Roosevelt Island, all we had to do was feed the three
resident goldfish. Between visiting the museums, catching a
Broadway show, eating at different restaurants, and seeing the
sights, we were horrified to discover that the goldfish had died.
There was nothing left to do but procure new goldfish to replace
the dead ones. But where did one buy goldfish in New York

City? I didn't know a soul, and Claire didn't want to call friends
for fear that word would reach her parents, who had already
been lecturing her about being responsible.

After calling every pet store in the yellow pages, we finally
discovered one in downtown Brooklyn that claimed to have
goldfish the same size and color as our dead ones. So Claire and
I got off the aerial tramway that connected Roosevelt Island to
Manhattan and hailed a cab. To my delight, I discovered that
the driver was from Kerala and quickly lapsed into Malayalam.
His name was Gopi. He had grown up near Vaikom, he said,
and in fact his parents still lived there. When I told him that we
were driving to Brooklyn to buy goldfish, he stared at me as if
I was mad.

"You're going to spend twenty dollars taking a cab to buy
three-dollar goldfish?" he asked.

"Well, not exactly," I stuttered. "You see, they have to be
a certain size and color."

"What color will goldfish be except gold?" he asked.

I didn't know what to say. Claire had made the calls, found
the shop, and negotiated the deal. She had seemed very excited
about pulling off the whole thing.

"This is ridiculous," the cabbie said in Malayalam. Before
I could say a word, he screeched to a halt and made a U-turn. "I
live right across the Queensboro Bridge," he said as we drove in
the opposite direction. "I have dozens of goldfish. You can come
to my house and pick out any that you like."

I jubilantly translated for Claire, proud that a fellow Indian
had come to our rescue, but she squirmed. This was our first
time in New York, she said, and she would much rather go to a
known shop than a stranger's home. She caught my eye and
shook her head.

"Tell your friend to trust me," Gopi said. "Guruvayur is my
family temple too. On the name of the Lord, I promise that you
will be safe."

Within minutes he pulled up in front of a ramshackle house in an alley just under the bridge. Three children rushed out, surprised and delighted. A woman followed, wiping her hands in a sari. "My wife, Shanti," Gopi said, and explained our mission to her.

In broken English and with a lot of smiles, she welcomed us into their home. Amidst the frayed carpet and the musty brown furniture was a giant aquarium filled with fish of different types.

"Kerala people can live without money, but they can't live without plants and water," Gopi said with a smile. "Please. Help yourself."

Claire and I stood on tiptoe and picked out three goldfish from the tank, which Gopi briskly packed in a plastic bag filled with water.

"You have come to our home for the first time," his wife said. "You must eat something."

Claire and I demurred, or rather, Claire demurred and I pretended to demur. I hadn't eaten Indian food since I came to Mount Holyoke some months ago, and the most delicious smells were wafting out of the kitchen. I would have liked nothing better than to plunk myself on the floor and eat, but I didn't want to impose on them. We had given enough trouble already, I said. But Gopi wouldn't take no for an answer. He would go out and try to get a local fare within Queens and come back in forty-five minutes, he said. That would give us some time to eat lunch.

Claire and I sat at the rickety brown table while Shanti set out a sumptuous *sadhya* (feast) for us. I fell on the food with the fervor of a parched desert traveler spotting an oasis. Red rice straight from Kerala, spicy onion *theeyal* with a dollop of ghee on top, and a delicate *olan* brimming with coconut milk. It was sublime, returning to me the memory of several bus trips that my parents and I had undertaken in Kerala.

I remembered attempting one such journey, when the bus arrived brimming with people and the harassed ticket collector told us that there was no room, especially not for a family of four carrying a dozen pieces of luggage. My parents glanced at each other, worried. The *ghat*-mountain road was narrow. We had to get to Cochin before dark. The cool mountain air carried the fragrance of turmeric and cloves, causing us to shiver. Desperate, my mother opened her tiffin carrier under the ticket collector's nose. The aroma of ginger, curry leaves, and coconut milk filled the bus. "All right, get in," the ticket collector said impatiently eyeing the thick white *olan*. Quickly we clambered on. As the bus careened through the drizzle, my mother mixed the *olan* with rice and passed it around in cone-shaped banyan leaves. No one refused, least of all the ticket collector. We got to Cochin by midnight.

Shanti's *olan* was just as fragrant and tasty. "If you had come after a few months, I could have served you lunch on a banana leaf," Shanti said with a smile.

As promised, Gopi returned in forty-five minutes to give us a ride back into Manhattan. I thanked Shanti profusely for the meal, the memory of which I was sure I would hoard during the long winter months at Mount Holyoke.

Gopi dropped us near the tramway and refused to accept any money, even though Claire and I insisted on paying for the cab ride at least.

"You are from my town," Gopi said. "You are like a sister to me. Does one take money from a sister?"

With that, he tooted his horn and took off into the zigzagging traffic.

ELIZABETH NUNEZ

Trinidad

Elizabeth Nunez (1944–) was born on the island of Trinidad, where her father was a government official and later a consultant for international oil companies. The eldest of her parents' children, Elizabeth began writing at an early age, and after graduating from high school, she was awarded a scholarship in 1963 to attend Marian College in Fond du Lac, Wisconsin.

Upon gaining independence in 1962, Trinidad and Tobago had its annual limit for immigration to the U.S. set at a mere one hundred, of which Nunez was one. These immigrants were primarily composed of white-collar workers, students, and people reuniting with families, a population of no more than 2,500 between 1960 and 1965. In the wake of the U.S. Civil Rights movement, the Hart-Cellar Immigration Reform Act set uniform quotas for immigration, enabling more than twenty-three thousand Trinidadians and Tobagonians to immigrate between 1966 and 1970.

Nunez completed her bachelor's degree and then took an MA and a PhD in literature from New York University. An award-winning author of eight novels, most notably Prospero's Daughter *(2006), Nunez is currently a Distinguished Professor of English at Hunter College. Her first full-length memoir delicately treats the passing of her mother, Una, and Nunez's four-day return to Trinidad for the burial. Reflecting on her immigrant life and its effect on her relationship with her family, Nunez derived the title* Not for Everyday Use *(2014) to describe the Nunez family's ascetic habit of withholding affection. Throughout the memoir, the author tries to reconcile the professional success that she and her siblings achieved with the negative effect that her parents' childrearing had on their personal lives.*

In the passages that follow, Nunez moves back and forth between her present and past to meditate on the so-called better life her parents expected her to achieve in the U.S. Her views shaped by the idyllic representations of the U.S. in 1950s cinema, Nunez's mother refused to believe her light-skinned children would encounter racism. Nunez also describes how upon returning to her parents' home in 2008, she began to recognize the complex price she paid by taking her parents' advice to remain abroad.

Excerpt from

Not for Everyday Use

— 2014 —

I have been tough on my mother. Resentful. I cannot seem to forgive her for turning me out of the house before I was old enough to understand the workings of the world. For turning me out of the house is what she did. I was just sixteen. In 1960, in colonial Trinidad, a girl like me was still a child, sheltered by her middle-class family and shielded by nuns in her convent school who knew next to nothing about the evils lurking in the world except what they had read in the Bible. I had never kissed a boy; I had never gone on a date. When the sun descended and the sky darkened, I returned home from wherever I had gone. I was always chaperoned: in the day by parents, relatives, teachers, and neighbors, at night by my brothers and older cousins. But my father had landed a big position at Shell, and my parents were moving to the south. They sent me to live with my grandmother in the north, in Diego Martin. Three years later, I was on my way to Fond du Lac, Wisconsin, on a scholarship from Marian College.

What an opportunity! What a better chance you'll be getting than the chances your mother had when she was your age! That was what the neighbors said, what my relatives said.

I am eternally grateful for that scholarship from Marian College. It set me on the path to my careers as an academic and a writer, professions that have given me much satisfaction. But the singular dream that persisted from my childhood until it was shattered irrevocably late into my adulthood was to have a loving family, a husband who shared my values and hopes, happy children we raised together. I have the child, a son who more than makes up for the happiness I could have had from children I denied myself when shortly after his birth, painfully aware that my marriage was doomed, I instructed my doctor to implant an IUD in my womb which I did not remove until I entered menopause.

A better life? Nothing could make up for my despair, my utter loneliness, at the time that should have been the happiest of my life, the time before and after the birth of my son. What can compensate me for the feeling of being set adrift in a strange and hostile land with no one to rescue me, no family in America to support me? I will skip the details of the actual birth of my son. I will go straight to the night before the morning I fully expected to take him home.

It is 1976. I am in Brookdale Hospital in Brooklyn, New York. Though I have no concrete proof, I suspect my husband D— is having an affair, has been having an affair for months now. He was angry when I told him I was pregnant. We had been married just over a year. I was thirty, he was thirty-seven. He had been married before; his wife had died, leaving him with a small son. He wasn't ready to be tied down with another child and he made me feel guilty for burdening him with the added responsibility. He wanted to have fun, he said, and rumors swirled in my college that he was having fun with one of my colleagues.

I went into labor on August 10, in the middle of a stormy night. D— drove me to the hospital and stayed by my side until I was taken on a gurney to the delivery room the next morning when my son was born, on August 11. I see D— once later that day, but he seems restless, anxious to leave. He will come and help me pack the next night, he tells me; we can take the baby home early in the morning. The next night, August 12, a nurse's aide brings me dinner, she clears my tray after I eat. I wait. I'm not worried. The nurse will bring my son to me soon so I can feed him. D— will be there for the feeding; in the morning we will take our baby home.

Half an hour later I hear footsteps, two sets; they are approaching my room. A woman enters. She is not a nurse. She is dressed in civilian clothes, a pretty bright blouse under a fashionable suit jacket. She is holding a clipboard in one hand, a pencil in the other. Behind her, in the shadows, I see a doctor. He is not my doctor. He is too young to be my doctor, and he is white. My doctor is middle-aged, and he is black.

I sit up. My heart sinks. I think the worst. "My baby! Is something wrong with my baby?"

The doctor steps forward. He is wearing a white coat; his stethoscope dangles professionally around his neck. "Mrs. H—, we know what you have done." His manner is that of judge pronouncing the verdict of the jury.

My jaw drops open. "Done?"

"No time for games, Mrs. H—. We have the proof."

The woman with the clipboard speaks up. Her tone is gentler, soothing, but her words unequivocal. "We have given the baby something, Mrs. H—. It will help him with the spitting up."

"Something?" I repeat foolishly.

"To counteract the effects of the methadone," the young doctor says sternly. He has other patients to see; he does not have time for niceties.

"Methadone?" I am in a nightmare. Soon I will wake up,

I tell myself. I repeat my question. The doctor does not answer me.

The woman with the clipboard begins to write something on what I can see is some sort of official form. "Of course, you can't take your baby with you," she says. "You'll have to leave him with us. We have already reported the situation. That's why I'm here. I'm a social worker. I'm here to help you."

The room begins to spin, faster and faster. I am in a whirlwind, voices bouncing and swirling against each other. I hear the words *heroin, needles, baby spitting up, methadone.* I am a wild woman now. I strip off my gown. I do not care who sees my body, my flabby belly, my pendulous breasts. "Where? Where?" I stick out my arms; my nails scratch long ashy lines across my veins. "Where are the needle marks? Where have I injected heroin into myself?"

The well-dressed, perfectly coiffed social worker is taken aback. She pulls her clipboard to her chest, armor to protect herself from the crazy woman I have become.

"Where?" I slide my hands down my bare legs. I am trembling all over.

The woman brings the clipboard closer to her chest. It is her heart she wants to protect now, the heart I can see is bleeding for me. "It's a mistake," she whispers to the doctor. "I think we made a mistake here."

D— arrives later. I am shaking, not so much with anger as with fear. *What have they done to my son? Why haven't they brought him to me?* I cannot speak. D— has to grab me roughly by my shoulders and shake me to get me to speak.

"They have given him methadone." I force the words through clenched muscles tightening my throat. "We have to stop them."

"Calm down, calm down," D— says.

My husband's girlfriend is waiting for him. He is impatient. This incident—that his child could have been given methadone—is an inconvenience for him. Though I do not know this now,

the day we bring our son home, he will disappear for a week. So
he does not need my craziness, my paranoia (he seems to believe)
interrupting his plans. "Calm down. Calm down," he repeats. I
cannot calm down.

We go to see the director of the hospital. He has heard
from the social worker and the doctor, of course. He is ready for
us, ready with his lies.

—No, not at all. We haven't given your son methadone.

—But the doctor said—

—He's an intern. He misunderstood. Misspoke.

—And the woman who was with him?

—She apologized. It was a mistake. She went to the wrong
room.

—Then I want to take my son home now. Not tomorrow.
Tonight.

—Well, we can't do that. Hospital rules.

—What rules?

—We have to get permission from the pediatrician.

—I'm his mother. I want to take him home now.

There is silence. I wait. The director shuffles some papers
on his desk.

—Mrs. H—. His voice is syrupy, patronizing. Mrs. H—, I
know how you feel. I would feel the same way if I were in your
situation, but I can assure you that we did not give your son
methadone. As I said, the doctor misspoke. He is young, he didn't
understand. We will take perfect care of your son, I promise. We
have to be sure that nothing is wrong with him. The spitting up,
you know . . . He shuffles the papers again. He avoids my eyes.

—All babies spit up, I say. I am glaring at him, my eyes on
fire.

—Go home, Mrs. H—. Come back Monday.

It is Friday. They have already reported me as a negligent
mother, an abusive mother, my son in need of government protection. The social services office is closed; the staff has gone

home for the weekend. I will have to wait until Monday. They do not tell me this, but I know that this is the case.

What did I expect my mother to do when I told her what had happened to me? I was in America, the land of opportunity. Everything will work out. Everything works out in America.

My mother does not understand American racism; she does not understand that here her class does not trump her color. I have been harsh with my brother Richard, but there is some truth in what he says. I rail against his insistence that only in America does he confront racism, arguing that it is his light skin that gives him a pass in Trinidad, privilege to enter the island's high society without question. But when I say this to him, I am also aware I am only partially right. If he were pitch-black and he were a doctor, the very same doors in Trinidad would be open to him.

I am a college professor. I was a college professor at the time I had my son, but my profession, my class, counted for nothing when that young, inexperienced white doctor, carrying with him years of American history, deep-rooted prejudices that define a black man or woman as less than a white man or woman, walked into my hospital room. He didn't have to ask who I was, what I did. He simply looked at me and assumed.

Fixed in my mother's mind are images of Americans she had seen in the 1950s movies she loves. She does not notice there are no black people in those movies, or if there are, they are saucer-eyed, big grins plastered on lips exaggerated to make them more servile and farcical. Those black people are not in her social class. My mother identifies with the Americans in her social class; it does not occur to her that all of them are white.

To my mother Americans are incredibly polite. Even the gas station attendant says thank you. In the department store, the saleslady follows her. I tell her the gas station attendant wants a tip; the saleslady is afraid she'll steal something. My mother doesn't believe me.

So I tell her that her son, the surgeon, cannot drive his Mercedes in New Jersey without being stopped by the police at least once a week. To avoid confrontation, he allows other cars to pass him; he drives strictly within the speed limit. "That's what he *should* do," my mother replies. "One should always obey the law." When I ask her about the other cars that were speeding, she shakes her head. "One cannot always count on luck," she declares.

What if I tell her what has happened to her son just recently, in 2011? She is no longer alive; I cannot tell her. So I'll tell you, Reader.

It's New Year's Eve, my brother's patient is in labor; it's a difficult case. The hospital calls; the woman is fighting for her life. My brother doesn't wait to change his clothes. He jumps in his Mercedes dressed as he is, in an old pair of jeans and a torn sweater, and he speeds down the turnpike. The inevitable happens: the police stop him. He shows the officer his ID. He is a doctor. "Oh yeah?" the officer sneers. It is clear he thinks the ID is a fake. "What hospital?" My brother explains the situation. It is urgent, dire. "Let me see your hospital papers." My brother has learned to hold his temper. He has learned to be cool. America's black president is cool, too cool, his critics say. He should show some real emotion, they say. How can we tell when he is really angry? Does he have real feelings? But black people in America know that emotions can get you locked up. They stay cool. They say, "Yes sir. No sir," when they speak to the police.

"Here is the phone number, sir," my brother says. "Call the hospital."

The officer grins and withdraws. He does not call the hospital. After all, it's New Year's Eve; everybody wants to party. "Okay, but let that be the last time," he warns, then winks at my brother. "Do me a favor, lay off the champagne. Okay, man?"

My brother tells us this story and we listen in silence. "I suppose it was because I was dressed so casually," he says.

"The officer couldn't imagine a doctor would be dressed the way I was."

We nod in agreement. No one believes what my brother has just said and neither does he, but for a moment we allow his excuse to take the edge off the humiliation we feel. No matter how high we may climb up the professional ladder, we will always be judged as inferior. My mother did not understand that. She was a brown-skinned woman, but doors parted for her in Trinidad. She belonged to the island's upper-middle class.

Why didn't my mother come to New York when I needed her, when I found myself accused of being a heroin addict, an abusive mother? Why didn't she take my side? "It was probably as the hospital said, a mistake. Your son is doing fine now." That's what she made herself believe.

Paul McCartney was sixteen when he wrote the lyrics to his song "When I'm Sixty-Four." A young man in love worries about the future. Will his girlfriend still love him when he's sixty-four? He asks the question that troubles his spirit: *Will you still need me, will you still feed me / When I'm sixty-four?* I am sixty-four.

Does my mother love me? I do not have my answer, though my future is here now. My mother sent me away when I was still a child, then she abandoned me again. Years have passed. I have allowed my resentment to simmer quietly, to fuse into the undying embers of an ancient grievance. But I am not a child now. It is 2008. My mother is still alive. There is time for me to rid myself of this stone in my heart.

And a miracle happens. I am a skeptic, but what else can I call the events that lead to my coming to Trinidad three times in 2008, the year my mother dies? What stars had to be aligned? *God moves in a mysterious way, His wonders to perform.* So writes the eighteenth-century English poet William Cowper. How often had I heard my Anglican grandmother sing the hymn that was set to those words!

I am awarded a sabbatical leave, and without much fore-thought I decide to spend the spring semester in Trinidad. I call my friend, the eminent scholar Dr. Kenneth Ramchand. He was then associate provost at the newly established University of Trinidad and Tobago and head of the arts department. He tells me I can teach a course in creative writing if I am willing to forgo my usual salary. Once we come to an agreement, I call my parents. I will be staying with them for three months. If my mother feels any trepidation, as is usually the case when any of her foreign-based children visit (she would repaint rooms, send Petra in a tizzy to clean and polish the brass, buff the tiled floors, bake special breads), she gives me no evidence. "Come," she says. "Your father and I would welcome a long visit from you. It's about time."

It's about time. Is she thinking what I am thinking? Is she thinking it's about time we resolve the unspoken tensions that persist between us?

I arrive in mid-February. In the lobby of the airport, returning Trinidad nationals are waving and shouting happily to families and friends who rush to greet them. Cars are waiting for them at the curb, engines throbbing. Young men—husbands, sons, uncles, nephews—fling open doors and dash out to grab suit-cases. Another explosion of greetings. More hugs and kisses. The parking police officer indulges them. He grins and waits patiently. Finally, he calls out to them: "Okay, okay. Enough now. You have time for all that when you get home."

There is no one at the airport to greet me. In the past my father would have been here, but he is too old to drive now and my two sisters and my brother are at work. I must take a taxi like the rest of the tourists. I am awash by deep feelings of loss. I have come back to Trinidad, but not to home. I turn away from the happy, raucous crowd.

The cabdriver senses my foreignness. "We just finish build-ing this airport," he says, his hand sweeping across the length of the new building. "You see the Carnival costumes inside? Nice, 'eh? You know we have the best carnival in the world." His face is aglow with pride.

I am tempted to say I'm a national too, I am part of "we"; I know our history, I know about Carnival, but I can tell he has rehearsed this speech for people who look like me. Even with my brown skin, I am pale from the cold winter months away from the sun. My white linen shirt is glued to my back, drenched with perspiration.

"Number one in the world, for sure. Better than Rio." He talks on, pacing his words, pronouncing them as carefully as he would for the tourists who have a hard time understanding the Trinidadian accent. In the end, the *th*'s prove too much of an effort for him and he gives up. "What you tink of de pictures of de prime ministers on de wall? We have one for de queen too? We was a colony of England, you know. But all dat done." When he drops me off, I give him a big tip. In American dollars.

My mother is all smiles when she sees me. She throws one arm around my neck, the other across my back, crushing my ribs. She kisses me. This time it's not the usual peck, her lips barely grazing my skin. It's a full kiss she gives me; it lingers, and I feel the warm, wet softness of her mouth on my cheek.

This is my first indication that my mother wants to break down the wall between us, that for her it's about time too. When we part, I reach for her hand; her fingers are icy cold.

My father shuffles to the gate to meet me, but there is no doubt he is delighted I am here. He can't seem to stop chuckling. His eyes twinkle mischievously. "You looking good or you good looking?" He laughs uproariously, tickled by his witticism.

Petra, too, is happy to see me. "The house get so quiet

sometimes," she says. I imagine it gets quieter when she leaves in the late afternoon. My mother and father are alone when she goes. Their old gardener has retired. With the exception of Petra, all the people who now work for my parents are strangers. My sisters and brother drop by, but not daily.

Is this the price for ambition? Did my parents think of this possibility, that they could be left virtually alone in their old age if all their children go abroad?

My father follows me to the girls' room. "Let her unpack, Waldo," my mother says querulously. "She's just arrived. Give her time." My father stands sheepishly at the door.

We have lunch. I sit next to my mother. She passes the dish of fried chicken to me. "I didn't know if you liked it stewed, so I told Petra to fry it. Like Kentucky Fried Chicken, you know." She grins shyly.

She means to say she does not know if I can still stomach Trinidadian food, the way they make stewed chicken with burnt sugar and lots of spices.

"I like fried chicken, but I love it stewed too," I respond. My mother clears her throat and exchanges knowing glances with Petra, who has been watching me too as I bite into the chicken.

After lunch, my mother goes to her room to watch the soaps. My father retires to the couch in the veranda. Soon he is asleep. My sisters tell me that lately his naps after lunch last until teatime. Old age, they say, the body preparing itself for the long sleep. I am glad I am here before it's too late.

We have tea at four with hot scones Petra baked and jam. My mother and I talk around each other, about the latest news in America, the latest news in Trinidad. She asks about my son, about my work, about my friends she has met on her trips to New York. She veers away from anything too personal. She does not ask about my life, though I know she wants to know if I am happy, if all is going well. If I have met someone who could be with me for the rest of my life. There is always hope; I could get an annulment like Jacqueline and remarry in the church. I could have a husband. I answer her questions but I tell her also that my life is full. I have good friends, and my son and his family are a comfort to me. Her eyes brighten. I am pleased to know I have put her at ease.

My sisters and brother visit but soon leave to be with their families. Darkness comes quickly and suddenly. I am shading my eyes from the glare of the sun one moment and the next I need clear glasses to find my way to the light switch on the wall. My father retires early. At exactly six thirty, he closes the drapes in the dining room and living room and switches off most of the indoor lights. He leaves one dim light on in the veranda. My mother complains. "It's like a tomb in here." But she follows my father to the bedroom.

I go to the den and switch on the TV. I find myself hungry for news from America. Only two American news stations are available, CNN and Fox. In New York I never watch Fox News, but now I am so anxious to hear American voices, I find myself switching back and forth from CNN to Fox. Two hours later, I am about to turn in for the night when I hear my mother's foot-steps padding along the corridor. "Is everything all right?" she asks me. I nod and smile. "I love you," she says, and turns away before I can respond.

But would I have responded? Would I have said, "I love you too," as my son always says to me?

It has been two years now since my mother has begun ending all my telephone calls to her with a quick and abrupt, "I love you." She puts down the phone before I can answer. Now she has said the same words to me in person and I am strangely uncomfortable.

I make up my mind to find some sort of distraction the next night. I call a friend who has lived many years abroad and has returned to retire in Trinidad. We cannot meet tomorrow but the following day she will have someone pick me up and bring me to a small dinner party she is hosting.

I teach the next day. By six thirty, the house is shrouded in silence and darkness again except for the insistent croaking of the frogs outside, the drone of voices on the TV in my parents' bedroom, and the light in the den where I find myself oddly entertained by the rantings of Bill O'Reilly. I can hardly wait to go to my friend's home tomorrow.

The man who picks me up the next evening tells me he cannot bring me back. My friend assures me she will, though I will have to wait until all her guests have left. It is two in the morning when she finally drives me back to my parents' home. My mother is up, waiting for me in the kitchen. "I was worried. I wanted to be sure you were safe. These are not good times in Trinidad. The crime, you know . . ." She had obviously not slept a wink. Old, her body failing, she had summoned the strength to stay awake for me. Still, I cannot get my tongue to say the words *I love you*, though they stir in my heart. My mother does not repeat them to me, though I am certain she wants to.

And so we continue day after day, night after night. We are stubborn, fixed in our habits. Or is it that we don't need words to express what we know each other feels? The proof is in the doing, in the behavior, I tell myself. I am here, in her house, to spend time with her.

Sometimes, when I do not have to teach, I sit with my mother in her bedroom as she follows the soaps on TV or watches the religious channel. Sometimes, instead of going to the veranda, my father stretches out on the bed, next to his wife, and naps. One afternoon, my mother's favorite soap is cut short for the simultaneous airing of the pope's visit to New York. My mother does not mind; she is anxious to see the pope. I am anxious too, but for a bit of New York, a bit of home. From the minute the program begins my mother's eyes are trained on the TV, tracking the procession that precedes the pope's entrance to the church. I am glued to the TV too, but not for the pope. I am searching the crowd pressed against the restraining ropes, hoping to see someone I know, a familiar face.

The pope arrives. Suddenly my mother, who has been sitting on the edge of the bed, rears back, her face wrinkled with disgust. She makes wide waving gestures with her arms, crossing them back and forth in front of the TV. "I don't believe in all that," she says, shaking her head vigorously.

I can barely trust my ears. "You don't believe in the pope?"

"All that gold around him, all those fancy vestments!"

I stare at her. "*Him?*"

"Yes, the pope. What does all that gold around him have to do with God, or the poor people who are dying of starvation and disease?"

My sentiments exactly! "Yes. What does all that gold have to do with God?"

"Or Jesus."

I hold my breath. My mother is criticizing the religion she has always obeyed slavishly, which she had made us, her children, obey slavishly when we lived under her roof!

"Jesus was born in a manger to a poor woman," she says, fanning the air dismissively.

I am more relieved than I am in shock. I release my breath. We are bonding, my mother and I. It is a baby step we take, to be sure, but a beginning.

Two days later, my mother's prayer group arrives. "One of the hardest things about growing old," my mother says to me, "is that by the time you are my age, all your friends have died." She has always been a social butterfly. My father was married to her and to his work, and when he could no longer do his work, all that was left for him was my mother. But my mother made new friends. She not only joined a neighborhood ladies club, she also became a member of a prayer group that is meeting in her home today.

The members arrive together in one car. I leave the veranda and go to my bedroom, but soon my mother calls out: "Elizabeth! Come! We have a question for you."

All the women in the prayer group are younger than my mother. One of them sits imperiously opposite her, her back ramrod straight. She turns to face me when I walk through the glass sliding door into the veranda, her eyes challenging mine. *Your mother may have a question for you, but I don't,* her eyes seem to say. *I'm the expert here. Don't you come with your liberal American foolishness and confuse my friends.*

"P— says . . ." My mother points to the woman with the ramrod back and repeats her interpretation of a passage in the Bible. "What do you think, Elizabeth?"

My first instinct is that she wants to show me off, Elizabeth her professor daughter, but something in her smile, sly like the proverbial Cheshire cat, tells me that this time is different. I sense a setup. She wants me on her side. The younger women have their darts pointed at her. She wants us to do battle together against them.

I sit down next to my mother. I can feel her body tensing up. *Will I play along? Or will I be her lost American daughter who is no longer on her team?* I smile at her and she relaxes. "I may not be right," I say to the group, "but this is what I think." I give my interpretation; I talk about metaphor, symbol, allegory. I pepper my response with historical, biblical, and literary references. I elaborate. I cite long quotes by heart. The women are impressed, even the imperious one backs down. My mother is pleased. "Why don't you stay for the rest of the discussion?" she suggests. I stay, proud that I have been there to help her.

We are getting along, inch by inch, day by day. I go to Sunday Mass with my parents. My mother does not have to ask me to join them. I'm dressed, ready to go, when Wally pulls up in the driveway to take us to church. I sit in the pew next to them. The church is crowded; there are people standing in the back and along the sides, but the place in the pew where my parents have sat for years is empty. The usher quietly asks strangers and newly arrived parishioners to move if by chance they have seen the empty spot and have not been forewarned. *That's Mr. and Mrs. Nunez's place.*

I have never seen my father pray, but at Mass he knows all the prayers, all the hymns. When the priest turns to the congregation for a response, my father's voice is the loudest. He sings off-key, the words warbling out of his mouth. Children giggle, parents admonish them sternly and send my mother sympathetic smiles.

For my father, the high point comes when the priest asks the congregation to give each other the sign of peace. My father kisses my mother quickly on the cheek, kisses me, and he is out of the pew, up and down the aisles, shaking hands, greeting the parishioners. They know him by name. *How are you doing, Mr. Nunez? How are your children?* My mother, ever elegant, remains standing in her place, acknowledging their good wishes with a gracious smile.

It takes my parents almost an hour to get into the car after Mass. I watch as people crowd around them, introducing relatives, visitors, children. Wally is patient. "This is the day they wait for all week," he tells me. "At least Dad does. Mum goes out, but Dad sticks to the house all week. He won't go anywhere, except to take long walks in the afternoon."

Later, as he does every Sunday, Wally drives my parents to the home of one my sisters, either to Jacqueline's home or Karen's. My sisters prepare an elaborate lunch. They put out their best dishes, their best silverware, their best stemmed glasses for my parents. The food they serve is beautifully prepared, color coordinated, and delicious. This Sunday, lunch is at Jacqueline's. My sisters and brother talk and laugh with each other, they exchange memories. When Jacqueline speaks of the distant past, I am animated; I find a space to break into their reveries. "Do you remember the times we spent in Toco?"

Every vacation—Christmas, Easter, the August holidays— my parents took us to the countryside to spend a week or more at the rest houses in Cedros, Mayaro, Blanchisseuse, Toco. The English had built these vacation cottages in the coastal villages in Trinidad, not for us of course, but for their expatriate employees, though my father could not be denied one of the perks that had been given to the Englishman he succeeded. The English, after all, took pride in their sense of fairness, especially when it was not inconvenient for them, and I had spent some of the happiest days of my youth at the rest house in Toco.

Karen cuts me short in the middle of my reminiscences. She remembers the great times they had on the other islands, in Tobago, St. Vincent, Grenada, Barbados. What fun they had staying at the hotels on the beach!

Hotels? I had known only rustic rest houses in the countryside in Trinidad. But I had long ago left the island; I was in America; I had missed those days.

"Your father believed in keeping the family together," my mother says.

How well I know the truth of what she says. In the box where I store my most treasured possessions there is a letter from my father. The stationery is elegant, most likely chosen by my mother. It is lime green in color, the insides of the envelope a darker green. A vine of flowers in shades of green runs along the sides of heavy expensive paper. My father thanks me in the letter for making the trip from New York to Trinidad to celebrate his fiftieth wedding anniversary. In his sweeping, handsome handwriting, stemmed letters flowing confidently below each line, he writes:

> Dear Elizabeth,
>
> Thank you for joining with your brothers and sisters to celebrate with us our Golden Anniversary.
>
> We trust you will always remain together as a closeknit family caring for each other.
>
> *May God bless you.*
> *Mom & Dad*

Just as I am sure, given my mother's exquisite taste, that she was the one who selected the stationery, I am sure too that it was she, forever hopeful, forever praying we would all return to the Catholicism of our childhood, who had my father add the words, *May God bless you.* She signs *Mom*; I recognize her handwriting. My father signs *& Dad*. Though my brothers and their wives have taken to calling them Mom and Dad, my sisters and I continue to address them as Mummy and Daddy, and with American television beaming daily into their bedroom, my parents too eventually began signing their holiday cards to us using the American shorthand. My siblings tell me that each of them, all eleven of us, received a similar handwritten letter. The letters are dated May 1, 1993, one week after our parents' anniversary.

Karen is sitting close to my mother. She will not allow my father to take all the praise for keeping the family together. She has told me more than once that our mother considered her her best friend. Now she interjects: "You too, Mummy. You kept the family together."

"Yes, me too," my mother concedes.

My father nods in agreement and then slips away to an armchair near a window. Soon he is fast asleep.

Talk turns to a past that is familiar to my sisters and brother, a past light-years ago when I was in my twenties, thirties, and forties, living in America. I have nothing to say; no memories to add. When I leave my sister's home I am sad, slightly depressed. How comfortable they are with each other! What history they share! They speak of people I do not know, have never met, of events I know nothing about. Their jokes fly over my head. I laugh with them, but I do not understand much of the humor in the stories they tell. Sometimes I am forced to ask them to slow down, my ears no longer tuned to the accents of my homeland. I want to make history; I want to connect the line from my childhood to my present, from Toco to this moment, but my history has been broken by my years in America.

Early the next morning, before the sun has had a chance to rise above the horizon, I am awakened by the clanging of dishes in the kitchen. I hear voices, female voices. I tiptoe to the kitchen. My mother is there, fully dressed in slacks and a loose silk shirt. Petra is next to her. They are huddled together packing sandwiches in a tin box. She is going on a picnic with her prayer group, my mother says. I run to my room and bring out my oversized designer handbag. "Here." I give her my brand-new Louis Vuitton bag. "Put the box in there," I say.

She is pleased. "I'll look real stylish today." And she does when she holds the bag against her tan slacks.

I ask her where the prayer group will be having the picnic. "At a retreat house on Salybia Bay," she answers.

I gasp. Salybia Bay is on the north coast. It is dark now; it will still be dark when she and her group reach the north coast and begin the dangerous trip to Salybia Bay through winding, narrow roads that plunge down steep precipices to a windswept sea hurling against gigantic black rocks scattered along the shoreline. My mother is eighty-nine, only a couple of months away from ninety. She may think of herself as young as the women in her prayer group, but she is not as agile.

"What if something happens to the car along the way?" I ask.

My mother, who I know to be afraid of rough seas, afraid of the dark, brushes me away. "You have such a vivid imagination, Elizabeth."

And I remember that in 1949, afraid of the sea, afraid of the dark, she went on a ship by herself across the Atlantic Ocean, no land in sight for days, because she missed her husband.

GUSTAVO PÉREZ FIRMAT
Cuba

A writer and scholar, Gustavo Pérez Firmat (1949–) was born in Ha-
vana, Cuba, to a family of wealthy warehouse owners, or almacenistas,
and was raised in a large house with servants, until the Cuban Revolution
on New Year's Day 1959. Communist leader Fidel Castro called families
like Pérez Firmat's gusanos *(worms), and they lived the following two*
years in "inner exile," shut in their homes as groups of triumphant guer-
rillas took over their affluent neighborhood. His parents sold off posses-
sions in order to smuggle funds out of Cuba in preparation for leaving,
and the family arrived in Miami in 1960 as part of the first wave of
Cuban immigration to the U.S., which was primarily composed of the
country's elite, or the "golden exiles." They lived in an area that would
become known as Little Havana, and Pérez Firmat attended primary
school, where his excellent English smoothed his way.

Later came a dramatic series of migrations, including the Mariel boat-
lift in 1980 (a six-month period when Castro removed restrictions against
emigration, including freeing prisoners, among other marginal popula-
tions, to facilitate an exodus of some 125,000 citizens) and the Rafter
Crisis in 1994 (a monthlong suspension of restrictions that enabled several
thousand Cubans who could find their own transportation, often flimsily
made balseros, *to escape to the U.S.). Currently, nearly nine hundred*
thousand Cuban-born immigrants live in the U.S., not to mention at least
two and often three subsequent generations of native-born descendants.
While other states have sizable populations, some two-thirds of the people
of Cuban descent live in Florida.

Pérez Firmat is currently the David Feinson Professor in the Hu-

manities at Columbia University. His scholarly study, Life on the Hyphen: the Cuban-American Way, *explores how his "1.5" generation of young immigrants has become successful hybrids of their inherited and adopted cultures. His Pulitzer Prize—nominated memoir,* Next Year in Cuba: A Cubano's Coming of Age in America, *pursues this issue more personally, describing his family's complex generational response to their immigration: although Pérez Firmat came to recognize himself as a Cuban American, his father continued to dream of returning to the island.*

Excerpt from

Next Year in Cuba

— 1995 —

For better and for worse, Cubans face hardship lightly. Confronted with difficult times, we fall back on *relajo* or *choteo*, a type of humor that deals with life's adversities by mocking them. I'm sure you've heard the proverb, if life gives you lemons, learn to make lemonade. As soon as Cubans arrived in Miami, we started making lemonade in industrial quantities. A spoonful of *choteo* made the Spam steaks go down. The *carne del Refugio* became the subject of endless jokes and stories, as did the *factorías* where many people had to work for subsistence wages. Just as my mother and her friends exchanged recipes for Spam and powdered milk, my father and his friends traded jokes about Fidel or life in exile. The Miami buses, notoriously untimely, became *la aspirina*—you took one every three hours. As *relajo* relaxed us, the town began to fill up with colorful characters. One man who had been a sergeant in Batista's army liked to walk the streets of Little Havana holding up a signed photograph of the ex-dictator; he became known as *el hombre del cuadro*, the man with the picture. A transvestite who hung out on Eighth Street was dubbed *La engañadora,* the deceiver, after the title of a fifties *cha-cha*. A woman nicknamed Beba de Cuba was famous for holding wild parties every May 20 to celebrate Cuba's day of independence. For the party Beba wrapped herself in a Cuban flag and tied her hands and feet. At around midnight, when Beba was good and tipsy, the partygoers would start the chant, "Beba, break the chains; Beba, break the chains." Beba would start to shake and shimmy and shudder until not only the chains but part of her clothing came off, symbolizing the liberation of Cuba.

As the sixties advanced into the seventies. Cubans began to take possession of the city, to make it our own in small but crucial ways. Like Adam in paradise, we named. In some cases American place names were hispanicized. Not only did "Southwest" become *la sagüesera* but "Northwest" became *la norgüesera*; Miami Beach was simply *la playa*. Tony Key Biscayne became Hialeah by the Sea, after a working-class neighborhood at the western edge of Dade County, or more simply, *el cayo*, the key. In other instances Cuban names were imported, so that a popular apartment complex off Eighth Street was rebaptized Pastorita, a take-off on the name of Castro's minister of housing. The corner where Cuban men congregated to talk politics was dubbed La ONU, the U.N.; and the corner where they played dominoes became *el parque del dominó*, Domino Park. Crandon Park turned into *"palito* beach," since that's where teenagers went to make out (*palito* is Cuban slang for intercourse). The fact that the streets in Coral Gables already had Spanish names—Sevilla, Granada, Alcazar, Romano—offered a kind of confirmation that Miami had been destined all along to become a Hispanic city. By the early seventies so many neighborhoods had been taken over by Cubans that the longtime Miami residents began to display bumper stickers with the question, "Will the last American to leave please take the flag?"

It's hard to describe now, more than twenty years later, the bizarre yet comforting atmosphere of those years. We spent our days in the mode of crisis, hyped to a continuous state of alert. Like zealots on the eve of the millennium, Cuban exiles were certain that something was going to happen to Fidel at any moment. Talk of Cuba was constant, and constantly wistful, for *regreso* was always around the corner. Miami was like an Irish wake, with the same admixture of festiveness and grief, but with the difference that we expected the corpse to come back from the dead at any minute. By the end of the sixties the rest of the country was in the throes of turbulent social changes, but for us the only thing that mattered was Cuba. Even the war in Vietnam was relevant only insofar as it had an impact on U.S. policy toward Fidel. Even though most exiles supported the war, we were puzzled by it: why go halfway across the world to fight communism when you can fight it on your doorstep? I wasn't anxious to get drafted and go to Vietnam, but I did sign up with Alpha 66, a paramilitary exile group that mounted raids to Cuba. (Since I had no prior military training, they never used me, but my nominal membership in this organization almost prevented me from becoming an American citizen a decade later.)

Inside our house, the radio was always tuned to one of the Cuban stations, where the political talk was relieved occasionally by an old song or two, or by a nostalgia program. Among the latter, one of the most popular was a call-in show featuring a man who had been a mailman in Havana. People would call in, give him an address, and ask him what building or landmark stood at that address. Sometimes they would give him the addresses of their own homes or places of business. The mailman usually knew the answer. I used to listen to this show with my grandmother Martínez, who herself had an impressive recall of

Havana streets, and marveled at the mailman's freakish memory of the smallest details of the city's topography. The only time I remember him stumped was when a clever caller asked him what stood across from a certain building on the Malecón, the coast-side avenue that girds the city. After hesitating for a moment, the mailman named some monument, but it was not what the caller had in mind. Across from the Malecón, he informed the mailman, was the Atlantic Ocean.

Years later, when Cubans of my generation reached adulthood, this kind of program was ridiculed with the slogan "*Más música y menos bla-bla-blá*," "More music and less blah-blah-blah." But at the time, all we wanted was to hear about Cuba. Reports from the island were our life's blood. The radio on my father's night table was always set to Radio Reloj, a station that told the time every minute and in between summarized the news. As the announcer read the latest from Cuba, the seconds ticked away in the background. This went on without surcease hour after hour, day after day, month after month, year after year. Every morning my father woke to the sound of Radio Reloj droning in his ear, and every night he went to sleep the same way. It was eerie. Ticking away, Radio Reloj was like a time bomb set to explode at any moment, except that it never did. The one piece of news we all craved was never broadcast.

And yet each day brought new signs of the Revolution's deterioration. There would be rumors of an uprising outside the capital, or a recent arrival would share horror stories about food shortages or political repression, or the State Department would release a strongly worded statement about the Revolution. These rumors swept across Little Havana like hurricane gusts. Someone would call our house with a news flash and my father would in turn call his friends and relatives. Even though most likely it was a *bola*, a false alarm, the rumor bounced around unchecked. For years *bolas* of all shapes and sizes filled the Miami air, launched not only by ordinary citizens but by radio stations and the numerous exile tabloids, or *periodiquitos*. Since many *bolas* started out as practical jokes, *relajo* played a part here also. I doubt that there are any Cuban exiles who at one time or another have not received a call from a friend telling them, in an agitated voice, that Fidel is dead. And if you were the one who got the *bola* rolling, chances are that within the hour someone would phone *you* with the same rumor that you set in motion. My father got a kick out of doing this to my gullible aunt Cuca, who lived in New York and was therefore chronically starved for the latest exile gossip. When he called her with the *bola* that there had been a coup in Cuba, half an hour later someone else called my house with the news that Fidel was dead.

For years we lived like this, in booms and busts, having a ball with our *bolas* and grieving when they fell flat. Nourishment as well as narcotic, news from Cuba jolted us, made us buzz with anticipation, fed our hopes and blunted our frustrations. All this gossip helped us cope with exile, but it also diminished our need to move beyond it. Perhaps if we had been less prone to wishful thinking, we would have paid more attention to the American here and now; but instead, here and now collapsed into nowhere, and we lived dreaming about the island across the water.

Miami is a city of mirrors and mirages. Under the relentless Florida sun the ubiquitous chrome and glass splinter into myriad reflections. Barely touching the earth, the city floats in a sea of images, a swelter of illusions. In the sixties and seventies, when the return to Cuba was foremost on everyone's mind, hardly a few weeks went by without the arrival of a new savior. These monthly messiahs always promised the same thing: to lead us from the wilderness of the Everglades back to our Cuban paradise. Some of these men were honest and well-meaning, while others were crooks and opportunists. But one man, the illusionist par excellence, fits none of these labels. His may have been the greatest *bola* of all.

José Francisco Alabau Trelles was born in 1924 into a prominent family from the province of Cienfuegos. Graduating at the head of his class from the University of Havana Law School, he went back to Cienfuegos and opened a law practice. Soon he became involved in politics, appearing frequently on radio panels and contributing editorials to newspapers and magazines. He first came to national prominence in 1958, when, as a magistrate in Havana, he indicted two of Batista's henchmen for the murder of four students. Always a devout Catholic, that same year he published a modern adaptation of the life of Jesus Christ, but he was destined to become another prophet without honor in his own country. When his indictments were quashed by Batista's minister of justice, Alabau went into exile. Returning to Cuba in 1959 right after the triumph of the Revolution, he was appointed by Fidel to the Cuban Supreme Court. Like many other early supporters of the Castro regime, Alabau Trelles quickly became disenchanted with Fidel's Marxist leanings and joined the thousands of Cubans already living in Miami.

In exile for a second time, Alabau Trelles remained active in Cuban politics. As a former justice on the Cuban Supreme Court, he was a figure of some prominence, and his name surfaced sporadically in newspaper columns and political gatherings. Joining the Republican Party in 1968, he campaigned for Nixon among Cuban exiles. By then he had formed a political organization called Movimiento Unitario Invasor (United Invasion Movement), and the scuttlebutt had it that he enjoyed Nixon's backing. His plan was to infiltrate Cuba and establish a provisional government in the expectation that the United States would recognize it and offer military assistance.

One morning in September 1971 Alabau Trelles showed up at a radio station in Little Havana wearing battle fatigues and a bloodied bandage around one arm. "Two nights ago," he began his broadcast, "forty soldiers of the United Invasion Movement disembarked on the southern coast of the province of Camagüey, where we occupied the town of Guayabal and killed more than thirty communist soldiers." He went on: "After completing our mission, we withdrew in perfect order and returned to the place from which we had come, whose name I cannot reveal, for obvious reasons. On our side we suffered only one casualty, José Rodríguez Zafra, who will forever remain in our memory as a martyr to our homeland. I myself was wounded in one arm by a piece of shrapnel." He concluded with an appeal to all Cuban exiles: "The end of the Cuban nightmare is at hand. With this heroic feat the Movimiento Unitario Invasor has begun the last stage of the war. Now is the time for all Cubans who love their country to join together in support of our cause!"

This stunning news was greeted with a mixture of euphoria and disbelief. If the attack occurred two days ago, on September 19, why did Alabau look like he had just gotten off the boat? And why had there been no *bolas* about the sortie beforehand? Cubans are notoriously bad at keeping secrets; we have many virtues, but discretion is not one of them. But Alabau's tale was too good to be false. After all, he came from a good family; he was educated and articulate; he had been a judge on the Supreme Court in Cuba; and he was friends with President Nixon.

To top it off, Alabau had pictures of the attack, which he distributed to the newspapers. The photographs showed a damaged building and a large cement mixer engulfed by flames. Could it be that Alabau, who was known as Frank to his friends, was indeed telling the truth? Perhaps the war for the liberation of Cuba had begun at last.

During the hours that followed Alabau's revelations, the denizens of Little Havana, my parents included, talked about nothing else. Although by then we had been in Miami for ten years, in some ways our life hadn't changed much. Pepe and I had already graduated from La Salle. After attending a local community college for two years, I was in my first semester at the University of Miami and living at home. Pepe had gotten a scholarship to New College in Sarasota, one of those progressive sixties institutions where the professors gave no grades and held class in their living rooms. Carlos was a junior at La Salle and Mari had just started at Immaculata. My mother was working as a secretary at St. Hugh and my father was still selling Datsuns at a dealership on Calle Ocho. Rego had moved with his parents to New Orleans and Constantina had gone back to the upstairs apartment. Abuela Martínez still lived with us, on the other side of the partition in the Florida room. By then she had gone almost completely blind, and we could hear her at night crashing into the metal closets looking for the way to the bathroom.

In a feat worthy of Fidel himself, Alabau stayed on the radio for nine hours straight, answering questions about the attack, making cryptic comments about future operations, and asking for support. The action became known as the Battle of Guayabal, after the town where it had taken place. I spent that evening listening to the radio with my father. Although Gustavo Sr. is not a talkative man, that night he was full of hopeful words about Cuba, about his *almacén* and the life we had left behind. There were rumors of other attacks. Alabau would not say for certain, but he hinted that more military operations were in the offing. Many people, my parents included, called in to the radio station with contributions; others, including me, wanted to know where to sign up to fight.

Then, as always, the *bola* burst. Two days after Alabau's supposed return from Cuba, one of the city's American newspapers published photos exactly like those that Alabau claimed to have taken at Guayabal. Some intrepid reporter had invaded a toy store in Little Havana, where he commandeered a Tonka truck and a miniature building. He doused them with lighter fluid and put a match to them. Wild! The photographs he took were indistinguishable from those of the ministry building and the cement mixer.

There were other problems with Alabau's account. His

"military communiqué" claimed that the attack had occurred at one o'clock in the morning; yet in his photographs the truck and the building cast long shadows. And if one looked closely, some of the soldiers in the photographs weren't wearing army boots but sneakers! Moreover, no one could find any record in Miami of José Rodríguez Zafra, the martyr whose body had been riddled by sixteen communist bullets.

In the next few days the whole truth came out—that there was no truth in the story at all. A member of Alabau's high command confessed that everything had been a fabrication. There had been no attack. Alabau had not been wounded. No buildings had been blown up. No one had been killed. Nobody in the United Invasion Movement had gotten closer to Cuba than Coral Gables. Alabau made the whole thing up—he had gone mad. Obsessed with the liberation of Cuba, he had spent too many years away from his homeland. It was rumored later that Alabau was terminally ill and that he had just a few weeks left to live.

The local *choteo* mill was quick to seize Alabau and grind him to a mango pulp. Wags remarked that in Cuban slang a *guayaba is* not only a fruit but a tall tale, a fib. No wonder, then, that the attack had taken place in a town called Guayabal! The story was nothing but a patch of guavas, an orchard of lies. Others compared him to Don Quijote, the mad knight who tilted at windmills and courted Dulcinea. Fidel was his evil giant; Cuba was his Dulcinea; he was determined to win her at any cost.

Like Don Quijote himself, Alabau was undaunted by all the ridicule. Resurrecting his old hagiographic vocation, he compared himself to Jesus Christ. Those doubting Thomases who didn't believe his story were free to stick their hands into the wound on his arm. Two months to the day after the supposed attack, Alabau began publishing a tabloid called *Invasión*. The first issue declared in big bold letters, "THE BATTLE OF

GUAYABAL HAS JUST BEGUN." Undeterred by the incontrovertible proof that the attack had been a hoax, Alabau continued to speak of it as a great victory. This went on for two years, until Alabau fell ill and passed away. It was rumored that he died crazy.

But was Alabau really insane? Was he all that different from thousands of other Cuban exiles? Miami Cubans have never thought it crazy to re-create Havana at the edge of a swamp. We thought nothing of opening a store in the United States and putting up the sign "The same one from Cuba" or "Here since 1935." We take it as a matter of course that distance is not destiny, that our ways of life transcend geography. To one degree or another, haven't all of us enacted our own Guayabal?

Exiles live by substitution. If you can't have it in Havana, make it in Miami. The Cuban-American poet Ricardo Pau-Llosa writes, "The exile knows his place, and that place is the imagination." Life in exile: memory enhanced by imagination. Like Don Quijote, every exile is an apostle of the imagination, someone who invents a world more amenable to his ambitions and dreams. It's no accident that for over twenty years the most popular eatery in Little Havana has been the Versailles restaurant, which is all cigar smoke and mirrors. Surrounded by reflections, the exile cannot always tell the genuine article from the hoax, the oasis from the mirage. Exile is a hall of mirrors, a house of spirits. In that sense, Alabau may have been the quintessential exile.

During the 1960s and 1970s Calle Ocho, or Eighth Street, was a busy, bustling one-way thoroughfare lined with restaurants, supermarkets, gas stations, bakeries, florists, fruit stands, barbershops, car dealerships, furniture showrooms, appliance stores, *botánicas* (stores for religious artifacts used in Afro-Cuban rituals), funeral parlors, and schools. Anything one needed could be found on Calle Ocho, which was located in the heart of Little Havana. As sociologists put it, the community that sprang up around this street was institutionally complete. An individual who lived there could be delivered by a Cuban obstetrician, buried by a Cuban undertaker, and in between birth and death lead a perfectly satisfactory life without needing extramural contacts. Little Havana was a golden cage, an artificial paradise, the neighborhood of dreams.

Many of the establishments on Calle Ocho were *mami*-and-*papi* stores that supported and employed a whole family. While the grandmother stayed home with the small children, Mami and Papi worked the store. Once the children were old enough, they too came to work after school and on Saturday mornings. Some of the businesses in Little Havana had not existed in Havana, but others had been re-created in their Cuban image. One of the most prestigious private schools in Havana had been the Jesuit-run Colegio Belén, which many middle- and upper-class Cubans attended, including my father and Fidel Castro (Fidel graduated, Gustavo was kicked out). Shut down in Cuba, Colegio Belén resurfaced at the far end of Eighth Street in Miami, across the street from a Buick dealership. So it was with other well-known Havana establishments like the Rivero Funeral Parlor, the Centro Vasco and Casablanca restaurants, and radio stations such as Radio Progreso. La Ocho, as Cubans called it, was the location of Domino Park, as it was of the memorial to the soldiers who died at the Bay of Pigs.

Before the Cuban exodus began, Eighth Street had been a quiet, out-of-the-way street between Downtown Miami and Coral Gables; by the late sixties it had developed into the hub of a thriving community of energetic and ambitious exiles. Calle Ocho was where my father worked, where my mother shopped, where my grandmothers went to the doctor. When I was in college and went out on a date with a Cuban girl, that's where I headed, usually to the Pekín, a Cuban-Chinese restaurant that combined standard Cuban fare with Chinese dishes, so that you could begin your dinner with fried wonton and end it with

guava shells and espresso. The Pekín was owned by two brothers, Rafael and Federico, who had been born in Cuba of Chinese parents and spoke Spanish with a thick oriental accent. As
thin as bamboo reeds, they greeted their customers at the door,
introducing themselves as "Lafael" and "Felelico." After dinner
my date and I would go to a movie, perhaps at the Tower Theater a few blocks up the street, and then, if I got lucky, to *palito*
beach (a whimsical name, because nobody ever got that lucky).
If it was a special occasion and we stayed out really late, the
evening would end with *café con leche* at the Versailles, which was
open until four or five in the morning.

Since so many establishments in Little Havana had their
roots across the sea, one tended to think of this neighborhood as
a mirror image of its Cuban original. Cuba was everywhere—in
the taste of food, in the sound of the voices, in the drawings on
the place mats. You could walk into Lila's restaurant and almost
pretend that you were still in Havana. Behind the counter was a
map of the Cuban capital; on the walls, pictures of the Cuban
countryside. All of the patrons, and all of the employees, were
Cuban. The pungent smell emanating from the kitchen was vin-
tage *criollo*: sweet plantains frying in olive oil.

At the same time, however, Little Havana was much more
than a substitute city. Our neighborhoods didn't just emulate
Havana, they completed it. Engendered by the coupling of
memory and imagination, Little Havana was not only a copy but
an alternative. Things that Havana lacked—food and freedom—
Miami had in abundance. Some years ago a Cuban museum in
Miami set up an exhibit detailing the history of the Cuban capital from its foundation in the sixteenth century. The striking
thing was that the exhibit ended abruptly in 1958. There wasn't
one artifact, one photograph, from the last thirty years, as if
Cuba's largest city had disappeared from the face of the earth the
day Fidel's *milicianos* marched in. To judge by the exhibit, on
January 1, 1959, Havana vanished.

In one respect this view of Cuban history testifies to the exile's capacity for comforting delusion. We console ourselves with the thought that, while we have remained the same, it's our homeland that has changed. We often feel that we haven't abandoned our country, but that our country has abandoned us. Countless songs and poems play variations on this theme: Cuba changed. I didn't. Years ago an exile song told the story of a *guajiro*, a Cuban peasant, who visited Havana after the triumph of the Revolution. He found the place unrecognizable—the Malecón was deserted; the people looked different; no one sang or danced. The reason was that the son, the musical soul of the island, had left the country. With the son in exile, Cuba was no longer itself. From the *guajiro*'s—that is, the exile's—perspective, the city that survived the Revolution was a different place.

But I don't think that this way of thinking is merely delusional. The exhibit ended in 1958 because in certain concrete, substantive ways the history of Havana ended with the Revolution. The break with the past was so sharp that the city acquired a new identity. Even the names of streets and buildings changed: Carlos III became Salvador Allende Avenue; the Havana Hilton became the Habana Libre; the Casino Deportivo was renamed the Sierra Maestra. Go to Havana and try to get directions to Club Náutico, and perhaps only an old-timer would be able to tell you. I ask myself: how much does the new socialist man who walks those streets and uses those buildings resemble his old *cubano* ancestor? Cuban exiles mockingly divide the island's history into A.C. and D.C., *antes del caballo* and *después del caballo* (a *caballo* is a horse, and the horse, of course, is Fidel—and never, ever confuse a Cuban *caballo* with an American *yegua*). This isn't only *choteo*. The changes brought by the aptly named Revolution have been so profound that one may well wonder whether it still makes sense to speak of Cuba as one country. Although I often wonder whether I'm still Cuban enough to pick up where I left off decades ago, I also ask myself whether the Cubans who didn't go into exile are themselves still Cuban enough to pick up where we all left off. One doesn't have to emigrate to become an exile—sometimes the most acute estrangement results from staying right where you are. Just as a man can look into the mirror and not recognize the face that stares back, a city can become a stranger to itself.

So it is with Havana: some of it has remained what it always had been, and some of it moved. Perhaps the Cuban museum's exhibit did not include a post-1958 display because that history was unfolding in the very neighborhood where the museum was located. To continue the overview of the city, all one had to do was step out on Calle Ocho. Little Havana U.S.A. was perhaps small in size, but it was large enough to contain some of what was best and most typical about Cuba. The diminished city, the truly little Havana, was the one that languished in the Caribbean. Compared to other Latin American nations, pre-Castro Cuba was a fairly prosperous nation. Pick the index you like— literacy, per capita income, the number of hospital beds or TV sets or Cadillacs or radio stations—and then compare the figures for fifties Cuba with those of other Latin American nations. My favorite stat: by 1950 Cuba had more movie theaters per capita than any other country in the Western Hemisphere, including the United States. The Blanquita theater in Havana, which had 6,600 seats, was reputed to be the largest in the world. In the 1950s Cuba wasn't a typical third-world country; it became one only as a result of the Revolution, whose remarkable feat has been turning this formerly prosperous island into one of the hemisphere's poorest nations.

Exile mutilates the country that is left no less than the people who leave it. Even those exiles who arrived with only the clothes on their backs brought with them all kinds of precious baggage, a *cache* of expertise and talent whose loss changed the island, for the worse. Thirty-some years later residential Cuba is still paying the price of exile, and so are we. But the ultimate lesson of Little Havana is that, regardless of the costs, distance is not destiny. The true Havana is a movable city; its foundations slide on shifting grounds. The Little Havana of years ago, the one I grew up in, reminds me of Philip Larkin's definition of home: "a joyous shot at how things ought to be." Never mind that the words that wafted in the air weren't always intelligible. Never mind the cooler winters and the unusually muggy summers. Never mind that the sky was less blue and the sand less fine than in Cuba. In some ways Miami was closer to the heart of Havana than Havana itself. In Spanish there are two verbs of being: *ser*, which denotes existence, and *estar*, which denotes location. No matter how much geography may confine us, *ser* cannot be reduced to *estar*—a state of being cannot be reduced to a geographical place. Melding essence and residence, Miami Cubans picked up where history had dropped them off (or perhaps, where we had dropped ourselves off). Little Havana became the greater Havana.

By the early 1980s the Cuban enclave in Miami had expanded far beyond Little Havana. In April 1961, when the Bay of Pigs invasion took place, there were 135,000 Cubans in Miami; five years later, that figure was 210,000. By 1973 more than half a million Cubans had left the island and most of them were living in Miami. In the 1980s the number of Cubans in Miami swelled to about two-thirds of a million.

As the first waves of exiles prospered, many sold their modest homes in *la sagüesera* and moved south or west to upscale suburbs like Coral Gables or South Miami; more recently they have moved farther away to Kendall or Perrine, which lie at the southern edges of Dade County. Hialeah, a working-class neighborhood located on the northwest portion of Dade County, grew into a large Cuban enclave, as did Westchester, Carol City, and other neighboring municipalities. When the first-wave Cubans moved out, more recent arrivals moved in. Some were the so-called *marielitos*, Cubans who came to this country in the summer of 1980 via the Mariel Boatlift; others were immigrants from other parts of Spanish America, particularly Colombia and Nicaragua. The Nicaraguans, who began to stream into Miami after the triumph of the Sandinistas in 1979, have become the second largest Hispanic group in Miami.

Currently, Dade County has well over a million Hispanic residents, and about two-thirds of them are Cuban. The influx of Hispanics of other nationalities has turned Miami into a more diverse, and in some ways a more interesting, city. Now, on a given Friday night, you can choose from the Colombian discotheque that plays *cumbia*, the Dominican one that plays *merengue*, and the Cuban one that plays *son* and *guaracha*. But I must confess that I miss the "old" Miami, the Miami of the sixties and seventies, which wasn't as Hispanic as it is now, but where every Hispanic that you met was certain to be Cuban. Now I can no longer go into a gas station in Little Havana and address the attendant with the familiarity that Cubans habitually use with each other; I may be talking to a Nicaraguan, who may not appreciate it if I address him as *tú* and call him *mi sangre*. These days you have to feel out the territory first, decide whether you are among Cubans or not, and act accordingly. Years ago Miami consisted of us, the Cubans, and them, the Americans. We were an upwardly mobile tribe, tightly knit and ambitious. Now things are more complicated, for it's not so clear where the "us" ends and the "them" begins. And to muddle things further, some of us Cubans, the younger ones, were actually born in this country. No longer the Cuban tribe, we're fast becoming part of the Latino community. We're making the difficult transition from exiles to ethnics. As an exile, I'm not sure I like it. Because I already lost Havana once, I don't want to lose my city again.

My trouble is that I don't see myself as Latino, but as Cuban—*cubano, cubiche, cubanazo, criollo*. To tell the truth, the Latino is a statistical fiction. Part hype and part hypothesis, the Latino exists principally for the purposes of politicians, ideologues, salsa singers, and Americans of non-Hispanic descent. The Latino's brown face has greenbacks plastered all over it, and in fact most of the people to whom the label is applied reject it, opting instead for a national designation: Mexican, Puerto Rican, Cuban, Dominican, Venezuelan, Colombian. (Ironically, the survey where these findings were reported was called the Latino National Political Survey—some professors never learn.) Although this diversity may be inconvenient for some, it reflects reality: Hispanics of different national origins have divergent features, customs, foods, temperaments, and traditions. A common language doesn't ensure a common culture. A Mexican is like a Cuban no more than an American is like a New Zealander or a Frenchman is like someone from Port-au-Prince.

As advertisers have discovered to their dismay, there's no such thing as a Latino market. There's a Cuban market (we call it *bodega*) and a Mexican market (they call it *mercado*) and a Puerto Rican market (they call it *colmado* and sometimes *marketa*), but there's no single, indivisible Latino market that can be reached with one sales pitch. Try to sell me a *coche*, the Latin American word for car, and I won't bite, for in Cuba *coche* is baby carriage. Try to sell me a pesticide that kills *gusanos*, worms, and I'll think you are my enemy. Put a lovely *mestiza* in your ad for skin cream, and Cuban and Dominican women won't pay attention. Like other Americans, when I want to eat exotic food I go for burritos and enchiladas. It's a pleasant experience, but it's not like having black beans and rice at a Cuban restaurant.

Not long ago I spent an afternoon walking around Little Havana with Roberto Fernández, a Cuban-American novelist who also grew up in the neighborhood. We went into a little restaurant on Calle Ocho that we both used to patronize, one that Fernández put into one of his novels. The decor and the menu hadn't changed much in twenty years, but the Cuban sandwich I ordered tasted nothing like the way it was supposed to. Roberto said it was because my Cuban sandwich had become a Latino sandwich. He's right. By now Little Havana is as much a part of urban American folklore as the French Quarter or Little Italy. The quaint lampposts on the street corners bear the names of politicians and patriots, Hollywood film crews shoot movies in front of coffee stands, and presidential candidates put in obligatory appearances at old folks' homes and cigar factories. But Little Havana, the Little Havana that I knew, doesn't exist anymore.

GUILLERMO REYES
Chile

Guillermo Reyes (1961–) was born in the rural town of Mulchén in southern Chile and soon moved with his single mother, María, to Santiago, the nation's capital. Reyes was an intelligent boy whose mother doted on him and encouraged his interest in the arts. After María's cousin, Nelly, secured employment in the U.S., she sponsored his mother to work as a nanny for a family in Bethesda, Maryland. Adventurous and recognizing the chance to improve their life, María eagerly accepted the offer, arriving in 1970. The author was left for a short while in the care of his mother's family until she could secure his immigration, when he was ten years old.

During this time, Chilean immigration to the U.S. was primarily composed of upper-class college students, but those numbers steadily increased in response to the passage of the 1965 Immigration and Nationality Act. The average annual number of immigrants between 1953 and 1973 was nine hundred, but in 1965, more than twice as many Chilean immigrants made the passage to the U.S. Although California is by far the most desirable destination for Chileans, New York, Florida, New Jersey, and Texas also boast large immigrant populations. Most Chilean Americans in the U.S. immigrated within the past twenty-five years for economic and political reasons. A major exodus in 1973 followed dictator Augusto Pinochet's rise to power, although the U.S. received comparatively fewer of these than other countries.

After a leaving Maryland, Reyes and his mother traveled across the country, eventually moving to Hollywood in 1976. An exceptional student, Reyes was also a sensitive youth who suffered from body-image *problems and struggled to hide his homosexuality from classmates. After graduating from high school, Reyes attended UCLA, where he began writing plays; he later took an MFA from the University of California at San Diego. Reyes is currently a Professor in the School of Film, Dance, and Theatre at Arizona State University, where he is also the Coordinator of New Work Development.*

The following excerpt is from Madre & I *(2010), a collection of essays on both his challenges and accomplishments and his mother's; it received an Honorable Mention for Best Autobiography in English by the International Latino Book Awards, appearing in a series entitled "Writing in Latinidad: Autobiographical Voices of U.S. Latino/as."*

Excerpt from

Madre & I

— 2010 —

In 1970 my mother came to the United States to work as a nanny for an American family in Bethesda, Maryland. I'd been left in the care of Tata and Grandma and the many extended family members around them. But my grandmother's health deteriorated. Pancreatic cancer quickly tore through her, and she died a month after my mother's departure. A war of words ensued between Tata and my mother through international mail, and I was in the middle of it. That was one of the reasons I was hounding my great-grandmother Natalia that summer. I'd been sent to stay with her and her granddaughter, also named Natalia, or Nati for short, and they and several family members had to cope with my growing curiosity about everything.

No need to buy this child puzzles. He had an entire family to unscramble and put back together.

Tata grieved my grandmother's death in the most peculiar way, by planning to remarry almost immediately. During the wake, his best friend, Don Elmer, stepped up to him in front of my great-grandmother and great-aunt Tecla and offered his un-married daughter, Teresa, as Tata's new wife.

"Teresa, come here," said Don Elmer, at least according to my vociferous aunt Tecla, who remembered this too vividly. His daughter, in her thirties, came forth toward the dining table, looking apprehensive, as if she knew what was to come. She had come to the wake at my grandfather's house to mourn his wife's death. She didn't expect her father to tell her, "Don't you want to marry Don José now?" It sounded more like a command than a question. She blushed, smiled, and could only politely say, "If he'll have me."

The scandal tore through the family and isolated my grand-father immediately. First, my great-grandmother Natalia left town, then her two granddaughters, Eva and Nati, taking me along with them. My grandfather felt the loss so tremendously and the emptiness in his bed and his home so intensely that the grieving process became about filling the void as soon as possi-ble. This widower's grief wasn't paralyzing, but, conversely, it became a call to action. He announced an engagement in less than a month and married within three. And, no, this was not a Chilean custom. It was not a "cultural thing." This was a bizarre personal call on his part, which would cost him dearly in family ties and in sympathy. My grandmother's family thought his actions inconsiderate and plainly shocking. I became torn between the Cáceres family and my grandfather, who felt the need to stand up to the family alone. If my great-grandmother considered his actions madness, even lust for a younger woman,

I also understood his sense of abandonment. My grandmother was dead, and my mother had left for the United States. I shared the feeling, too.

I know that Tata did make an attempt—no matter how futile—to put the happy family we'd known back together again without having to marry. He wanted my mother back, to begin with, and at least this would have delayed the need to find a new wife, and my grandmother's family would have been mollified and less inclined to denounce him as a scoundrel. Tata could barely write full sentences so instead he dictated his letters to me. I wrote them down like a faithful scribe. I was nine years old, felt extremely useful to be writing down Grandpa's thoughts, and I couldn't help but feel the excitement as I became caught up in a grand epistolary struggle between my mother and my grandfather.

Tata demanded that my mother renounce all her U.S. "pretenses," as he saw them, and return to Chile to take over household duties, which meant Mother would need to return to take care of him and the house, cook, clean, and sew and all the stuff that was expected of her as a woman. Of course, I missed my mother, but I couldn't help cheer for her as she wrote back angrily, dismissing his taunts and threats. I knew a raw deal when I saw one, and I believed she was doing much better in the United States, earning "big bucks" by Chilean standards and having a good time with her cousin, Nelly, who'd been the first to leave for the United States. They were single girls out on the town in Washington, D.C., and they were far from home and on their own. They considered it a privilege to live and work in the United States, even if they were doing "only" domestic duties. Poor people have their logic, and that was theirs. They were grateful to be in the United States, because, ultimately, they felt that was their start to do something venturesome with their lives. The United States provided a break from what they considered to be a provincial or unpromising way of life in Chile. It made no sense to my grandfather, however, why any Chilean woman would risk her pride to work as a nanny or a maid in the United States. We were supposedly above such things. We were lower middle class really, but a notch above the masses. It seemed to matter to some people, like my conservative and himself peasant-bred Tata.

My mother resisted. Her letters proved unfriendly. So that's when I started wondering. Her attitude appeared disrespectful—and I had to read the letters out loud to him with the flair a hyper, dramatically inclined child like me could give it. *No puedo volver y prefiero traerme a mi hijo lo más pronto posible.* "I can't go back, and I'd prefer to bring my son over to the U.S. as soon as possible." Talk about *armar toda una película.* I didn't have to film the movie of these events. She won me over immediately because I also sought to travel, and it would be a true adventure, not a fantasy. Grandpa had to accept the fact that Mother not only wasn't coming back but now also threatened to take me along with her. She never called Tata "Querido Padre" in her letters. She addressed him as "Estimado Don José," as if he'd been the local landowner somewhere. He was a retired policeman, and a man who'd never been without a woman in his house. This type of treatment hurt. I felt for him as well. I read the letters to him, and I watched his reaction, which brought him to tears every time. I felt like the midget who humors the king, and this king was turning into Lear.

Tata finally and with great trepidation accepted my mother's decision, and immediately determined—as if to do it hastily before he could change his mind—to marry the youthful and pretty Teresa. They held a wedding party barely three months after my grandmother died. It made sense to him. My mother's own decision to stay in the United States had pushed him into it, and he claimed to be the victim here. He was alone; he needed a woman. It seemed logical to him to marry immediately. Some—I would say most—of the Cáceres family would refuse to speak to him for the rest of his life. First of all, Teresa had been a childhood friend of my mother. They'd grown up together, become teenagers, and had flirted with the same young men at dances and at the beach together. And now she had become, practically overnight, my mother's stepmother. Her father, Don Elmer, was my grandfather's buddy from the days he'd spent in the *carabineros*, the Chilean military police, which would soon help rule the entire country through a military putsch, which my grandfather stubbornly supported. Don Elmer's attitude toward his own daughter was one of possessiveness, even jealousy. Many years later, Teresa would tell me: "My father would not approve of any suitor for me. I brought home men my age, and he would find fault with each and every one of them. But when your grandmother died, he thought his buddy, your Tata, or Don José, as I knew him, would make a good husband. I said yes. At the time, I even had a job in an office that I enjoyed, but they made me quit immediately. I was given no choice." My grandmother's family was too busy maligning Teresa as a ruthless conspirator. She had planned it this way, they said, to immediately move in after my grandmother's death. My mother observed the events from Washington, D.C., with some wicked bemusement. Teresa pairs up with my stepfather? she wondered. What a joke.

Teresa was married to my grandfather for nearly twenty-seven years until he passed away. She bore him two children, a boy and a girl, who themselves are now adults. These are the Bravo family, not a blood-related family, but nonetheless a product of one of those arrangements that most young people today in Chile would consider bizarre, even alien. At the time, Teresa bore the brunt of people's disdain. I was the only one on my mother's side of the family who spoke to her and treated her with respect. Even as a child, I understood her dilemma. She was only allowed to marry an older man, and now the Cáceres family maligned *her* for it, without taking into account that she had little to say in this arrangement between the older men.

This period was an odd one in my life as well. My mother, in the United States, had put into motion the paperwork needed to obtain a visa for me while I was in the midst of this major family struggle. With my grandfather rushing into a quick marriage, I was being taken care of by female cousins, Eva and Nati at times, other times by my great-grandmother Natalia. But the cousins decided to follow Natalia out of our Santiago home after my grandfather made his fateful decision to marry. One morning I woke up, and the two sisters were packing my things along with theirs. You're coming with us, they let me know. You're not going to some stupid wedding.

I ended up with my great-grandmother Natalia in the south: in Mulchén to be exact, a cool, thickly forested town that leads into the heart of Chile's Lake District, where my great-grandmother Natalia had lived since childhood. Natalia had, of course, also chosen to boycott the wedding. She called Teresa *la otra*, which is something you would call a mistress. She theorized that Teresa had conspired to be first in line to marry my grandfather to gain access to his military pension as soon as my grandmother died. "We're a poor country," she said. "People will do anything for a pension. We need security, and we need men to survive in this country. This woman. She was waiting in the wings, waiting for your grandmother to die. Her parents proposed the day of the funeral. I was there; I heard it all. The mourning wasn't over, and they were already telling your grandpa to marry their Little Teresa. I wouldn't be surprised if she'd been his mistress before my daughter died."

I fought back, however, as a loquacious and oppositional nine-year-old was wont to do. "She didn't do anything wrong," I told Natalia. "She just needed to get married because she was getting too old!"

"But why wouldn't men marry her to begin with?" My

great-grandmother insisted on following her line of reasoning. "They didn't want used goods."

"But I like her!"

"You would!"

This entire summer, the south-of-the-equator summer of December–March, was spent in a battle of wills between an eighty-year-old woman and a loquacious kid. I was an *atrevido*, a loudmouthed disrespectful child, and I must admit, without my mother's powers of persuasion and discipline, I was a contentious child, but for a good cause, or so I thought.

It angered me to know there was so much ill will in our family, which led me to naturally question the family's history and its secrets, particularly as I began to discover the issues of bastardy, related to signs of cruelty throughout the family. I didn't have the wherewithal as a nine-year-old to provide intellectual perspective into illegitimacy, but even at that age I seemed to be trying hard to get to know the facts. First of all, I resented plenty of things and said so. The dismissal of Teresa as the evil other one (*la otra*) struck me as extremely unfair, and it led to plenty of fights. But I also had to call into question Natalia's treatment of her granddaughter Nati, who told me her story that summer with a casual tone, a matter-of-factness that seemed resigned to her fate at the time. Young Natalia, in her late teens by then, had gone to Santiago as a little girl to take care of her grandmother. She was basically the sacrifice of a large poor family born to Uncle Ismael, my grandmother's (also illegitimate) brother, who lived with his family in a poor, working-class neighborhood in Santiago. Grandmother Natalia had visited one day and had set her sights on Little Natalia. She will take care of me, the older woman decided, and took her back home to Mulchén with her as a prize, separating her from the rest of her family when she was six years old.

"I cried for days on end," Little Natalia eventually told me much later as a fifty-year-old adult. "I didn't know where they were taking me. I wanted to be with my mother, not my grandmother. She took me back home and taught me how to cook, make breakfast, clean up, make beds, and all sorts of other things, such as buy charcoal and warm up the place in a small coal brazier. I actually loved my grandmother, but I didn't think that I should be taking care of her alone. A year later, I was allowed to visit my family in Santiago. When I entered my parents' home, my sister Eva came out and looked at me as if I'd been a complete stranger. 'I'm here to see my mother,' I said. 'She's *my* mother,' said Eva, and ran inside, afraid I'd take away her mother. My own little sister had forgotten me!"

This same shuffling of women that had made Teresa marry my older grandfather had also affected the Younger Natalia, and it made me aware as a child that there was cruelty in all these arrangements, products of poverty perhaps, but which threatened us all with a certain imposition of authority, making us all feel like bastard children. We certainly had plenty of those. Even legitimate children had reasons to fear. They could be taken from their immediate families at any time to fulfill some larger family duty.

But I still had one form of privilege and I sensed it: my mother was in the United States, and she would send modest amounts of cash that looked hefty in a child's hand and—more importantly—she also sent down promises to take me with her. I clearly had something—big travel and adventure—to look forward to, and during this summer that I spent away from her, I had time to form my impressions of this rather bizarre society of intricate family entanglements, which often grew into scandals. I kept a record of impressions in a series of notebooks, which my stern great-grandma called "nonsense" when she flipped through them, because I would draw family portraits, along with those of sports figures, politicians, and mostly American movie stars, and it became a rather surreal world of images without much of a narrative (an early style had been born). . . .

• • •

At school, the usual bullying, pushing, and pulling continued unabated for the remaining time of my residence. At first, my mother's personal tutoring appeared to complement whatever I learned at school, but in reality, it was school that ended complementing, if barely, everything my mother taught me at home. Whatever the teacher tried at school, my mother did better, including reading, writing, and arithmetic. Her tutoring ensured I got perfect scores. But my local school would remain an unhappy place for most of the children. Poverty—and the poverty of imagination among most parents and teachers—seemed to ensure failure. I don't remember these children talking about the future except to dread it. I sensed the sadness and the frustration in my peers' lives, and I felt distinctly set apart. My mother made it clear I was destined for greater things, and my ego was swollen enough in this one aspect of my life to make me feel that attitude. I refuse to believe I was haughty and condescending toward the rest of the students, but I simply felt that with better grades, I would get out of such an environment. I at least held on to the hope that being different would make me special, a cut above, even though paradoxically I was a sissy, not quite a man, not quite human. I made the best of my distinction nonetheless. I knew I had it better than most of these kids. My mother's imagination—her unique enthusiasm and curiosity for everything—allowed her to stir up mine. Imagination was the one resource we had plenty of. But it was difficult to share it with children in my school, a place most went to fail.

Another important difference, which worked in my favor for once, was that my mother was single and felt no qualms about leaving everything behind and going to the United States. This aspiration began early enough for me to sense hope during all those years of attending the same school. I had reasons to believe I would one day leave my abusive peers behind and start a new life far away.

The first glimpse of this life was the announcement that my aunt Nelly had landed in Valparaíso on a ship in the middle of the winter in 1968. She was making her way back to Santiago, and we would catch a glimpse of this traveler at her sister's—Aunt Gladys's—house. It meant taking a bus downtown and dressing up, which was part of the event. She had returned, this much-vaunted, talked-about cousin who had left to go work in the United States. She already inhabited a special place in my imagination. I imagined her as one did a foreign visitor, an adventurer, or a worldly traveler, someone with stories to tell and maybe gifts. She had flown away to the United States once, and now she had returned in an ocean liner. I remembered her vaguely as a figure from earlier in my childhood, mostly a plump woman with small eyelids and a big infectious grin. She had been one of us, a commoner. But years had passed, and my grandmother said everything changes about you once you travel abroad. Some grand transformation would bring her back to us in some charmed new form. I expected a leaner, taller woman looking like a dancer from one of the Elvis Presley movies, dancing the go-go while wearing miniskirts, boots up to her knees, and a fat ribbon to keep her long hair away from her forehead.

I was wrong about the look. She still looked like the aunt Nelly I remembered, but the changes were in her attitude, her smile, the way she could answer questions about Washington, D.C. She had walked the streets and seen the monuments, and yet her work was altogether humble. The disparity between what a maid could expect in Chile—mostly abuse, poor wages, and a classist condescension verging on disdain—and this maid from the United States made the jobs seem like worlds apart. She was the live-in maid for a Bethesda, Maryland, couple, and yet she could somehow afford international travel. Aunt Nelly had just landed on a Chilean commercial ship, not a cruise liner. She and a Chilean friend (a lovely, humorous, warm, older lady, La Chepita, who also worked in the D.C. area as a live-in maid) had managed to get a cabin on a ship that normally didn't carry passengers. It was bringing back auto parts from Detroit and other American exports. La Chepita was blessed with contacts, one of whom happened to get a friend to grease the wheels, and they were allowed to ride with Chilean merchant mariners who serenaded them as the only women on the ship.

My mother explained it this way: "La Chepita has a son who's now a lawyer, and he knows people." That was it. That was supposed to explain it all. But what was odd to me was that a lawyer in Chile was considered a prestigious position, and yet it was no secret that his studies were paid for by the hardworking woman who spent considerable time working as a maid in the United States. And now these two women had undertaken a virtual cruise that allowed them to visit their family in Chile. They crossed the Panama Canal and arrived in Valparaíso, Chile, rested, tanned, and full of life. A country that allowed the domestic help enough leisure time to undertake such an adventure seemed miraculous. Aunt Nelly was still the plump, lively woman in her thirties, but she showed the stamina and spark of Nell Carter singing "The Joint Is Jumping" in *Ain't Misbehavin'*, a monolith of a hard-drinking, hard-partying woman during the Harlem Renaissance. Nell and Nelly became one person in my imagination.

During this get-together, I noticed Aunt Nelly approach my mother and, handing her an envelope, say, "My boss sent you this letter." Why would the boss do that? Correspond with my mother? I discovered that Aunt Nelly had been planning to bring somebody to the United States to work alongside her. She had been alone for a long time in a neighborhood in which nobody else spoke Spanish. Her boss, a matronly woman with a protective, motherly attitude, had advised her, through a translator, "Stop crying, Nelly, I'll bring you one of your sisters to the U.S. so you won't be so alone." None of her sisters was available. They were married or had some other commitment that prevented them from coming. Instead, they found a cousin, my mother, eager, willing, ready to undertake the adventure. That evening the two women conferred about future plans. I didn't know my mother was preparing to go to the United States. "I didn't want to disappoint you," my mother told me years later. "If things didn't come through, it would have seemed premature to get you all excited beforehand."

For at least two more years, I heard my mother talk about her visits to the U.S. Embassy in Santiago. After the passage of the 1965 Immigration and Nationality Act, Chile got its quota of resident alien visas, and my mother had been among the first to apply. Knowing her, she was probably the first in line. With the sponsorship of Aunt Nelly's boss, my mother was offered a job in the United States. Some time in June 1970, my mother went to another routine meeting with the embassy people, who had been holding her off for nearly two years. To her surprise, she was presented with the paperwork that would later finalize the steps to get her an official green card at a time when such cards were still green. She had become a legal, fully documented immigrant to the United States.

One reason to hesitate was that my grandmother had become gravely ill. She had undergone gall bladder surgery and suffered cardiac arrest during the operation. The doctors revived her, yet she was left in a critical state. She gradually recovered during that winter but spent most of her time in bed. My mother decided that my grandmother was dying of "cancer of the pancreas," but the doctors never confirmed that. They could never point at anything other than gastrointestinal difficulties. My mother's diagnosis was based on symptoms she had read in a book. A Chilean doctor, el Doctor Elizalde, had written a best-selling book about the vegetarian lifestyle that also prescribed a specific diet for every malady one could imagine. Fruits, whole grains, and vegetables would cure just about everything. (That was the general thrust of his argument.) But my grandmother was too far along in a diet that included red meat and animal fats to be resuscitated with a change to vegetarianism. Nor did she make an effort to stop eating meats. My mother's diagnosis ended up being just as good as anybody else's because the doctors had no clear answers either.

Whatever her malady, it was killing her. With an ailing mother and a child who was to be left to the care of a public school system that horrified him, María could have been easily persuaded not to go, but my grandmother herself spoke out against changing her mind.

"My mother didn't want to hear me complaining that I had a great opportunity and didn't take it because of her," María said, decades later. "She didn't have long to live, and she knew it. There was no point in me passing up this sudden chance to work abroad and do something different with my life. She herself had left the countryside to go settle in a new life in Santiago. Unlike my stepfather, she didn't beg me to change my mind, and instead encouraged me to take the plunge, so I did."

During an evening in late September 1970, a few weeks after the historic election of the Socialist president Salvador Allende, a flock of Cáceres family members and friends accompanied my mother to the airport for some history making of her own. Today's Santiago doesn't allow for family members to watch a plane pull away and then take off. Security concerns prevent one from walking a member to the actual gate of departure, and one has to watch behind a glass panel where no one will hear a bon voyage shout. Back then, Mother left the gate on a bus that transported her and other passengers to the plane. She gave us a final wave before boarding, and then she was off. We were like a fan club—a crowd of twenty-five or so—waving and applauding, creating a ruckus that people associated with celebrities. The plane disappeared into the darkness. My mother was gone to the other edge of the world.

My mother would not have left me alone, however, without knowing I was well accompanied. An entire family, of aunts, cousins, even my great-grandmother, would contribute their share of coping with a difficult, moody kid such as myself. The family was already rallying around my ailing grandmother, known to everyone as "La Jerny." A death watch began as soon as my mother left. Visitors invaded the house from every corner of the country. There was no time to be alone. La Jerny held on for an entire month and got a chance to receive one of her daughter's vivid, detailed letters, revealing the long plane ride to Miami, where she changed planes for Washington, D.C., the taxi drive to the house in Bethesda, Maryland, where Aunt Nelly worked, and then her introduction into a house where she had been set up to work for another family. My mother fulfilled the purpose of keeping Aunt Nelly company, but another cycle of preparations would begin. My mother intended to bring me along.

A month after my mother's departure, La Jerny died. Her prolonged ailment had slowly taken the light out of her. She kept her daughter's letter nearby on her lamp table and made me read it out loud every night before she went to bed. Then one morning in October she did not wake up.

Shadowing these circumstances, at the school—the prison, as I had begun to call it—a small miracle occurred during my final year. Our teacher, a severe, regal, thin, but pretty woman, Señora Arriagada, had fallen ill and required an operation. She was gone for the rest of the year. A substitute arrived, briefly, who added to the usual horror with his bullying and humiliation of students. On the first day he decided discipline would be his theme. Every question that was answered badly netted a slap on the palm of the hand with a ruler—for just about everyone except me. I would pay for that in the schoolyard, but by then I was used to it. This gentleman, rather pudgy and red faced, lasted only a few days. For some inexplicable and merciful reason, he was reassigned to another classroom. And the next day, into our classroom of nearly thirty students, both male and female, walked a certain Mr. Mendoza. He was a short, dark-looking gentleman with a thin moustache. He entered smiling with a comfortable stride, which already revealed a different disposition. A sincere, warm smile went a long way to pacify a classroom.

He initiated his lesson plan by writing out some words on the entire chalkboard. We thought: Oh no, homework of some kind, words to memorize, and whoever gets it wrong would be severely beaten. Instead, he made us get up and sing the words. What he had written down were simply lyrics to some folkloric song about Chilean heroes. It didn't matter really what the song was. He made us get up, to sing loud and proud. What a concept! From then on, Mr. Mendoza began the day's lesson with two or three songs, sometimes repeating ones we'd already learned just to get them right. He created, of all things, a chorus out of us. But more importantly, he created, for the first time, a contented class. I didn't think my schoolmates would ever walk around looking cheerful or generous. I remember that year—even as my mother left and my grandmother was ill—as a time of contentedness, at least at school. The songs we learned woke us up for the first hour, and then we would happily work with Mr. Mendoza on the inevitable math assignments or the memorization of vocabulary. Whatever he cared to address, he had our attention. He had earned it. We knew the reward would be one more song at the end of the school session. We sang about everything—about waking up in the morning to plough the fields (a Victor Jara song, most likely), or some distant heroic battle, or a religious song about brotherhood. Somehow, this incredible teacher managed to salvage school for us all. For the first time, I believed my peers were beginning to learn, and I would not have to stand out and be punished for it.

Mr. Mendoza prepared us for a presentation in front of the entire school, songs about the heroes we were supposed to re-member from the fight for Chilean independence. He chose me to deliver a eulogy. I read the words from some book, about two heroic brothers who martyred their lives in the struggle against Spanish oppression. The words hardly mattered. The fact that we created a spectacle, did it in an organized manner, rehearsed meticulously, and then presented it to the rest of the school, which applauded us, seemed miraculous to me. That he chose me to deliver the words was also flattering, but what was more important was the teamwork that went into making this event.

I left for the United States not long after. Visiting Chile in September 1980, barely nine years later, I spotted Mr. Mendoza in downtown Santiago as he rushed to catch his bus. I thought about catching up with him and letting him know that he had saved my public schooling from the daily session of abuse it had become. I would have liked to explain the importance of finding a teacher like him at a time when my mother—my real teacher—had left, and I was in need of mentoring. But the bus whisked him away, and I never saw him again.

I flew alone into the United States at ten years of age, and the first word that caught my attention upon my arrival at JFK International Airport glowed in the various signs that pointed toward the world outside: *Exit*. The Spanish word for "success" is *éxito*. My translation was, of course, wide of the mark, but my child's eye saw something else: what a great country, I thought; it wishes you success as you leave the building. Today, I would advocate changing all the exit signs to *success*. Give your best wishes to people. Let them feel confident as they go out of the building into those streets where they might well be devoured by people who lack success or, conversely, zealously cling to their own. Be an optimist, and let your best wishes prevail. I would eventually learn the flat, unadorned meaning of "exit," but I haven't forgotten the translation that amused me at that age and that I thought was so original, an optimistic one for a child who constantly sought to bend the world to his imagination.

The United States felt welcoming to a child of ten, impressions colored by my mother's rosy disposition, her Maria von Trapp aura of seeing the world through a wide angle and Cinemascope lens with a bouncy soundtrack playing in our heads. The music and the rhythm of the streets invited one to think in terms of music and dance. The jukebox in the diner across from the Manhattan hotel featured the hits of the times, and I could choose Diana Ross's "Surrender," the Jacksons' "Going Back to Indiana," or Joan Baez's "The Night They Drove Old Dixie Down" with haunting lyrics by Robbie Robertson that I wouldn't understand until I learned English. My mother didn't hesitate to give me enough quarters to play all three selections and then poured raspberry syrup on my pancakes. That's how she welcomed me into the country, through a glimpse of the Big Apple, both my taste and aural buds appeased. We took the bus to D.C., where we settled down in the nation's capital—for a short while anyway. Settling down did not suit us well. We turned out to be restless immigrants on the go. We started in D.C. and then bounced around the country until we reached L.A., the last station for fidgety people before the ocean put a stop to us.

My mother had arrived a year ahead of me like a scouting agent looking at the schools and the way of life. She had been working for a family in Bethesda, Maryland, as their house- and life-keeper. Mother claimed she ran the house, the lives, and the everyday rhythm and traffic of her chosen home. Housekeepers

try to believe this, but I suspect my mother was right. She had
yet to learn English fluently, but an irrepressible smile conveyed
plenty of meaning, and she could communicate loudly with her
broken new language. She was well loved by the American family for whom she worked, but she couldn't surrender her need
for independence and self-sufficiency. Within a year, she had
saved enough money and moved out. She continued to work for
several families in the Bethesda–Chevy Chase area as a live-out
domestic, but only for families she'd select. She shared a di-
minutive apartment with a Mexican woman on Bradley Boule-
vard within walking distance of a bus stop that took her to the
various homes she cleaned. Her roommate was Flora, a hair-
dresser, who let her stay in a foldout bed in the living room. No
problem. While Americans see overcrowding and poverty, an
immigrant sees an opportunity. Americans who bothered to notice may have wanted to define us as underprivileged. But poverty is a way station on our road into the American way of life.
María appreciated the United States and considered herself lucky
to be sleeping on a foldout bed in a cramped Maryland apartment. She bought herself a modest camera with a flashcube. On
weekends she and her cousin Nelly hopped on the bus to Washington, D.C., where they posed for pictures in front of national
monuments and mailed them to Chile. A picture of my mother
standing next to anti–Vietnam War protestors shows her smiling
in sweet innocence. The hippie protestors struck her as exotic
creatures, part of the free-love lifestyle that she had once seen in
the movies, and that she could now join in as a shy young Catholic woman who had no trouble getting male admirers, yet kept
her distance. Another picture is a glamour shot. My mother
poses in a miniskirt in front of an average home in the Maryland
suburbs, showing plenty of legs and a sensual pout with painted
lips. On the back, a dedication to her son. All the homes look
like this, she writes, in front of a cobblestone entrance to a gorgeous house.

What is remarkable in all the pictures she leaves behind is the adventurous spirit of an immigrant woman chronicling her eagerness to see it all for herself. The Lincoln Monument: we must stand in front of it. The Washington Monument: make sure it appears in the background. The Jefferson Memorial: let me move to the side for you to catch the cupola. It was a long way from the girls' school in Santiago in which food shortages had forced her to eat spicy ants off a stick.

A year's worth of paperwork, and I became entitled to join her in the adventure. I've always been grateful for this, even today when immigrants get attacked, and conservative politicians write that we're unwilling to learn English, that we refuse to assimilate. My mother and I arrived in a confident country that still welcomed immigrants. We sensed it. We felt right at home. We had trouble believing that there were Americans who resented us, who felt threatened by us. That's not the people we met in this suburb of D.C. Americans seemed sane. Anti-war protests revealed a democratic process, not chaos or hatred. Learning the language would take time, but there'd be no deep alienation for us (maybe mild befuddlement at times), no obligatory inner-city malaise that required us to, say, denounce our oppression as Third World people. That type of thing wouldn't come up until I went to UCLA, a shocking new political reality that tried to tear down my American childhood, deconstruct it for me, and spit it back as an imperialist, oppressive reality. My childhood had been the mirage. The luminous world into which I thought I had immigrated, in which my "poverty" seemed brighter, cleaner, more comfortable than any middle-class status I had experienced in Chile, would eventually be ridiculed—by more than one professor and several of my classmates. A Marxist history professor asked me about my background, and when he heard Chile, he was overjoyed. U.S. intervention, the CIA, the martyr Salvador Allende. When I told him we immigrated before the military coup, he was unfazed. He said I needed to pick up the struggle. When I told him I liked moving to the United States, that's when he replied, "That's all bourgeois illusion."

"You need to struggle anyway. You must find out the truth about Chile."

I agreed. "But I don't want to seem ungrateful to the U.S."

"The CIA destroys your country, and you're supposed to be grateful?"

"I'm getting an education because of the U.S."

"Milk it for all it's worth," he followed. "The Republicans are going to cut down on student aid, and then don't come tell me you feel grateful."

I couldn't argue. I didn't want to come across as naive, as I continued to cling to memories of my initial days as an immigrant as days of liberation. I also came from a school in Chile where bullying was practically required as a social norm. I have learned plenty about bullying in the United States, especially in the aftermath of the Columbine tragedy, but I thought that any meanness I encountered in U.S. schools did not compare to my childhood perceptions of cruelty in Chile. I wanted to listen to everybody and learn from all my teachers, but I often felt that they wanted me to fulfill their image of the victimized minority. I was poor. I was supposed to be angry. But my mother and I experienced exhilaration instead, a honeymoon with the much-denounced Empire. Even my Socialist aunt in Chile had warned me: the moment you get there you'll turn into a *gringo*. This was her specific lament. Still, my Socialist aunt was practical. She talked of a Cuban Revolution but understood with some fatalism the lures of the capitalist empire. She sent me to the United States to experience it for myself. She claimed one day the Socialist countries would also be ready to welcome immigrants, but for now, people tried to flee Cuba and the Soviet Bloc countries and risked their lives doing so. She recognized it as a temporary historical phenomenon: people wanted to live in the United States, but one day they would actually choose socialism.

Until that happened, off I went into the United States, and she found that perfectly acceptable, for the historical moment.

The Chilean relatives who put me on the plane wished me luck. Success, they whispered among themselves, *éxito*. *Hacerse la América*, they said, yet another expression that connotes success. It literally means "to make yourself an America," your own America, your own creation of the Big Time. The expression started with the European newcomers, for whom all the Americas meant finding gold. That's how you made your own America, by migrating to it, but now the term had turned north. Latin Americans used it to imply the United States, where you went to make yourself an America. To leave for the United States was considered a lucky break, leading inevitably to making it. My relatives, dozens of them, came to bid me farewell at the then-called Pudahuel International Airport of Santiago. Most had never seen a plane up close. There were still literal gates, the type that swing open, not simply the holes in the wall in which a movable unit (a jetway) connects travelers to the plane. They could stand behind those gates, and I—a little person traveling alone—went with my ticket and my legal residence papers into a bus that transported me and the other passengers to the plane. I got out of the bus and gave a final farewell to this throng of supporters cheering me on. The stewardesses gave me a suspicious look: a child traveling alone, something for us to take care of. But I gave them no problem. I was too busy inspecting the plane, playing with the buttons, and then admiring the clouds and the moon outside the window. I was an astronaut. I was Neil Armstrong. There had been a time when our teacher had made us memorize the names of American astronauts.

A friend of my grandmother, the indomitable Mother Lolita, who lives on into her nineties and looks as spirited and lovely as ever, slipped a bottle of her homemade liqueur into my backpack, a sweet concoction she called *dulce Lolita*. This was her farewell gift—meant for my mother. I chose to sip *dulce Lolita* on

the plane ever so slowly, to calm my nerves. The stewardesses
kept looking at it. At a distance, it might have looked like a sug-
ary drink, yet they didn't realize I was a ten-year-old enjoying
a happy hour. Once I landed in New York City, the customs
officials smelled it and gave me a strange look. Half the bottle
was gone. Then, when they looked into my suitcase, they found
herbs. Yet another aunt had slipped in bags of herbal remedies,
which were packaged in loose plastic bags. The customs inspector smelled them just to be certain but determined that those
suspicious-looking products were what they were, rural medicine. They're good for your mother's digestion, the aunt had
said. To top it off, an uncle had crowned me with a *huaso* (Chilean cowboy) hat at the airport, and I had boarded the plane
wearing it. As I slept on the plane, it slipped somewhere into the
crevices. I forgot about it altogether, and it disappeared into
the night. At JFK customs, I suddenly remembered. I told an
official who spoke Spanish that my *huaso*, my hat, was missing.
She let another officer know. The officer made a phone call. "Go
find some wa-zoo hat," he ordered somebody. Nothing turned
up. I had moved on to notice the impressive exit signs with their
wishes of success.

I was in New York City. My mother stood above, waving
from a viewing station overlooking the customs desks. I recognized her face immediately, a glowing, welcoming smile. We
hadn't seen each other in over a year. My mother's first action
was to walk me into the city, to 32nd Street, where we'd hitch
a ride to the top of the Empire State Building, something I'd
seen in the movies, with Deborah Kerr and Cary Grant kissing.

"How was your plane ride?" Mother asked.

"I barely slept," I said. "I kept playing with all the buttons,
then I read all my magazines, Archie comics, Batman, Lone
Ranger, and Barrabás (the Chilean cartoon about an indefati-
gable soccer team). Then the mean stewardess came by and
turned off my light and told me to sleep, but I couldn't. I looked

out the window and stared at the moon and the clouds the entire night."

It was the longest trip of my life, in child's time, which slows down to the minute and split seconds. Awake and aloft while cruising through clouds, I was an introspective child, ascertaining the meaning of this new life, imagining who knows what—excitement, glory, glamour? I felt no sense of loss. I didn't miss my native country. I didn't think I had left Chile forever. People talk about their exile, their need to abandon their homelands, perhaps for political reasons, perhaps risking their lives on rafts or, worse, walking by foot through a desert. I had left Chile on a joyride, with a full set of papers because my mother had planned it that way. Luck had allowed it to happen precisely as she planned it. Boring immigrants, that's what we were, ones who came without the drama of danger, risk, potential oppression, or alienation as "illegals." We felt the welcome and the transformation of a new life. Our optimism was probably justified—although today I have learned enough skepticism to ridicule it myself before others do. We were trained by Julie Andrews to think of our favorite things, and even our local church in Santiago had adopted the song in a Spanish translation. The American nuns who presided over the church kept up the Maria von Trapp allure of thinking good things. "Raindrops on roses, whiskers on kittens." Not much of a believer nowadays, I'm still grateful for the songs and the music the nuns gave us, like gifts wrapped in good wishes. There was something unhip about us, immigrants who actually enjoyed their immigration. I've learned today, through my academic friends, that a rosy disposition is considered square, even reactionary. In intellectual circles, I've learned to turn on the heavy sarcasm and irony, if only to hide a Catholic childhood in which we could sing songs such as "My Favorite Things" without being ridiculed.

In Maryland, we were newcomers, and yet we felt, of all

things, at home. Mother and I shared a sense of excitement and adaptability. The first lesson: other immigrants complain about everything; we annoyed them by liking everything. What better lesson than to find the *West Side Story* soundtrack in the mobile library that parked in front of our building every week. A mobile library was exciting enough—did we also make people sick by being excited by that, too? There were no public libraries in my neighborhood in Santiago at the time. The only library was the used book and used magazine store we ran ourselves. We were the facilitators of culture in the La Palmilla neighborhood at a time when television hadn't yet established itself in Chile. We didn't sell books. We rented them along with magazines. That was the essence of the economy. People were too poor to buy them, and the content was populist—cartoons, serial illustrated romances, movie gossip. But in Bethesda, the library came to us with books, for free.

"There are some books in Spanish in the back," I remember the librarian saying. Was she a librarian or just a driver? I didn't know the difference. There were indeed children's books in Spanish, which I checked out. But I plunged into English-language books at the same time. I didn't have to know the language. I wanted to stare at the words and the illustrations and try to match them. My first "Cat in the Hat" books were a surreal experience, drawings of a funky cat with language that expressed who knows what. The early playwright in me was writing his own script.

But much more important for the long-term imprint upon my imagination was another finding: the soundtrack of the Sondheim/Bernstein/Robbins musical *West Side Story*.

"I like to be in America," said the lyrics. One group of immigrants yearned to go back to San Juan, and the other wanted to give them "a boat to get on." I have spent the rest of my life acting out those lyrics. My mother was Anita, the lively Puerto Rican woman in love with Manhattan, singing about how much

she likes to be in America. The rest would be the other people—
the morose, the pessimists, the realists, the academics—who
tried to point out all the problems with life in the United States.

"But there is a reason why we came," Mother said. Gatherings included friends from Peru, Mexico, Guatemala, and
other Latin American countries. "Let's not forget that we left
behind countries that had no future for us (in Sondheim's
words: "Always the hurricanes blowing, always the population
growing").

This basic lesson was never lost on me. Our native countries would fall into the hands of dictators throughout the 1970s,
one by one, with the help of the CIA. The economies could not
catch up with the basic human yearning for some breathing
space, even a small touch of magic, of hope for oneself and family. Out of frustration, people rioted or joined revolutionary
movements, in which case the ruling class cracked down, im-
posing curfews, then dictatorship. The pattern repeated itself
over and over again throughout this period. Relatives from
Chile wrote short narratives, a paragraph here and there, revealing food shortages, riots, police brutality, and eventually the
tragic military coup.

My mother had no time to look back. For her the United
States was the place to dream first and then to work to pursue
those dreams. That night at the Empire State Building, she laid
it on the line: "*Ay, pero mira esta gran ciudad*, how the lights shine
up into the night. People who worked hard put up those buildings, not some *flojos* who do nothing all day. You build it day by
day, brick by brick; it's about the choices you make every single
day, from the moment you wake up."

It dawned on me that she always introduced a new task in
the context of play. A free afternoon? Why not go over the abc's?
Or the multiplication tables? Or use that new movie with Liz
Taylor to talk about the history of Rome and Anthony and
Cleopatra? A certain dutifulness came attached to the everyday

life, but she always made it seem as fun as riding the elevator to the top of the Empire State Building.

In looking back, I questioned her tone, her tendency to dismiss people as *flojos* the way some Republicans dismissed "welfare queens." I understood eventually why she didn't consider herself a Republican and still voted for Reagan. She resented the people who she thought dismissed hard work and who supposedly glorified dependency. I never met a "welfare queen" personally. But my mother recognized that I couldn't get an education without government aid, and that free lunches helped us make it through the day without experiencing hunger. She was a hardworking woman, but she could certainly use the subsidy. It became simply a matter of style—it was optimism that got you through the day, and the mantra was obligatory. Make fun of that optimism, and María made the unsuspecting victim get back that dismissive attitude Anita perfected so well: "I know a boat you can get on."

I still didn't know exactly what success entailed, but I knew early on in my first days in the United States that all the exit signs wished it for me. It was time to exit the building and start living out there in the new country, and to start getting the translations right.

MARCUS SAMUELSSON

Ethiopia

Marcus Samuelsson (1970–) was born Kassahun Tsegie, the second child of a poor single mother in the farming village of Abrugandana in east-central Ethiopia. Two years later, he, his mother, Ahnu, and his older sister, Fantaye, all contracted tuberculosis during an epidemic. In "the most mysterious and miraculous of ways," Anhu walked for days with Kassahun in her arms, seventy-five miles to a hospital in the nation's capital, Addis Abba. The children recovered, but Ahnu did not survive, and shortly after her death, Anne Marie and Lennart Samuelsson of Sweden adopted the children and renamed them Linda and Marcus.

Samuelsson's childhood in Gothenburg was a happy one, with a loving extended family, especially Mormor, his adopted maternal grandmother, who fostered his love of cooking. The boy's soccer prowess helped him to overcome the racial discrimination he suffered outside the home. Later, after graduating from the Culinary Institute in Gothenburg, Samuelsson apprenticed in various European restaurants before securing a job at the Swedish restaurant Aquavit in New York City in 1991.

A relatively new ethnic group to the U.S., Ethiopians have only recently begun immigrating. Many Ethiopians in the 1980s initially sought to escape famine and the repressive government of Mengistu Hale Mariam by migrating to neighboring African countries like Sudan, at least until the unsuccessful resettlement period forced them to seek better conditions in the U.S. when the opportunity arose following the passage of the 1980 Refugee Act. The annual limit accorded to Ethiopia has risen over the years, yet the number of refugees admitted per year is considerably lower than the number from other countries, partly the result of immigration officials' worry over the threat of uncommon communicable diseases. The majority of the estimated seventy-five thousand Ethiopians admitted by 1992 were educated Christian men, who were thought to be better prepared for assimilation; by 2007, gender parity was achieved.

Upon landing in New York, Samuelsson experienced a new sense of belonging. While he was often the only person of African descent in his Swedish community, he was one of the many in New York. Samuelsson felt a further sense of belonging at Aquavit, where he enjoyed both the familiarity of the Swedish cuisine and the comfort of the restaurant's multicultural, bilingual atmosphere. In 1995, Samuelsson rose to executive chef and soon earned recognition as a world-class chef. He has since opened his own restaurants, written an award-winning cookbook, appeared on television, and served as guest chef for President Barack Obama's first state dinner. Currently, he lives in Harlem, near his newest restaurant, Red Rooster.

The following passage from Samuelsson's bestselling memoir, Yes, Chef, describes his first few months in New York as he acquaints himself with the diverse culinary offerings of the city's ethnic enclaves. While the city was more accepting of Samuelsson, the restaurant world was not; and he describes the discrimination he faced as well as his resolve to break into the upper echelon of fine dining.

Excerpt from

Yes, Chef

— 2012 —

My plane touched down at New York's John F. Kennedy International Airport, and when I stepped into the terminal, the first thing I noticed were all the black people. They were everywhere. Black gate agents, black flight attendants, black baggage handlers, black cashiers, black cabdrivers. Black people, everywhere I turned. The second thing I noticed was that no one was looking at me differently. No, scratch that: No one was looking at me at all.

Right then, I knew I'd come to the right place.

In the weeks after my grief-stricken departure from Switzerland, I'd scrambled to find another restaurant placement. I was still aiming for France, but while I looked for a three-star spot that would have me, I needed to keep moving forward, not to mention keep some money rolling in. I followed up on every lead except for the ones that would have kept me in Sweden. Ironically, the apprenticeship I finally secured was in a Swedish restaurant . . . in New York. In fact, this restaurant was more Swedish in its menu than any I had ever worked in. Aquavit, housed in a former Rockefeller mansion, had opened in 1987, back when I was still a student at Mosesson. It was the brainchild of a food-loving Swedish businessman named Håkan Swahn who had settled happily in New York some years before but had missed the flavors of his homeland. In collaboration with the famous Swedish chef Tore Wretman, Håkan opened a restaurant that would be the first in the United States to serve more than smorgasbord and meatballs. Aquavit found a receptive audience among adventurous patrons who appreciated the pairings of sour, sweet, and savory that were, on the one hand, slightly exotic but, on the other, crafted from ingredients familiar to the European palate.

I'd landed the job at Aquavit thanks to my old friend Peter, a former *commis* at Belle Avenue. Peter had gone on to do well, and now he was a *sous-chef* at Aquavit. He got the executive chef, Christer Larsson, to offer me a nine-month apprenticeship, and so here I was at the airport, with nothing more than a telephone number and an address.

I threw my two duffels into the luggage hole of the bus, handed my ticket to the black bus driver, squeezed past a black woman nodding along with whatever was streaming out of her earphones, and sat by a window. I was more well-traveled than the average middle-class Swedish kid, thanks to soccer and my apprenticeships, but I'd never been anywhere that seemed as exotic as this. Over the course of the half-hour drive in from Queens, the enormity of the city started to sink in. There was just . . . more of everything. More congestion, more cars, more people, more skyline, more garbage. I don't think I looked away until the bus emptied out at Grand Central.

My first apartment was on the east side of the island, on Fifty-second Street and Third Avenue. Peter was not only my direct boss at work, he was my roommate, generously letting me bunk with him and his brother Magnus, a massage therapy student at the Swedish Institute College of Health Sciences, in their second-floor walk-up. Technically, the apartment was in midtown, but really, it had none of the business-world cachet of that label. We were more or less on the edge of the world then, in a tenement apartment so small I slept on the massage table set up in their living room.

"You can stay as long as you like," Peter offered, and while I knew he was generous enough to mean it, I also knew I should find my own place as soon as I could.

Peter's apartment was not far from the restaurant, which was then half a block west of Fifth Avenue and between Central Park and the Museum of Modern Art, all easy landmarks. But even with clear directions and a city laid out on a strict and logical grid, I got lost on my first day. I was distracted by everything. Especially the street people. In Göteborg, there was only one man who slept in the street. Everybody knew him and knew that he was rich—he *chose* to sleep there. In New York that first day, I saw homeless people on every block, stationed outside ATM lobbies and supermarkets, some holding Styrofoam cups, some passed out in entryways and alleys. I saw people smoking covertly, which meant, I figured, that they were not smoking tobacco. In Sweden, even though we had drugs, they were done in private, not out on the street. I was so turned around and discombobulated on the first day that even though I'd left the house after lunch and the commute was only a twenty-minute walk, I didn't arrive at the restaurant's doors until after my three p.m. shift start time. Not a good start.

Aquavit had two levels, a booth-filled ground-floor café adjacent to the bar, and a formal dining room downstairs. The dining room felt like a solarium: It was the onetime courtyard of the house, now closed in by glass, and its central feature was a Zen-like waterfall against one wall, which kept the mood of the room subdued and soothing.

The kitchen was smaller than any I'd ever worked in, a dozen cooks crammed shoulder-to-shoulder, pot racks overhead and screwed onto every available inch of wall. Manhattan real estate was too expensive to waste on the back of the house; there wasn't enough room for a kitchen with discrete stations and a traditional *chef de partie* system. We had Chef Christer and a couple of *sous-chefs* overseeing the rest of us, who were simply called line cooks. The other distinction was the smell, which was different from any kitchen I'd ever known. No matter how diligent we were in our cleaning, one odor lingered underneath: roach spray.

In many ways, Aquavit was the most comfortable work environment I'd had in years. I now had the skills to do most tasks automatically, which allowed me to pay attention to the overall rhythm of the kitchen, to the way Chef Christer worked through a week's worth of inventory, putting a glazed salmon with potato pancakes on Monday's menu and, by Friday, offering a tandoori-smoked salmon. The kitchen languages were English and a sprinkling of Swedish; the social culture was Swedish and American, a combination of familiar and relaxed; the flavor palate was in my bones. The informal café stuck to traditional Swedish fare: meatballs with mashed potatoes and lingonberries, vegetable and cheese-filled blini, rolls from the northern regions. In the dining room we used classical French techniques, with Christer applying Tore Wretman's brilliant philosophy of taking regional and folk specialties and elevating them to a more sophisticated plane. We'd make venison just as my mother's people did in the Skåne region, but instead of smoking it, we'd pan-roast it with olive oil, aquavit, thyme, garlic, allspice, and juniper berries. Instead of serving it with the traditional cream sauces, we'd lighten it up with a fruit and berry chutney. In another house favorite, Christer paired avocado and lobster, a melding of two worlds that worked so well it was hard to imagine no one had done it before.

On the line, I was able to hold my own from day one. I was more precise and probably a better cook than a lot of the guys, but they were fast and I had to get up to speed. We would churn out ninety covers for the pre-theater crowd, something I'd never seen before. In Göteborg, Belle Avenue was practically next door to the concert hall and city theater, but no self-respecting Swede would have considered eating until after the shows. At Aquavit, we got the ticketholders in and out in under an hour, then turned around and fed another ninety people right after that. The first few times I was on a pre-theater shift, I thought, Holy shit. I was drowning, constantly behind, constantly playing catch-up to the guys around me. So what if I was cleaner? It was speed that counted.

When I was at work, I gave everything I had to Aquavit, but when I was off the clock, I was a full-time student of New York. Here, it seemed, was everything I ever wanted. At first, I tried to make my $250 weekly paycheck go further by buying a used bike to get around. It got stolen almost instantly, which led to my first big American purchase: a pair of Rollerblades. I hardly rode the subway after that. The energy of the city was infectious, and I took to Rollerblading all over town on everything but the wettest and iciest of days. Skating was a way to save money and satisfy a lifelong addiction to exercise, but it was also a way to learn the map of the city, its architecture and topography, its neighborhoods and, most exciting of all, its foods. To get to work, some days I'd skate uptown first and cut back through Central Park, sailing through the aromas wafting from the chestnut-roasting vendors, the hot dog and shawarma carts, the syrupy burnt sugar of the peanut and cashew men. Other days I'd dip down into the thirties so that I could skate through Koreatown, with its smells of kimchi and its modest barbecue joints in the shadow of the Empire State Building. All those years of playing hockey on bumpy pond ice were finally paying off.

If I worked the early shift, I'd take off after lunch service and skate down the east side of the island, stopping in the Indian groceries to wander through the spice aisles, once in a while treating myself to something unfamiliar, like the pungent, gummy asafetida, which went from having a truly objectionable stink when raw to a pleasant garlic-meets-leeks vibe when cooked. One week I'd try yellowtail sushi in the East Village, and the next week I'd save up money to sample the tamarind-dipped crab rolls at Vong.

My favorite of all the ethnic-food areas, though, was Chinatown. Manhattan's was the biggest enclave I'd ever seen (at least until I ventured off the island to discover the South Asian neighborhoods of Jackson Heights, Queens), and I had my first dim sum at Golden Unicorn, a two-floor restaurant a couple of streets below Canal that was so vast and well-trafficked that it will probably outlast any other on the island. Chinatown's curbside stalls reminded me of the fishmongers in Göteborg's Feskekörka and along the Bryggan up on Smögen Island. There weren't just snails on offer here, but five different kinds of snails that had been graded into three sizes each. Some of the fish I could recognize, but many vendors didn't know how or didn't bother to translate their signs into English—besides, the bustling shoppers that jockeyed for service suggested that language was not a barrier to commerce. I went into basement supermarkets on Mott Street where I found entire aisles of dried mushrooms, and varieties of ingredients that I'd never known came in more than one version, like sea salt, which I now saw packaged in different grinds—fine, coarse, and flake—and in colors from white to pink to black.

My old boss Paul Giggs kept me company on many of these adventures—in my mind, at least. I'd look at the dish section of the supermarket, noting the graceful curves of teapots, the thousands of chopstick designs, and I'd recall his instructions to draw our food, to study the gemstones in Bern. "Food is not just about flavor," he'd lecture us. "It has countless dimensions, and one is visual. What do you want it to *look* like? What do you want the customer to *see*? Your job is to serve all the senses, not just the fucking taste buds, OK?"

In the aisles of Kalustyan's, a spice market on Lexington Avenue that continues to be one of New York's best exotic food sources for everything from *farro* to Kaffir lime leaves, I'd hold different dry curry blends up to my nose, committing their distinct aromatic structures to memory, but also remembering that they wouldn't release their full powers until they met up with heat.

"Toast your spices in the pan first or don't even bother,"

Giggs would say when he made a curry for Victoria Jungfrau's staff meal.

One spring day, I skated by a greengrocer in the northern corner of Chinatown, a block from the part of the Bowery where lighting supply stores alternated with restaurant equipment warehouses, chandeliers and exhaust fan hoods spilling onto the sidewalks. The unusually patient and orderly line of patrons stopped me. They were watching a woman with a large knife who stood at a makeshift counter between bins. Wearing a thick glove, from a stack by her side she picked out a green, spiky orb the size of a soccer ball, then sliced it open and into wedges, sliding her knife between the thorned skin and a milky interior flesh. In one fluid motion, she dropped the flesh into a plastic bag, secured the bag with a knot, and exchanged the bag for cash, only to start the process over again.

I watched for a minute or two, trying to locate a sign that would tell me the name of this object that resembled a medieval weapon. No luck. Was it a melon? A squash? I was upwind of the counter, but now and then I caught a whiff of something that cleared my sinuses. I smelled something nutty and fetid. The odor was repellent, but so tantalizingly strange that I couldn't break away. Finally, I tapped the shoulder of the last person in line, a young woman holding the hand of a toddler who looked to be her son. In her other hand, she held a bouquet of plastic shopping bags, pinks and greens and blues, all spilling out with leafy vegetables and paper-wrapped packages.

Not knowing if she spoke English, I combined raised eyebrows, pointing fingers, and speech.

"What is that?" I asked.

"Durian," she said, in an English far less accented than my own. "Green durian. It just came in this week. You like the smell?" She smiled as she asked this, but even as she wrinkled up her nose in shared disgust, I could see she wasn't about to give up her spot in line.

Again, Giggs's voice spoke to me.

"Cat piss," he'd once said, describing durian, a popular Asian fruit he'd first had in Singapore. "Smells like cat piss mixed with garlic, but the custardy texture is pure velvet and, if you hold your breath while you eat it, the flavor is sublime."

I slipped my hand in my pocket to make sure I had some bills, then took my place behind the mother and her son.

The more ground I covered in New York and the more people I met, the more I came to see the difference between international and diverse. Interlaken was international, and I got off on the energy of being around so many different cultures and languages there. But in the end, they were all going back to where they came from. The American waiters would head back to LA after one too many cold winters; the Portuguese dishwashers would be allowed work visas only as long as Switzerland needed their labor; the hoteliers and chefs in training, like me, would learn how to make fondue and *röschti*, then go on to the next kitchen, the one with more stars or a more famous executive chef. New York was different. There were divides along lines of race and class, but whereas the ethnic Swiss owned Switzerland and the ethnic Swedes owned Sweden, everybody in New York had a stake in where they were. Maybe you had to have a place this big to allow there to be a hundred different New Yorks living side by side, but almost everyone I saw seemed to move with a sense of belonging. This was their city whether you liked it or not.

I had an Italian-American friend named Anthony, a kid a couple of years younger than me whom I'd first met in Switzerland. Anthony was a good kid, if a little rich and bratty, the son of a hotelier who came from Garden City, a classic Long Island suburb. Sometimes I'd go visit him on a day off, which was like going back to the quiet of Partille or any other Swedish suburb, except even more removed. Anthony and his buddies drove everywhere, the girls sprayed their bangs into place and wore Reeboks, and when they weren't listening to Taylor Dayne, they listened to black music, even though they didn't have any black friends. I knew that Anthony genuinely liked me—I had his back the whole time we were working for Stocker—but I also knew that I was something of a prize he could parade around his friends to up his coolness factor. Almost none of Anthony's buddies ever went into New York City, except the adventurous few who'd snuck out one night to go in and hang out under the bright lights of Times Square.

All in all, I couldn't have asked for a better launch pad into the United States than Aquavit. My friend Peter watched out for me. Chef Christer was kind to me. The work, the food, the familiar culture, and the easier languages gave me a serious comfort zone, but I came to America to be with Americans, not Swedes. I was still working on getting to France, but I had an inkling that I might come to live in the United States someday, and this was my chance to check it out and make sure.

Apparently, I made my enthusiasm and curiosity plain, because I quickly made friends who volunteered to show me their versions of New York. One of the most influential was Casey, a line cook at Aquavit who was the only African American there. He came from a working-class background, and in the summer, he'd take me to family cookouts. His parents lived in the city of White Plains, a short train ride north from Grand Central Station, and I felt like I was entering an MTV video set when I saw their backyard table laden with fried chicken, coleslaw, and potato salad, with the guys my age able to drop in and out of any song lyric blasting from the DJ mixes on the stereo, everyone joining in when their girl from Mt. Vernon, Mary J. Blige, came along. "*What's the 411? / What's the 411? / I got it goin' on . . .*"

Every experience Casey showed me was hard-core. He took me to late-night hip-hop clubs in distant corners of Queens. We'd change trains three times so that we could see every kind

of act, from unknowns to Run-DMC. New York wasn't as polished back then as it is now, and those three a.m. train rides
home felt like scenes from *The Warriors*, where a gang rides subway after subway in its quest to get back to Coney Island. Casey's
friends either worried that I was some kind of cop or were
amused by me: I was black but not black. I played soccer and
they played basketball. I had darker skin than almost all of them
but poor command of their language and even poorer command
of style—my Levi's were too close-fitting, my Doc Martens
were not Tims, and it took me a while to shift from my blown-
out Hendrix fro to the fade I finally adopted for the rest of my
stay.

The more time I spent with Casey, the more I realized how
quaint my own upbringing had been. From the outside looking
in, I was fascinated that these guys who lived inside the law and
weren't broke still related to the hip-hop world where everyone
was on the lam and out of work. Casey's buddies identified with
that world and stuck with it the way I've since seen the alumni
of black colleges or fraternities stick together.

We'd go to the outer boroughs to hear music but also to
play basketball. I'd say, "There is basketball in Manhattan," but
they never wanted to play there. Manhattan was where they
worked. They called it "money-making Manhattan," and they
didn't know anyone who lived there, except for maybe in Harlem. When we went to parties in Harlem, I realized their whole
world was completely black. Maybe there'd be some Puerto Ri-
cans involved, but otherwise, it was all black. On the one hand,
that was opposite from my own upbringing. On the other, it was
just as homogenous.

Casey became my window into African American experiences, and I was so happy to be invited along; this was what I
came to America for. At times, it felt like a cultural test: What
would it take for me to belong? Was the color of my skin
enough?

Casey had a serious side, too, and he knew more about the Black Panther movement than anybody I've ever met. We would have these big arguments about how to fight for racial equality—MLK or Malcolm, early Malcolm or late Malcolm, violent or non-. Casey was intrigued by Sweden, and listened to my stories as if I were telling him about living on Mars. I realized how his world, so full and rich in some ways, was also like my pal Anthony's in that it was so completely cloistered, cut off from the rest of the world. As cosmopolitan as Casey and his homeboys seemed to me, they were also sheltered. It was 1993 and we didn't have the Internet; they didn't see black movers and shakers outside the classic professions of entertainment or sports. They had very little in the way of role models aside from Biggie Smalls and Tupac Shakur, men who, right or wrong, came across as powerful and self-made.

Another New York came to me through Aquavit, the New York of Central Park. I found it through Carlos, the Guatemalan fry guy who had fingers made of asbestos and would reach into the fryer to pull out pieces of fish and remain unscathed. Carlos turned out to be a serious soccer player. Plenty of guys in Aquavit's kitchen came from soccer-loving cultures. They had a favorite team or strong opinions of who was or wasn't worth shit, but not too many actually played with any regularity. Carlos was good.

"I'll show you where you can play," he offered, and the next day we both had off, he took the train into Manhattan from his Red Hook apartment, where he lived in close proximity to twenty or thirty people from his hometown of Guate, or Guatemala City. "We have better teams in Brooklyn, but this is easier for you."

We met at a field in Central Park, just above the Ninety-seventh Street transverse and in the lower part of the North Meadow. It was a series of fields, actually, all of them in use and with squadrons of players waiting to take over when any match finished.

I towered over many of my Central American teammates, which was the exact and pleasant opposite of my lifelong Swedish soccer experience. Even though I had no Spanish and some of them had no English, we were all fluent in our sport. We held our own against a crew of well-practiced Brazilians, then trounced a team of American yuppies whose training was no match for those of us born to the sport.

Afterward, I was with my teammates, shooting the shit, goofing on each other's mistakes and re-creating the great passes and goals. I got so worked up about a bad call that I started cursing in Swedish. "*Värsta* fucking *domare någonsin. Du måste vara jävla blind att ha missat det!*" Worst fucking call ever. You'd have to be fucking blind to have missed it!

I saw a group of black guys headed toward me. The smallest of the bunch, a light-skinned guy with a shaved head, looked me in the eye.

"*Svenne?*" Are you Swedish?

"Yeah," I said in English. "Are you?"

Teddy told me he was an Ethiopian raised in Sweden and Israel, and the guys with him were equally international, some part Swedish, some Somalian. The tallest one, a guy named Mesfin, was from an Ethiopian family that had moved to Stockholm. Mes was an aspiring photographer in New York, currently working at a coffee bar and schlepping backdrops at a fancy photo studio in the West Village.

Teddy, Mes, and I started hanging out right away. They were more like me in terms of experience and culture than anyone I'd ever met, and they also knew how to navigate the city. Mes had a coworker at the coffee bar, a handsome Somali Swede named Sam. Sam and Mes roomed together in a quirky arrangement they had with a model friend. The model let them stay in her apartment for free when she was doing the seasons in Paris and London, and it was several steps up from anything they could have afforded on their own: a doorman one-bedroom on Twenty-fifth and Park. At that point, I'd left Peter and Magnus's to stay in a series of word-of-mouth apartments with roommates I didn't know and where my stuff, what little of it there was, constantly went missing. When Mes suggested I join him and Sam in their one-bedroom, I packed my bags and went.

We rotated sleeping arrangements; one person got the couch and two shared the bed. At first we were suspicious of the doorman, assuming he knew we were not legitimate tenants, but he didn't seem to care and opened the door for us just as promptly as he did for the little old ladies with their little old dogs. That apartment was my first home in New York, a place where my Swedish-English patois was the common language.

My new roommates brought me into their world, which was every bit as exotic as my adventures into Queens. This was the era of the supermodel, and Mes's studio would regularly bring in Christy Turlington or Naomi Campbell for shoots. Eddie Murphy would be in one day, TLC the next. Often, the shoot day would end with a party, and under the guise of being staff, I'd join them behind the bar, pouring coffee and beers. If we didn't have a posh party to crash, we'd go to the one-dollar beer place in the Village where we could play pool and the jukebox gave you seven songs for a buck. We loved going high and low, and between the three of us, we had enough charm to get in almost anywhere. In Manhattan at the time, there was an ongoing underground party called Soul Kitchen that played soul music and switched locations every Thursday or Tuesday. One of us always figured out where that party was going to be. We'd go to Nell's on Fourteenth Street, a club that had live bands upstairs and hip-hop on the floor below, and where you got in not by wearing a suit, like so many clubs these days, but by wearing an attitude.

None of us talked about it—we were guys, after all—but

we all felt freer in New York than we had at home; we were no longer such oddballs. We all had other black friends and other people of color as friends and everybody did his thing. Everything we moved to New York for was happening for us: diversity, music, excitement, creativity.

Not everything went my way in New York, of course, and some of those disappointments were greater than others. On the lighter side of failure, my attempts at love, American style, flopped. I had this idea, when I arrived, that I wanted to date a typical American girl. (Whatever that was.) I wasn't more specific than that in my desire; I was just ready to change up from the Swedish au pairs I'd met through *Svenne* buddies at work. Casey hooked me up, of course—I'd have had no other way into that world.

The deck was stacked against me from the start, since I knew almost nothing about dating, much less American dating. In Sweden, we hung out in groups, and whoever ended up as couples still traveled as part of the group. Whoever had money paid; there were no expectations, and no one kept track. Once I got to America, my Garden City buddy Anthony filled me in on the high school prom rituals of the boy asking the girl, the corsage, the limo, the bow tie having to match the dress.

"For a high school *dance*?" I kept asking him.

When I met up with my first proper American date, an African American woman a couple of years younger than me, she seemed ready for adventure.

"Let's go places," she said. Cool, I thought, and headed for the nearest subway.

"No, I can't," she said, looking down at her high heels. "Not in these."

So we cabbed down to the Village to have a drink and some food at a skanky place on Bleecker Street. Then she wanted to go uptown to the Shark Bar, so we cabbed up to the Upper West Side and had another drink. Then she wanted to go back

downtown to listen to late-night music, and when we stepped
out onto Seventh Avenue, I counted out the fare for our third
taxi of the night and I realized I had only eight dollars left. I
panicked, then I got mad. Screw this, I thought.

"This has been nice," I lied. "But I have to get up early
tomorrow."

It's not in my nature to give up easily. I met another girl
and came up with what I figured was a surefire plan. One of
Aquavit's Brazilian waiters had gone back to Rio for vacation,
and I was apartment-sitting for him. He had a nice place, so I
figured, OK, rather than go on a date to some bad restaurant, I
should invite the girl over so I can cook for her. I get to show off
what I'm good at, and we'd eat better and cheaper than any restaurant I could afford. I called and proposed the dinner.

"What are you talking about?" she said, as if I were crazy.
For me that wasn't a weird thing, just to invite someone over and
cook a big meal. She finally agreed to come—as long as she
could bring a girlfriend/bodyguard.

"No problem," I said.

I did a four-course meal, with appetizer and soup and a
potato-wrapped salmon.

The girls oohed and aahed at every course. I figured I'd put
the girl I liked at ease, but as soon as dinner ended, and I asked
if she wanted to hang out, she and her friend announced they
had to go. I guess they'd figured they'd eat with me and then go
hang out with the guys who were serious prospects, guys with
enough loot to wine and dine them.

That wasn't me. My salary wasn't going to increase anytime
soon, so I had to figure out how to have fun on the cheap, and
find girls who would go along with that. By the end of my nine-
month stint, I'd tracked down the best hot dog stand in the city,
and that's where I'd take my dates. Afterward, if a girl hadn't
given up on me yet, I'd invite her to take a walk with me
through Central Park. You'd be surprised how many New

Yorkers have never really *been* to Central Park—or if they have, haven't visited it in years.

I love Central Park like only an immigrant could. It's an American masterpiece. I explored every corner of it: I'd skate up to 100th and Fifth to sit in the rose garden or hang out at the east-side plaza where roller skaters of every shape and size danced all day long. People were making out, picnicking, jogging. There was every color and ethnicity. Back then, you'd see lots of Vietnam vets, too, guys who'd checked out of society and made their home there. On the soccer field, I'd play one day against some of the best soccer players I've ever competed against in my life, and the next day, I'd be playing against some bum who would drop out to go smoke weed and then come back in. No one cared. No one was there to judge.

Being broke and living in a city like New York was no problem, once I realized you could still find plenty of stuff to do if you knew where to look. If I was going out and had fifty dollars to spend, I'd grab the *Village Voice* events calendar, scoping out whatever was cheap or free—concerts in the park, clubs with no cover, off-off-Broadway shows that needed butts in the seats. I got it down to an art form: how to have a good time for forty-nine dollars or less.

The best place to start was Chinatown, which was busy and energetic, with a sidewalk scene that provided plenty of visuals and smells and a totally exotic soundtrack. I found spots where my date and I could get a tasting menu for five dollars each, if you ordered right, and since I was the cook, I always ordered. We would share noodles, dumplings, steamed buns, barbecue ribs, hot and sour soup, and one noodle dish for the grand sum of ten dollars. Add in some really bad plum wine and a tip: sixteen dollars and you were good to go. For me, the best dish of all was the sweet pork buns, which were such a new combination of textures and flavors. The big white buns were light and airy with a slightly toothy skin caused by the steaming process.

I watched as the cooks loaded up bamboo steamer baskets with buns, put on their lids, and then set them over heats much higher than we ever used at Aquavit. At the center of the bun was a filling of roasted pork and a sweet sauce.

It came with a side dish of soy sauce, and into this I'd mix every condiment on the table: mustard, chili sauce, and a bit of chili vinegar. We'd dip the buns in the sauce and get through the obligatory first bite—all dough—to get to the mind-blowing second bite, which combined dough and filling. It's still one of my favorite dishes to eat. I always wondered who created this dish, how it came about.

The whole experience of the Chinese restaurant was so intriguing to me that I never minded being treated rudely or made to wait. And yes, the lighting was usually operating room fluorescent and the floor was linoleum and the service would have gotten you kicked out of restaurant school, but if you were lucky enough to be able to see into the kitchen, even glimpses through swinging doors, you saw a fury of activity, cooks working at top speed putting out tremendous volume and quality. That work ethic, along with a price I could afford, kept me coming back.

Chinatown was just one of a hundred food destinations I'd discovered, and almost day by day, my desire to stay in New York grew stronger. I was intrigued by what I was seeing in the American approach to food. It clearly started with the traditions of Europe but was not bound by them. Europeans I'd worked with scoffed at American cuisine, claiming it was nothing more than burgers. I knew that was bullshit. I was having one unbelievable food adventure after another, and I didn't want that to stop.

In New York, I was surrounded by people who were on their way somewhere. I wanted to be on my way, too, but it turned out that the rest of the New York cooking world wasn't quite as easy to crack as Aquavit had been. While I was still waiting to hear from places I'd written to in France, it seemed silly not to explore some American options while I was in the country. I aimed high. Jean-Georges Vongerichten was at Lafayette and Daniel Boulud was at Le Cirque, and while they were clearly geniuses, they were not at center stage. Center stage, at that moment, belonged to David Bouley, a chef from Connecticut who had made his mark in the city when he ran the kitchen at Montrachet, a TriBeCa restaurant owned by the then fledgling restaurateur Drew Nieporent. Bouley won raves for stuffing cabbage rolls with foie gras one night and pairing red snapper with a tomato-and-coriander pasta the next. Both Bouley and Nieporent were about to build food dynasties, but, due to mismatched temperaments, not together. In 1987, Bouley opened his own restaurant—Bouley—on West Broadway and Duane, practically around the corner from Montrachet. He knocked it out of the park, too, earning four stars from *The New York Times*, repeatedly coming in at number one in the reader-driven *Zagat Survey*, and winning awards from the industry's benchmark-setting James Beard Foundation. Customers reserved months in advance to taste Bouley's locally sourced fingerling potatoes or his roasted wild salmon with sesame seeds in tomato water.

I wanted to work for David Bouley.

I took the subway down to Canal Street one afternoon to see if I could secure a *stage* with him. I was fairly sure Christer Larsson would let me off for a couple of weeks; it was a kind of gentlemen's agreement among chefs to let your hard workers train with someone else when the opportunity arose.

The first thing I noticed about the restaurant was a crate of fresh apples sitting out on the sidewalk, waiting to be taken inside. I made my way back to the kitchen and recognized in every detail—the decor of the dining room, the freshness of the herbs that an intensely focused *commis* was chopping, the quiet seriousness of the staff—the same level of commitment I had known at

Victoria Jungfrau. I found the *sous-chef*, a German guy who would go on to have his own successful restaurant in the West Village some years later. I told him my history and asked if they'd let me *stage*.

"No," he said, and I realized that his gaze had stopped short of actually focusing on me, that he wasn't putting any effort into seeing beyond an instantaneous judgment he'd made that I was not worth his time. It was the look. I'd seen it everywhere from Gburg to Nice. "I don't think so."

"You could let me do a tryout before you decide," I suggested, feeling emboldened by my recent successes at Aquavit. I was offering a couple of weeks of free, skilled labor. If they let me work just one shift, they'd see what I could do.

"I don't think so," he repeated, and turned his back.

Had they ever had a black cook in that kitchen? Would they ever?

It was becoming clearer and clearer to me that black people were almost by design not part of the conversation about fine dining. In New York, I'd only heard of one black man to pull a chair up to that table, and that was Patrick Clark, a second-generation chef from Canarsie, Brooklyn. In 1980, when he was only twenty-five, Clark brought nouvelle cuisine to TriBeCa via the Odeon, and *The New York Times* gave him two stars in its very first review of the place. Clark would go on to do stints in LA and DC, he'd turn down an invitation to become the White House chef for the Clinton administration, and he'd eventually be named executive chef for Central Park's iconic Tavern on the Green restaurant.

Sometimes, when Christer Larsson took me along to swanky cooking events, I would see Clark there. He seemed like a nice guy with a big personality, built like a boxer. A well-fed boxer. He was always, without fail, the only black man among his peers, but he seemed at ease in any environment, confident that he deserved to be in the room, on equal footing with other food-world luminaries who left me starstruck, like Park Avenue Café's David Burke and Aureole's Charlie Palmer. Clark always seemed to be accompanied by people of color, people who probably would never have gotten into the room without him.

Back then, as a black man in the world of fine dining, Patrick Clark was truly the exception to the rule. His food was solid and well-executed, his passion and personality were larger than life, and yet he would never get more than two stars. I wanted more. I wanted four stars. The upper echelon among chefs was still reserved for white men, but I knew, in my heart, that that could change. I was the Lion of Judah, as Ethiopians sometimes referred to themselves, born into one of the oldest, proudest civilizations on the planet. And I was raised with the truth of equality, by white parents who lived out their belief in racial equality through their love and protection and support. I believed in myself as a chef. I just needed to get through the door. The key, I knew, was to have the one credential that still mattered above and beyond anything else: France. If I could get to France, then even a jerk-off *sous-chef* couldn't afford to ignore me.

KATARINA TEPESH

Croatia

Women's rights advocate Katarina Tepesh (1950–) was born on the Slovenian side of the Sutla River in the city of Rogatec, the fourth of six children of Ivan and Bozena. Before World War II, Ivan was already an abusive alcoholic who relied on patriarchal traditions and violence to assert his authority over the family, but his abuse escalated upon his return from his brutal experiences as a soldier. After years of mistreatment and poverty stemming from Ivan's alcoholism, Bozena began to fear for the lives of her adolescent children and fled with them to Samobor, Croatia.

Living in a decrepit, illegally rented room and struggling to find work, Bozena contacted her sister, Anica, then living in the United States as a mail-order bride, for monetary assistance. Anica recognized that sending money was only a temporary salve for her sister's problems and hired an immigration lawyer to petition for the family's permanent resident status; however, Bozena could not legally take the children out of Yugoslovia without getting divorced from Ivan, who opposed the step.

Penniless, the Tepesh family landed in New York City in 1968, and Katarina discovered the women's rights movement, through which she learned to assert herself and work her way out of menial factory labor by attending evening classes at City College. Tepesh worked in finance and is now an accounting supervisor for the YWCA in addition to volunteering with the National Organization for Women.

Tepesh has said that her inspiration for writing the memoir Escape from Despair *was to break the circle of silence that surrounds violence against women, a topic she began exploring in "My Father's Funeral," an essay written for a class at the Gotham Writers' Workshop. Like the authors of many other selections in this volume, Tepesh links her family's immigration to the turbulent politics of her homeland but goes a step further by linking her country's fate to her family's history of abuse and their desire for freedom. The following excerpt describes how her older brother began emulating his abusive father, while her mother once again submitted to traditional gender roles.*

Excerpt from

Escape from Despair
— 2007 —

Much to my surprise, one of my school professors asked me to visit her apartment on my day off from the beauty parlor, to help manage her very long black hair, which her husband never let her cut. I tried to tell her that it wasn't a good idea and came up with all kinds of excuses. When nothing worked, I went so far as to tell her that I needed to do homework. "You doing homework?" she sneered. "That will be the day!"

These bloody Communist teachers! I thought. *They all talk to each other!* She was fairly new in school but must have found out that I wasn't a good student. I couldn't focus on school because I desperately needed someone to talk to about my mother. Nothing they taught helped me with the problems I faced in everyday life.

I had no choice but to go to the address the professor had given me in a part of town I had never visited before. I stood

there and just stared at the brand-new apartment complex reserved only for Communists.

It got much worse as I entered her apartment and saw for
the first time how the Communists lived. It was beautiful and
sunny, with huge windows, three bedrooms full of furniture, a
balcony, a shiny parquet floor, and a kitchen with all kinds of
machines. I felt sick to my stomach contrasting that apartment
with our miserable living conditions.

The professor wanted her hair in a French twist, which was
fashionable then. When it was done, she innocently asked,
"How much do I owe you?"

Shifting my weight uncomfortably, I silently cursed her.
What a hypocrite, I thought. If she wanted to pay, she should have
come to our beauty salon instead of making me come to her
luxury apartment with its beautiful American-style kitchen, just
like the ones in the Doris Day movies. She pushed some money
into my purse and asked if I could come again next week.

I shrugged my shoulders, mumbling that Mama might
need me.

Later, I made all kinds of excuses to avoid going to her
apartment. It disturbed me greatly to see how well the Communists lived in a country promoting brotherhood and equality.

I used the money to see another Doris Day movie. After
the movie, I went home and talked endlessly about marvelous
kitchens, a topic that we, as a family without a kitchen, fantasized about. I didn't say a word about what I saw in the movie of
romance, flirting, and sexual attraction.

Joza mailed us French Francs stuck between pages notify-
ing us that he temporarily worked in a garage in France while
he applied for legal papers to go to America. Mama had a most
difficult time exchanging French Francs because Mr. Abramovic
only wanted U.S. dollars. Mama had no choice but to go to the
government bank where she received little money in exchange
for Francs.

The only good thing about my life was the handsome teen-ager Ljubimko, who was always smiling and waving. I was attracted to his smile and endlessly fascinated that he could smile so much. Like me, he was from the working class. He was the same age I was, going to the same school, living in the same town. What did he have to smile about?

When Mama forced me to go to Mass, the presence of Lju-bimko made it bearable. I had a secret crush on Ljubimko, pre-ferring to look in his direction as opposed to pray during the Latin mass. When he wasn't there, I had to look at the seven-teenth-century frescoes and beautiful stained-glass windows. Built in 1675, the parish church of Saint Anastasia was a spacious Renaissance structure with three side chapels and a sanctuary supported by pillars. I loved the sound of the church bells, but I disliked the endless sermons telling us that we must procre-ate and that women must submit to their husbands. Each time the priest reminded us that Jesus suffered for us, I would glance toward Mama and see her wiping away tears and hang-ing her head in prayer, clutching her rosary. She had obeyed all her life and become a martyr. That was the last thing I wanted to do.

After a long and bitter court fight, the committee deter-mined that the divorce was our father's fault. He signed the legal papers on November 28, 1967, giving up the custody of his minor children as long as he was never obligated to pay child support.

Later, we miraculously passed a medical exam ordered by the American government. Knowing that the doctors would expect to be bribed, Mama told them, "Even if you shoot me, I don't have a penny to give you!"

Next, we were called to the American embassy in Zagreb. We entered the room, shabbily dressed and sickly looking. The cocky American representative, smoking a smelly cigar with his feet on top of his official mahogany desk, addressed our mama in broken Croatian. "Are you now or have you ever been a member of the Communist party?"

This question was so preposterous that Mama just kept quiet.

"Are you now or have you ever been a member of the Communist party?" the man repeated.

Glancing nervously at all of us, Mama said, "I am a mother to six children!"

"Are you now or have you ever been a member of the Communist party?" he asked again.

"No! I am a mother to six children!"

Slamming down his hand, he stamped the official papers that would allow us to leave the country and reside permanently in the United States of America.

As soon as we stepped outside the American Embassy, we ran to the main post office in Zagreb to send a telegram to Anica in New York: "Received papers. Stop. Need airline tickets. Stop."

Anica mailed us the airline tickets, along with a note explaining, "Once you arrive in America, you'll get some kind of a job and gradually repay me."

Either because she was riddled with guilt for leaving or because she just wanted to forgive her husband before she left him forever, Mama ordered us children to take a train to Rogatec to say good-bye to our father. I hated to go back to the horror house in Rogatec, not knowing whether he would scream hate-filled obscenities or pull a knife on us.

Shyly, we extended our hands for our father to shake and ran out the door. He called us back and insisted that we eat some soup and fried chicken, with rice and salad prepared by his new girlfriend, Marica, a local woman whom we all knew as a friend of the family. I thought, *He never had any love for us, his children, but* now *he's taken up with Marica*. But, within minutes, I realized that he was barking orders at Marica, just as he did with us.

Marica looked and behaved much like Mama. She wore practically the same clothes, reflecting the limited choices available in communist Yugoslavia, and had the same quiet manner, bordering on submissiveness—anything to please him so that he wouldn't throw a tantrum or, worse, beat her up.

We spent the day saying good-bye to our schoolmates and coworkers. On our final night in Samobor, Zorica invited us to her farm for a feast of roast lamb, baked potatoes and fresh, crispy green salad. When *tamburitza* melodies floated through the air, the music touched our hearts and tears rolled down our faces.

Zorica bought food and delicious desserts that we could never afford but wanted to eat during our two years living in a shack.

We were deeply grateful to Zorica for feeding us and for her inspiring motto: "One day, you'll be out of here!" which now came true.

We expected our landlord, a slightly tipsy Vuk, to be delighted to get rid of us. But, no, he gave us a lecture instead.

"I swear I'm not talking about my rent money. But I'll say this to you: I object to your moving to America. Now we live in Communist Yugoslavia but one day we will have a free and independent Croatia. And I only talk like this among friends; otherwise I would go to jail. You're Croatians, and you should stay here. You're deserting our homeland, our dear Croatia. Imagine if every Croatian family with difficulties moved overseas. What would happen to our beloved Croatia? We can't allow Croatians to disappear. We need more of God's children to build up our country. No, I say, stay, get married, have babies, and work like the rest of us."

Officially, in 1968, Croatia still belonged to Yugoslavia, but many Croatians, including Vuk, wanted a free and independent Croatia. I rolled my eyes and thought, *Bloody Fascist Vuk! He wants us to stay and suffer.*

The next day, early in the foggy morning, we took a bus to the Zagreb airport, shivering from the cold and crying all the way. All of us were terribly nervous and afraid. We had never seen a plane except very high up in the blue sky.

We had to leave Croatia. Mama, a good, decent, and law-abiding citizen, was forced to leave to survive. The corrupt Communists, who lied, stole and cheated, stayed behind to do more damage.

On the plane, we were nauseated and throwing up all the way to New York. The American stewardesses tried to be sympathetic. Smiling pleasantly and politely, they kept offering us Coca-Cola and ginger ale to soothe our nervous stomachs. None of us in the family spoke English. I was dying to drink a soda, but I thought that the stewardess would ask us to pay for it. Knowing we had no money, I just kept shaking my head, indicating that I couldn't accept a soda.

Finally, after a long and tiring plane ride, we descended at sundown, watching the flickering lights of eight million New Yorkers and listening to Frank Sinatra singing "Strangers in the Night" from the airplane speakers.

We landed at JFK Airport on April 6, 1968, without luggage, money, or any possessions except the legal papers in our pockets. Those were worth gold, or at least we thought so.

As soon as we landed on American soil, Mama made the sign of the cross, moving her right hand to her forehead and muttering, "In the name of the Father, and of the Son, and of the Holy Spirit. Amen."

As we went through customs, Mama, looking older than her forty-five years with a peasant handkerchief around her head, clutched her rosary. Standing beside her was my older sister, Ljubica, who was nineteen, followed by my two younger brothers, Slavek, sixteen, and Ivek, twelve, and me, seventeen years, five months, and eight days. Marijana was still in Yugoslavia, waiting for her new husband, Niko, to get his legal papers so they could join us.

We were greeted by Joza, age twenty-two, who arrived from France a couple of months earlier. We shook hands with Joza, who looked skinny and tall, fashionably dressed in a new pair of jeans, grey sweater and a dark brown leather jacket. In contrast, our family was dressed shabbily in the cheapest clothes Mama could find. As the youngest of the three girls, I wore hand-me-downs from my older sisters.

Next, we kissed our aunt Anica and her second husband, Walter, who met us at the airport with two of their cars. Anica, who had arrived in America eighteen years earlier as a mail-order bride to her first husband, Louis, was our godmother and had supported us financially our whole life. Anica had lent us the money to buy one-way tickets to America and signed the legal papers certifying that our family would not be a financial burden to the United States.

Anica started preaching to us immediately. "We're Catholic Croatians," she said, as much to herself as to us. "Poor but decent people. We don't steal, lie, or cheat. No welfare for us! Everybody is going to work and school later this week. So, we resolve to be good citizens: obey the laws, pay our taxes, and, eventually, vote. Now that you're in America, you must understand that voting is a privilege and an obligation. Always be punctual and neat going to work and Mass. Your upbringing— a combination of your parents, the Communist system, and the Catholic Church—was not so bad."

After a short pause, my aunt continued, "After all the horrors you went through in Communist Yugoslavia, don't even think about drinking alcohol, smoking cigarettes, or taking illegal drugs. It would kill you. Instead, look for ways to heal yourselves by praying."

Squashed between my brothers in the back of Anica's silver Buick, still feeling nauseated from flying, emotionally drained, I thought, *The woman is right!* We needed to be healed, physically and emotionally. The entire family had viral Hepatitis A and B and chronic viral tuberculosis. Most of us had rheumatoid arthritis, and some of us had a chronic eye infection called blepharitis after a history of repeated styes. We had the promise of a new life, but we also had haunting memories.

Meanwhile, from the airport, Mama was riding in a car with Uncle Walter and Joza. Already at the airport, as soon as they closed the car door, Joza turned to Mama, angrily asking, "Why doesn't everybody thank me for the French Francs I mailed to the family in Samobor?"

Mama felt uncomfortable, "Oh, Joza, we are grateful, but we could not write to you because we had no return address. Worse, I had so much trouble exchanging your French Francs on the black market in Yugoslavia. Nobody wanted them. They asked for American dollars."

"What?" Joza screamed at her. "I almost killed myself escaping from Yugoslavia to Italy, dealing with snow storms on my way, hiking over the mountainous Alps border to France. In Nice, I took a big risk by working on the black market fixing probably stolen cars and I mailed you my hard-earned French Francs." Gnashing his teeth, Joza shook his head in disapproval, bitterly hurt at what he perceived as our disrespect and ungratefulness. He envisioned himself as our family savior, and demanded to be acknowledged as such. He avoided direct eye contact with Mama, while her lips trembled at this new development of events reminding her of similar troubled behavior from Ivan.

Our family had been deeply hurt by our father's chronic verbal and sexual abuse of our mother. We were bleeding from wounds and each of us carried a big chip on our shoulders, but we were still standing!

Our entire family settled down in a two-bedroom walk-up apartment in a working-class section of Ridgewood. Our apartment was officially in Queens, but our post office, two blocks away, was in Brooklyn.

Our new neighborhood consisted of gritty avenues lined with factories and sprawling row houses inhabited by blue-collar families, most of them immigrants from Italy, Ireland, or Germany. The area was a mix of small brick and stone buildings, old and new, bisected by Myrtle Avenue, the main commercial strip. The private homes had adjacent garages, with cars in the driveways, little gardens in front and back, and barbecue grills during the summer.

The railroad-style apartment cost $347.45 a month. Our aunt arranged for us to receive a $75.00 monthly discount for cleaning the hall and steps once a week, as well as taking out the garbage from the basement every Monday and Thursday.

We kids bickered constantly about who was going to take the foul-smelling garbage from the basement and leave it at the curb. The heavy aluminum garbage cans had a handle on each side, and it took two people to pick them up. "It's not my job!" we screamed at each other, holding our noses.

"I don't want the landlord to get angry at us, so I'll clean the halls myself," our mother said. From then on, she cleaned twice and sometimes three times a week, to the delight of the three other families that lived in the building.

Mama looked tired and thin, with dark circles under her eyes and puffy eyelids. Her face was riddled with worry lines, and her blue eyes appeared bloodshot from tossing and turning all night. She had a tendency of talking slowly and making nervous hand gestures. Women her age were going through menopause, a true change of life. Her health had suffered after she gave birth to six children and was forced to deal with additional unwanted pregnancies, all of which had been aborted. The complete hysterectomy at age thirty-seven saved her life, but she was left with debilitating monthly migraine headaches resulting in part from severe beatings that had fractured her skull. She felt dizzy and her vision became blurry. Month after month, she complained, "The migraine feels like someone is hitting a hammer inside my head."

Mama hated going to doctors. Anica admonished her, "Don't be so stubborn. I insist and am going with you." After a checkup, Mama was given a B-1 injection to improve her immune system and received a high dosage of hormone replacement therapy tablets.

Mama had been taught by nuns to pray every morning, as soon as she opened her eyes, by making a cross with her right hand and saying, "*Majka Bozja koja si v nebesah*. Holy Mary, Mother of God . . ." She repeated the prayers every night before closing her eyes.

By the time we reached America, Mama was burned-out. In addition to her poor health, she felt overwhelmed with learning English. Her once-bright smile, which I had seen only in the black-and-white photos taken before her marriage, was gone.

Other members of the family, particularly Joza, reacted to our new country in unexpected ways.

The first time we shopped at the A&P supermarket, walking alongside the huge glass window, I saw tremendous amounts of food, very different from the markets in our old country. Just as we approached the entrance, the door opened automatically. The sudden, jerky movement startled me, and I stared in amazement. Joza snickered. "Aha, I knew that America has automatic doors. I was watching your face. You're stupid because you didn't know it was automatic."

"Don't call me stupid. We're in America now."

Joza looked down at me, laughing loudly and jabbing his finger in my face. "You're stupid and ugly."

Offended, I rushed home, crying, "Mama, Joza called me stupid and ugly."

Wearing a beige housedress two sizes too big for her, Mama was kneeling on the kitchen floor, scrubbing the white-and-gray-checkered linoleum. She tilted her head to look up at us. "Oh, I don't know what to do with you children. Why can't you get along?"

"Why don't you punish Joza?"

"Ah, boys will be boys." She waved her hand and continued cleaning.

"This isn't right," I protested. "Our father called us stupid and now it's our brothers. They're no better than our father."

"Don't say that! Don't say anything! You're no better than your brothers."

"Shut up!" Joza screamed at me on his way to the kitchen refrigerator to pick up a cold Budweiser. Flicking the beer can open, he raised his hand and proclaimed in a loud voice, "Listen to me, everybody! From now on, I want my own room. My brothers can sleep on the living room couch. I'm the oldest son, so I'm the boss now. I make more money than any of you, and I want my own room."

Except for the two youngest boys, who attended school, we had all found jobs, and we divided the expenses for rent and food equally. Joza was earning $3.25 per hour as a tool and die maker, but the rest of us were earning the minimum wage of $1.68.

"If you want your own room, you should contribute a larger portion toward the rent," said Ljubica.

"Shut up! I make decisions in this family, not you. I'm the boss now, and I'm not going to pay more," screamed Joza. "Like our father always said, women are witches. I won't listen to you."

"If you have the money to buy *Playboy* magazine . . ." continued Ljubica.

"I told you to shut up!" screamed Joza. "I won't listen to

you. You talk like a motor mouth. You're stupid and ugly!" He slammed the door and left to take tennis lessons at the nearby park.

Ljubica and I jumped up from the table and circled Mama, both of us talking in urgent tones. "You have to talk to Joza! Tell him he can't have his own room while the rest of us are cramped in the other bedroom. It's not fair that all of us have to sleep in one bedroom while he has a room of his own."

"Oh, what can I do? Joza is the oldest. Well, he's a man and has his needs. Nothing I can do. He can have his own room." Mama, wearing her ever-present flowery apron, clasped her hands in the sign of prayer and looked toward heaven. "Oh, Majka Bozja, help me," she mumbled and turned back to the kitchen to continue cooking. After a while, she called out her mantra from the small kitchen, "I just want all of you children to get along."

My job, stacking woolen material before it was cut and sewn into sweaters at the Ridgewood Knitting Shop on Putnam Avenue, was monotonous and boring. I was worried sick that I would never escape factory work. But, like the rest of the family, I was also taking English 101, which I hoped would lead to better things.

With the help of my Croatian/English dictionary, I could read the labels on the bottles of over-the-counter medication sold in the numerous drugstores. To my intense relief, I discovered that my chronic, extremely painful menstrual cramps had a name: endometriosis. Cells from the inner lining of the uterus, called the endometrium, sometimes form into small growths or benign tumors outside the uterus. These growths normally form around the pelvic area and affect the ovaries and the fallopian tubes. During menstruation, the tissue breaks down and bleeds just like the cells in the uterus. The problem is that the blood outside the uterus has nowhere to go and remains in the body, causing organ inflammation, which, in turn, causes severe pain and cramps on the first day of menstruation. That's what had happened to me in Rogatec and continued in Samobor, occasionally keeping me out of school or away from work. Now, with over-the-counter medication available, my menstrual suffering was over. I no longer had to listen to Mama's "Trust in God."

"On Sunday, we're all going to church," Mama announced just before our first weekend in America. "I would like all three boys to serve God as ministrants."

"No, I'm not going!" I said in my stubborn way. "I want to see Manhattan."

Ljubica joined me with, "Me, too."

The boys exclaimed that they had plans of their own. "We discovered a nearby public park that has twelve free tennis courts! It also has a soccer field. We'll be playing tennis and soccer all day on Sunday."

This was the day Mama discovered that none of her children shared her religious beliefs. We had seen too much hypocrisy in our family to truly believe. Our father had forced us to go to Mass. After we escaped him by running away and moving to another town, Mama, who was even more religious, forced us to attend just as our father had. Now, however, we were older and we were in New York. No one could force us to attend Mass if we chose not to go.

Ljubica and I were curious to see Manhattan. Our first adventure was trying to find the Statue of Liberty from our Queens neighborhood. Not speaking the language, we were thoroughly confused: uptown, downtown, exit, entrance, east, and west. It took us practically all day, but we finally found it. That's when I cracked my first smile, right in front of the Statue of Liberty.

Two weeks later, along with Ljubica, I visited Central Park. Finding it, without speaking English, was quite an adventure.

Older women in the factory warned me, "Whatever you

do in New York, don't ever go to Central Park!" As soon as I heard that, like a typical rebellious teenager, I wanted to see it for myself. Yes, it was dirty, with cans and papers strewn all over the grass, but there were beautiful things, as well: musicians strumming on guitars, hippies walking everywhere, girls dressed in miniskirts, the Alice in Wonderland and Hans Christian Andersen statues, the Belvedere Castle, a lake for boating, the Vanderbilt gardens. . . .

During my very first walk in our Queens neighborhood, I saw signs reading, "Welcome Home, Johnny," for Vietnam vets. The signs were all the same; only the names varied. Of course, most soldiers did come home, some unharmed, others wounded, and some in body bags.

Within the first month of our life in America, Mama opened the apartment door, crying and looking crushed. "Anica told me that the boys might be drafted for Vietnam," she cried hysterically. "If that happens, they must go because the government makes those decisions. But what if something happens to them?"

In Communist Yugoslavia, we were constantly surviving one crisis after another. Now, in America, the possibility of danger lurked again, only this time, it was in faraway Vietnam, killing the Communists or being killed.

At the factory, I befriended a woman who invited me to a picnic. "It's the Fourth of July, Independence Day! You have to come to our picnic and try our delicious, juicy hamburgers, French fries, and coleslaw. For dessert, we'll serve apple pie à la mode. Do you know what that is?"

I looked at her blankly.

"Oh, never mind. It's vanilla ice cream on top of warm apple pie," she explained.

When I arrived at her backyard, she exclaimed to the small crowd of relatives, "Hey, everybody! This girl just arrived in April from Communist Yugoslavia!"

A fat man smoking a smelly cigar approached me. Smiling wickedly, he said, "How is the old dictator, Tito?"

I nearly collapsed, my knees buckling. I had just spent my youth hearing nothing but praise for Josip Broz Tito, the heroic figure who fought the Nazis, and suddenly here was an American calling him a dictator. It left me speechless, literally and figuratively.

Later that week, our family had a huge surprise. All of us except Joza, who was working overtime, were sitting around the table finishing dinner, when suddenly we heard a knock. We didn't expect anyone and didn't react. The door opened and in stepped a tall, stunning blond woman wearing a white tennis outfit and holding a Wilson tennis racket. Her short tennis dress had a vertical red line on the sides, accentuating her long, sun-tanned legs.

Smiling sweetly, she said, "Hello, I'm Elsie. Is Joza home?"

We shook our heads and wondered how in the world Joza, whose English was not much better than ours, had managed to meet Elsie.

We fumbled nervously with the dishes on the table, and Ljubica said to Elsie, "Coffee?"

"Oh, no. I don't drink coffee. Please tell Joza that Elsie was looking for him to play tennis. By the way, Mrs. Tepesh, it's wonderful that you have six children. I'm an only child and always wanted a brother or sister."

I thought, *If only Elsie knew what a mess it is to have a huge family.*

Later, when Joza came home and we told him about Elsie, he laughed. "Yeah, I met her at the park, playing tennis. I was pretty sure she threw her tennis balls toward me on purpose, just to meet me. She's German. I think she said that her family escaped from East Germany. Eh, she's wild about me. I could have thirteen girls like Elsie; they're all over the place."

"Don't talk like that," Mama admonished him. "Your

father always said he could have thirteen women at any time. And now . . ." Her lips trembled and she ran out of the kitchen, crying.

Our feelings toward our father were confusing, full of guilt. On the one hand, we were relieved to be away from him in a safe place, remembering how he used to beat us up, while at the same time we worried about how he was getting on. Our mama made us write letters to him, but we didn't know what to say.

The most important thing I tried to learn, besides English, was typing. In class, we used clunky old IBM typewriters. To practice and memorize the keyboard at home, I circled a penny on a blank piece of paper and stenciled in the letters as they appeared on the keyboard. Riding the subway, I stared at the paper until I memorized the location of each key and could type without looking (what the teacher called "blind typing"), using all ten fingers.

During this time, I changed jobs frequently among textile knitting factories. A German woman taught me how to use a sewing machine, a job that paid a dime per hour more than I was paid as a plain apparel worker. Sometimes I was fired when the capitalist boss objected to my going to night school, suggesting that I concentrate only on the factory work and produce more work faster.

My budget was so tight that I had no money for luxuries like movies. If a boy didn't take me to the movies, I just couldn't go. My first year in America, I earned $2,546.73 before taxes.

The biggest discovery in America for me was the women's rights marches. Even though I didn't fully understand the details, I grasped the overall idea and saw it as the solution to our family's problems, as well as the way women were treated in my old country.

The first time that I saw American women marching in protest on television, I couldn't believe my eyes. I was surprised just to see so many women walking peacefully along the streets. Immediately, I started comparing the diversity, openness, and free speech in the United States with the silence and total obedience demanded in the Communist bloc.

The idea of sisterhood did not work very well in our home. Now that they were living nearby in New York, the two sisters, Anica and Bozena, like our siblings, didn't get along smoothly. Occasionally, their disagreements erupted into arguments.

Every day, as I did my monotonous factory work, I kept thinking about our turbulent family life: how Mama had endured one pregnancy after another. How our neighbors, both the Communist authorities and the Catholic priest and nuns, had tolerated the violence with hardly a word to our father.

Now, in America, our family continued to keep silent among ourselves about father's abuse. He had threatened us to keep quiet, which we did in order to survive. When Americans asked us why we came to America, we felt extremely uncomfortable, avoiding eye contact and trying to change the subject. All of us were trapped in a vicious circle of pain. Most of the time, we expressed our frustration and anger by blaming each other, all of us dancing the same dance over and over again without knowing how to stop.

I kept thinking, *If only Mama had had the same rights in Communist Yugoslavia that she has here, our father would never have gotten away with beatings and unwanted pregnancies.*

What had rattled me throughout my childhood in Yugoslavia didn't stop in America. I was one of too many children in the family who didn't count. All of us had medical problems that our destructive father and our helpless, subservient mother had not attended to. Our three brothers picked up where our father left off, abusing us verbally. They behaved like macho bullies, always needing to be right. When we fought, Mama would cry and wring her hands. I wanted her to defend me, but she never stepped forward.

When we were financially dependent on our sadistic father, I always fantasized that, if we ever managed to get out and away, Mama would know how to be the head of our family, how to be affectionate toward us, as she was not allowed to do when we lived with our troubled father. I wanted and needed her to be the captain of our ship, steering us through a turbulent sea. But with her long history of sexual abuse, she couldn't. Worse, our ship was suddenly hijacked by the pirate Joza, committing treachery against the rest of our family. Back in Rogatec, Joza had been part of our team, trying to figure out how to rescue us from the clutches of our cruel father. Now that we were finally in America, Joza turned against us by continuing our father's abusive behavior every day. Just like our father, Joza was pugnacious, yelling threats and curses. In front of strangers, Joza put up a charming front, especially to women. But at home with us, he was capricious. His moods were unpredictable, his anger petty and vicious. Within three months after coming to America, our family broke apart. I moved out and didn't speak to my mother or my brothers for a year. I rented a furnished studio in the basement of a modest two-family house in Queens, with a black-and-white television set, a single bed, an armchair, and a drawer. One of the closets had a built-in kitchen with a gas stove, a sink, and a small refrigerator. The shower was outside the studio, a mere five steps away. One of my childhood fantasies—to live in a safe place where I wasn't constantly being dictated to—was coming true.

I was sick of seeing so much violence, first in our own home in Communist Yugoslavia and later on American TV. I was shocked by the news coverage of Vietnam and by the tragic assassinations of Martin Luther King, Jr., and, later the same year, Robert F. Kennedy. The Communist-controlled media in Yugoslavia didn't report all the crime taking place. In my new country, news broadcasts reported someone killed practically every day.

One Saturday, while I was shopping for food, I suddenly saw a huge convertible approaching with the top down. A woman wearing a beautiful white hat was talking into a loudspeaker, speaking passionately about women's rights. Her name was Bella Abzug, and I regretted that I had to wait five years to become a citizen before I could vote for her.

As I was exiting the subway in Ridgewood, I overheard two girls speaking my language. I shyly approached them, and one girl said, "My name is Maja Kramaric, and this is my sister, Nena. We have lived here in New York for a long time, attending high school and college." After chatting for a few minutes, they asked me, "Hey, do you want to go camping with us?"

"No, thank you," I said. "I camped for seventeen years in Communist Yugoslavia. I would enjoy going to a beach, though, but I don't have a car."

A week later, Maja and Nena borrowed an old silver Chevrolet from their father, and we drove off to Jones Beach. The salty water and sandy beach, along with a clear blue sky and a refreshing breeze, were a far cry from the polluted River Sutla back in Rogatec.

Such leisure moments were rare, however. Attending college classes after work was expensive and demanding, with study and homework. On the first day of the fall semester, our professor suggested that every student briefly introduce themselves. When it was my turn, I told them my name and mentioned that I came from Yugoslavia. I had barely finished the sentence when I heard a tremendous noise behind me. Startled, we all turned around. A man a few years older than me threw down all his books in a fit of anger and screamed at me, "There is no Yugoslavia! Free Croatia! I demand free Croatia!"

This man scared me to death. In a private setting only our old landlord from Samobor, Franjo Vuk, who was a little tipsy that night, spoke of "free Croatia." At that time, Croatia was officially one of six republics within Communist Yugoslavia, where any political discussion among the common people was stifled and punished.

"Sit down and calm yourself, Ante," the professor said.

The young man obeyed and the class resumed as if nothing had happened.

After class, Ante followed me. I asked him in Croatian where he was from.

"Herzegovina," he answered.

"Oh, you're Bosnian!" I answered.

He angrily shouted that I was stupid. "People from Herzegovina, we're true-blue Croatians," he said. "I'm a Croatian freedom fighter. I demand free Croatia!"

I was stunned and confused. It was hard for me to comprehend that it was perfectly legal for people in America to express their opinions.

Ante claimed that a huge political organization, which I had never heard of, would free Croatia very soon. When I voiced some reservations about this organization, he again became angry with me. He kept calling himself a freedom fighter, willing to die for "free Croatia."

My family had barely escaped our violent father, who wanted to kill us. I wanted to live! It was preposterous to hear Ante saying that he was willing to die for a cause.

When Ante mentioned that his father had died during the 1945 withdrawal of Croatian soldiers, including Ustashe at Bleiburg, on the Austrian border, I mentally connected his story with my family's story about Domobrani, the National Guard for the Independent State of Croatia, and Ustashe soldiers passing through our region of Zagorje at the end of World War II, during May of 1945. They had never been seen or heard from again. Local Croatian peasants were left wondering what had happened to them. Under the Communist system, it was taboo to talk about the Ustashe. They had sided with the Nazis against the Communists, and anyone who discussed the Ustashe was sent to jail.

Meeting this troubled man reminded me of the saying, "I have met the enemy and it is us." He was nasty and mean, full of hatred like my father, and I was horrified when he asked me for a date. Instead of the peace and kindness I craved, he offered political violence. He kept stalking me around the campus. I was so afraid of him that I stopped going to class.

I was surprised to see all this political turmoil in New York City between the Croats and the Serbs. Across town, on the West Side of Manhattan, the Serbian community was plotting how to achieve greater Serbia. The Serbs wanted to impose their culture and language on everyone living within the Yugoslavian border. Rumor had it that the most popular man in the Serbian community in New York was a printer who produced and sold so many maps of greater Serbia that he became rich.

Joza got married to the beautiful, high-cheeked and long-legged, Elsie, who was pregnant with their first child. None of our family attended the church wedding or reception because Joza was raving and ranting against us, telling everyone who would listen to him how he had risked his life roaming the Alps for us, but received no respect. We were critical of his behavior toward us and he did not invite us.

At a Christmas singles party, my friend Suzana from Hungary introduced me to a young man named George. Five years older than I, George had arrived in America from Hungary via France six months before me. Tall and skinny, with a Marlboro cigarette dangling from his mouth and sporting a fashionable mustache, George loved to wear Wrangler blue jeans and soccer T-shirts. We dated, mostly in a group setting. George taught me how to drive his car and I passed the written and driving tests on the first try. When George asked me if I wanted to get married, I blurted out, "I just got divorced." I was referring to my emotional reaction to my parents' bitter divorce and also to my newfound freedom in America. I was finally *divorced* from the oppressive Communist system and—even more important—

finally, I was *divorced* from the iron chains that our father had imposed on us.

George didn't understand and kept arguing with me, "What do you mean by *divorced*? Why not get married?"

"I'm too young."

"Oh, my mother was fifteen when she got married," said George.

Deep inside, I felt insecure, totally isolated and alone. But I was very sure I didn't want, at eighteen, to live in an apartment in Brooklyn and have babies while George worked at a dirty garage fixing cars and pumping toxic gasoline.

Our godmother, Anica, was another person who pressured us girls into marriage.

Instead, I was thrilled to receive my first job in an office, typing numbers all day as a keypunch operator. The computer company I worked for serviced unions, producing union members' paychecks. I was impressed with the huge and loud IBM computer system, using punch-cards.

I kept daydreaming about having a better, more diversified office job that would make me financially independent and free to travel. Above all, I wanted to avoid my mother's fate.

One day in 1970, when I was in the college cafeteria ordering French fries and a soda, I met another student my age, a twenty-year-old Puerto Rican named Angel.

"I remember seeing you last week," he said, staring at my legs. "You wore the same blue outfit."

It was true. Short on money, I always wore the same clothes. My hair was long because I couldn't afford a haircut, so I just let it grow, as most kids did in the 1970s.

Angel was tall and slim, handsome with short curly hair,

and dark skinned. Wearing jeans and a plain white T-shirt, he appeared friendly and talkative, speaking in Spanish to other students. He asked me out on a date, but I said no because I was uncomfortable in the presence of this stranger. I felt over-whelmed by the lifestyle changes I was going through in a new country.

The next week, I saw Angel again. Sitting at my table, he asked me about my family, and I hesitantly told him that my parents were divorced.

"Mine, too," he exclaimed and then corrected himself. "Ah, uh, actually, my parents were never married. You know, he already had a wife and children. There was a lot of trouble. My mother is light-skinned, like you, with blue eyes. My father is very dark, actually black. You see, I look like him."

"Did you ever meet your father?"

"Not really. He never acknowledged me. But one time on the street, my mother pointed him out to me and said 'Mira, mira. You look just like him.'"

Listening to Angel talk about his difficult life, I felt we had a lot in common. When he asked me about my family again, I told him honestly, "We arrived recently from Eastern Europe. I was one of many children in a troubled family."

I was ashamed to tell Angel the whole truth—that my sisters and brothers and I, along with our deeply religious and submis-sive mother, had fled our home to escape from our abusive, alco-holic father. Then, finding ourselves without money or jobs, we'd had to escape the Communist country that had failed to help us.

Alone, without any support, I thought I could never tell anyone that within three months after our arrival in America, my family had split up and everyone had gone their own way. Since I had very little money, I was living with other students, even sharing a bedroom. I worked in an office during the day at a full-time clerical job and attended evening classes—English 101, communication, and history—at City College.

Week after week, Angel and I kept running into each other in the cafeteria. One time, I could swear he was waiting for me at the exit. As he walked me home, Angel started to talk about sex, suggesting all his friends were sexually active. I disagreed, but kept quiet, thinking, *I'm a virgin*.

I was shy and insecure with low self-esteem resulting from the verbal abuse I'd received from my father. Considering how hatefully my father had behaved toward us, it wasn't surprising I didn't trust men.

Angel invited me to a casual party with his friends to celebrate someone's birthday. They spoke mostly Spanish and I felt out of place. Another time he invited me for a paella dinner at a Spanish restaurant owned by his uncle. Angel did not have to pay for dinner.

One evening, instead of dropping me off, Angel insisted on coming into the apartment I shared with three other students. No one else was home. We talked for a while, and then it was time for him to leave. Instead, he came toward me, obviously intending to kiss me, which he did. But he didn't stop there. Suddenly, he grabbed me by the shoulder and violently threw me on the floor. He was pulling my clothes off, ripping them. I struggled frantically, but being much bigger and stronger than I was and very rough, he soon overpowered me.

Angel got on top of me, and I struggled to get him off. I started to cry and put my arms up to stop him, yelling, "No!" but Angel covered my mouth with his hand and hissed for me to be quiet. I kicked, but Angel used his legs to hold mine apart. I screamed and called for help.

The rape was violent. It hurt and I was bleeding profusely, crying hysterically, and shaking from trauma. When it was over, I crawled to the bathroom, where I shut the door and quickly locked it. I took a shower, mostly sitting instead of standing. Still trembling, I examined my body and found bruises around my neck and arms.

Much later, when I opened the bathroom door, Angel was gone. He had cleaned up the evidence, all the blood from the floor. I thought about calling the police. Would they help me? Back in Communist Yugoslavia, the police were used for political purposes. They were not there to help women or children in need.

Bitterly, I said to myself, "There are eight million people in New York City. Why didn't anyone hear me?"

I remembered my parents forcing us to go to the Catholic church to learn catechism and the priest telling us that angels are there to protect us. Where were the angels now?

I remembered, too, how my father had roughly and violently pulled my mother into their bedroom, sometimes in the middle of the day. She was always pregnant, and now here I was, also violated.

Too humiliated to seek help, I never called the police or went to the emergency room. Petrified of being pregnant, I couldn't sleep, and I felt totally isolated. I couldn't call my family, knowing that they would blame me, as always. I could just hear my mother's voice: "What did you do? Why did you talk to him?"

A few days later, I finally summoned enough courage to confide in another student, Suzana, who was a year or so older and an immigrant from Hungary. When I told her, with great hesitation, that Angel had raped me, she shrugged her shoulders and said, "That's life! Guess what happened to me? I escaped from Hungary with my male friend, and as soon as we reached Austria and stopped in a motel, he raped me."

Suzana never called the police because she didn't have the papers required to cross Austria legally. Nor did she speak fluent German. Like me, she was terrified of being pregnant. Later, Suzana had an abortion and spent a year in a refugee camp in Austria before coming to America.

I was luckier. After feeling fearful and nervous for weeks, I went alone to a clinic for a pregnancy test. It was negative! Just as I was walking out of the clinic to go back to work, I got my period. It was an immense relief.

After telling Suzana, I kept quiet about the date rape. I told no one until after the bloody collapse of the Communist federation of Yugoslavia. More than two hundred fifty thousand people died during the wars of the 1990s, when Serbs violated some twenty thousand to fifty thousand women to "ethnically cleanse" the Muslims through forced pregnancy.

Without community support in former Yugoslavia, shame and silence prevailed and no one will ever know the exact number of rape victims. Most of the babies were aborted, others given to orphanages. Some of the rape victims killed themselves in distress and others gave birth and kept the babies.

Reading about it in the newspaper in 1993 in New York, I felt deeply upset and shocked. I collected hundreds of signatures to petition the United Nations to include systematic rape in former Yugoslavia as a war crime.

In America, we held a fund-raiser during which we collected money for rape survivors. Each contributor received a T-shirt with the slogan "*Ja sam tvoj svjedok!* I am your witness!" which referred to Serb perpetrators denying the systematic rapes.

"Women's bodies," said the speaker at the fund-raiser, "historically have been and continue to be the source of great trauma, ridicule, torment, and violence. Women, specifically women from the former Yugoslavia, have witnessed or grievously experienced firsthand the use of their bodies as tools of war."

It has taken me forever to write this chapter because it's the hardest thing I've ever had to do. Some people say that silence is golden, but in certain instances it is not. Rapists thrive on the silence of women like me.

GILBERT TUHABONYE
Burundi

Gilbert Tuhabonye (1974–) was born in the southern province of Bururi in Burundi into a relatively well-off family of Catholic Tutsi subsistence farmers. Largely removed from the ethnic violence between the Tutsi and Hutu in other parts of the country, Tuhabonye began running competitively while attending Lycée Kibimba, becoming a national champion by the eleventh grade and dreaming of an athletic scholarship to an American college. On October 21, 1993, units of the Tutsi-dominated army overthrew and executed President Melchior Ndadaye, who was Hutu, and key cabinet members. As news of the president's death spread, enraged Hutu made all Tutsis the targets of ethnic cleansing, killing tens of thousands of civilians. When the violence broke out, Tuhabonye's high school was invaded, the students hacked to death or burned; Tuhabonye was the only survivor.

After an agonizing recovery from his burns, Tuhabonye returned to competitive running at Burundi University, where his success brought an invitation to attend the Olympic training camp held in La Grange, Georgia, prior to the 1996 Atlanta games.

Although many of Tuhabonye's early experiences in the U.S. were mediated by his track coaches and limited by his rigorous training schedule, his intermittent social activities confirmed his assumptions of Americans' fabled affluence and introduced him to American perceptions of Africans. Reluctant to return to war-torn Burundi following the Olympics, Tuhabonye applied for political asylum. Ultimately, he attended Abilene Christian University (ACU) on an athletic scholarship. Despite his limited English skills, the outpouring of support from the ACU community eased Tuhabonye's sense of marginality and helped him overcome his traumatic past. His success as a long-distance runner and his compelling personal narrative made him a celebrity, even leading to a citation from President Clinton in 1999. Upon graduating from ACU, Tuhabonye moved to Austin, Texas, where he is now the head cross-country and track coach at St. Andrew's Episcopal School. The retired runner also cofounded the Gazelle Foundation, whose mission is to provide Burundians access to clean water.

Alternating between accounts of his running career and the massacre and its aftermath, Tuhabonye's memoir This Voice in My Heart *was published in 2006.*

Excerpt from

This Voice in My Heart
— 2006 —

The university had a school-sponsored drum team and football team but no track team. Once I was feeling like I could come close to the times I had run before this, I went to see Adolphe. I surprised him in his office. I wore a loose-fitting long-sleeved shirt and a pair of warm-up pants. Adolphe assumed that my visit was a social one. We exchanged greetings and he kept telling me how well I looked. I sat down and rolled up the right leg of my pants. I showed him the blackened scar tissue and ran my hand over its pebbled surface. I smiled and said, "They work far better than they look."

I don't know if Adolphe had heard through the grapevine that I was back running, but as was his custom, he got up from his desk, snatched up his clipboard and his stopwatch, and walked outside. I followed him to the track and stripped off my warm-up clothes. I saw his eyes surveying the relief map of my scars. Better to get this over with immediately. I stretched my arms over my head and waited for instruction.

"You know what to do."

After a few warm-up laps, I was in the infield stretching and then doing form running under Adolphe's watchful gaze. I detected no note of sympathy or letup in his assessments. He hounded me as he always had before. When I finally hit the track again for a few time trials, I was loose and feeling good. Bujumbura's saunalike heat threatened to draw every molecule of moisture out of my body, but as soon as he raised his arm for me to get into my starting position, I blocked out any thought of the weather. After I did two hundreds, four hundreds, and eight hundreds, a dozen total, Adolphe waved me over to where he stood in the infield. His arms folded across his chest shielding the clipboard where he had recorded my times, he issued his pronouncements. "Have you forgotten the metronome?"

I shook my head. How could I forget the metaphor he used all the time to describe our arm swing and the relentlessly consistent tempo he wanted it to have?

"No, sir. I haven't forgotten."

"Gilbert, I can't find the words to tell you how glad I am to see you running again. It brings me joy. Tomorrow."

The last was more a statement than a question, but I detected a note of uncertainty in his voice I had never heard before.

"I will be here. Will you?"

I waited to see his reaction, but none came for a moment. Then a slow, thoughtful nod confirmed what I'd already suspected.

By May 1995, I was ready for my first major international meet, in Kenya. I had never flown before, so I was both nervous and excited when Stany and Gertrude dropped me off at Bujumbura International Airport. The building was a single floor, no larger than most small-town American bus stations, and it had one runway. By the time I climbed aboard the Sabena Airlines jet for the flight to Nairobi, I was sweating nervously. Adolphe had made all the arrangements, gotten me a passport, and told me what to expect when I got to Nairobi, but all his words flew out of my head the moment I put my foot on the first step climbing into the jet's cabin. I was with two other runners, eight-hundred-and fifteen-hundred-meter specialist Gilbert Mvuyekure and Phydia Inamahoro, who ran the women's one hundred and two hundred meters. I thought of the few times I'd come to the airport to watch the planes take off and land. I had always wondered what it would be like to be inside and how it would feel to climb so steeply above the surrounding mountains. I was soon to find out. Of course, the three of us argued over who would get the window seat, and I won out. That was a battle I soon regretted winning. Once the plane was airborne and banked east to follow the route to Nairobi, we passed over Kibimba. Phydia was in the center seat, and she leaned over to see what I was staring at so intently, a scarred spot on the landscape that to most was little different from the rest of the land. She nudged Mvuyekure, and they both started reassuring me about Kibimba, letting me know I was far away from that place.

The airport in Nairobi was a far cry from the single gate at Bujumbura. As soon as we got off the plane, we heard announcements in English and Swahili. While I understood a little of both languages, this amplified mishmash of the two, combined with the crowd noise, came out sounding like an overly excited Bugs Bunny speaking backward at double speed. We were trying to find the person who was to take us to the Utari Hotel. As much as I tried to remain humble, I felt like a big deal.

I had a pocketful of American dollars, a per diem paid to me by the Burundi athletic association. I was in one of Africa's largest cities, and in addition to the track meet, we were to go on a couple of tours, including a visit to a national park, where I would see lions.

Unfortunately, language proved a problem during the meet. I had never seen so many runners gathered together in one spot. There were multiple heats for every event, many different divisions of competition, and I thought I heard my name being called to the start of the four hundred heat I was scheduled to run. I was wrong. The announcements were all in English, and I misunderstood which race was being called. I got in a four hundred heat that was open to all runners and not just university students. I finished a distant fourth and did not qualify for the finals. I had no complaints. I had gotten to fly for the first time, leave Burundi for the first time, and be exposed to the ins and outs of travel and international meets. I was probably most pleased that I was able to buy Dieudonné a good pair of Asics running shoes, and buy the sheets that Stany and Gertrude had asked me to get.

Triphine was thrilled for me but also worried for my safety—and not just because of the flight. I had a brief taste of what it would be like to be a competitive athlete and experience a bit of what Kwizera and the others had. To be honest, I was hooked immediately. I felt more comfortable outside of Burundi than I did inside its borders. I liked the anonymity I could enjoy there. I wasn't the runner who survived the horrible fire, I was the runner from Burundi. I had no real name or reputation, good or bad. No one was targeting me on the track as the one to beat, and no one was targeting me off the track.

My professors were not pleased that I had to miss classes, and I worked hard to make up any labs I skipped. But now, as had happened at Lycée Kibimba, school seemed more a means to an end than an end in itself. I was in school hoping to run and earn credits that would transfer to an American university. I needed more exposure, more chances for U.S. coaches to see me. Adolphe knew this as well, and so did a few other Burundian runners already in the States.

Fukuoka, Japan, held the 1995 World University Games, and just a few short days before the games were to begin, the dean of students learned that money had been freed for the school to send three people. Of course, he could not pass up the opportunity, so he went along with the two Gilberts. Once again I was to enter the four hundred and the eight hundred, and Gilbert M. was to compete in the eight hundred and the fifteen hundred.

I had enjoyed the trip to Nairobi, but now I was going to experience true international travel taking me halfway across the globe. Everything was arranged so last-minute, so I didn't have the opportunity to call my mother or Triphine. I found out a few days ahead of time, but I didn't want to tell them I was going and then have it prove not be true; that would have shamed me. They heard on the radio that I was going to Japan, but by that time I was somewhere between Bujumbura, Nairobi, Belgium, London, Tokyo, and Fukuoka. We crossed time zones, cultures, and cities, sometimes dashing from one airport gate to another only to sit and wait hours for the next flight. It took more than forty-eight hours for us to finally arrive. By that time, I'd discovered I had lost my wallet with the six hundred dollars that was to be my allowance for the next seventeen days. Fortunately, my two traveling companions helped me out when I wanted to buy gifts for family and friends. The rest of the time, I ate in the dormitory together with athletes from universities around the world. That year 162 nations sent athletes (the most ever) to the biannual event. I knew a little about Japan but only enough to assume I would be able to speak French once I got there—my English was still not very good.

When we got off the plane, I was groggy and in a near

stupor, but not even those factors could explain the sense of dislocation I felt. We were greeted by people who looked like no one I had ever seen. I had seen a few *muzungus* in Africa and many more on television, but most of them had been westerners. When a bowing and very pale young woman dressed in traditional Japanese garb—what looked to me like ceremonial pajamas—handed me a flower and said, *"Konnichiwa,"* I nearly fainted. Over the course of the next few weeks, thanks to the unfailing friendliness and politeness of our host families, the organizing committee representatives, and the people of Japan themselves, I was completely won over by what seemed to me the cleanest and most orderly country possible.

The three of us stayed in a dorm room. On either side of us were the delegations from Malta and Brazil, and our wing of the dormitory housed runners from many other African nations. One of the highlights of the trip off the track was getting to interact with so many athletes from so many countries. I also loved getting to know about the different cultures through their food. The Japanese had hired chefs from around the world to prepare the native cuisine from each country. We lived together, ate together, and trained together. I also spent a lot of time with the family who sponsored the Burundi team. A translator helped us to communicate. They gave me a lovely Seiko watch and made up for my loss of allowance.

The opening ceremony was especially memorable. I carried our flag in the parade of athletes and marched around the stadium in front of sixty thousand people. I was enormously honored, and despite all the troubles in Burundi, my chest swelled with pride when I watched its red, green, and white colors furling and unfurling against Fukuoka's brilliant blue skies. I had not trained well for the four hundred, and I didn't make it out of my opening-round heat—they only took the top two finishers from each preliminary round. I did learn something from that race, though, and from watching many of the others. They were far more tactical than what I was used to. By that I mean the races were often won by guile and not sheer speed. The pace would be slow, and then someone would kick into gear, or the pace would be strong at the start and you had to decide whether to stay with it or attack at the end.

I enjoyed greater success in the eight hundred. I was less nervous. When I went to the blocks, I spent far less time looking around and soaking in the atmosphere and checking out my opponents than I had in my first heat. Adolphe's admonition to focus, run my race, and dictate to others paid off. I made it through two rounds, and then in the semifinals I missed out on qualifying for the finals by less than a quarter of a second. When I crossed the line and saw that I had finished fifth, just one place away from the finals, I covered my face with my hands and folded at the waist. A runner from Namibia who had finished just in front me and who I'd told my story to draped his arm over my shoulders. Together we walked off the track and he held up my arm in victory.

In many ways, simply getting to the event had been a victory. I don't simply mean overcoming my injuries. Burundi is a very poor country and doesn't have the kind of infrastructure to support its amateur athletes the way so many so-called developed countries do. We often have to rely on the generosity and support of larger bodies (like the International Olympic Committee) or corporate sponsors (Nike, Adidas, Asics, and the like) to help fund us. I was so grateful for the opportunity to run in my first truly international meet. I made friends from South Africa, Kenya, Morocco, and nations outside of Africa. I still keep in touch with many of them. Being among athletes and outside of Burundi and not having a military presence near me helped me drop my defenses and enjoy myself. Because I shared a deep and abiding passion with these athletes, I trusted them. Many were curious about my scars, but they instantly accepted me as one of them. The truth was, I felt more like one of them—

an athlete or sportsman as many called themselves—than I did a Burundian. More than anything else, this trip confirmed my desire to go to the United States. One of the reasons Adolphe wanted me to compete internationally was to draw the attention of the U.S. coaches. I did not get the opportunity to speak to them, and my performance did not merit their attention. However, when I returned home (fully laden with gifts for everyone), I had a packet waiting for me from Tulane University with an application, a course catalog, and other materials.

I was excited about the opportunity, but I still had coursework to complete and training to do, so the package sat on my desk at Stany's place gathering dust. I don't know why I was reluctant to fill it out and send it in, but in the long run my reluctance paid big dividends.

For every amateur athlete, the Olympics are the pinnacle of achievement. No stage is more grand, and no honor is greater than to be an Olympic Gold Medalist. Running in the Olympics is the goal that motivates most of us, and though I fell short of that goal, I did get to have my own amazing Olympic experience nonetheless.

Prior to the Atlanta Games in 1996, the International Olympic Committee set up an Olympic development training camp in La Grange, Georgia. There, athletes from developing nations could send their athletes to live and to train prior to the games. The hope was that by exposing these athletes to top-notch facilities, coaches, and training methods, the economic playing field could be leveled. To be honest, I didn't think of the larger implications and consequences of the IOC's policies and programs. All I knew was that I was going to get a chance to go to the United States.

I could barely contain my excitement. From the moment I heard in January 1996 that I was one of the eight male athletes from Burundi who would be attending the development camp, everything else in my life paled in importance. My studies were effectively ended. From that point forward I was going to train in hopes of qualifying for the fifteen hundred meters. Though the Atlanta Games weren't going to start until August, we were scheduled to leave Burundi at the beginning of April. I counted down the days. My name was on the radio constantly with announcements about who was going to the Olympics. I would later regret this inaccuracy, but in the moment I reveled in the knowledge that everyone who knew me as the boy who had been attacked would now know that I had fully recovered. At that time I used the massacre as a source of strength. These people had done their best to kill me, but it was not enough. The strength of the Lord was greater than theirs.

When the plane touched down on American soil on April 8, 1996, I had no way of knowing that I would not be going back to Burundi for a very long time. Like my arrival in Japan, my arrival in Atlanta produced culture shock. Though I had studied English for so long in secondary school, it had been several years since I'd used it much. Language barriers are one thing, but the other cultural barriers are another. Americans look funny, dress funny, and sound funny. Their cars are strange, their music strange, their food an abomination. (What is the fascination with the hamburger all about?) They live in homes that look like boxes stacked atop one another, on plots of land that seemed to be stamped from a press. I could go on, but you get the point. Everything here was new to me.

When we were picked up at the airport by Jim Manhattan, head of the La Grange Track Club and one of the chief organizers of the development camp, we climbed into a huge twelve-passenger van and made our way through a maze of roads to exit the airport. In what I later learned was a deliberate attempt to introduce us immediately to American culture, and an experience they introduced every foreign athlete to, we stopped a little while later at a McDonald's. We had been given a few dollars upon arrival, and we were now left to fend for ourselves. Herded through the door, we faced the gleaming expanse of the counter and the gaudy display above the workers' heads. I came alone and Justine came two months later. Justine Nahimana, the lone woman in our group, was from the city originally and had traveled and studied in Europe before. She quickly assumed the role of guide and instructed us. With a few simple pointing gestures and a mumbled order, we got our food. That is all I will say about McDonald's—except to say that I did "enjoy" the bread and the pickle.

The rest of the trip to La Grange Community College, where we were to spend the next five months, was a whirlwind of concrete and tarmac, an endless stream of traffic, and lush greenery sectioned off into sharply divided rectangles and squares. Even flying over the country I noticed as we came farther east that the rectangles and squares below us grew gradually smaller and smaller. I wondered why everything seemed so divided and orderly. Our farmland tended to meander, and one crop sometimes spilled over into another, just as it did in nature. It would take me some time to get used to the rigidity of space and time Americans impose on themselves. Our schedule at the camp was segmented and precise. If the schedule called for us to be at an event that began at nine o'clock, you can be sure that at nine o'clock it began. Eventually, I heard Africans who were veterans in the United States talking about how the Americans teased us for living on "African time," and I wondered what they would think of some of my countrymen who were athletes. We were the most disciplined people I knew.

Our days were filled with training and social activities. One of the coaches at the camp, Abdi Bile, was a Somalian runner, and he took us into the city of La Grange and elsewhere to visit the local shops. We were all nearly overcome by the experience of an American shopping mall, but we quickly recovered. I had never seen so many items in one store, and then to have store after store after store stuffed to overflowing with them—

well, it was hard not to believe the stories we had all heard about how wealthy most Americans are. People in the streets would regard us with curiosity, but they were unfailingly nice to us. I did notice that some of the African Americans we met, not all but enough to notice, seemed a bit distant and less likely to approach us or to engage us in conversation. In some ways, I think they found us to be more strange than the whites did.

I grew to really like and admire Abdi Bile. In 1996 he was thirty-seven years old, on the downhill side of a career in which he had been a world champion in the fifteen hundred. He came to La Grange to coach but also to compete. He knew what he was talking about, and I picked up some very good training and racing tips from him. He was amazing to watch. He came into the training center with a best time that year in the fifteen hundred of 3:45. The A Olympic qualifying standard was 3:36. He needed to knock off nine seconds to qualify for the Olympics, and by the end of the camp, he had done it. Amazing.

To provide us with opportunities to run times that qualified us for the Olympics, various meets were held. I should explain to you about the Olympics and qualifying. Just because you are the fastest runner in your country at a certain distance, say, the fifteen hundred meters, doesn't mean you can race in the Olympics. (Bile won the 1987 world championship and holds an NCAA record, both in the fifteen hundred.) You must run an officially sanctioned race and meet or exceed the standard established. I wish that it was as simple as that, but some runners do get to compete in the Olympics without having run that qualifying time. The IOC wants to give runners (and athletes in other events) from countries with less-developed programs an opportunity to have an Olympic experience, so some spots are filled with athletes who meet a B standard. Sometimes athletes who do not meet either standard are allowed to compete. I will get to those special circumstances later on.

I did get to compete in a triangular meet among Burundi,

Rwanda, and Brazil. We beat everyone except the Brazilian 4-by-100 meter relay team, which would later earn a Bronze in the games. Unfortunately for me, I ran a 3:46 in the fifteen hundred, missing the qualifying standard by five seconds. I was disappointed, but I had been mostly running the four hundred and the eight hundred meters, and I just was not as strong in the fifteen hundred as I needed to be. I took some consolation in being the second-fastest fifteen-hundred runner in Burundi. The athletes from Burundi who had qualified were Charles Nkazamyanpi, Vénuste Niyongabo, Aloise Nizigama, Justine Nahimana, Arthémon Hatungimana, and Tharcisse Gashaka— an impressive number for a country like ours.

One honor you do not have to qualify for is carrying the Olympic torch in the relay prior to the games. I was chosen to carry the torch in Birmingham, Alabama. I traveled by bus from Atlanta to Birmingham and ran through the streets of Birmingham for a quarter of a mile. The symbolism and irony of the torch ceremony were not lost on me. As I ran along with the torch flames flaring just above my head, I felt a chill. I was glad to have had the opportunity, and equally glad to pass the torch on to the next person in line. Birmingham was an important trip in another way. I got to go to the National Civil Rights Museum there and was greatly inspired by seeing the exhibits dedicated to Martin Luther King, Jr. I had read much about him, and like most Africans I greatly admired that man of peace.

As the games drew closer, more athletes arrived. Though we did not live in the Olympic village with all of them, our status as part of the developmental camp allowed us access to all the Olympic venues as well as the village itself. I got to meet and work out with some of the most famous and fastest runners in the world. One of the guys I really liked because he was probably the most famous runner in the world at the time and had the most pressure on him to succeed was the Moroccan Hicham el-Guerrouj. Known as "King of the Mile," he holds the world record in the fifteen hundred, the two thousand, and the mile. Since we both spoke French, we were able to communicate. What impressed me the most about him was how normal he seemed. The guy was recognized around the world as perhaps the greatest middle-distance runner ever, and you would have never known it by how he carried himself. Just to show you what kind of guy he is, the same year as the Atlanta Games, the International Association of Athletics Federations honored him for his humanitarian efforts, and he remains a UNICEF ambassador. Along with Guerrouj, I got to know Frankie Fredericks of Namibia, Driss Mazouse, also from Morocco, and a host of other medal winners.

The highlights of the Olympics for me were attending the opening ceremonies and being in the stands when Vénuste won the Gold Medal in the five thousand meters. It was awesome! He was in the middle of the pack with six hundred meters to go and put on a finishing kick that had him breaking the tape and winning the Gold for Burundi. It was a thrill to hear our national anthem being played in the Olympic Stadium and watching our flag rise above the Kenyan and Moroccan. Vénuste was the only winner and medalist from Burundi, though Aloise Nizigama did finish fourth in the ten thousand, narrowly missing a medal.

Being interviewed on CNN was both a highlight and a lowlight. They did a story on my experiences and wanted to interview me. At that point my English still was not very good, so I was extremely nervous. Dieudonné Kwizera was with us acting as a kind of ambassador and translator, since he had been in the States for a few years. He accompanied me, as did Jim Manhattan. When I was asked how I thought I would do in the fifteen hundred, I froze and blurted out the first thing that came to my mind. I said I thought I could win a medal. In truth, I was not even going to run. I did not have the words to explain that to the reporter. I have felt foolish about that interview and the confusion it has caused ever since. Many people mistakenly believe that I ran in the Olympics, but I did not. I could have, but I didn't.

That leads to the other major disappointment. From the very beginning Vénuste did not want to run the fifteen hundred. He simply wanted to concentrate on the five thousand, which he eventually won. Because he ran a qualifying time in the fifteen hundred, if there was ever an opening in a heat, someone from his country who had not qualified for the event could run in the race. I had the second-best time in the fifteen hundred. I did not get the opportunity to run because Dieudonné Kwizera took the spot that in all fairness should have been mine. Kwizera spoke English well and was friendly with the officials, so when a spot needed to be filled in an opening-round heat, he signed himself up.

The best part of the experience was meeting all the other runners and realizing how much more work I needed to do to get to their level. While my fifteen hundred time of 3:46 was four seconds away from the qualifying standard, most of the runners in the finals were in the upper 3:20 range. I had a long way to go, and I grew more determined than ever to get there.

After the games, I remained in Georgia—first in La Grange and later in Savannah. In both places I attended small junior colleges and lived in off-campus housing. At first Jimmy Manhattan and the La Grange Track Club sponsored me, and later in Savannah, my host family at the Savannah International Training Center did. The Bossons were a great couple, extremely kind and generous with their time. On weekends they took me to movies and sometimes to church with them. They allowed me to phone home to talk to my mother and Triphine. I was in the United States on a student visa, and as long as I remained enrolled in school, I was eligible to stay. I wanted to have a more secure arrangement than that, so Bob and Susan Carlay, my host family in La Grange, helped me apply for political asylum. The process was long and tedious, but it would be worth it.

The longer I was away from Burundi, the better I felt. I realized that the stress of the violence and political upheaval was greater than I had imagined. I missed my family and Triphine terribly, but I knew I could make a better life for myself and eventually for them if I remained here. Though America had seemed so strange to me at first, and elements of life here always would, I saw that it was truly a land of great opportunity.

I was blessed to have benefited from the remarkable generosity of people like Jim Manhattan, the Carlays, the Bossons, and so many others that I can't name them all. Good fortune seemed to follow me wherever I went, and when I did a good turn for someone else, it seemed to come back to me many times over. For example, I was instrumental in helping Patrick Nduwimana join us in La Grange after our initial group had arrived. I knew Patrick from Adolphe's group, and though he was still in secondary school, he was an outstanding runner. I spoke of him to Jim, and he arranged to bring Patrick over. After the Atlanta Games, Patrick went to Sydney, Australia. There he competed in the World Junior Championship for runners under the age of twenty. He did so well that he attracted the attention of a number of American coaches. Several of them followed up with phone calls, and finally, in the fall of 1997, he asked me to go with him to visit Arizona State in Tucson, Abilene Christian in Texas, and the University of Georgia in Athens. I had not forgotten about Tulane University and my dream of attending an NCAA Division I school. Only one thing stood in my way—the TOEFL. The coaches there were eager for me to get out of the arrangement I had at Savannah State University, and so was I. I liked Savannah, but I was living with a group of foreign students and athletes in a wing of a nursing home. To put it bluntly, our accommodations were not good. I enjoyed living with the guys, but the arrangement was beginning to wear on me.

Eventually, Patrick and I met with the coaches of the track and cross-country teams at Abilene Christian University, Wes

Kittley and Jon Murray. They offered us both a full scholarship, and I accepted but Patrick decided to go to school in Tucson. I fell in love with Abilene as soon as I saw it, and dreams of Nouvelle-Orléans faded away. The campus was beautiful, and each day at noon the bells tolled and the students all went to chapel together. In many ways, Abilene reminded me of Burundi. I loved the hot, dry weather, so different from the humidity in Georgia. Mostly I liked the campus and how peaceful I felt there. I can't really explain my decision—it felt right, and I went there. Even the longhorn cows on the nearby ranches reminded me of home.

Abilene Christian had a long history of bringing in foreign students. Among its enrollment of five thousand were students from Algeria, Morocco, Jamaica, Zimbabwe, Russia, and Ukraine—and those are just the ones who competed in track and field. We all lived in the Center for International and Intercultural Education. Prior to enrolling at ACU, I had traveled to Marsala in Sicily to compete in my second World University Games. I was coming off a stress fracture in my foot and was not running at full speed, but once again I reveled in getting to know athletes from around the world. It seemed each time I went somewhere, I learned so much more about people, and the events of October 1993 receded further into the distance. I kept in constant communication with Triphine by phone, and the advent of e-mail and the Internet made it easier to keep up-to-date on what was happening around the world. It seemed I knew someone living in every far-flung region of the globe—Vénuste in Italy, Patrick in Arizona, Arthémon in France, Nizigama in Japan. In our own way, we were all refugees. We had not fled in the aftermath of the political upheaval, but we had scattered nonetheless. Adolphe was still at work patching together a team and then letting them go like seeds to drift on the wind and take root elsewhere. What was there to go back to? More assassinations? The presidents of Burundi and Rwanda had been shot down in April 1994, and Rwanda's genocide was then finally being widely reported. All these events saddened me and widened the gulf I felt between my home and me.

Into that gulf rushed a wonderful series of friends, teammates, professors, and strangers soon to be great friends and benefactors. I had been in the United States for nearly two years when I enrolled at Abilene in January 1998. With each day I was becoming more American. While in La Grange and Savannah I had been able to satisfy my taste for American movies. All of us learned to speak better English from films and television. One guy from Chad I lived with in Savannah took that to the extreme by watching Jerry Springer on cable television, switching from one channel to the next in hopes of catching another broadcast. I was enamored with the music of Tupac Shakur, Puff Daddy, and Biggie Smalls—I loved the pulsing energy of the rhythm and rhymes. Later, as my English improved and I could understand their lyrics, I stopped listening to them, but their infectious beats lingered in my mind long after the lyrics faded. One group whom I continued to listen to and admire for their positive message on all levels was Boyz II Men.

LOUNG UNG

Cambodia

Loung Ung (1970–) was born in Phnom Penh, the capital of Cambo-
dia, the sixth of seven children of a high-ranking military officer and his
wife. When the Communist Party of Kampuchea, more notoriously
known as the Khmer Rouge, rose to power in 1975, the new government
sought to erase class distinctions and finance rapid industrialization, order-
ing all Cambodians to the countryside to boost agricultural production.
The nascent government also began executing potential dissidents en
masse, including Ung's father. As Ung writes, "For three years, eight
months, and twenty-one days, we were made to live in villages more akin
to labor camps," suffering wide-scale starvation, exhaustion, and disease
that would cause some two million deaths, including those of her mother
and two of her sisters. After being liberated by the Vietnamese in 1979,
Ung joined her older brother Meng and his wife, Eang, in being smuggled
into Thailand. After six months in a refugee camp, they found immigra-
tion sponsorship in the Holy Family Church in Essex Junction, Vermont.
Prior to the rise of the Khmer Rouge, Cambodian immigration to the
U.S. was nearly nonexistent; only about sixteen thousand came before
1980. Subsequent to the Refugee Act of 1980, an estimated thirty-eight
thousand Cambodians immigrated to the U.S.; by 1990 the Cambodian
population had risen to approximately 150,000.

In Vermont, Meng, Eang, and Ung were provided with a modest
apartment, and they relied on the church for financial assistance, along
with language tutoring and moral support. Ung entered the third grade
and initially struggled as a result of her tentative English. Suffering bouts
of depression and flashbacks throughout her adolescence, she followed the

advice of a high school teacher and started a journal. Ung ultimately won a scholarship to nearby Saint Michael's College and took a bachelor's degree in political science.

Ung's trilogy of memoirs begins with the national bestseller First They Killed My Father *(2000), in which she recounts her traumatic memories of Cambodia; continues with the well-received* Lucky Child *(2005), which compares her difficult early years in the U.S. with her sister Chou's experiences in Cambodia after their separation; and concludes with* Lulu in the Sky *(2012), which chronicles Ung's college years and how she became a human rights activist. She has lectured at numerous universities and collaborated with humanitarian organizations worldwide. She helped to write the film* Girl Rising *(2013), a portrait of nine girls from underdeveloped countries and the value of education in battling poverty.*

In this excerpt from Lucky Child, *Ung narrates her departure from Cambodia with her brother and sister-in-law, reminisces about those she is leaving behind, and prepares to meet her sponsors. She then describes her struggles with nightmares and inevitable feelings of displacement and powerlessness.*

Excerpt from

Lucky Child

— 2005 —

June 10, 1980

My excitement is so strong, I feel like there are bugs crawling around in my pants, making me squirm in my seat. We are flying across the ocean to resettle in our new home in America, after having spent two months living in a houseboat in Vietnam and five months in a refugee camp in Thailand.

"We must make a good impression, Loung, so comb your hair and clean your face," Eang orders me as the plane's engine drones out her voice. "We don't want to look as if we've just gotten off the boat." Her face looms in front of me, her nails working furiously in their attempts to pick crusty sleepy seeds out of the corners of my eyes.

"Stop, you're pulling out my eyelashes! I'll clean my own face before you blind me." I take the wet rag from Eang's hand.

I quickly wipe my face and wet the cruds on my lids before gently removing them. Then I turn the rag over to the clean side and smooth down my hair as Eang looks on disapprovingly. Ignoring her scowl, I ball up the rag, run it over my front teeth, and scrub hard. When I'm finished, I wrap the rag around my pointing finger, put it in my mouth, and proceed to scrape food residue off my back teeth.

"All finished and clean," I chime innocently.

"I do have a toothbrush for you in my bag." Her annoyance is barely contained in her voice.

"There just wasn't time . . . and you said you wanted me clean."

"Humph."

Eang has been my sister-in-law for a year and generally I don't mind her; but I just can't stand it when she tells me what to do. Unfortunately for me, Eang likes to tell me what to do a lot so we end up fighting all the time. Like two monkeys, we make so much noise when we fight that my brother Meng has to step in and tell us to shut up. After he intervenes, I usually stomp off somewhere by myself to sulk over how unfair it is that he takes her side. From my hiding place, I listen as she continues to argue with him about how they need to raise me with discipline and show me who has the upper hand or I'll grow up wrong. At first, I didn't understand what she meant by "wrong" and imagined I would grow up crooked or twisted like some old tree trunk. I pictured my arms and legs all gnarly, with giant sharp claws replacing my fingers and toes. I imagined chasing after Eang and other people I didn't like, my claws snapping at their behinds.

But no, that would be too much fun, and besides, Eang is bent on raising me "right." To create a "right" Loung, Eang tells Meng, they will have to kick out the tomboy and teach me the manners of a proper young lady—which means no talking back to adults, fighting, screaming, running around, eating with my mouth open, playing in skirts, talking to boys, laughing out loud, dancing for no reason, sitting Buddha-style, sleeping with my legs splayed apart, and the list goes on and on. And then there is the other list of what a proper girl is supposed to do, which includes sitting quietly, cooking, cleaning, sewing, and babysitting—all of which I have absolutely no interest in doing.

I admit I wouldn't fight Eang so hard if she followed her own list. At twenty-four, Eang is one year older than Meng. This little fact caused quite a stir when they married a year ago in our village in Cambodia. It also doesn't help that Eang is very loud and outspoken. Even at my age, I'd noticed that many un-married women in the village would act like little fluttering yellow chicks, quiet, soft, furry, and cute. But once married, they'd become fierce mother hens, squawking and squeaking about with their wings spread out and their beaks pecking, es-pecially when marking their territory or protecting their chil-dren. Eang, with her loudness and strong opinions, was unlike any unmarried woman I'd ever spied on. The other villagers gossiped that Meng should marry a young wife who could give him many sons. At her advanced age, Eang was already thought of as a spinster and too old for Meng, a well-educated and hand-some man from a respected family. But neither one cared too much for what the villagers said and allowed our aunts and un-cles to arrange their marriage. Meng needed a wife to help him care for his siblings and Eang needed a husband to help her survive the aftermath of the Khmer Rouge war, Cambodia's poverty, and increasing banditries. And even though they got married because of those needs, I do think they love each other. Like the two sides of the ying and yang symbol, together they form a nice circle. Whereas Meng is normally reserved and quiet, Eang makes him laugh and talk. And when Eang gets too emotional and crazy, Meng calms and steadies her.

"Thank you for the rag." I smile sweetly, handing it back to Eang.

"Did you see what she did, Meng?" Eang crunches her face in disgust as she rolls up the wet rag and puts it in her bag. On my other side, Meng is quiet as he pulls a white shirt from a clear plastic bag and hands it over to his wife. The shirt gleams in Eang's hands, crisp and new. When Meng found out we were coming to America, he took all the money we had and bought us all new white shirts. He wanted us to enter America looking fresh and unused despite our scraggy hair and thin limbs. Eang kept the shirts in a plastic bag so they would stay fresh and unwrinkled for this very special occasion.

At twenty-three, Meng wears a somber expression that makes him look many years older. The Meng I remember from before the war was gentle, with a ready smile and an easygoing manner. This new Meng seems to have left his sense of humor in Cambodia when we waved good-bye to Chou, Kim, and Khouy nine months ago. Now, only deep sighs escape his lips. At the refugee camp, there were many times when I was in our hut, lost in my world of words and picture books, when suddenly I would hear this long intake of breath, followed by a rushing exhale. I knew then that Meng was hovering somewhere nearby, and I would turn to find him looking at me with his long face and sagging shoulders.

When I ask Meng why we had to leave our family behind, he sighs and tells me I'm too young to understand. My face burns red by his put-offs. I may be too young to understand many things but I am old enough to miss Khouy's voice threatening to kick anyone's bottom who dares mess with his family. No matter how far we leave them behind, I still miss Chou's hand clasped warmly in mine, and Kim's fingers scratching his ribs in manic imitation of a monkey, kung fu style. I am young but sometimes, when I would float alone in the ocean near the refugee camp, I'd feel old and tired. I'd sink to the bottom of the ocean, staring up at Ma, Geak, and Keav's faces shimmering on the water's surface. Other times, as I bobbed up and down, I'd imagine my tears being carried by the waves into the deep sea. In the middle of the ocean, my tears would transform into anger and hate, and the ocean would return them to me, crashing them against the rocky shoreline with vengeance.

At night at the refugee camp, I would gaze at the full moon and try to bring forth Pa's face. I'd whisper his name into the wind and see him as he was before the war, when his face was still round and his eyes flashed brightly like the stars. With my arms around myself, I'd dream of Pa holding me, his body full and soft and healthy. I'd imagine his fingers caressing my hair and cheeks, his touch as gentle as the breeze. But before long, Pa's face would wither away until he was only a skeleton of his former moon-self.

If Meng also could see Pa's face in the moon, he didn't tell me. I don't know how or when it started, but Meng and I somehow have found ourselves in a place where we don't talk about the war anymore. It's not as though we sat down one day and decided not to talk about the war—it happened so gradually we barely noticed it. At first he asked me questions I was not ready to answer, and I would ask him for answers he could not explain, until eventually the questions and talking just stopped. There are times that I still want him to tell me more about Pa and Ma and what kinds of people they were before I was born. But I do not ask because I cannot bear to watch his face light up at the memory of them, only to see it dim and darken when he remembers they are no longer with us.

When Meng and I do talk, we speak about our present and future. Of my past, Meng says only that he thinks I am ten years old but he is not sure. He shares that when he was a boy, Pa and Ma were so poor that they sent him to live with our aunts and uncles in the village. He says that each time he visited home, there was another little brother or sister to greet him until, in the end, there were seven of us. He tells me that what papers or records we had of our births the Khmer Rouge destroyed when they entered the city on April 17, 1975. Without the papers, Ma and Pa were our only memories of our entrance into the world, but now they're gone, too. In Thailand, when Meng was required to pick a new birthday for me in order to fill out the refugee papers, he chose April 17—the day the Khmer Rouge took over the country. With a few strokes of his pen, he made sure I will never forget Cambodia.

In the time that I've lived with Meng and Eang, it is clear to me that Meng's thoughts are always focused on Cambodia and our family there. We have no way to send or receive word, so we do not know if Khouy, Kim, and Chou are still with us. In the Ung clan, Pa was the firstborn son in his family, and since Meng was Pa's firstborn son, he now holds the title role not only as the head of our family, but as the eldest brother to all the Ungs of our generation. Meng wears this title with pride and constantly worries about the well-being of the younger Ungs and how he can be a good role model. Before leaving Cambodia, Meng painted a bright picture of our future to our aunts and uncles to justify our leaving for America. Once en route and on the boat, however, Meng's eyes brimmed with tears and his face fell.

On the plane, I climb on my seat and turn around to wave at my friend Li Cho, seated a few rows behind me. Only a year younger than me, Li is part of the seven-person Cho family also on their way to make a home in Vermont. Because Meng and Eang mostly kept to themselves at the Lam Sing Refugee Camp, they did not know the Chos before today. However, Li and I met the first night I arrived there. Behind the walled prison fence of the refugee camp and in the midst of the porous thatched-roof huts, Li and I explored our temporary homes together and became friends. We shared our secrets by the ocean while spying on grown-up women and making fun of their large breasts. Li told me she was born in Cambodia to a Chinese father and a Vietnamese mother. Her mother and her father passed away when Li was young and now she lives with her adult brothers, sisters, and nephews. Fully clothed and with our sweaty hands clasped tightly together, Li and I would run into the ocean and talk about how much we wished we could buy a bottle of Coke and a bowl of noodles. I would tell her about how my father would hold my fried crickets for me at the movies, and she would tell me how her father used to read to her.

As the plane rocks and sways, Li looks green from motion sickness. Li's small body slumps over in her seat as her sister Tee pats her fine black hair. Even in sickness, Li is pretty with her large eyes and a small chin. Watching her, I remember a time when I thought I was pretty, too. It seems unreal that only five years ago in Phnom Penh, Ma and her friends would coo and pinch my cheeks when I entered the room wearing a new dress or a bow in my hair. They would comment on my full lips, large almond eyes, and wavy hair. To this, I'd smile and extend my hands until they emptied their purses of candies and money, before Ma shooed me away.

I turn back to look at Li. "Poor Li," I think. She has been sick and throwing up the entire plane trip. Awake, she is a sweet and mild-mannered girl, exactly the kind of girl Eang wishes I would be. With that thought, I sit down in my seat and open another bag of peanuts. Though Li cannot keep her food down, my stomach has no such trouble and like a good friend, I happily volunteer to eat her food.

As our plane begins its descent, the soft fluffy clouds part and open the world below to me. I lean over Meng to peer out the window and catch my first glimpse of my new home. Scanning the land, I am disappointed to see only mountains, trees, and water. I guess we are still too high up to see the tall, shiny buildings. My hands grip the armrest tightly, and I daydream about the America I hope I'm going to. In their attempts to prepare us for life in the United States, the refugee workers would show us Hollywood movies, where each plot took place in a large, noisy city with tall, shiny buildings and big, long cars racing down crowded streets. On the big screen, Americans are loud-talking, fast-moving people with red, blond, brown, or black hair, weaving in and out of traffic wearing heels or roller skates. In my seat, I imagine myself walking among these people and living an exciting new life far from Cambodia. These images set my heart racing with anticipation until Eang's voice brings me out of my reverie. Eang brushes her hand over the front of my shirt and complains about the falling crumbs. Meng hurriedly primps his hair with a small black plastic comb just as the captain announces we are landing.

On the ground, my hands lock in Meng's and Eang's, and we enter the airport lobby to bursts of flashes and loud whispers. Bright lights blind and scare me, and I lose eye contact with Li as she and her family are swallowed up by the crowd. With white spots swimming in my retinas, I shield my eyes with my forearm and take a step backward. The room falls silent as the throngs of pale strangers shift their feet and strain their necks to take their first peek at us. From behind Meng, I focus on one woman whose long white neck reminds me of a defrocked chicken, all skinny and leathery. Next to her, another woman stares at us from a face so sharp and angular that I name her "chicken face." Behind "chicken face" stands a man with round cheeks and a big nose whom I identify as "pig cheeks." Surrounding them are more people I can only distinguish with my special nicknames: lizard nose, rabbit eyes, horse teeth, cow lips, and cricket legs.

"Welcome!" a man calls out and walks toward us. His body is sturdy like a tree trunk and he towers one head taller than Meng as they shake hands.

After him, one tall person after another gathers around us. Making use of his English classes in Phnom Penh before the war, Meng smiles widely and answers questions as he pumps everyone's hand with vigor and energy. Standing beside him, Eang takes people's hands limply and nods her head. Not wanting to be crushed, I step out of the crowd and stand alone until a red-haired woman walks up to me. Remembering to show her my respect, I bow to greet her; at the same moment, she extends her hand and hits me square on the forehead. The cameras stop flashing and the room grows quiet as I stand there rubbing my forehead. From his corner, I hear Meng laugh and assure everyone I'm okay. A few seconds later, the room erupts into laughter. Instead of casting my eyes on the floor, I stare at the crowd with anger until Eang tells me to smile. Weakly, I curl my lips upward for the crowd. Suddenly, the red-haired lady steps forward again and hands me a brown teddy bear as more cameras flash to capture the moment. In that instant, I realize that I've buttoned my shirt wrong, leaving my white shirttail jagged and crooked, and me looking like I've just gotten off the boat.

In the car, Meng talks with our sponsors, Michael and Cindy Vincenti. As Meng speaks, Michael nods his head while Cindy answers with a series of "uh-huhs." Behind her, I stifle a laugh at her silly sound and pretend to cough. Sensing Eang's warning eyes burning the back of my head, I stare out the window and watch the world go by. Outside, the scenery moves at a slow speed, as short grass is replaced by thick shrubs and trees. Every once in a while, the rolling hills are dotted with small houses and running dogs. There are no tall shiny buildings in sight.

After twenty minutes, the Vincentis pull their car into the driveway of a small, two-story apartment building. The building looks old and dreary with white paint flaking off its front like dead skin. And right next to it, on the other side of the driveway, is a large cemetery where, inside, the summer wind blows gently on the trees and makes the branches sway and the leaves dance as if possessed by spirits. My skin warms at the sight of the cold, gray stones jutting out from the earth like jagged teeth. Beneath the stones, I imagine decomposed bodies trapped in dirt, waiting for nightfall before they can escape.

"You're home," the Vincentis announce.

Meng tells Eang and me to get out of the car as I direct a steely gaze at the back of Michael's head.

"Eang," I grab her hand, "it's bad luck to live next to a cemetery. The ghosts will not leave us alone!"

"The ghosts here cannot speak Khmer," she says. "They'll make no trouble for us."

"But . . ." I refuse to give up. "What if there is a common language all the dead use?" Before I can continue, Eang tells me to be quiet and motions for me to hurry. Glancing back tentatively at the cemetery, I slowly follow the adults into the apartment.

The Vincentis climb the stairs to the second-story apartment and wait for Meng, Eang, and me to catch up. While the adults talk, I take in the layout of our apartment. With rooms connecting in a long row, our new home feels like a train, and its narrow rooms look like boxcars. To the left of the stairs, Meng and Eang's room resembles a square tan box furnished with a simple wood dresser and a queen-sized bed. Walking up to its one window, I am glad to see that it faces the parking lot.

To the right of the stairs the kitchen is filled with all the modern amenities—a stove, oven, and refrigerator. In the middle of the room sit a small metal rectangular table and four matching chairs. Next to the kitchen, the bathroom is clean from the top of its ceiling to the white-yellow linoleum tiled floor. A few steps forward take me into the dining room.

"This will be your room," Cindy tells me cheerily.

With my hands clasped together in front of me, I turn a full circle to inspect my room. A frown forms on my face when I notice that the walls are not made of actual wood but a glued-on brown paper designed to look like fake wood. I have never seen such wall coverings before and reach out to slide my hand over its slippery surface. Suddenly I think of Chou living in a wooden hut in Cambodia. In an instant, I feel heavy and drag myself to the corner of the room where there is a small walk-in closet. Though I spy hinges on the frame, for some reason there is no door for the closet. My room is empty except for a small twin bed against the wall. I walk over and sit on the bed, testing its bounce with my weight while gazing quizzically at the drawings on my sheet. The drawings appear to be of girl and boy mice, ducks, dogs, elephants, and other animals, each playing or holding a musical instrument. All the characters are dressed in red, white, and blue costumes and smiling broadly. Covering my hands over my mouth, I giggle at the animals.

"Those are cartoon characters," Cindy offers. "See, they're at a circus."

"*Gao-ut taa ay?*" I ask Meng what she says.

With Meng as our interpreter, Cindy then goes on to tell me their names and that they belong to the Disney family. Tracing my finger over the mouse's large round ears and the duck's protruding fat beak, I smile and think what fun it would be to belong to such a family. When I imagine myself dancing and playing with these funny creatures, my insides swirl and unexpectedly giggles burst forth out of my mouth. As another chortle breaks to the surface, I think of Chou, who always thought it was silly that I remember people by giving them animal names and characteristics. I wish Chou were here with me so I could show her this great new world where animals do look like people.

I get off my bed, cross my room, and enter through another large doorway into the living room. With its three bay windows, the living room is bright and attractive. Filling up the space is a couch and chair set, both covered in tropical floral prints. Standing in front of the middle window, I flatten my hands on the glass and stare at the traffic below before heading back to my room. It occurs to me that with no doors separating my room from the kitchen or the living room, there will be no sleeping in late for me with early riser Eang. I drop my shoulders in resignation and walk back to my room, then cringe at what I see—my window looks directly into the cemetery.

"I am home," I whisper. I have traveled so very far and for so long to reach America and now the journey is over! I close my eyes and breathe a sigh of relief, expecting feelings of calm and contentment to flow into my body.

"I'm home!" I tell myself, but the world remains strange to me.

I lie in bed with my arms wrapped around my belly and glance out the window at the dark sky. Outside, the wind sleeps and the air travels quietly as if they, too, are afraid to disturb the spirits. It is a silence that I find unnatural; in Cambodia, night is always accompanied by the shrill mating songs of crickets. I turn my face to the wall and pull the blanket over my head. Eyes closed, I wait for sleep to come and make me unconscious until the time when the living can reclaim the world. But instead of sleep, the mouse and the duck dance on my sheets in their full circus regalia and top hats. Beside them, their female counterparts twirl their batons and parade to tunes I cannot hear. Soon the other Disney family characters begin to come to life, but I blink them away and force them back into the cloth.

The clock on the wall says it's eleven P.M. This is bad news. It is now close to the dark hours—the hours when spirits and ghosts roam the world and walk among the living. A long time ago, Kim told me never to be awake from twelve A.M. to five A.M., but I couldn't help it. He warned that if I needed to pee, then I should do my business quickly and quietly and get back to bed. He said the more noise or movements I made, the more I would attract the spirits and ghosts. And once that happens, they won't let me go. Kim didn't tell me what he meant by the ghosts not letting me go. He never finished his story but preferred to let the ending form a life of its own in my mind. I used to get so mad at him for this that I would chase him, my arms swinging karate chops at him. Thinking about Kim makes my heart feel tight, as if too many things are being pushed into it.

In the dark, I sit up and lift the blanket off my body. I take the flashlight out from under my pillow, shine a beam on my ankle, and locate the black X on it. Kim told Chou and me that by marking Xs on our ankles and the soles of our feet, we let the ghosts know that our bodies are taken. It is our mark of ownership. Satisfied that the Xs are still there, I tuck the sheet back under my feet and pray the ghosts will not unloose them. Ghosts are very fond of bothering people by tickling their feet with the purpose of waking them.

When sleep does not come, my mind drifts off to find Chou. It is eighteen months since the Vietnamese defeated the Khmer Rouge and chased them into the jungle, and nine months since I pulled my hand out of her grasp. Though she is two years older than me, Chou had the luxury to weep openly at our separation, as was expected of her for being the more fragile sister. But I had to stay strong and smile for her.

In Vermont, alone in my bed, I grind my teeth knowing that I now have to stay strong for myself. . . .

• • •

July 1980

Last night I dreamt I was in the middle of gunfire. There were
people running after me, trying to kill me. I ran and ran but
they were always nipping at my heels. I woke up sweating and
full of fear. But in my closet, I am not afraid. The day after we
moved in, Meng put up a curtain, gave me a chair, and turned
the three-by-four-foot space into my own private world. Here,
I am the creator, taker, and giver of life. My sun, the one light-
bulb above my head, shines brightly at the flick of my wrist. At
my command, it illuminates my box and bestows life to the
shadow creatures on my floor. Like mischievous ghosts, they beg
me to play with them. But I ignore them and bend my head
closer to my sketch pad, my hand busily drawing away.

Outside my sanctuary, Eang clangs our pots and pans as she
scrubs them spotlessly clean in the sink. I suppose I should be a
good girl and go see if she needs my help, but for now the bad
girl wins and I stay put. I tug my curtain to close it tighter and
focus on my paper. In my closet, I know things and things are
known to me. Outside of it, the world is big and bright and so
full of things I need to learn that sometimes my brain feels like
the cream-filled doughnuts Meng sometimes brings home, all
crammed up and mushy. I envision that if I squish the side of my
head with my hands, the overstuffed filling will shoot out of
my nose. But inside my closet, my world is controlled and my
brain pulses firmly and gently under my skull.

I lean back on my chair and stare at my creation. My brows
furrow with frustration and my teeth gnaw at a thumbnail. Under my blue pajama pants, the gray metal pull-out chair cools my
butt, sending a chill up my spine. Involuntarily, I shake out my
shoulders to let loose the energy before returning to my task.
My left arm cradling my small pad, I finish the mouse by adding

its circle ears. Once I finish, I place the pencil behind my ear and observe my drawing at arm's length.

My feet start their rhythmic tapping on the hardwood floor. Normally, if Eang is within visible distance, I stop my feet by resting my hands on my knees. When my legs are still, my thighs and calves tingle as if hundreds of millipedes and their thousands of legs are crawling on my skin. Their friction creates static electricity, making the hair on my body stand up. From my knees, the millipedes' microscopic legs travel down my feet until their electrical current becomes a tickle in my toes. At this point, I imagine if I don't twitch to release the energy, the voltage will explode like ten tiny rockets out of my toes.

But Eang cannot see me in my closet so I let my knees knock and my feet tap to their content. I take my No. 2 pencil and shade in the pants, shirt, ears, and nose. My pencil presses down on the shape, darkening the circle ears, taking care to shade within the lines. Then I place the tip of the pencil in my mouth and wet the lead with my spit. With the wet tip, I blacken my figure's eyes until they stare back at me like two black coals. Sitting back on my chair, I observe my drawing with a smile of satisfaction.

"Minnie Mouse," I roll the name off my tongue. The name floats in the air like a catchy song.

"Minnie Mouse," I repeat. Minnie does not answer me. Staring at her, I daydream about how fun it must be to look like a cartoon character and make people smile. I wish people would like me the way they like Minnie. When people look at Minnie, they are happy. I wonder what people see when they look at me. Eang says I look like an street kid, all dark and thin with my spindly arms and legs and bloated belly. Meng is afraid my growth may have been stunted because of the years of starvation and malnutrition. When I look in the mirror, I don't see the girl they see. Instead, my hands pinch and pull at my features to bring forth Ma's nose, Pa's eyes, Keav's smile, and Chou's lips. I crave to hold their image in my hand and stare at their faces until their imprints are permanent in my brain. But we do not have a single picture of them and my face is now the only image I have to remember them by.

From the white sheet, Minnie stares up at me with her wet eyes and pleads for friends. As I begin to draw her some friends, Eang's voice booms above me. I lift my head to see her standing in my closet's doorway, my tan cotton curtain all bunched up in her hand.

"What are you doing?" she demands, sounding irritated.

"Drawing," I reply nonchalantly.

"I've been calling you for the past fifteen minutes. Didn't you hear me?"

I want to scream out. *Of course I heard you! No amount of banging pots and pans can mute the shrill sound of your voice!* But instead, I cast my eyes down and say, "I'm sorry."

"All right," she sighs. "Come help me clean the house. The McNultys will be here soon to pick us up for a barbecue at their house. We don't want them to think we live in a messy house."

"Can I have fifteen minutes? I want to pick up my closet first."

"Oh, all right." With another resigned sigh, she exits my space.

I drag the curtain across the copper rod and shut myself in again. I close my sketch pad and lay it on the floor, then fold up the metal chair and lean it against the wall. Picking up a clothes hanger from the ground, I hang it on a wooden rod stretched across the back of the closet. Next to the other skeletal hangers, my one white shirt, now wrinkled and slightly stained, looks lonely and sad. I pull out a drawer where I store my few sets of clothes and gently place my drawing in among them. Above the drawers, on one shelf, I adjust my small rectangular standing mirror, straightening out my comb, brush, and pencil box so that they line up evenly next to one another, careful not to knock over the glass of water nearby. On another shelf, I pick up stray bobby pins, rubber bands, and safety pins and put them in a wooden bowl already filled with colorful ribbons for my hair.

I pick out a red ribbon and smooth it between my thumb and index finger. As the silky satin glides over my skin, my mind travels back to Cambodia, where for four years we lived without colors and wore only the official Khmer Rouge black pants and shirts. The soldiers said that sporting colorful clothes separates people and breeds contempt and distrust among its citizens. They warned that children who longed for a red skirt, pink shirt, or blue pants were vain, and therefore had to have their vanity beaten out of them. I wonder what the soldiers would say if they saw my bowl of colorful ribbons. Whatever they would say, I hope they spew their words from their dead lips and decomposed flesh. I tie a red ribbon in my hair, thinking how happy I am to be in America.

It seems so strange sometimes that I have lived in America for two weeks now. And even though I have learned to live with the ghosts and spirits next door, at dusk each night I still take out my pen and mark Xs on my heels and ankles before the sun hides completely behind the mountains. Under the blanket, with Mickey, Minnie, and the gang on top of me, I escape to a troublesome and restless sleep. In the morning before Meng and Eang see me, I rush to the bathroom and scrub off my Xs so they will not scold me for being crazy. But sometimes we are surprised with an early visit from one of our sponsors and I have to resort to other means to erase the Xs.

One such surprise arrived on our second day in Vermont when we were awakened by a loud knock on the door. While Meng went down to open the door, I groggily rushed into my closet and changed out of my pajamas and into my brown shirt and pants. I cleared my throat and attempted to spit but my mouth was dry; instead of saliva, a glob of mucus landed on my palm. I smeared it over my ankles and rubbed out my Xs. I fumbled for the comb and brushed down my fly-away hair before securing it down with bobby pins. Finished with my primping, I hurriedly left my closet to make my bed.

All the while, the cheerful lady huffed up the stairs, explaining to Meng that she was a member of the parish from the Holy Family Church that sponsored our family to America. Meng smiled and thanked her. She then walked into our kitchen and proceeded to show us how to operate the stove, oven, and refrigerator. Crossing the kitchen to the sink, she opened our cabinets and pulled out a mug. She explained that it is used to drink tea or coffee. She then pointed to cups, bowls, and plates, and with each item, she told us what they are used for. When she got to the new tableware set, she instructed us that for everyday use, we were to use the old set: we were to use the new set when we have guests. By the end of her speech, Meng and Eang's faces were tight and their smiles forced.

When the sponsor lady left, I asked Meng why so many people assume we don't know about such things as fine china and cups. Yes, it was true that during the Khmer Rouge regime, our plate sets and silverware consisted mostly of coconut shells, banana leaves, our fingers, and our table was the rice fields. But before the war, our family sat for dinner at our big mahogany table and high-backed teak chairs while our house help served us food on fine china. Young as I am, I felt my ego bend like a bamboo tree each time the lady picked up another item, until in the end the reed was too heavy with burden and snapped, causing my face to darken and my eyes to harden.

"These people know nothing! They think we're backward villagers and peasants!" I blurted out.

Meng bent down to my level. His eyes bulged and his head expanded with hot air so that he resembled a praying mantis. He ordered me to be quiet.

"These people have busy lives. They don't have to help us at all but they do, so you be grateful." His voice low, he continued. "They may only know about Cambodia's war and poverty. They have no way of knowing we once came from a high-class family. Without them we wouldn't be here, so unless you want to return to Cambodia, you better show them gratitude." With that, he turned and left me. Ashamed and embarrassed, I vowed to be nicer and more grateful, and not complain anymore.

The next day, Michael Vincenti returned carrying a small, nine-inch TV. I followed on his heels and watched him set the TV down on the coffee table in the living room. As he pushed the plug into the wall, I bounced on the couch and waited for the magic pictures to appear. A few seconds later, the TV buzzed like a thousand bees, and black-and-white lines swam across the screen. Fascinated, I stared at Michael's fingers as they fumbled with the knobs and dials until finally a clear voice came through and with it a cartoon cat chasing after a little mouse. I clasped my hands together in a praying gesture and glued my eyes to the magic box.

For the next two weeks, the sponsor visitors kept arriving, each time to give us new life lessons on everything from how to take a bus to the grocery store to operating the machines to wash our clothes at the Laundromat. In between these visits Sarah, our English tutor, would come to our home to teach us the English language. In her mid-twenties, Sarah was all smiles and big eyes that looked buggy behind her thick glasses. Each day, she would sit across from Meng, Eang, and me at our kitchen table and play cards with us. From her old cloth bag, she would retrieve her cards and teach us Go Fish and Memory. Each time we flipped a card, we would repeat the word after her. After we finished with our games, Sarah would take out of her bag many books with bright pictures of the rooms in the house, numbers, and letters. She would point to the various pictures or numbers and ask us to repeat after her.

As nice as Sarah is, I am happy when it's time for her to leave because it means I can turn on the TV. Although I don't understand the reason, Meng and Eang have a very strict policy that while there are guests in the house the TV must be turned off. This makes for many awkward and silent visits with our guest peppering Meng with questions as Eang and I sit silently nearby. Sometimes, a visitor looks in my direction and I smile, pretending to pay attention to words I do not understand. While the adults talk, in my mind's eyes I flatten, pull, stretch, and reshape their human faces into cartoon characters. A man with a big nose becomes a pig, a round face turns into a monkey, and a thin-lipped person transforms into a chicken. At times, I have a whole farm of animal people, all of them pecking, hissing, or spitting noises at me as I nod my head in reply.

When we have no visitors, I stay in my closet; outside, the sun makes the white people brown, the birds chirp their wake-up song, and the clouds roll by as soft as cotton balls across the blue sky. At three, I leave my closet and turn on the TV in time to hear the familiar Looney Tunes theme. Then for an hour I follow Bugs Bunny, Daffy Duck, and Tweety Bird as they chase, kill, and bash one another without bloodshed or anybody getting hurt. In shows where a cartoon character dies, it usually comes back to life in the next episode or flies up to heaven with its tiny white wings while strumming a harp.

Each time the Road Runner comes on, I hope for the coyote to catch the bird and sink its teeth into the bird's long neck. After all, I reason, the coyote isn't being mean; it is hungry and only wants something to eat. If I could create a show, I'd draw the Road Runner plucked of its feathers and hanging on a hook, all naked and skinny. Slowly, I would deep-fry the bird in hot grease until it was golden and crispy. Then the coyote and I would crunch on it, bones and all, like it was a pheasant.

The days I don't think about deep-frying the bird, I daydream about roasting the pig, barbecuing the duck, and steam-

ing the fish. This usually means that I need to fill my stomach
with chips and cookies until the next mealtime. With my stomach full, I sit in front of the TV lost in a world where everything
is light, silly, and young again. In the evening, when there are
no more cartoons to keep me company, I tune in to the Brady
family and laugh at their antics. Although I cannot understand
their words, the largeness of their family and their crowded
house make me feel less alone in mine. For half an hour each
night, I live their lives and enjoy their family bonding and sibling rivalries. Watching them, I am taken back to a time and
place when I, too, was part of a large family. But now, I am the
only child of Meng and Eang.

As much as I like the show, I sometimes fantasize about
beating up the Brady girls. In my mind, I lift their stick figures
up in the air, their golden hair flowing like silk threads over my
shoulders as I send them crashing on my knee, snapping them
like dry old twigs. I think of doing this not to hurt them but to
save them. In my mind, I worry that if fighting suddenly erupts
in America, many of its frail citizens with their weaknesses will
not survive. And I want them to live because it is so much harder
to see them die. I know that in my new home, there is no war,
hunger, or soldiers to be afraid of. Yet in the quiet recesses of my
mind, the Khmer Rouge lurks and hovers in dark alleys, waiting
for me at the bend of every corner. No matter how far I run, I
cannot escape the dread that they have followed me to America.

To escape the soldiers, I sometimes find myself in a field not
far from our apartment. With my hair loose and free, I run
through elephant grass as tall as my thighs until I come to a
brook. The sound of the gurgling water soothes and relaxes my
mind, shutting out the thoughts of war. On the edge of the
rushing stream stands a tree that reaches up high into the heav-
ens with branches that dip toward the earth. I run and wrap my
arms around its trunk, pressing my body against its hard bark.
My eyes closed, I imagine Chou on the other side, her cheek

smashed against the tree, her fingers reaching out for mine the way she used to when we were together. When I open my eyes, Chou is not there and my mind races to find her, wherever she is.

As I focus my thoughts on Chou, in the kitchen Eang is being noisier than ever.

"Loung! Come help me clean the kitchen!" Eang wakes me from my daydreaming. I ignore her call.

"Loung, come help me now!" she yells.

In the past few months, I'd noticed that Eang had been more impatient and spent a lot of time throwing up in the bathroom. Then last week, while Meng waited quietly outside our apartment, Eang told me that she was pregnant and that the baby will come in December. I burst out laughing then because I now knew the reason for her bloated face and bad moods.

"All right! I'm coming!"

I turn around and survey my closet to make sure all is neat and orderly. In my sanctuary, my world is decorated with a single picture—a drawing I made of Mickey holding Minnie's hand. Pulling the curtain open, I enter the big world.

KAO KALIA YANG

Thailand

Kao Kalia Yang (1980–) was born in Thailand in the Ban Vinai refugee camp, a haven for the ethnic Hmong from Laos. During the Vietnam War, the United States had recruited the Hmong as allies in what became known as the "Secret War," a CIA-led effort against the communist Pathet Lao faction in the Laotian civil war. When the U.S. forces withdrew from the region in 1975, Pathet Lao sought to exterminate Hmong people the U.S. had not evacuated. Rather than face harsh re-education camps, many Hmong fled into the jungles or made the dangerous journey across the Mekong River to refugee camps in Thailand, as Yang's parents did in 1979. Yang describes her seven years at the refugee camp as "wait[ing] in the dust," sleeping in wooden shacks, and subsisting on meager U.N. rations. Yang's father was the first of his extended family to register the family for migration to the U.S., and they spent two years in the Phanat Nikhom Processing Center before arriving in St. Paul, Minnesota.

The Yangs were part of the much larger second Hmong immigration following the passage of the Refugee Act of 1980; before that, approximately thirty thousand Hmong lived in the U.S., but the population soared to 186,000 in 2000. Initially dispersed across the country, many Hmong sought to reunite with their extended families in agricultural areas with moderate climates throughout California. In the 1980s, the Minneapolis–St. Paul area became a center for Hmong people as a result of the support of volunteer agencies in Minnesota, where the Yang family located, relying on state assistance and local charitable organizations. Yang quickly displayed a skill for writing in English, surprising her instructors because she was so reluctant to speak. Yang later received a BA in American studies from Carleton College before studying creative writing at Columbia, where she took her MFA.

The first Hmong memoir to be published nationally, The Latehomecomer: A Hmong Family Memoir *(2008) won many awards for its chronicle of the family's harrowing history in Laos and Thailand and their subsequent immigrant experiences. She also wrote the short documentary* The Place Where We Were Born *(2008) and cofounded* Words Wanted, *a writing and translation service for refugees. The following passages describe her family's first years in St. Paul, where Yang's parents could find only factory work and were embarrassed to be receiving public assistance. Then the author ruminates on her relationship to Hmong culture and compares herself to her American-born siblings and relatives.*

Excerpt from

The Latehomecomer

— 2008 —

The McDonough townhouses had been built after World War II for returning soldiers and their families. The first low-income housing units in the state of Minnesota, the buildings were made of concrete. Everything was cold and strong, meant to last a long time. And so they had, and they had waited for us, soldiers from a different war, not returning to families but to remnants of them.

Located in St. Paul, the John J. McDonough Housing Project housed many Hmong families. The housing project was smaller than Ban Vinai Refugee Camp, but it was on high ground, and in this way it recalled the other places the Hmong had lived on, cried on, and died on. When imagination struck, I fancied that the grass hills were really mountains, the resting place of our ancestors. In the silent moments when my hands and feet weren't busy, I knew our townhouse was different from the homes of the American children on television and along the highways.

All the buildings in the project were rectangular and made of cement, all were the same shade of tan with brown roofs and had small windows covered with steel screens. The symmetry of the place was similar to the sameness of our lives, each family caught up in school and English, each family visiting thrift stores and driving used cars, living on the monthly welfare and disability checks from the government. The truth was dawning: the lives we were living in America were far from the life that the adults had imagined from the camps in Thailand.

My family lived at 1475 Timberlake Road, Apartment C. It was a small unit for families with few children. Our segment of the townhouse consisted of two bedrooms, one bathroom, a small living room, a kitchen, and a bare, cold, concrete basement. The bedrooms had no closets, just spaces pushed into the walls with a rod across the front. Onto thin, rusty wire hangers my mother hung our better clothes from Thailand. Into plastic hampers she folded our pants and the few pieces of everyday clothes we'd gotten from church basements. The bathroom was tiny and the site of perfect showers, but otherwise uninteresting. The living room was my favorite room. It held a black-and-white television and two couches from the early 1970s, one a dark forest green that smelled of cigarettes and the other a musty orange with cat and dog hair embedded in the tough fibers. The kitchen belonged to my mother, who stood often at the sink or the stove. It held our first American-bought appliance, a rice cooker from Japan that we got from an oriental store. The base-ment belonged to no one. It was dark and empty. Sometimes I stood in the open doorway, looking down the shadows that cloaked the stairs, feeling the cold air seeping up and into the pores of my skin, shivering before the darkness, challenging and shirking away from its unhesitating reach. Each time I stood at the top of the stairwell and looked down, I wondered: why were rooms made to hold darkness in America when lights could be shined on everything?

It was as if our time in Thailand—the way we had lived and played and waited—had not been a part of the world.

My family was part of the biggest wave of Hmong refugees to enter the country; many of us were settling into California, Wisconsin, or Minnesota. In 1980, the U.S. Census recorded 5,204 Hmong in America. By 1990, that number would grow to a substantial 90,082. But the story of the Hmong lives in America hadn't changed very much by 1987. On October 20, 1980, the *St. Paul Dispatch* published a story titled "Hostility Grows Toward Hmong." On June 11, 1987, the headlines read similarly, "Hmong Gardens Vandalized for the Third Time This Spring." My family arrived in July; we were just beginning. On the streets, sometimes people yelled for us to go home. Next to waves of hello, we received the middle finger.

My mother and father told us not to look at the Americans. If we saw them, they would see us. For the first year and a half, we wanted to be invisible. Everywhere we went beyond the McDonough Housing Project, we were looked at, and we felt exposed. We were dealing with a widespread realization that all Hmong people must do one of two things to survive in Amer-ica: grow up or grow old. In the case of the noticeably young, the decision was made for us. For those who were older, the case was also easy to figure. Those marred by the war, impaired by the years of fighting, social security and disability were options. For my mother and father, already adults who had waited on life long before it was their time, the government stepped in and told them: the welfare clock was ticking. She was twenty-five. He was twenty-eight. They knew they wanted a chance to work, but they did not know how to keep that chance safe, so on the streets, before the slanted brows of mostly white men, they held us close for security.

On the hills of the McDonough Housing Project, the sun high in the summer sky, Hmong people practiced walking in America, children struggling with their parents holding on to them harder than ever. Dawb and I could no longer walk as we always had. The hands holding ours were more determined than before, and also full of pressure. When I skipped, my mother told me falling on the pavement would hurt, so I struggled to match her rapid nervous gait. When Dawb limped, my father placed himself before her, protecting her with his body, and I watched her learn to stand strong for him. At night, the children looked at the white ceilings and remembered how it had been long ago and far away. We wondered if our parents, on the high mountains of Laos, had to relearn the basics of walking when they were our age, when the bombs fell and the craters broke into the earth, the paths of their lives shattered forever.

That very first summer, I encountered the challenge of not getting what I wanted most: to see my grandma in California. I also wanted her to sit with me on our small front porch, talk with me from the windows of the townhouse, and tell me about how it had been when we were still together. Money, something that I had begged like a monk for, in the dress of innocence, became a stumbling block. She'd arrived in America in late August with Uncle Hue's family. On the phone, her voice trilled in the distance, and though I could not see her tears, I felt them on my own face. Dawb clamored with me for this thing that we both dearly wanted: please let us all go see Grandma. Our mother and father shook their heads. It was not an explanation— it was a new fact in our lives. We did not have enough money.

Facts are not enough for children. We asked questions.

They tried to explain facts: "Money is not something the heart makes."

We were not convinced, but we knew that they wanted to see Grandma, too, so we accepted it. On the telephone, with Grandma's tears in her voice, our tears on our faces, we promised each other a future in America.

We said, "One day, we'll find our way to you. This country is big. But it is not as big as our love for you."

She cried. We could not hear what she was trying to say. We cried with her. I got teardrops on the receiver. I wanted to believe that the tears would reach her, but I knew they wouldn't. Only human beings can reach each other; tears are just water; salty water that I cannot control, so they slip out of my eyes, down my cheeks, to my lips, to the tip of my tongue, until I wipe them away on my sleeve.

I started dreaming about money, dollar bills that folded into cylinders, looked like trashcans, and rolled around in my head, loud and angry, smooth and gentle. After my dreams, I made decisions. When I grow up, I'm going to have money. When I grow up, I'm going to never need money. When I grow up, I'm going to treat money so well that it will always want to stay with me. When I grow up, I'm going to hate money so much that it will be afraid of me and stay away from me. Money was like a person I had never known or a wall I had never breached before: it kept me away from my grandma. I saw no way to climb this wall. Sometimes I thought so much about money that I couldn't sleep. Money was not bills and coins or a check from welfare. In my imagination, it was much more: it was the nightmare that kept love apart in America.

The welfare check arrived in our mailbox near the first of the month. We were a family of four, so we got $605 a month. Rent was $250, and our sponsor was teaching my father how to drive because a family cannot survive without a car in America.

My parents had bought an old brown Subaru on monthly payments. After we paid for the car insurance, electricity, and natural gas, we were left with only $150 to spend on gas for the car, on Dial soap and Pert Plus shampoo, on extra lightbulbs and vacuum bags for the old Eureka we received from a church basement, on Vaseline lotion and powder detergent so my mother could wash our clothes in the bathtub. Then there was the money we had to save to help pay for clan dinners to talk about life in America and for emergencies like sickness or death. We'd learned a lesson from our history: hard times were inescapable, but when they came, Hmong people would have to help Hmong people survive.

In our new life of not looking closely at Americans, of walking carefully on paved streets, of living without money, my family sat in front of the black-and-white television and watched soap operas. My cousin's wife, who did not know English well, came over with her children and translated the dramas for us. The American people on television kissed and kissed and kissed, and I slipped my hands over my eyes and then carefully spaced my fingers apart and looked between them. My cousin and his wife had young children that cried all the time and drank bottles of cow milk; I worried that they would become like cow children. I watched the television, and the days passed, one after another.

At night, the families gathered for long conversations, which were always about surviving in America, the same topic that the adults in my family started the first night we arrived in the country. It was a conversation that would continue for the next twenty years. How do we survive in America and still love each other as we had in Laos? We must have yearly family picnics to discuss our problems and progress. What are safe things a family can do to save money? If a family purchases a one-hundred-pound bag of Kokuho Rice from a Hmong store (only around twenty dollars then) and goes to Long Cheng's Butchering Complex to buy a pig for one hundred dollars to put in the freezer, the family will not starve. Which program was the best one to help a man find a job, the Lao Family Organization, formed by General Vang Pao, or the Hmong American Partnership, led by Hmong men who were on their way to being established already? Go to Hmong American Partnership, because they are less political than Lao Family. Politics had destroyed our lives too many times. To make lives in America, let us all try and focus on the things we can control: ourselves. I grew drowsy during these conversations.

Life without money became more than the things we wanted or could not do. It became the things I smelled and touched, the people I loved. We shopped from secondhand stores. Together, we discovered the aisles of Goodwill and Savers. We learned about church basements. The piles of badly folded clothes and the smell that hung in the air, dust and mold mingling in dry places that had not seen sunlight or fresh air for a long time. Instead of colorful skirts, my mother wore solid-colored pants, and instead of soft-fabric pants, my father wore jeans. My fingers crumpled the fabric of their changing wardrobe, and my eyes noted the absence of color.

Amid all this, my mother and father tried to protect our visions of America. They said the used clothes were road maps of successful paths out of being poor, signs toward our happy futures in this country. They said watching television was a luxury. We should pay attention and learn something. Their smiles and laughter were for us, to cover up the nothing in our lives.

I missed my grandma, and I saw the used clothes on my parents. I felt the weight of the road before us. The only road signs I liked were the red ones put out by the ice cream truck when children came answering its melody. When the ice cream truck started calling the children, my mother gave Dawb and me quarters to buy the sweet treats. We handed the man in white clothes our quarters and he handed us Kemps banana-flavored

Popsicles—cold in the palms of our hands, in the hold of our eager fingers. Every day the ice cream man came with his song and his road sign. Every day I waited eagerly.

One day, I asked my mother how it was that we did not have money to visit Grandma in California, but she had quarters for ice cream.

She answered me flatly, "Because I do not like to see you watching other children run to the truck. Because even from the window, a child can taste the sweetness of sugar. Your throat swallows when other children lick their ice cream."

The truck came every day, and then the days got a little cooler and the call for ice cream became less frequent. The only road sign that I liked in America went away as summer became fall.

I have an image of my mother and father on a bridge over a highway. They are looking down at the busy people on the road, but they have nowhere to go. The sky is a rumbling gray, perhaps in anticipation of the fall rain. They are little more than two outlines, standing together, not touching, facing the same direction, standing still. In their thin jackets, the sizes all wrong, too big and too long, they watch people with work to do and places to go, young children buckled safely in backseats. That first year, and for many years after, my parents spent a lot of time yearning to be strangers. I felt it then, and I feel it now. It is hardly ever enough to simply be alive. This image, played time and again that entire first year in America, is how my father learned about the types of cars that didn't leave families behind on the road, which cars, even when old, ran strong. This is how he became an advocate of the Toyota and Honda brands. This is how my mom's fear of driving began. Everybody was so trained, so fast, trusting one another, but things could go wrong—the sound of far-off ambulances and police sirens. I watched my mom and dad stand on the highway bridge from a distance, safe on the sidewalk of my youth.

• • •

When the days and nights grew colder, and summer changed to fall, my parents began talking about Dawb and me becoming educated people. They stopped talking about money almost entirely. They became hopeful. For my mother, the thinking was simple: we all had to go to school so we could all learn about America. For my father, the thinking was more complicated, snagging more emotions and giving rise to more questions than answers. He said we could no longer wait. We could no longer play all the time—even if it was just in our heads. We had to practice growing up to be good people. The Hmong had traveled farther to America than we had to any other land. We would live here longer than we've ever lived in another country. The only way to live in America was to learn of its possibilities, and the way to do that was school.

My parents knew that Dawb had been good at school in Ban Vinai Refugee Camp and Phanat Nikhom Transition Camp to America. They had one strong learner. They were confident that I would do well, too. When they saw me gnawing my lips, contemplating school, they reassured me. I had learned how to speak early. I asked hundreds of questions a day. They told me a story about a cat. I asked: Does the cat in the story have one mouth? Two eyes? Paws for hands and feet? What about a tail? They didn't know education well but they knew it was tied to curious questions. I would do just fine in school.

A cousin took us to register at Battle Creek Elementary first. There was a white woman with curly hair wearing a red turtleneck and a sweater with a reindeer on it. She wore white stockings and black heels. Her skirt was made out of denim. She was the tester, and she told us to say our ABCs. I had to go first. I said, "A, B, C." Then I stopped. She said for me to say my ABCs again and my cousin said for me to say the letters again, so I repeated them again, "A, B, C." The woman tried more

times and then she shook her head. She held up cards with different colors and I smiled each time she changed the card. Say
the color. I said them in Hmong. She shook her head. She held
up numbers, but I didn't know them, so I smiled some more. She
shook her head, so my cousin took my hand and pulled me gently to his side, and pushed Dawb before me. Dawb said her
ABCs. She said every color was "yellow." She said the numbers
in English up to ten, and then she offered to keep on saying the
numbers in Hmong and Thai. Battle Creek Elementary let us in.
They placed Dawb in second grade and me in first. . . .

Dawb ran outside. I put my spoon in my aunt's hand, and I
ran after Dawb. We reached them at the same time. My
mother was carrying our brother in her arms, walking slowly.
He was not asleep. I could tell because he was looking at me
with small, dark eyes, but as if he were sleeping, my mother said
very quietly, in a whispering voice, "His name is Xue. Someday,
when he is old, we are going to call him Zong Xue."

They had given him a strong name. In Hmong, *xue* is the
word for knowledge, for skill. *Zong xue* means forest of knowledge, forest of skill. I wanted to hate him a little, but I was un-
sure of what hate felt like. I listened to my heart: no erratic
jumps, just the regular pounding response. I couldn't find the
hate inside of me. But I didn't love him immediately, as Dawb
did. But he was small and weak, and I couldn't hurt such a baby.
I even wanted to hold him. My mother and father were smiling,
happy the whole time. I asked them why they never told me my
mother was pregnant. They said I was too young. I didn't believe
them. They just wanted to keep me from knowing. I was too
young to know that my mother was pregnant, but I was not
too young to be a big sister? There was no sense in that.

I tried to look for changes in the beginning. Xue, the son they had waited so long for, the baby boy whose spirit made it to our world when six others had not. Xue, the tiny round head and the red lips like a chili pepper, whose breath smelled like fresh sugarcane and warm jasmine rice steam. My mother treated him gently, gentler than she treated me, like he was softer and more fragile, but I was not jealous. It made sense. He scared easily. If I was loud, he whimpered in his sleep. If I was rough, he winced, little brown eyebrows furrowed in a wrinkled forehead. My father treated him like a regular child. I paid attention to the way my parents talked and treated me. I noted that there were no significant changes.

It didn't take me long to conclude that Xue's coming into our lives changed many things but not the way my parents loved Dawb and me. My uncles, my grandma, and the whole family were excited for us; they all called and said how happy they were at the arrival of a little son at last. I started feeling proud, as if I had something to do with the calling of Xue's spirit from the clouds into our world. If I had been a gift when my mother and father didn't dare dream of presents, Xue was a miracle that they had hoped a long time for.

Like the year I was born, 1989 was a big year for babies in my family. All my aunts and uncles except for one pair had a baby that year. It felt like everybody wanted to have a baby in America. The adults continued to say that we were lucky to be here in America, to have new lives opening before us, but they added a different phrase for the new children.

They all said, "These new children are Americans."

All these new children would know was America. They would have no refugee camps in Thailand to compare life here with. The stories from Laos they would only hear, as I had heard them, from the adults. The war and the tragedy and the difficulty of our early lives, they would feel only via our filtered memories. It was our duty, all the big brothers and sisters, even the mothers and fathers, to make sure that these young Americans had a better world than we'd ever known. It was a big obligation, and I took it seriously.

Xue shapes the memories I carry from that time. He cried at night. My mother and father were always walking him around the house trying to shush him. He cried during the day. My mother would sit with him on her lap close to a small electric water heater they had bought just for him. There was no more real fire to hold babies by, as there had been in Thailand and Laos, but in America there were substitutions for the real things. Sometimes my mother told me to sit very still, and she placed him in my arms. He wiggled and looked at me, and I smiled down at him. It took him a long time to learn how to smile back. I don't remember taking care of him as a baby, only that he was in my life. Maybe I was too busy in school, trying to become educated, overwhelmed by my growing silence.

I was becoming good in different subjects: math, English, social studies, science, and art. My report cards were full of 4s for "great" and 3s for "good." I had learned how to be a good student in America, except for an important thing. I got 2s for "needs improvement" for all things that had to do with making friends and talking. I realized I was forgetting how to talk, and things got immediately more complicated. There were Hmong kids who were not any better than I was in English, but they were trying to speak English left and right, which made them look young and silly and new. There was a part of me that felt old. Instead of talking, I focused on listening.

In third grade, the serious teacher with the brown hair didn't care. The other Hmong girl in class spoke English well, so maybe that's why the teacher noticed that I was not talking. There were American kids everywhere. I was embarrassed trying to speak their language in front of them because sometimes when I whispered something wrong, a few of them laughed. The teacher encouraged me to speak and frowned when I an-

swered her questions without words, when I shook or nodded
my head instead of using my voice. She made me feel that my
silence was a bad thing. I tried to respond to her in whispers,
which I kept as short as possible. I neglected the embellishments
of my life to keep it simple:

"Kao."

"Here."

"Yes."

"No."

"Fine."

"O.K."

"Thanks."

"Welcome."

"Bye."

My vocabulary list was short, and I never volunteered to
speak. Inside, I grew angry at myself: Why didn't I speak? Why
couldn't my voice sound normal in English? It always felt stuck
in my throat, and it showed on my face that I was trying too
hard. The words came out with rust all over them.

Despite my silence, I knew my grasp of English was growing. I no longer needed Americans to repeat themselves or speak
slower. I understood, only I didn't respond, so my understanding
didn't show. The American people at school did not trust that I
knew what they were saying.

At home, I had to use my English. It was not a matter of
choice. My mother and father had become shy in America, especially when it came to English. They were taking care of us
in the important ways: buying us food and clothes, making sure
the welfare check came, and being careful about money so that
we could have plastic rulers to do our math with and winter
boots for the Minnesota snow. But whenever there were interactions with random American people, at Kmart when we were
looking to buy electrical outlet plugs so Xue couldn't get his
fingers into the sockets, or at Wal-Mart when we needed to

know the aisle for the replacement vacuum cleaner bags, Dawb became the speaker. If Dawb wasn't there, I would have to speak.

It's hard to watch your parents stumble before other adults. We wanted to protect them and our visions of them as competent people who knew what we needed and the best ways to love us. So we took the fall into the language. We did not think about how this would change our roles as children or their abilities as parents. It was one more necessary step in surviving as a family.

My parents knew that I was not speaking much at school, but they both knew that I was learning English. They had seen me write letters to Grandma in California. They had noticed when I laughed at the funny parts of *Tom & Jerry*. But the thing that gave me away most was my anger. Whenever I got angry, I spoke in English, unless I was angry at them, in which case I would want them to know everything I was saying, so I would try my best at being angry in Hmong:

"Dawb is a lazy bum, and you never ask her to do anything. You always ask me because I do it. I make it too easy for you! You are being unfair! You are parents, and you are not doing your job well!"

I did not know enough bad words in Hmong to satisfy my anger. The words I knew justified it but did not show it. My parents had made it a point not to say any bad Hmong words in front of us. In English, though, I was learning. Every time kids got mad at school, they usually said "fuck" and "bitch" and "shit." When I was angry, when my feelings were hurt, or I felt injured and weak, I used these words in a fierce whisper just for me. My parents hated it. They, too, had learned the meaning of these words. They said that if I wanted to use English, then use it for a worthy cause: our survival.

My parents tried their best at English, but their best was not catching up with Dawb's and mine. We were picking up the language faster, and so we became the interpreters and translators for our family dealings with American people. In the beginning, we just did it because it was easier and because we did not want to see them struggle over easy things. They were working hard for the more important things in our lives. Later, we realized so many other cousins and friends were doing the same.

I remember being at the grocery store with my father, buying diapers for Xue. They didn't have his size on the shelves. I hated to speak English outside the house. Even to my cousins I did not like speaking the language. My father was still looking on the shelves. A deep breath. I'm a big sister. It is the least I can do. I had started calling my father "Daddy."

"Daddy, I'll go ask them if they have any in the back."

"I'll go with you."

I put my hand in his, and we walked over to the clerk at the customer service counter. I was self-conscious that my father was going to hear me talk. I could barely see over the top of the counter. I stood on tiptoes, with one hand on the counter for balance. I tried to look brave. I was hesitant and quiet when the words came out.

"Do you have a box of number one Pampers? We didn't see any on the shelf."

I shook my head to support my words. I couldn't trust myself in English; my mother and father could barely trust me.

My father said in a louder voice, "Pampers number one."

He held up one finger. He didn't trust himself in English, either.

The fact that so few people trusted themselves in English was a big problem for my whole extended family. Over time, the kids were invited to the family meetings on how to improve our lives in America. We gathered at an aunt or uncle's house; they usually called the meetings because they were worried that their children were wasting opportunities to become educated people in America. All the young cousins were to learn not to become like the bad older cousins—bad usually because they had friends and went out with them and had started speaking English at home, and sometimes when they were angry with their parents, they would go into their rooms and slam the doors and say that their lives were horrible and that they wished they hadn't been born. The adults would point out the good role models for us to follow at these family meetings—good usually because they went to school every day and came home on time and spoke Hmong at home, and sometimes when they were happy with their mothers and fathers, they talked about how lucky they were to be in America and have opportunities to make a good life. High school was the highest educational level of the children in our family then. When we went to these family meetings, I usually sat with the cousins who were close to my age. The meetings were always the same. They began with the same words, in Hmong, by an uncle (they took turns):

"We almost died in the war. Many Hmong people died in the war. We are fortunate to have made it to America. Many died trying to get to this country of opportunity. Now we are in America. There are schools for children to go to. There are universities. Your mothers and fathers are not educated people. Maybe you go to school and you see that your classmates have parents who are doctors and lawyers and you wonder why your mother and father do not work and have disability checks and cannot help themselves, let alone help you. We are not doctors and lawyers. We never had the chance. We do not speak English. You can."

They would say how much they loved us and hoped that we became great people in America. They said they understood that some of us may feel embarrassed at school because we got free lunches and our parents were on welfare. Sometimes they cried. At these meetings, I learned that what made our parents sad was not so much the hardness of the life they had to lead in America, or the hardness of the lives they had led to get to

America, but the hardness of *our* lives in America. It was always about the children. And so the pressure built.

The children would sit and listen. I always thought the talks went on for a little too long and that they were much the same each time, but I enjoyed these gatherings because the family was together. Even then I knew that not many American families got together and tried to speak to each other about becoming better people in America. It was something special that my family did. Some of my cousins didn't enjoy the talks at all, especially the ones whose parents had called the meeting. They felt it was public ridicule. They complained about the comparisons among children.

We had one cousin, the one my family had lived with when we first came, who had graduated from high school. We were all proud of him. He looked older and wiser and more stylish to me than any other cousin because he carried a yellow notepad and a pen at the family meetings. Sometimes he wore a suit. He said he was going to go to college if the family would support him. Of course we all would—even children nodded. Then yes, he would go. He would go to a community college and then transfer to the University of Minnesota. He would blaze a trail for us in America toward education, so that when it was our turn, we could follow his lead. He had learned the term "role model" and used it with authority and a resounding eloquence that made the adults pause in pride. Dawb really listened to this part of the conversation. I could tell because she would nod her head as he said each word, her eyes following his pen on the paper as he marked each point he had made.

At home Dawb told me that we had to work hard so we could go to the University of Minnesota, too. It was a great school, she said. It was *the* University of Minnesota—smart Americans went there, like her teachers. Only the luckiest and smartest Hmong people could go. We had to work very hard so that we could make our father proud. Dawb said it was ambi-

tious and that we shouldn't tell our parents or Grandma or anybody else that we wanted to go there. She understood how it was
when people did not turn out as expected. I didn't contradict
her. I wasn't even sure I wanted to go forward with the plans
at all. Dawb said that people might laugh if we told them. That
part, I agreed with. Dawb pressed on, said that we could remind
each other if one of us forgot that the University of Minnesota
was a great school. She said that maybe we could qualify and get
in if we studied hard and really learned English. I knew there
were no problems with her English. She was trying to be kind
by saying "we." I saved my words: I didn't tell her that I didn't
really care about the University of Minnesota or college. I wasn't
even in junior high yet.

I think each of us cousins still remember the words that
were spoken at the family meetings. We could see the dreams of
our parents in their words. It was often hot, and the windows
would be open, and the panes would fog up as the night wore
on. The aunts prepared food: warm rice and fried chicken wings,
beef vegetable stir-fry seasoned with oyster sauce, and pots of red
chicken curry and green salad, and always an assortment of pop.
My favorite was Sunkist, and I always had a can, although I could
never finish it, only drink it halfway and then sit and look at the
adults and the good cousins and bad cousins and know that I did
not want to be either. I knew that if I couldn't carry the pressure
of being good, then surely I would be bad. But I didn't let on.

Sometimes at the meeting the adults went around and
asked each child to stand up and say in front of the entire family
what they were going to work hard to be in America, what they
were going to do to make the trip that their mothers and fathers
had taken worthwhile. The air got heavier, and our bodies were
on alert. Before the meetings, my mother would tell us that if
we were asked, we should modestly say, we girls especially:

"I will try my best in school. I cannot know what I will
become. Thank you for telling us to be good children."

I think my mother wasn't the only one telling her children what to say at the meetings. I remember the different cousins standing up, trembling a little, clearing thick throats, speaking their dreams and ambitions in shaky voices, but I have no memory of doing so myself. A part of me knew that these meetings were more for the boys of the family than the girls. We were told to be good girls. We were told to dream of school. We knew that the boys would carry on the family name, be called to life and death for the Yang name we all carried.

My father told us that we were his future in America, that it didn't matter if we were boys or girls. He had called our spirits from the clouds, and we would be his future on the earth (never mind that our children would carry other men's last names and live in legacies he couldn't own). We were in America and the small size of our feet would not determine how far we could travel in life. Xue was only a baby, he said, and added, sincerely, "I will be very happy if one day Xue could grow up to be just like you two. No less, no more, just like his sisters."

Grandma visited us the summer after Xue's birth and saw this first son in our family. Xue didn't reach for her, and she didn't reach for him—they were like strangers to each other. She did not stay long enough to know him the way we all had—there was little time to bond—and so Grandma left kissing Dawb and me, holding us close, and looking at Xue only a little as he smiled from my mother's arms. A part of me grew protective of the little boy and the unspoken expectations of the man he would have to become. I wondered if she found him as cute as I did. After the hug, I held Xue's little hand and we both waved good-bye.

ACKNOWLEDGMENTS

I would like to thank Noel Zavala for his indispensable aid in preparing this collection.

ABOUT THE EDITOR

Gordon Hutner is a professor of English at the University of Illinois, where he teaches American literature. Previously, he was on the faculty of the Universities of Wisconsin and Kentucky. He has written and edited many books and articles on American fiction and culture, including *Immigrant Voices: Twenty-four Narratives on Becoming American* (Signet Classic). Professor Hutner is also the founder and editor of *American Literary History*, a scholarly journal published by Oxford University Press.